ARTELLIA

IRON ISLANDS

Thayos

Thrane

OUTER ISLANDS

Stormhammer

Thar Kril

Far Hunderlin

Broken Ring

N

THE EMBERS

Map by James Sinclair

Windhaven

Wind

Bantam Books
New York Toronto London Sydney Auckland

haven

George R. R. Martin
and
Lisa Tuttle

This edition contains the complete text
of the original Simon & Schuster edition.
NOT ONE WORD HAS BEEN OMITTED.

Windhaven

A Bantam Spectra Book

PUBLISHING HISTORY
Simon & Schuster edition published 1981
Bantam Spectra edition / June 2001

Lisa Tuttle:

This book is dedicated with love and gratitude to
my mother and father, even if they don't read it.

George R. R. Martin:

This one is for Elizabeth and Anne and Mary Kaye
and Carol and Meredyth and Ann and Yvonne and
the rest of my *Courier* troublemakers, in the hope that they
will continue to make trouble, ask questions,
and get thrown out of offices.

Contents

For once you have tasted flight you will
walk the earth with your eyes turned skyward;
for there you have been,
and there you long to return.

—LEONARDO DA VINCI

Prologue

THE STORM HAD RAGED through most of the night.

In the wide bed she shared with her mother, the child lay awake beneath the scratchy woolweed blanket, listening. The sound of the rain against the thin lemonwood planks of the cabin was steady and insistent, and sometimes she heard the far-off boom of thunderclaps, and when the lightning flashed thin lines of light leaked in between the shutters to illuminate the tiny room. When they faded, it was dark again.

The child could hear the patter of water against the floor, and she knew that the roof had sprung another leak. It would turn the hard-packed earth to mud, and her mother would be furious, but there was nothing to be done. Her mother was not good at patching roofs, and they could not afford to hire anyone. Someday, her mother told her, the tired cabin would collapse in the violence of the storms. "Then we will go and see your father again," she would say. The girl did not remember her father very well, but her mother spoke of him often.

The shutters shook beneath a terrible blast of wind, and the child listened to the frightening sound of creaking wood, and the thrumming of the greased paper that served them for a window, and briefly she was afraid. Her mother slept on, unaware. The storms were frequent, but her mother slept through all of them.

The girl was afraid to wake her. Her mother had a fierce temper, and she did not like being awakened for something as small as a child's fear.

The walls creaked and shifted once again; lightning and thunder came almost together, and the child shivered underneath her blanket and wondered whether this would be the night that they went to see her father.

But it was not.

Finally the storm subsided, and even the rain stopped. The room was dark and quiet.

The girl shook her mother into wakefulness.

"What?" she said. "What?"

"The storm is over, Mother," the child said.

At that the woman nodded and rose. "Get dressed," she told the girl, as she hunted for her own clothing in the darkness. Dawn was still an hour away, at least, but it was important to get to the beach quickly. The storms smashed ships, the child knew; little fishing boats that had stayed out too late or ventured too far, and sometimes even the great trading ships. If you went out after a storm, you might find things washed up on the beach, all kinds of things. Once they had found a knife with a beaten metal edge; when they had sold it they had eaten well for two weeks. If you wanted to find good things, though, you could not afford to be lazy. A lazy person would wait till dawn, and find nothing.

Her mother hung an empty canvas sack over her shoulder, for carrying things. The girl's dress had big pockets. They both wore boots. The woman took down a long pole with a carved wooden hook on its end, in case they saw something in the water, floating just out of reach. "Come on, child," she said. "Don't dawdle."

The beach was cold and dark, with a chill wind blowing steadily from the west. They were not alone. Three or four others were already there, prowling up and down the wet sands, leaving bootmarks that quickly filled with water. Occasionally one would stoop and examine something. One of them was carrying a lantern. They had owned a good lantern once, when her father was alive, but they had to sell it later. Her mother complained of that often. She did not have her daughter's night vision, and sometimes she stumbled in the darkness, and often she missed things she ought to have seen.

They split up, as they always did. The child went north along the beach, while her mother searched to the south. "Turn back at dawn," her mother said. "You have chores to do. Nothing will last past dawn." The child nodded, and hurried off to search.

The findings were lean that night. The girl walked for a long time, following the water's edge, eyes on the ground, looking, always looking. She liked to find things. If she came home with a scrap of metal, or perhaps a scylla's tooth, long as her arm, curved and yellow and terrible, then her mother might smile at her and tell her what a good girl she was. That did not happen often. Mostly her mother scolded her for being too dreamy, and asking foolish questions.

When the vague predawn light first began to swallow up the stars, she had nothing in her pockets but two pieces of milky seaglass and a clam. It was a big heavy clam, large as her hand, with the rough pebbly shell that meant it was the best kind for eating, the kind whose meat was black and buttery. But she had only been able to find one. Everything else that had washed up was worthless driftwood.

The child was about to turn back, as her mother had told her to, when she saw the flash of metal in the sky—a sudden silver gleam, as if a new star had come to life, outshining all the others.

It was north of her, out above the sea. She watched where it had been, and a moment later it flashed again, a little to the left. She knew what it was: a flyer's wings had caught the first rays of the rising sun, before they quite touched the rest of the world.

The child wanted to follow, to run and see. She loved to watch the flight of birds, the little rainbirds and the fierce nighthawks and the scavenger kites; and the flyers with their great silver wings were better than any birds. But it was almost dawn, and her mother had told her to turn back at dawn.

She ran. If she hurried, she thought, if she ran all the way there and all the way back, she might have time to watch for a while, before her mother could miss her. So she ran and ran, past the lazy late-risers who were just coming out to wander on the beach. The clam bounced in her pocket.

The eastern sky was all pale orange by the time she reached the flyers' place, a wide expanse of sandy beach where they often landed, beneath the high cliff from which they launched. The child liked to climb the cliff and watch from up there, with the wind in her hair and her little legs dangling over the edge and the sky all around her. But today there was no time. She had to go back soon, or her mother would be angry.

She had come too late, anyway. The flyer was landing.

He made a last graceful pass over the sand, his wings sweeping by thirty feet above her head. She stood and watched with wide eyes. Then, out above the water, he tilted himself; one silver wing went down and one went up, and all at once he came around in a wide circle. And then he straightened and came on ahead, descending gracefully, so he barely touched the sand as he came skimming in.

There were other people on the beach—a young man and an older woman. They ran alongside the flyer as he came in, and helped to stop him, and afterward they did something to his wings that made them collapse. The two of them folded up the wings, slowly and with care, while the flyer undid the straps that bound them to his body.

Watching, the girl saw that he was the one she liked. There were lots of flyers, she knew, and she had seen many of them and even learned to recognize some, but there were only three that came often, the three who lived on her own island. The child imagined that they must live high on the cliffs, in houses that looked something like the nests of birds, but with walls of priceless silver metal. One of the three was a stern, gray-haired woman with a sour face. The second was only a boy, dark-haired and achingly handsome, with a pleasant voice; she liked him better. But her favorite was the man on the beach, a man as tall and lean and wide of shoulder as her father had been, clean-shaven, with brown eyes and curling red-brown hair. He smiled a lot, and seemed to fly more than any of them.

"You," he said.

The child looked up, terrified, and found him smiling at her.

"Don't be frightened," he said. "I won't hurt you."

She took a step backward. She had often watched the flyers, but none of them had ever noticed her before.

"Who is she?" the flyer asked his helper, who was standing behind him holding his folded wings.

The young man shrugged. "Some clam digger. I don't know. I've seen her hanging around before. Do you want me to chase her off?"

"No," the man said. He smiled at her again. "Why are you so afraid?" he asked. "It's all right. I don't mind your coming here, little girl."

"My mother told me not to bother the flyers," the child said.

The man laughed. "Oh," he said. "Well, you don't bother me. Maybe someday you can grow up and help the flyers, like my friends here. Would you like that?"

The girl shook her head. "No."

"No?" He shrugged, still smiling. "What would you like to do, then? Fly?"

Timidly, the child managed to nod.

The older woman sniggered, but the flyer glanced at her and frowned. Then he walked to the child and stooped and took her by the hand. "Well," he said, "if you're going to fly, you have to practice, you know. Would you like to practice?"

"Yes."

"You're too little for wings just now," the flyer said. "Here." He wrapped strong hands about her, and hoisted her up to his shoulders, so she sat with her legs dangling on his chest, and her hands fumbling uncertain in his hair. "No," he said, "you can't hold on if you're going to be a flyer. Your arms have to be your wings. Can you hold out your arms straight?"

"Yes," she said. She raised her arms up and held them out like a pair of wings.

"Your arms are going to get tired," the flyer warned, "but you can't lower them. Not if you want to fly. A flyer has to have strong arms that never get tired."

"I'm strong," the girl insisted.

"Good. Are you ready to fly?"

"Yes." She began to flap her arms.

"No, no, *no*," he said. "Don't flap. We're not like the birds, you know. I thought you watched us."

The child tried to remember. "Kites," she said suddenly, "you're like kites."

"Sometimes," the flyer said, pleased. "And nighthawks, and other soaring birds. We don't really fly, you know. We glide like the kites do. We ride on the wind. So you can't flap; you have to hold your arms stiff, and try to feel the wind. Can you feel the wind now?"

"Yes." It was a warmer wind, sharp with the smell of the sea.

"Well, catch it with your arms, let it blow you."

She closed her eyes, and tried to feel the wind on her arms.

And she began to move.

The flyer had begun to trot across the sand, as if blown by the wind. When it shifted, he shifted as well, changing directions suddenly. She kept her arms stiff, and the wind seemed to grow stronger, and now he was running, and she bounced up and down on his shoulders, going faster and faster.

"You'll fly me into the water!" he called. "Turn, turn!"

And she tilted her wings, the way she had watched them turn so often, one hand going up and one down, and the flyer turned to the right and began to run in a circle, until finally she straightened her arms again, and then he was off the way he had come.

He ran and ran, and she flew, until both were breathless and laughing.

Finally he stopped. "Enough," he said, "a beginning flyer shouldn't stay up too long." He lifted her off his back and set her on the sand again, smiling. "There now," he said.

Her arms were sore from holding them up so long, but she was excited almost to bursting, though she knew a spanking was waiting at home. The sun was well above the horizon. "Thank you," she said, still breathless from her flight.

"My name is Russ," he said. "If you want another flight, come see me sometime. I don't have any little flyers of my own."

The child nodded eagerly.

"And you," he said, brushing sand from his clothes. "Who are you?"

"Maris," she replied.

"A pretty name," the flyer replied pleasantly. "Well, I must be off, Maris. But maybe we'll go flying again sometime, eh?" He smiled at her and turned away, and began walking off down the beach. The two helpers joined him, one carrying his folded wings. They began to talk as they receded from her, and she heard the sound of his laughter.

And suddenly she was running after him, churning up the sand in her wake, straining to match his long strides.

He heard her coming and turned back to her. "Yes?"

"Here," she said. She reached into her pocket, and handed him the clam.

Astonishment broke over his face, then vanished in the warmth of his smile. He accepted the clam gravely.

She threw her arms around him, hugged him with a fierce intensity, and fled. She ran with her arms held out to either side, so fast that she almost seemed to fly.

PART ONE

Storms

MARIS RODE THE STORM ten feet above the sea, taming the winds on wide cloth-of-metal wings. She flew fiercely, recklessly, delighting in the danger and the feel of the spray, not bothered by the cold. The sky was an ominous cobalt blue, the winds were building, and she had wings; that was enough. She could die now, and die happy, flying.

She flew better than she ever had before, twisting and gliding between the air currents without thought, catching each time the updraft or downwind that would carry her farther or faster. She made no wrong choices, was forced into no hasty scrambles above the leaping ocean; the tacking she did was all for joy. It would have been safer to fly high, like a child, up above the waves as far as she could climb, safe from her own mistakes. But Maris skimmed the sea, like a *flyer*, where a single dip, a brush of wing against water, meant a clumsy tumble from the sky. And death; you don't swim far when your wingspan is twenty feet.

Maris was daring, but she knew the winds.

Ahead she spied the neck of a scylla, a sinuous rope dark against the horizon. Almost without thinking, she responded. Her right hand pulled down on the leather wing grip, her left pushed up. She shifted the whole weight of her body. The great silver wings— tissue thin and almost weightless, but immensely strong—shifted

11

with her, turning. One wingtip all but grazed the whitecaps snapping below, the other lifted; Maris caught the rising winds more fully, and began to climb.

Death, sky death, had been on her mind, but she would not end like that—snapped from the air like an unwary gull, lunch for a hungry monster.

Minutes later she caught up to the scylla, and paused for a taunting circle just beyond its reach. From above she could see its body, barely beneath the waves, the rows of slick black flippers beating rhythmically. The tiny head, swaying slowly from side to side atop the long neck, ignored her. *Perhaps it has known flyers,* she thought then, *and it does not like the taste.*

The winds were colder now, and heavy with salt. The storm was gathering strength; she could feel a trembling in the air. Maris, exhilarated, soon left the scylla far behind. Then she was alone again, flying effortlessly, through an empty, darkening world of sea and sky where the only sound was the wind upon her wings.

In time, the island reared out of the sea: her destination. Sighing, sorry for the journey's end, Maris let herself descend.

Gina and Tor, two of the local land-bound—Maris didn't know what they did when they weren't caring for visiting flyers—were on duty out on the landing spit. She circled once above them to catch their attention. They rose from the soft sand and waved at her. The second time she came around they were ready. Maris dipped lower and lower, until her feet were just inches above the ground; Gina and Tor ran across the sand parallel to her, each beside a wing. Her toes brushed surface and she began to slow in a shower of sand.

Finally she stopped, lying prone on the cool, dry sand. She felt silly. A downed flyer is like a turtle on its back; she could get on her feet if she had to, but it was a difficult, undignified process. Still, it had been a good landing.

Gina and Tor began to fold up her wings, joint by foot-long joint. As each strut unlocked and folded back on the next segment, the tissue fabric between them went limp. When all the extensors were pulled in, the wings hung in two loose folds of drooping metal from the central axis strapped to Maris' back.

"We'd expected Coll," said Gina, as she folded back the final strut. Her short dark hair stood out in spikes around her face.

Maris shook her head. It should have been Coll's journey, perhaps, but she had been desperate, longing for the air. She'd taken the wings—still *her* wings—and gone before he was out of bed.

"He'll have flying enough after next week, I expect," Tor said cheerfully. There was still sand in his lank blond hair and he was shivering a little from the sea winds, but he smiled as he spoke. "All the flying he'll want." He stepped in front of Maris to help her unstrap the wings.

"I'll wear them," Maris snapped at him, impatient, angered by his casual words. How could he understand? How could *any* of them understand? They were land-bound.

She started up the spit toward the lodge, Gina and Tor falling in beside her. There she took the usual refreshments and, standing before a huge open fire, allowed herself to be dried and warmed. The friendly questions she answered curtly, trying to be silent, trying not to think, This may be the last time. Because she was a flyer, they all respected her silence, though with disappointment. For the land-bound, the flyers were the most regular source of contact with the other islands. The seas, daily storm-lashed and infested with scyllas and seacats and other predators, were too dangerous for regular ship travel except among islands within the same local group. The flyers were the links, and the others looked to them for news, gossip, songs, stories, romance.

"The Landsman will be ready whenever you are rested," Gina said, touching Maris tentatively on the shoulder. Maris pulled away, thinking, Yes, to you it is enough to serve the flyers. You'd like a flyer husband, Coll perhaps when he's grown—and you don't know what it means to me that Coll should be the flyer, and not I. But she said only, "I'm ready now. It was an easy flight. The winds did all the work."

Gina led her to another room, where the Landsman was waiting for her message. Like the first room, this was long and sparsely furnished, with a blazing fire crackling in a great stone hearth. The Landsman sat in a cushioned chair near the flames; he rose when

Maris entered. Flyers were always greeted as equals, even on islands where the Landsmen were worshipped as gods and held godlike powers.

After the ritual greetings had been exchanged, Maris closed her eyes and let the message flow. She didn't know or care what she said. The words used her voice without troubling her conscious thought. Probably politics, she thought. Lately it had all been politics.

When the message ended, Maris opened her eyes and smiled at the Landsman—perversely, on purpose, because he looked worried by her words. But he recovered quickly and returned her smile. "Thank you," he said, a little weakly. "You've done well."

She was invited to stay the night, but she refused. The storm might die by morning; besides, she liked night flying. Tor and Gina accompanied her outside and up the rocky path to the flyers' cliff. There were lanterns set in the stone every few feet, to make the twisting ascent safer at night.

At the top of the climb was a natural ledge, made deeper and wider by human hands. Beyond it, an eighty-foot drop, and breakers crashing on a rocky beach. On the ledge Gina and Tor unfolded her wings and locked the struts in place, and the tissue metal stretched tight and taut and silvery. And Maris jumped.

The wind caught her, lifted. She was flying again, dark sea below and rumbling storm above. Once launched she never looked back at the two wistful land-bound following her with their eyes. Too soon she would be one of them.

She did not turn toward home. Instead she flew with the storm winds, blowing violently now, westerly. Soon the thunder would come, and rain, and then Maris would be forced up, above the clouds, where the lightning was less likely to burn her from the sky. At home it would be calm, the storm past. People would be out beachcombing to see what the winds had brought, and a few small dories might be casting off in the hope that a day's fishing might not be entirely lost.

The wind sang in her eyes and pushed at her, and she swam in the sky-stream gracefully. Then, oddly, she thought of Coll. And suddenly she lost the feel. She wavered, dipped, then pulled herself up sharply, tacking, searching for it. And cursing herself. It had been so good before—did it have to end this way? This might be her last flight ever, and it had to be her best. But it was no use: she'd lost the certainty. The wind and she were no longer lovers.

She began to fly at cross-purposes to the storm, battling grimly, fighting until her muscles were strained and aching. She gained altitude now; once the wind-feel left you, it was not safe to fly so near the water.

She was exhausted, tired of fighting, when she caught sight of the rocky face of the Eyrie and realized how far she had come.

The Eyrie was nothing but a huge rock thrust up from the sea, a crumbling tower of stone surrounded by an angry froth where the waters broke against its tall, sheer walls. It was not an island; nothing would grow here but pockets of tough lichen. Birds made their nests in the few protected crevices and ledges, though, and atop the rock the flyers had built their nest. Here, where no ship could moor, here where no one but flyers—bird and human—could roost, here stood their dark stone lodge.

"Maris!"

She looked up at the sound of her name, and saw Dorrel diving on her, laughing, his wings dark against the clouds. At the last possible moment she turned from him, banking sharply, and slipped out from under his dive. He chased her around the Eyrie, and Maris forgot that she was tired and aching, and lost herself in the sheer joy of flying.

When at last they landed, the rains had just begun, howling suddenly from the east, stinging their faces and slapping hard against their wings. Maris realized that she was nearly numb with cold. They came down in a soft earth landing pit carved in the solid rock, without help, and Maris slid ten feet in sudden-mud before coming to a stop. Then it took her five minutes to find her feet, and fumble with the triple straps that wrapped around her body. She tied the wings carefully to a tether rope, then walked out to a wingtip and began to fold them up.

By the time she had finished, her teeth were chattering convulsively, and she could feel the soreness in her arms. Dorrel frowned as he watched her work; his own wings, neatly folded, were slung over his shoulder. "Had you been out long?" he asked. "I should have let you land. I'm sorry. I didn't realize. You must have been with the storm all the way, just in front of it. Difficult weather. I got some of the crosswinds myself. Are you all right?"

"Oh, yes. I was tired—but not really, not now. I'm glad you were there to meet me. That was good flying, and I needed it. The last part of the trip was rough—I thought I would drop. But good flying's better than rest."

Dorrel laughed and put his arm around her. She felt how warm he was after the flight and, by contrast, how cold she was. He felt it too and squeezed her tighter. "Come inside before you freeze. Garth brought some bottles of kivas from the Shotans, and one of them should be hot by now. Between us and the kivas we'll get you warm again."

The common room of the lodge was warm and cheerful, as always, but almost empty. Garth, a short, well-muscled flyer ten years her senior, was the only one there. He looked up from his place by the fire and called them by name. Maris wanted to answer, but her throat was tight with longing, and her teeth were clenched together. Dorrel led her to the fireplace.

"Like a woodwinged idiot I kept her out in the cold," Dorrel said. "Is the kivas hot? Pour us some." He stripped off his wet, muddy clothes quickly and efficiently, and pulled two large towels from a pile near the fire.

"Why should I waste my kivas on you?" Garth rumbled. "For Maris, of course, for she is very beautiful and a superb flyer." He made a mock bow in her direction.

"You should waste your kivas on me," Dorrel said, rubbing himself briskly with the big towel, "unless you would care to waste it all over the floor."

Garth replied, and they traded insults and threats in laconic voices. Maris didn't listen—she had heard it all before. She squeezed the water from her hair, watching the patterns the wetness made on the hearth stones and how quickly they faded. She looked at Dorrel, trying to memorize his lean, muscular body—a good flyer's body—and the quick changes of his face as he teased Garth. But he turned when he felt Maris watching him, and his eyes gentled. Garth's final witticism fell limply into silence. Dorrel touched Maris softly, tracing the line of her jaw.

"You're still shivering." He took the towel from her hands and wrapped it around her. "Garth, take that bottle off the fire before it explodes and let us all get warm."

The kivas, a hot spice wine flavored with raisins and nuts, was served in great stone mugs. The first sip sent thin lines of fire down her veins, and the shivering stopped.

Garth smiled at her. "Good, isn't it? Not that Dorrel will appreciate it. I tricked a slimy old fisherman out of a dozen bottles. He found it in a shipwreck, didn't know what he had, and his wife didn't want it in the house. I gave him some trinkets for it, some metal beads I'd picked up for my sister."

"And what does your sister get?" Maris asked, between sips of kivas.

Garth shrugged. "Her? Oh, it was a surprise, anyway. I'll bring something from Poweet the next time I go. Some painted eggs."

"If he doesn't see something else he can trade them for on his way back," Dorrel said. "If your sister ever gets her surprise, Garth, the shock will kill all pleasure. You were born a trader. I think you'd swap your wings if the deal was good enough."

Garth snorted indignantly. "Close your mouth when you say that, bird." He turned to Maris. "How is your brother? I never see him."

Maris took another sip of her drink, holding on to calm with both hands. "He'll be of age next week," she said carefully. "The wings will be his then. I wouldn't know about his comings and goings. Maybe he doesn't like your company."

"Huh," said Garth. "Why shouldn't he?" He sounded wounded. Maris waved a hand, and forced herself to smile. She had meant it lightly. "I like him well enough," Garth went on. "We all like him, don't we, Dorrel? He's young, quiet, maybe a bit too cautious, but he should improve. He's different somehow—oh, but he can tell some stories! And sing! The land-bound will learn to love the sight of his wings." Garth shook his head in wonder. "Where does he learn them all? I've done more traveling than he has, but . . ."

"He makes them up," said Maris.

"Himself?" Garth was impressed. "He'll be our singer, then. We'll take the prize away from Eastern at the next competition. Western always has the best flyers," he said loyally, "but our singers have never been worthy of the title."

"I sang for Western at the last meet," Dorrel objected.

"That's what I mean."

"*You* shriek like a seacat."

"Yes," said Garth, "but I have no delusions about my ability."

Maris missed Dorrel's reply. Her mind had drifted away from their dialogue, and she was watching the flames, thinking, nursing her still-warm drink. She felt peaceful here in the Eyrie, even now, even after Garth had mentioned Coll. And strangely comfortable. No one lived on the flyers' rock, but it was a home of sorts. Her home. It was hard to think of not coming here anymore.

She remembered the first time she'd seen the Eyrie, a good six years ago, just after her coming-of-age day. She'd been a girl of thirteen, proud of having flown so far alone, but scared too, and shy. Inside the lodge she'd found a dozen flyers, sitting around a fire, drinking, laughing. A party was in progress. But they'd stopped and smiled at her. Garth had been a quiet youth then, Dorrel a skinny boy just barely older than she. She hadn't known either of them. But Helmer, a middle-aged flyer from the island closest to hers, had been among the company, and he made the introductions. Even now she remembered the faces, the names: red-headed Anni from Culhall, Foster who later grew too fat to fly, Jamis the Senior, and especially the one nicknamed Raven, an arrogant youth who dressed in black fur and metal and had won awards for Eastern in three straight competitions. There was another too, a lanky blonde from the Outer Islands. The party was in her honor; it was seldom any of the Outers flew so very, very far.

They'd all welcomed Maris, and soon it seemed almost as if she'd replaced the tall blonde as the guest of honor. They gave her wine, despite her age, and they made her sing with them, and told her stories about flying, most of which she'd heard before, but never from such as these. Finally, when she felt very much part of the group, they let their attentions wander from her, and the festivities resumed their normal course.

It had been a strange, unforgettable party, and one incident in particular was burned golden in her memory. Raven, the only Eastern wing in the group, had been taking a lot of needling. Finally, a little drunk, he rebelled. "You call yourselves flyers," he'd said, in a whiplash voice that Maris would always recall. "Come, come with me, I'll show you flying."

And the whole party had gone outside, to the flyers' cliff of the Eyrie, the highest cliff of all. Six hundred feet straight down it plunged, to where the rocks stood up like teeth and the water churned furiously against them. Raven, wearing folded wings, walked up to the brink. He unfolded the first three joints of his wing struts carefully, and slid his arms through the loops. But he did not lock the wings; the hinges still moved, and the opened struts bent back and forth with his arms, flexible. The other struts he held, folded, in his hands.

Maris had wondered what he was up to. She soon found out.

He ran and jumped, out as far as he could, off the flyers' cliff. With his wings still folded.

She'd gasped, run to the edge. The others followed, some looking pale, a few grinning. Dorrel had stood beside her.

Raven was falling straight down, a rock, his hands at his sides, his wing cloth flapping like a cape. Head first he flew, and the plunge seemed to last forever.

Then, at the very last moment, when he was almost on the rocks, when Maris could almost feel the impact—silver wings, suddenly, flashing in the sunlight. Wings from nowhere. And Raven caught the winds, and flew.

Maris had been awed. But Jamis the Senior, the oldest flyer Western had, only laughed. "Raven's trick," he growled. "I've seen him do it twice before. He oils his wing struts. After he's fallen far enough, he flings them away as hard as he can. As each one locks in place, the snap flings loose the next one. Pretty, yes. You can bet he practiced it plenty before he tried it out in front of anyone. One of these days, though, a hinge is going to jam, and we won't have to listen to Raven anymore."

But even his words hadn't tarnished the magic. Maris often had seen flyers, impatient with their land-bound help, draw their almost-open wings up and shake out the last joint or two with a sharp snap. But never anything like this.

Raven had been smirking when he met them at the landing pit. "When you can do *that*," he told the company, "then you can call yourselves flyers." He'd been a conceited, reckless sort, yes, but right at that moment and for years afterward Maris had thought herself in love with him.

She shook her head sadly, and finished her kivas. It all seemed silly now. Raven had died less than two years after that party, vanished at sea without a trace. A dozen flyers died each year, and their wings usually were lost with them; clumsy flying would down and drown them, long-necked scyllas had been known to attack unwary skimmers, storms could blow them from the sky, lightning hunted out the metal of their wings—yes, there were many ways a flyer could die. Most of them, Maris suspected, just lost their way, and missed their destinations, flying on blindly till exhaustion pulled them down. A few perhaps hit that rarest and most feared menace of the sky: still air. But Maris knew now that Raven had been a more likely candidate for death than most, a foolish flashy flyer with no sky sense.

Dorrel's voice jarred her from her memories. "Maris," he said, "hey, don't go to sleep on us."

Maris set down her empty cup, her hand curved around the rough stone, still seeking the warmth it had held. With an effort, she pulled her hand away and picked up her sweater.

"It's not dry," Garth protested.

"Are you cold?" asked Dorrel.

"No. I must get back."

"You're too tired," Dorrel said. "Stay the night."

Maris drew her eyes away from his. "I mustn't. They'll worry."

Dorrel sighed. "Then take dry clothes." He stood, went to the far end of the common room, and pulled open the doors of a carved wooden wardrobe. "Come here and pick out something that fits."

Maris did not move. "I'd better take my own clothes. I won't be coming back."

Dorrel swore softly. "Maris. Don't make things—you know

that—oh, come, take the clothes. You're welcome to them, you know that. Leave yours in exchange if you like. I won't let you go out in wet clothes."

"I'm sorry," Maris said. Garth smiled at her while Dorrel stood waiting. She got up slowly, pulling the towel more closely around her as she moved away from the fire. The ends of her short, dark hair felt damp and cold against her neck. With Dorrel she searched through the piles of clothes until she found trousers and a brown woolweed sweater to fit her slender, wiry frame. Dorrel watched her dress, then quickly found clothes for himself. Then they went to the rack near the door and took down their wings. Maris ran her long, strong fingers over the struts for weakness or damage; the wings seldom failed, but when they did the trouble was always in the joints. The fabric itself shone as soft and strong as it had when the star sailors rode it to this world. Satisfied, Maris strapped on the wings. They were in good shape; Coll would wear them for years, and his children for generations after him.

Garth had come to stand beside her. She looked at him.

"I'm not so good at words as Coll is, or Dorrel," he started. "I . . . well. Goodbye, Maris." He blushed, looking miserable. Flyers did not say goodbye to each other. But I am not a flyer, she thought, and so she hugged Garth, and kissed him, and said goodbye, the word of the land-bound.

Dorrel walked outside with her. The winds were strong, as always around the Eyrie, but the storm had passed. The only water in the air was the faint mist of sea-spray. But the stars were out.

"At least stay for dinner," Dorrel said. "Garth and I would fight for the pleasure of serving you."

Maris shook her head. She shouldn't have come; she should have flown straight home and never said goodbye to Garth or Dorrel. Easier not to make the ending, easier to pretend that things would always be the same and then to vanish at the end. When they reached the high flyers' cliff, the same from where Raven had leapt so long ago, she reached for Dorrel's hand, and they stood awhile longer in silence.

"Maris," he said finally, hesitantly. He looked straight out to sea, standing by her side, holding her hand. "Maris, you could marry me. I would share my wings with you—you needn't give up flying entirely."

Maris dropped his hand, and felt herself go hot all over with shame. He had no right; it was cruel to pretend. "Don't," she said in a whisper. "The wings aren't yours to share."

"Tradition," he said, sounding desperate. She could tell he was embarrassed also. He wanted to help her, not to make things worse. "We could try it. The wings are mine, but you could use them . . ."

"Oh, Dorrel, don't. The Landsman, your Landsman, would never allow it. It's more than tradition, it's law. They might take your wings away and give them to someone with more respect, like they did to Lind the smuggler. Besides, even if we ran away, to a place without law or Landsmen, to a place by ourselves—how long could you bear to share your wings? With me, with *anyone*? Don't you see? We'd come to hate one another. I'm not a child who can practice when you're resting. I can't live like that, flying on sufferance, knowing the wings could never be mine. And you would grow tired of the way I would watch you—we would—oh . . ." She broke off, fumbling for words.

Dorrel was silent for a moment. "I'm sorry," he said. "I wanted to do something—to help you, Maris. It hurts unbearably knowing what is about to happen to you. I wanted to give you something. I can't bear to think of your going away and becoming . . ."

She took his hand again and held it tightly. "Yes, yes. Shh."

"You do know I love you, Maris. You do, don't you?"

"Yes, yes. And I love you, Dorrel. But—I'll never marry a flyer. Not now. I couldn't. I'd murder him for his wings." She looked at him, trying to lighten the bleak truth of her words. And failing.

They clung to each other, balanced on the edge of the moment of parting, trying to say now, with the pressure of their bodies, everything they might ever want to say to each other. Then they pulled away, and looked at each other through tears.

Maris fumbled with her wings, shaking, suddenly cold again. Dorrel tried to help, but his fingers collided with hers, and they laughed, haltingly, at their clumsiness. She let him unfold her wings for her. When one of them was fully extended, and the second nearly so, she suddenly thought of Raven, and waved Dorrel away. Puzzled, he watched. Maris lifted the wing like an air-weary elder, and threw the final joint into lock with a clean strong snap. And then she was ready to leave.

"Go well," he said, finally.

Maris opened her mouth, then closed it, nodding foolishly. "And you," she said at last. "Take care, until . . ." But she could not add the final lie, any more than she could say goodbye to him. She turned and ran from him, and launched herself away from the Eyrie, out on the nightwinds into a cold dark sky.

It was a long and lonely flight over a starlit sea where nothing stirred. The winds were steady from the east, forcing Maris to tack all the way, losing time and speed. By the time she spotted the light tower of Lesser Amberly, her home island, midnight had come and gone.

There was another light below, turning on their landing beach. She saw it as she coasted in, smooth and easy, and thought it must be the lodge men. But they should have gone off duty long ago; few flyers were aloft this late. She frowned in puzzlement just as she hit the ground with a jarring shock.

Maris groaned, hurried to get up, and set to work on the wing straps. She should know enough not to be distracted at the moment of landing. The light advanced on her.

"So you decided to come back," the voice said, harsh and angry. It was Russ, her father—stepfather, really—coming toward her with a lantern in his good hand, his right arm hanging dead and useless at his side.

"I stopped by the Eyrie first," she said, defensively. "You weren't worried?"

"Coll was to go, not you." The lines of his face were set hard.

"He was in bed," Maris said. "He was too slow—I knew he'd miss the best of the storm winds. He would have caught nothing but rain, and it would have taken him forever to get there. If he did. He's not good in rain yet."

"Then he must learn to be better. The boy must make his own mistakes now. You were his teacher, but soon the wings will be his. He's the flyer, not you."

Maris winced as if struck. This was the man who had taught her to fly, who had been so proud of her and the way she seemed to know instinctively what to do. The wings would be hers, he'd told her more than once, though she was not of his blood. He and his wife had taken her in when it seemed that he would never father a child of his own to inherit the wings. He'd had his accident and lost the sky, and it was important to find a flyer to replace him—if not someone of his blood, then someone he loved. His wife had refused to learn; she had lived thirty-five years as a land-bound, and she did not intend to jump off any cliffs, wings or no. Besides, it was too late; flyers had to be taught young. So it was Maris he had taught, adopted, and come to love—Maris the fisherman's daughter, who would rather watch from the flyers' cliff than play with the other children.

And then, against all probability, Coll had been born. His mother had died after the prolonged and difficult labor—Maris, very much a child, remembered a dark night full of people running, and later her stepfather crying alone in a corner—but Coll had lived on. Maris, suddenly a child-mother, came to care for him, love him. At first they didn't expect him to live. She was happy when he did; and for three years she loved him as both brother and son, while she practiced with the wings under their father's watchful eyes.

Until the night when the same father told her that Coll, baby Coll, must have *her* wings.

"I am a far better flyer then he will ever be," Maris told him now, on the beach, her voice trembling.

"I do not dispute that. It makes no difference. He is my own blood."

"It's not fair!" she cried, letting out the protest that had been lodged inside her since the day she had come of age. By then Coll had been strong, healthy; still too small to bear the wings, but they would be his on his coming-of-age day. Maris had no claim, no right at all. That was the law of the flyers, stretching back through generations to the star sailors themselves, the legendary wingforgers. The first-born child of each of the flying families would inherit the wings of the parent. Skill counted for nothing; this was a law of inheritance, and Maris came from a fishing family who had nothing to leave her but the scattered wreckage of a wooden boat.

"Fair or no, it is the law, Maris. You've known it for a long time, even if you chose to ignore it. For years you've played at being a flyer, and I've let you, because you loved it, and because Coll needed a teacher, a skilled one, and because this island is too big to rely on only two flyers. But you knew all the while this day would come."

He could be more kind, she thought wildly. He must know what it means, to give up the sky.

"Now come with me," he said. "You'll not fly again."

Her wings were still fully extended; only one strap was undone. "I'll run away," she said madly. "You'll never see me again. I'll go to some island where they don't have a flyer of their own. They'll be glad to have me, no matter how I got my wings."

"Never," her father said, sadly. "The other flyers would shun the island, as they did after the mad Landsman of Kennehut executed the Flyer-Who-Brought-Bad-News. You would be stripped of your stolen wings no matter where you went. No Landsman would take the risk."

"I'll break them, then!" Maris said, riding the edge of hysteria. "Then he'll never fly either, any more than . . . than . . ."

Glass shattered on rock and the light went out as her father dropped the lantern. Maris felt his grip on her hands. "You couldn't even if you wanted to. And you wouldn't do that to Coll. But give me the wings."

"I wouldn't . . ."

"I don't know what you wouldn't do. I thought you'd gone out to kill yourself this morning, to die flying in the storm. I know the feelings, Maris. That's why I was so frightened, and so angry. You mustn't blame Coll."

"I don't. And I would not keep him from flying—but I want to fly so badly myself—Father, please." Tears ran down her face in the dark, and she moved closer, reaching for comfort.

"Yes, Maris," he said. He could not put his arm about her; the wings got in the way. "There is nothing I can do. This is the way of things. You must learn to live without wings, as I have. At least you've had them for a time—you know what it is like to fly."

"It's not enough!" she said, tearful, stubborn. "I used to think it would be, when I was a little girl, not even yours yet, just a stranger, and you were Amberly's greatest flyer. I watched you and the others from the cliff and I used to think—if I could have wings, even for a moment, that would be life enough. But it isn't, it *isn't*. I can't give them up."

The hard lines were all gone now in her father's face. He touched her face gently, brushing away tears. "Perhaps you're right," he said, in a slow heavy voice. "Perhaps it was not a good thing. I thought if I could let you fly for a while, a little bit—that would be better than nothing, it would be a fine bright gift indeed. But it wasn't, was it? Now you can never be happy. You can never be a land-bound, really, for you've flown, and you'll always know how you are imprisoned." His words stopped abruptly and Maris realized that he was talking of himself as much as her.

He helped her unstrap and fold the wings and they walked back home together.

Their house was a simple wood frame, surrounded by trees and land. A creek ran through the back. Flyers could live well. Russ said goodnight just inside the door and took the wings upstairs with him. Has he really lost all trust? Maris thought. What have I done? And she felt like crying again.

Instead she wandered into the kitchen, found cheese and cold meat and tea, and took them back into the dining room. A bowl-shaped sand candle sat in the center of the table. She lit it, ate, and watched the flame dance.

Coll entered just as she finished, and stood awkwardly in the doorway. " 'Lo, Maris," he said uncertainly. "I'm glad you're back. I was waiting." He was tall for a thirteen-year-old, with a soft, slender body, long red-blond hair, and the wispy beginnings of a mustache.

" 'Lo, Coll," Maris said. "Don't just stand there. I'm sorry I took the wings."

He sat down. "I don't mind, you know that. You fly a lot better than me, and—well—you know. Was Father mad?"

Maris nodded.

Coll looked grim and frightened. "It's only one week away now, Maris. What are we going to do?" He was looking straight down at the candle, not at her.

Maris sighed, and put a gentle hand on his arm. "We'll do what we must, Coll. We have no choice." They had talked before, she and Coll, and she knew his agony as much as her own. She was his sister, almost his mother, and the boy had shared with her his shame and his secret. That was the ultimate irony.

He looked up at her now, looking to her again as the child to the mother; although he knew now that she was as helpless as he, still he hoped. "Why don't we have a choice? I don't understand."

Maris sighed. "It's law, Coll. We don't go against tradition here, you know that. We all have duties put upon us. If we had a choice I would keep the wings, I would be a flyer. And you could be a singer. We'd both be proud, and know we were good at what we did. Life will be hard as a land-bound. I want the wings so much. I've had them, and it doesn't seem right that they should be taken from me, but maybe—maybe the rightness in it is something I just don't see. People wiser than we decided that things should be the way they are, and maybe, maybe I'm just being a child about it, wanting everything my own way."

Coll wet his lips, nervous. "No."

She looked a question at him.

He shook his head stubbornly. "It's not right, Maris, it just isn't. I don't want to fly, I don't want to take your wings. It's all so stupid. I'm hurting you and I don't want to, but I don't want to hurt Father either. How can I tell him? I'm his heir and all that—I'm *supposed* to take the wings. He'd hate me. The songs don't say anything about flyers who were scared of the sky like I am. Flyers *aren't* afraid—I'm not meant for a flyer." His hands were shaking visibly.

"Coll, don't worry. It will be all right, really it will. Everyone is frightened at first. I was, too." She wasn't thinking about the lie, only saying words to reassure him.

"But it's not fair," he cried. "I don't want to give up my singing, and if I fly I can't sing, not like Barrion, not like I'd like to. So why are they going to make me? Maris, why can't *you* be the flyer, like you want to be? *Why?*"

She looked at him, so close to crying, and felt like joining him in tears. She didn't have an answer, not for him or for herself. "I don't know," she said, her voice hollow. "I don't know, little one. That is the way things have always been done, though, and that is the way they must be."

They stared at each other, both trapped, caught together by a law older than either and a tradition neither understood. Helpless and hurt, they talked long in the candlelight, saying the same things over and over again until, late, they parted for bed, nothing resolved.

But once in bed alone, the resentment came flooding back to Maris, the sense of loss, and with it, shame. She cried herself to sleep that night, and dreamt of purple storm-skies that she would never fly.

The week went on forever.

A dozen times during those endless days Maris walked up to the flyers' cliff, to stand helplessly with her hands in her pockets looking out over the sea. Fishing boats she saw, and gulls, and once a hunting pack of sleek gray seacats far, far off. It made her hurt the more, the sudden closing of the world she knew, the way the horizons seemed to shrink about her, but she could not stop coming. So she stood there, lusting for the wind, but the only thing that flew was her hair.

Once she caught Coll watching her from a distance. Afterward neither of them mentioned it.

Russ had the wings now, *his* wings, as they had always been, as they would be until Coll took them. When Lesser Amberly needed a flyer, Corm answered the call from the far side of the island, or gay Shalli who had flown guard when Maris was a child first learning simple sky sense. As far as her father was concerned, the island had no third flyer, and would have none until Coll claimed his birthright.

His attitude toward Maris had changed too. Sometimes he raged at her when he found her brooding, sometimes he put his good arm around her and all but wept. He could not find a middle ground between anger and pity; so, helpless, he tried to avoid her. Instead he spent his time with Coll, acting excited and enthusiastic. The boy, a dutiful son, tried to catch and echo the mood. But Maris knew that he too went for long walks, and spent a lot of time alone with his guitar.

On the day before Coll was to come of age, Maris sat high on the flyers' cliff, her legs dangling over the edge, watching Shalli wheel in silver arcs across the noonday sky. Spotting seacats for the fishermen, Shalli had said, but Maris knew better. She'd been a flyer long enough to recognize a joy-flight when she saw one. Even now, as she sat trapped, she could feel a distant echo of that joy; something soared within her whenever Shalli banked, and a shaft of silvered sunlight blazed briefly from a wing.

Is this the way it ends? Maris asked herself. It can't be. No, this is the way it began. I remember.

And she did remember. Sometimes she thought she had watched the flyers even before she could walk, though her mother, her real mother, said that wasn't so. Maris did have vivid memories of the cliff, though; she'd run away and come here almost weekly when she was four and five. There—*here*—she'd sit, watching the flyers come and go. Her mother would always find her, and she would always be furious.

"You are a land-bound, Maris," she'd say, after she had administered a spanking. "Don't waste your time with foolish dreams. I won't have my daughter be a Woodwings."

That was an old folktale; her mother told it to her anew each time she caught her on the cliff. Woodwings was a carpenter's son who wanted to be a flyer. But, of course, he wasn't in a flying family. He did not care, the story said; he did not listen to friends or family, he wanted nothing but sky. Finally, in his father's shop, he built himself a beautiful pair of wings: great butterfly wings of carved and polished wood. And everyone said they were beautiful, everyone but the flyers; the flyers only shook their heads silently. Finally Woodwings climbed to the flyers' cliff. They were waiting for him up there, wordless, circling and banking bright and quiet in the dawn light. Woodwings ran to meet them, and fell tumbling to his death.

"And the moral," Maris' mother would always say, "is that you shouldn't try to be something you're not."

But *was* that the moral? The child Maris didn't worry about it; she just dismissed Woodwings as an oaf. But when she was older, the story came back to her often. At times she thought her mother had gotten it all wrong. Woodwings had won, Maris thought. He *had* flown, if only for an instant, and that made it all worthwhile, even his death. It was a flyer's death. And the others, the flyers, they had not come out to mock him, or warn him off—no, they flew guard for him, because he was just a beginner, and because they understood. The land-bound often laughed at Woodwings; the name had become a synonym for fool. But how could a flyer hear the story and do anything but cry?

Maris thought of Woodwings then, as she sat in the cold watching Shalli fly, and the old questions came back. Was it worth it, Woodwings? she thought. An instant of flight, then death forever? And for me, was it worth it? A dozen years of stormwinds, and now a life without?

When Russ had first begun to notice her on the cliff, she was the happiest child in the world. When he adopted her and pushed her proudly into the sky, she thought she would die from joy. Her real father was dead, gone with his boat, killed by an angry scylla after a storm had blown him far off course; her mother was gladly rid of her. She leapt at the new life, at the sky; it seemed that all her dreams were coming true. Woodwings had the right idea, she thought then. Dream anything hard enough, and it can be yours.

Her faith had left after Coll came, when she was told.

Coll. Everything came back to Coll.

So, lost, Maris brushed all thought aside, and watched in melancholy peace.

The day came, as Maris knew it must.

It was a small party, though the Landsman himself was the host. He was a portly, genial man, with a kind face hidden by a full beard that he hoped would make him fierce. When he met them at the door, his clothes dripped wealth: rich embroidered fabrics, rings of copper and brass, and a heavy necklace of real wrought iron. But the welcome was warm.

Inside the lodge was a great party room. Bare wooden beams above, torches flaming bright along the walls, a scarlet carpet underneath. And a table, groaning under its burden—kivas from the Shotans and Amberly's own wines, cheeses flown in from Culhall, fruit from the Outer Islands, great bowls of green salad. In the hearth, a seacat turned on a spit while a cook basted it with bitterweed and its own drippings. It was a big one, half again the size of a man, its warm blue-gray fur skinned away to leave a barrel-shaped carcass tapering to a pair of powerful flippers. The thick layer of fat that protected the seacat against the cold had begun to crackle and hiss in the flames, and the curiously feline face had been stuffed full of nuts and herbs. It smelled wonderful.

Their land-bound friends were all at the party, and they clustered around Coll, offering congratulations. Some of them even felt compelled to talk to Maris, to tell her how lucky she was to have a flyer for a brother, to have been a flyer herself. *Have been, have been, have been.* She wanted to scream.

But the flyers were worse. They were there in force, of course. Corm, handsome as ever, dripping charm, held court in one corner, telling stories of far-off places to starry-eyed land-bound girls. Shalli was dancing; before the evening had run its course she would burn out a half-dozen men with her frantic energy. Other flyers had come from other islands. Anni of Culhall, the boy Jamis the Younger, Helmer of Greater Amberly, whose own daughter would claim his wings in less than a year, a half-dozen others from the West, three cliquish Easterners. Her friends, her brothers, her comrades in the Eyrie.

But now they avoided her. Anni smiled politely and looked the other way. Jamis delivered his father's greetings, then lapsed into an uncomfortable silence, shifting from foot to foot until Maris let him go. His sigh of relief was almost audible. Even Corm, who said he was never nervous, seemed ill at ease with her. He brought her a cup of hot kivas, then saw a friend across the room that he simply *had* to talk to.

Feeling cut off and shunned, Maris found a leather chair by the window. There she sat and sipped her kivas and listened to the rising wind pull at the shutters. She didn't blame them. How can you talk to a wingless flyer?

She was glad that Garth and Dorrel had not come, nor any of the others she had come to love especially. And she was ashamed of being glad.

Then there was a stir by the door, and her mood lifted slightly. Barrion had arrived, with guitar in hand.

Maris smiled to see him enter. Although Russ thought him a bad influence on Coll, she liked Barrion. The singer was a tall, weather-beaten man, whose shock of unruly gray hair made him look older than he was. His long face bore the marks of wind and sun, but there were laugh lines around his mouth as well, and a roguish humor in his gray eyes. Barrion had a rumbly deep voice, an irreverent manner, and a penchant for wild stories. He was Western's best singer, so it was said. At least Coll said it, and Barrion himself, of course. But Barrion also said he'd been to a hundred islands, unthinkable for a wingless man. And he claimed that his guitar had arrived seven centuries ago from Earth, with the star sailors themselves. His family had handed it down, he said, all serious, as if he expected Coll and Maris to believe him. But the idea was nonsense—treating a guitar as if it were a pair of wings!

Still, liar or no, lanky Barrion was entertaining enough, and romantic enough, and he sang like the very wind. Coll had studied under him, and now they were great friends.

The Landsman clapped him roundly on the back, and Barrion laughed, sat down, and prepared to sing. The room grew quiet; even Corm stopped in mid-story.

He began with the Song of the Star Sailors.

It was the oldest ballad, the first of those that they could rightly call their own. Barrion sang it simply, with easy loving familiarity, and Maris softened to the sound of his deep voice. How often she had heard Coll, late at night, plucking at his own instrument and singing the same song. His voice had been changing then; it made him furious. Every third stanza would be interrupted by a hideous cracked note and a minute of swearing. Maris used to lie in bed and giggle helplessly at the noises from down the hall.

Now she listened to the words, as Barrion sang sweetly of the star sailors and their great ship, with its silver sails that stretched a hundred miles to catch the wild starwinds. The whole story was there. The mysterious storm, the crippled ship, the coffins where they died awhile; then, driven off course, they came *here*, to a world of endless ocean and raging storms, a world where the only land was a thousand scattered rocky islands, and the winds blew constantly. The song told of the landing, in a ship not meant to land, of the death of thousands in their coffins, and the way the sail—barely heavier than air—had floated atop the sea, turning the waters silver all around the Shotans. Barrion sang of the star sailors' magic, and their dream of repairing the ship, and the slow agonizing dying of that dream. He lingered, melancholy, over the fading powers of their magic machines, the fading that ended in darkness. Finally came the battle, just off Big Shotan, when the Old Captain and his loyalists went down defending the precious metal sails against their children. Then, with the last magic, the sons and daughters of the star sailors, the first children of Windhaven, cut the sails into pieces, light, flexible, immensely strong. And, with whatever metal they could salvage from the ship, they forged the wings.

For the scattered people of Windhaven needed communication. Without fuel, without metal, faced by oceans full of storms and predators, given nothing free but the powerful winds: the choice was easy.

The last chords faded from the air. The poor sailors, Maris thought, as always. The Old Captain and his crew, they were flyers too, though their wings were star-wings. But their way of flying had to die so a new way could be born.

Barrion grinned at someone's request, and began a new tune. He did a half-dozen songs from ancient Earth, then looked around sheepishly and offered up a composition of his own, a bawdy drinking song about a horny scylla who mistook a fishing ship for its mate. Maris hardly listened. Her mind was on the star sailors still.

In a way, they were like Woodwings, she thought; they couldn't give up their dream. And it meant they had to die. *I wonder if they thought it was worth it?*

"Barrion," Russ called from the floor. "This is a flyer's age-day. Give us some flying songs!"

The singer grinned, and nodded. Maris looked over at Russ. He stood by the table, a wine glass in his good hand, a smile on his face. *He is proud,* she thought. *His son is soon to be a flyer, and he has forgotten me.* She felt sick and beaten.

Barrion sang flying songs; ballads from the Outer Islands, from the Shotans, from Culhall and the Amberlys and Poweet. He sang of the ghost flyers, lost forever over the seas when they obeyed the Landsman-Captain and took swords into the sky. In still air you can see them yet, wandering hopelessly through the storms on phantom wings. Or so the legends go. But flyers who hit still air seldom return to talk of it, so no one could say for sure.

He did the song of white-haired Royn, who was past eighty when he found his flyer grandson dead in a lover's quarrel, and took the wings to chase and kill the culprit.

He sang the ballad of Aron and Jeni, the saddest song of all. Jeni had been a land-born, and worse, crippled; unable to walk, she had lived with her mother, a washerwoman, and daily she sat by the window to watch the flyers' cliff on Little Shotan. There she fell in love with Aron, a graceful laughing flyer, and in her dreams he loved her too. But one day, alone in her house, she saw him play in the sky with another flyer, a fire-haired woman, and when they landed they kissed each other. When her mother came home, Jeni was dead. Aron, when they told him, would not let them bury the woman he had never known. He took her in his arms and carried her up to the cliff; then, slinging her beneath him, he rode the winds far out to sea and gave her a flyer's burial.

Woodwings had a song too, though not a very good one; it made him a comical fool. Barrion sang it, though, and the one about the Flyer-Who-Brought-Bad-News, and Winddance, the flyers' wedding song, and a dozen others. Maris could hardly move, so caught was she. The kivas was rain-cold in her hand, forgotten in the face of the words. It was a good feeling, a restless disturbing glorious sadness, and it brought back to her memories of the winds.

"Your brother is a flyer born," a soft voice whispered by her side, and she saw that Corm was resting on the arm of her chair. He gestured gracefully with his wine glass, to where Coll sat at Barrion's feet. The youth had his hands folded tightly around his knees, and his look was one of rapture.

"See how the songs touch him," Corm said easily. "Only songs to a land-bound, but more, much more, to a flyer. You and I know that, Maris, and your brother too. I can tell by watching. I know how it must be for you, but think of him, girl. He loves it as much as you."

Maris looked up at Corm, and all but laughed at his wisdom. Yes, Coll looked entranced, but only she knew why. It was singing he loved, not flying; the songs, not the subject. But how could Corm know that, smiling handsome Corm who was so sure of himself and knew so little. "Do you think that only flyers dream, Corm?" she asked him in a whisper, then quickly glanced away to where Barrion was finishing a song.

"There are more flying songs," Barrion said. "If I sang them all, we would be here all night, and I'd never get to eat." He looked at Coll. "Wait. You'll learn more than I'll ever know when you reach the Eyrie." Corm, by Maris' side, raised his glass in salute.

Coll stood up. "I want to do one."

Barrion smiled. "I think I can trust you with my guitar. Nobody else, maybe, but you, yes." He got up, relinquishing his seat to the quiet, pale-faced youth.

Coll sat down, strummed nervously, biting his lip. He blinked at the torches, looked over at Maris, blinked again. "I want to do a new song, about a flyer. I—well, I made it up. I wasn't there, you understand, but I heard the story, and well, it's all true. It *ought* to be a song, and it hasn't been, till now."

"Well, sing it then, boy," the Landsman boomed.

Coll smiled, glanced at Maris again. "I call this Raven's Fall."

And he sang it.

Clear and pure, with a beautiful voice, just the way it happened.

Maris watched him with wide eyes, listened with awe. He got it all right. He even caught the feeling, the lump that twisted in her when Raven's folded wings bloomed mirror-bright in the sun, and he climbed away from death. All of the innocent love she had felt for him was in Coll's song; the Raven that he sang of was a glorious winged prince, dark and daring and defiant. As Maris once had thought him.

He has a gift, Maris thought. Corm looked down at her and said, "What?" and suddenly she realized that she'd whispered it aloud.

"Coll," she said, in a low voice. The last notes of the song rang in her ears. "He could be better than Barrion, if he had a chance. I told him that story, Corm. I was there, and a dozen others, when Raven did his trick. But none of us could have made it beautiful, as Coll did. He has a very special gift."

Corm smiled at her complacently. "True. Next year we'll wipe out Eastern in the singing competition."

And Maris looked at him, suddenly furious. It was all so wrong, she thought. Across the room, Coll was watching her, a question in his eyes. Maris nodded to him, and he grinned proudly. He had done it right.

And she had decided.

But then, before Coll could start another song, Russ came forward. "Now," he said, "now we must get serious. We've had singing and talk, good eating and good drink here in the warmth. But outside are the winds."

They all listened gravely, as was expected, and the sound of the winds, forgotten background for so long, now seemed to fill the room. Maris heard, and shivered.

"The wings," her father said.

The Landsman came forward, holding them in his hands like the trust they were. He spoke his ritual words: "Long have these wings served Amberly, linking us to all the folk of Windhaven, for generations, back to the days of the star sailors. Marion flew them, daughter of a star sailor, and her daughter Jeri, and her son Jon, and Anni, and Flan, and Denis" . . . the genealogy went on a long time . . . "and last Russ and his daughter, Maris." There was a slight ripple in the crowd at the unexpected mention of Maris. She had not been a true flyer and ought not have been named. They were giving her the name of flyer even as they took away her wings, Maris thought. "And now young Coll will take them, and now, as other Landsmen have done for generations, I hold them for a brief while, to bring them luck with my touch. And through me all the folk of Lesser Amberly touch these wings, and with my voice they say, 'Fly well, Coll!' "

The Landsman handed the folded wings to Russ, who took them and turned to Coll. He was standing then, the guitar at his feet, and he looked very small and very pale. "It is time for someone to become a flyer," Russ said. "It is time for me to pass on the wings, and for Coll to accept them, and it would be folly to strap on wings in a house. Let us go to the flyers' cliff and watch a boy become a man."

The torch-bearers, flyers all, were ready. They left the lodge, Coll in a place of honor between his father and the Landsman, the flyers close behind with the torches. Maris and the rest of the party followed further back.

It was a ten-minute walk, slow steps in other-worldly silence, before they stood in a rough semicircle on the stage of the cliff. Alone by the edge, Russ, one-handed and disdaining help, strapped the wings onto his son. Coll's face was chalk white. He stood very still while Russ unfolded the wings, and looked straight down at the abyss before him, where dark waves clawed against the beach.

Finally, it was done. "My son, you are a flyer," Russ said, and then he stepped back with the rest of them, close to Maris. Coll stood alone beneath the stars, perched on the brink, his immense silvery wings making him look smaller than ever before. Maris wanted to shout, to interrupt, to do something; she could feel the tears on her cheeks. But she could not move. Like all the rest, she waited for the traditional first flight.

And Coll at last, with a sharp indrawn breath, kicked off from the cliff.

His last running step was a stumble, and he plunged down out of sight. The crowd rushed forward. By the time the party-goers reached the edge, he had recovered and was climbing slowly up. He made a wide circle out over the ocean, then glided in close to the cliff, then back out again. Sometimes young flyers gave their friends a show, but Coll was no showman. A winged silver wraith, he wandered awkward and a little lost in a sky that was not his home.

Other wings were being broken out; Corm and Shalli and the others prepared to fly. Shortly now they would join Coll in the sky, make a few passes in formation, then leave the land-bound behind and fly off to the Eyrie to spend the rest of the night in celebration of their newest member.

Before any of them could leap, though, the wind changed; Maris felt it with a flyer's perception. And she heard it, a gale of cold that screeched forlorn over the rocky edges of the peak; and most of all she saw it, for out above the waves Coll faltered visibly. He dipped slightly, fought to save himself, went into a sudden spin. Someone gasped. Then, quickly again, he was back in control, and headed back to them. But struggling, struggling. It was a rough wind, angry, pushing him down; the sort of wind a flyer had to coax and soothe and tame. Coll wrestled with it, and it was beating him.

"He's in trouble," Corm said, and the handsome flyer flung out his last wing struts with a snap. "I'll fly guard." With that, he was suddenly aloft.

Too late to be of much help, though. Coll, his wings swaying back and forth as he was buffeted by the sudden turbulence, was headed toward the landing beach. A wordless decision was made, and the party moved as one to meet him, Maris and her father in the lead.

Coll came down fast, too fast. He was not riding the wind; no, he was being pushed. His wings shook as he dropped, and he tilted, so one wingtip brushed the ground while the other pointed up toward the sky. Wrong, wrong, all wrong. Even as they rushed onto the beach, there was a great spraying shower of dry sand and then the sudden horrible sound of metal snapping and Coll was down, lying safe in the sand.

But his left wing was limp and broken.

Russ reached him first, knelt over him, started to work on the straps. The others gathered around. Then Coll rose a little, and they saw that he was shaking, his eyes full of tears.

"Don't worry," Russ said, in a mock-hearty voice. "It was only a strut, son; they break all the time. We'll fix it easy. You were a little shaky, but all of us are the first time up. Next time will be better."

"Next time, next time, next time!" Coll said. "I can't do it, I can't do it, Father. I don't *want* a next time! I don't *want* your wings!" He was crying openly now, and his body shook with his sobs.

The guests stood in mute shock, and his father's face grew stern. "You are my son, and a flyer. There will be a next time. And you will learn."

Coll continued to shake and sob, the wings off now, lying unstrapped at his feet, broken and useless, at least for now. There would be no flight to the Eyrie tonight.

The father reached out his good arm and took his son by the shoulder, shaking him. "You hear? You *hear?* I won't listen to such nonsense. You fly, or you are no son of mine."

Coll's sudden defiance was all gone now. He nodded, biting back the tears, looked up. "Yes, Father," he said. "I'm sorry. I just got scared out there, I didn't mean to say it." He was only thirteen, Maris remembered as she watched from among the guests. Thirteen and scared and not at all a flyer. "I don't know why I said it. I didn't mean it, really."

And Maris found her voice. "Yes, you did," she said loudly, remembering the way Coll had sung of Raven, remembering the decision she had made. The others turned to look at her with shock, and Shalli put a restraining hand on her arm. But Maris shrugged it off and pushed forward to stand between Coll and his father.

"He did mean it," she said quietly, her voice steady and sure while her heart trembled. "Couldn't you see, Father? He's not a flyer. He's a good son, and you should be proud of him, but he will never love the wind. I don't care what the law says."

"Maris," Russ said, and there was nothing warm in his voice, only despair and hurt. "You would take the wings from your own brother? I thought you loved him."

A week ago she would have cried, but now her tears were all used up. "I do love him, and I want him to have a long and happy life. He will not be happy as a flyer; he does it just to make *you* proud. Coll is a singer, a good one. Why must you take from him the life he loves?"

"I take nothing," Russ said coldly. "Tradition . . ."

"A stupid tradition," a new voice interjected. Maris looked for her ally, and saw Barrion pushing through the crowd. "Maris is right. Coll sings like an angel, and we all saw how he flies." He glanced around contemptuously at the flyers in the crowd. "You fly- ers are such creatures of habit that you have forgotten how to think. You follow tradition blindly no matter who is hurt."

Almost unnoticed, Corm had landed and folded up his wings. Now he stood before them, his smooth dark face flushed with anger. "The flyers and their traditions have made Amberly great, have shaped the very history of Windhaven a thousand times over. I don't care how well you sing, Barrion, you are not beyond the law." He looked at Russ and continued, "Don't worry, friend. We'll make your son a flyer such as Amberly has never seen."

But then Coll looked up, and though the tears flowed still, sud- denly there was anger in his face too, and decision. "*No!*" he shouted, and his glance at Corm was defiant. "You won't make me anything I don't want to be, I don't care who you are. I'm not a coward, I'm not a baby, but I don't want to fly, *I don't, I DON'T!*" His words were a torrent, all but screamed into the wind, as his se- cret came pouring out and all the barriers fell at once. "You flyers think you're so good, that everybody else is beneath you, but you're not, you know, you're not. Barrion has been to a hundred islands, and he knows more songs than a dozen flyers. I don't care what you think, Corm. He's not land-bound; he takes ships when everybody else is too scared. You flyers stay clear of scyllas, but Barrion killed one once with a harpoon, from a little wooden boat. I bet you didn't know that.

"I can be like him, too. I have a talent. He's going to the Outer Islands, and he wants me to come with him, and he told me once that he'd give me his guitar one day. He can take flying and make it beautiful with his words, but he can do the same thing with fishing or hunting or *anything*. Flyers can't do that, but he can. He's *Barrion!* He's a *singer*, and that's just as good as being a flyer. And I can do it too, like I did tonight with Raven." He glared at Corm with hate. "Take your old wings, give them to Maris, she's the flyer," he shouted, kicking at the limp fabric on the ground. "I want to go with Barrion."

There was an awful silence. Russ stood mute for a long time, then looked at his son with a face that was older than it had ever been. "They are not his wings to take, Coll," he said. "They were my wings, and my father's, and his mother's before him, and I wanted—I wanted—" His voice broke.

"You are responsible for this," Corm said angrily, with a glance at Barrion. "And you, yes *you*, his own sister," he added, shifting his gaze to Maris.

"All right, Corm," she said. "We are responsible, Barrion and I, because we love Coll and we want to see him happy—and alive. The flyers have followed tradition too long. Barrion is right, don't you see? Every year bad flyers take the wings of their parents and die with them, and Windhaven is poorer, for wings cannot be replaced. How many flyers were there in the days of the star sailors? How many are there today? Can't you see what tradition is doing to us? The wings are a trust; they should be worn by those who love the sky, who will fly best and keep them best. Instead, birth is our only measure for awarding wings. Birth, not skill; but a flyer's skill is all that saves him from death, all that binds Windhaven together."

Corm snorted. "This is a disgrace. You are no flyer, Maris, and you have no right to speak of these matters. Your words disgrace the sky and you violate all tradition. If your brother chooses to give up his birthright, very well, then. But he won't make a mockery of our law and give them to anyone he chooses." He looked around, at the shock-still crowd. "Where is the Landsman? Tell us the law!"

The Landsman's voice was slow, troubled. "The law—the tradition—but this case is so special, Corm. Maris has served Amberly well, and we all know how she flies. I—"

"The *law*," Corm insisted.

The Landsman shook his head. "Yes, that is my duty, but—the law says that—that if a flyer renounces his wings, then they shall be taken by another flyer from the island, the senior, and he and the Landsman shall hold them until a new wing-bearer is chosen. But Corm, no flyer has ever renounced his wings—the law is only used when a flyer dies without an heir, and here, in this case, Maris is—"

"The law is the law," Corm said.

"And you will follow it blindly," Barrion put in.

Corm ignored him. "I am Lesser Amberly's senior flyer, since Russ has passed on the wings. I will take custody, until we find someone worthy of being a flyer, someone who will recognize the honor and keep the traditions."

"*No!*" Coll shouted. "I want *Maris* to have the wings."

"You have no say in the matter," Corm told him. "You are a land-bound." So saying, he stooped and picked up the discarded, broken wings. Methodically he began to fold them.

Maris looked around for help, but it was hopeless. Barrion spread his hands, Shalli and Helmer would not meet her gaze, and her father stood broken and weeping, a flyer no more, not even in name, only an old cripple. The party-goers, one by one, began to drift away.

The Landsman came to her. "Maris," he started. "I am sorry. I would give the wings to you if I could. The law is not meant for this—not as punishment, but only as a guide. But it's flyers' law, and I cannot go against the flyers. If I deny Corm, Lesser Amberly will become like Kennehut and the songs will call me mad."

She nodded. "I understand," she said. Corm, wings under either arm, was stalking off the beach.

The Landsman turned and left, and Maris went across the sand to Russ. "Father—" she began.

He looked up. "You are no daughter of mine," he said, and turned on her deliberately. She watched the old man moving stiffly away, walking with difficulty, going inland to hide his shame.

Finally the three of them stood alone on the landing beach, wordless and beaten. Maris went to Coll and put her arms around him and hugged him. They held on to each other, both for the moment children seeking comfort they could not give.

"I have a place," Barrion said at last, his voice waking them.

They parted groggily, watched as the singer slung his guitar across his shoulders, and followed him home.

For Maris, the days that followed were dark and troubled.

Barrion lived in a small cabin by the harbor, just off a deserted, rotting wharf, and it was there they stayed. Coll was happier than Maris had ever seen him; each day he sang with Barrion, and he knew that he would be a singer after all. Only the fact that Russ refused to see him bothered the boy, and even that was often forgotten. He was young, and he had discovered that many of his own age looked on him with guilty admiration, as a rebel, and he gloried in the feeling.

But for Maris, things were not so easy. She seldom left the cabin except to wander out on the wharf at sunset and watch the fishing boats come in. She could think only of her loss. She was trapped and helpless. She had tried as hard as she could, she had done the right thing, but still her wings were gone. Tradition, like a mad cruel Landsman, had ruled, and now kept her prisoner.

Two weeks after the incident on the beach, Barrion returned to the cabin after a day on the docks, where he went daily to gather new songs from the fishermen of Amberly and sing at wharfside inns. As they ate bowls of hot, meaty stew, he looked at Maris and the boy and said, "I have arranged for a boat. In a month I will sail for the Outer Islands."

Coll smiled eagerly. "Us too?"

Barrion nodded. "You, yes, certainly. And Maris?"

She shook her head. "No."

The singer sighed. "You can gain nothing by staying here. Things will be hard for you on Amberly. Even for me, times are getting difficult. The Landsman moves against me, prompted by Corm, and respectable folk are starting to avoid me. Besides, there is a lot of world to see. Come with us." He smiled. "Maybe I can even teach *you* how to sing."

Maris played idly with her stew. "I sing worse than my brother flies, Barrion. No, I can't go. I'm a flyer. I must stay, and win my wings again."

"I admire you, Maris," he said, "but your fight is hopeless. What can you do?"

"I don't know. Something. The Landsman, perhaps. I can go to him. The Landsman makes the law, and he sympathizes. If he sees that it is best for the people of Amberly, then . . ."

"He can't defy Corm. This is a matter of flyers' law, and he has no control over that. Besides . . ." he hesitated.

"What?"

"There is news. It's all over the docks. They've found a new flyer, or an old one, actually. Devin of Gavora is en route here by boat to take up residence and wear your wings." He watched her carefully, concern written across his face.

"Devin!" She slammed down her fork, and stood. "Have their laws blinded them to common sense?" She paced back and forth across the room. "Devin is a worse flyer than Coll ever was. He lost his own wings when he swooped too low and grazed water. If it hadn't been for a ship passing by, he would be dead. So Corm wants to give him another pair?"

Barrion grinned bitterly. "He's a flyer, and he keeps the old traditions."

"How long ago did he leave?"

"A few days, the word says."

"It's a two-week voyage, easily," Maris said. "If I'm going to act, it must be before he gets here. Once he has worn the wings, they'll be his, and lost to me."

"But Maris," Coll said, "what can you do?"

"Nothing," Barrion said. "Oh, we could steal the wings, of course. Corm has had them repaired, good as new. But where would you go? You'd never find a welcome. Give it up, girl. You can't change flyers' law."

"No?" she said. Suddenly her voice was animated. She stopped pacing and leaned against the table. "Are you sure? Have the traditions *never* been changed? Where did they come from?"

Barrion looked puzzled. "Well, there was the Council, just after the Old Captain was killed, when the Landsman-Captain of Big Shotan passed out the new-forged wings. That was when it was decided that no flyer would ever bear a weapon in the sky. They remembered the battle, and the way the old star sailors used the last two sky sleds to rain fire from above."

"Yes," said Maris, "and remember, there were two other Councils as well. Generations after that, when another Landsman-Captain wanted to bend the other Landsmen to his will and bring all of Windhaven under his control, he sent the flyers of Big Shotan into the sky with swords to strike at Little Shotan. And the flyers of the other islands met in Council and condemned him, after his ghost flyers had vanished. So he was the last Landsman-Captain, and now Big Shotan is just another island."

"Yes," Coll said, "and the third Council was when all the flyers voted not to land on Kennehut, after the Mad Landsman killed the Flyer-Who-Brought-Bad-News."

Barrion was nodding. "All right. But no Council has been called since then. Are you sure they would assemble?"

"Of course," said Maris. "It is one of Corm's precious traditions. Any flyer can call a Council. And I could present my case there, to all the flyers of Windhaven, and . . ."

She stopped. Barrion looked at her and she looked back, the same thought on both minds.

"Any flyer," he said, the emphasis unvoiced.

"But I am not a flyer," Maris said. She slumped into her chair. "And Coll has renounced his wings, and Russ—even if he would see us—has passed them on. Corm would not honor our request. The word would not go out."

"You could ask Shalli," Coll suggested. "Or wait up on the flyers' cliff, or . . ."

"Shalli is too much junior to Corm, and too frightened," Barrion said. "I hear the stories. She's sad for you, like the Landsman, but she won't break tradition. Corm might try to take her wings as well. And the others—whom could you count on? And how long could you wait? Helmer visits most often, but he's as hidebound as Corm. Jamis is too young, and so on. You'd be asking them to take quite a risk." He shook his head doubtfully. "It will not work. No flyer will speak for you, not in time. In two weeks Devin will wear your wings."

All three of them were silent. Maris stared down at her plate of cold stew, and thought. No way, she asked, is there really no way? Then she looked at Barrion. "Earlier," she began, very carefully, "you mentioned something about stealing the wings . . ."

The wind was cold and wet, angry, lashing at the waves; against the eastern sky a storm was building. "Good flying weather," Maris said. The boat rocked gently beneath her.

Barrion smiled, pulled his cloak a little tighter to shut out the damp. "Now if only you could do some flying," he said.

Her eyes went to the shore, where Corm's dark wood house stood against the trees. A light was on in an upper window. Three days, Maris thought sourly. He should have been called by now. How long could they afford to wait? Each hour brought Devin closer, the man who would take her wings.

"Tonight, do you think?" she asked Barrion.

He shrugged. He was cleaning his nails with a long dagger, intent on the task. "You would know better than I," he said without looking up. "The light tower is still dark. How often are flyers called?"

"Often," Maris said, thoughtful. But would Corm be called? They had already floated offshore two nights, hoping for a summons that would call him away from the wings. Perhaps the Landsman was using only Shalli until such time as Devin arrived. "I don't like it," she said. "We have to do something."

Barrion slid his dagger into its sheath. "I could use that on Corm, but I won't. I'm with you, Maris, and your brother is all but a son to me, but I'm not going to kill for a pair of wings. No. We wait until the light tower calls to Corm, then break in. Anything else is too chancy."

Kill, Maris thought. Would it come to that, if they forced their way in while Corm was still at home? And then she knew it would. Corm was Corm, and he *would* resist. She'd been inside his home once. She remembered the set of crossed obsidian knives that gleamed upon his wall. There must be another way.

"The Landsman isn't going to call him," she said. She knew it, somehow. "Not unless there's an emergency."

Barrion studied the clouds building up in the east. "So?" he said. "We can hardly make an emergency."

"But we can make a signal," Maris said.

"Hmmmm," the singer replied. He considered the idea. "Yes, we could, I suppose." He grinned at her. "Maris, we break more laws every day. It's bad enough we're going to steal your wings, but now you want me to force my way into the light tower and send a false call. It's a good thing I'm a singer, or we'd go down as the greatest criminals in the history of Amberly."

"How does your being a singer prevent that?"

"Who do you think makes the songs? I'd rather make us all into heroes."

They traded smiles.

Barrion took the oars and rowed them quickly to shore, to a marshy beach hidden by the trees but not far from Corm's home. "Wait here," he said, as he climbed out into the knee-deep, lapping water. "I'll go to the tower. Go in and get the wings as soon as you see Corm leave." Maris nodded her agreement.

For nearly an hour she sat alone in the gathering darkness, watching lightning flash far off to the east. Soon the storm would be on them; already she could feel the bite of the wind. Finally, up on the highest hill of Lesser Amberly, the great beacon of the Landsman's light tower began to blink in a staccato rhythm. Barrion knew the correct signal somehow, Maris suddenly realized, even though she'd forgotten to tell him. The singer knew a lot, more than she'd ever given him credit for. Perhaps he wasn't such a liar after all.

Short minutes later, she was lying in the weeds a few feet from Corm's door, head low, sheltered by the shadows and the trees. The door opened, and the dark-haired flyer came out, his wings slung over his back. He was dressed warmly. Flying clothes, thought Maris. He hurried down the main road.

After he was gone, it was a simple task to find a rock, sneak around to the side of the building, and smash in a window. Luckily Corm was unmarried, and he lived alone; that is, if he didn't have a woman with him tonight. But they'd been watching the house carefully, and no one had come and gone except a cleaning woman who worked during the day.

Maris brushed away loose glass, then vaulted up onto the sill and into the house. All darkness inside, but her eyes adjusted quickly. She had to find the wings, *her* wings, before Corm returned. He'd get to the light tower soon enough and find it was a false alarm. Barrion wasn't going to linger to be caught.

The search was short. Just inside the front door, on the rack where he hung his own wings between flights, she found hers. She took them down carefully, with love and longing, and ran her hands over the cool metal to check the struts. At last, she thought; and then, They will never take them from me again.

She strapped them on, and ran. Through the door and into the woods, a different road from the one Corm had taken. He would be home soon, to discover the loss. She had to get to the flyers' cliff.

It took her a good half hour, and twice she had to hide in the underbrush on the side of the road to avoid meeting another night-time traveler. And even when she reached the cliff, there were people—two men from the flyers' lodge—down on the landing beach, so Maris had to hide behind some rocks, and wait, and watch their lanterns.

She was stiff from crouching and shivering from the cold when, far over the sea, she spied another pair of silvered wings, coming down fast. The flyer circled once low above the beach, jerking the lodge men to attention, then came in smoothly for a landing. As they unstrapped her, Maris saw it was Anni of Culhall, with a message, no doubt. Her chance was here, then. The lodge men would escort Anni to the Landsman.

When they had gone off with her, Maris scrambled to her feet, and quickly moved up the rocky path to the flyers' cliff. It was a cumbersome, slow task to unfold her own wings, but she did it, though the hinges on the left wing were stiff and she had to snap it five times before the final strut flung out. Corm didn't even take care of them, she thought bitterly.

Then, forgetting that, forgetting everything, she ran and jumped into the winds.

The gathering gale hit her almost like a fist, but she rolled with the punch, shifting and twisting until she caught a strong updraft and began to climb, quickly now, higher and higher. Close at hand, lightning flashed behind her, and she felt a brief tremor of fear. But then it was still. Again, she was flying, and if she were burned from the sky, well, no one would mourn her on Lesser Amberly save Coll, and there could be no finer death. She banked and climbed still higher, and despite herself she let out a laughing whoop of joy.

And a voice answered her. "Turn!" it said, shouting, hot with anger. Startled, losing the feel for an instant, she looked up and behind.

Lightning slashed the sky over Lesser Amberly again, and in its light the night-shadowed wings above her gleamed noonday-silver. From out of the clouds, Corm was coming down on her fast.

He was shouting as he came. "I knew it was you," he said. But the wind blew every third word away from her. "... had to ... behind it ... never went home ... cliff ... waited. *Turn!* I'll force you down! Land-bound!" That last she heard, and she laughed at him.

"Try, then," she yelled back at him, defiantly. "Show me what a flyer you are, Corm! Catch me if you can!" And then, still laughing, she tilted a wing and veered out from under his dive, and he kept on down as she rose, still shouting as he passed her.

A thousand times she'd played with Dorrel, chasing one another around the Eyrie, tag games in the sky; but now, this time, the chase was deadly earnest. Maris toyed with the winds, looking only for speed and altitude, and instinctively she found the currents and rose higher and faster. Far below now, Corm checked his fall, tilted up, banked and came at her from below. But by the time he reached her height, she was far ahead. She intended to stay that way. This was no game, and she could afford no risks. If he got above her, he was angry enough to begin forcing her down, inch by inch, until he pressed her right into the ocean. He would regret it afterward, grieve for the lost wings, but Maris knew that he would do it nonetheless. The traditions of the flyers meant that much to him. Idly, she wondered, how would she have acted, a year ago, toward someone who stole a set of wings?

Now Lesser Amberly was lost behind them, and the only land in sight was the flashing light tower of Culhall off to the right and low on the horizon. That too was soon gone, and there was nothing but black sea below and sky above. And Corm, relentless, still behind her, outlined against the storm. But—Maris looked back and blinked—he seemed smaller. Was she gaining on him? Corm was a skilled flyer, that much she was sure of. He had always performed well for Western in the competitions, while she was not allowed to compete. And yet now, clearly, the gap was widening.

Lightning flashed once more, and thunder rolled ominously across the sea a few seconds later. From below a scylla roared back at the storm, hearing in the boom an angry challenge. But for Maris, it meant something else indeed. The timing, the timing; the storm was growing more distant. She was heading northwest, the storm due west perhaps; at any rate, she was angling out from beneath it.

Something soared inside her. She banked and flipped just for the joy of it, did a showman's loop from sheer exultation, jumping from current to current like an acrobat of the sky. The winds were hers now; nothing could go wrong.

Corm closed in while Maris was playing, and when she came out of her loop and began to climb again, she saw him close at hand and dimly heard his shouts. He was yelling something about her not being able to land, about her being an outcast with her stolen wings. Poor Corm! What did he know?

Maris dove, until she could all but taste the salt, until she could hear the waters rolling a few feet below. If he would kill her, if he would force her into the waves, well, she had made herself vulnerable now, as vulnerable as she could be. She was skimming; all he had to do was catch up, get above her, swoop.

She knew, she *knew*, he could not do it, no matter how much he might like to. By the time she flew out from under the churning cloud cover, into a clear night sky where the stars winked on her wings, Corm was only a tiny dot behind her, dwindling fast. Maris waited until she could see his wings no longer, then caught a new upwind and changed course to the south, knowing that Corm would continue blindly ahead until he gave up and circled back to Lesser Amberly.

She was alone with her wings and the sky, and, briefly, there was peace.

Hours later, the first lights of Laus burned at her through the dark; flaming beacons set atop the rocky island's Old Fortress. Maris angled toward them, and soon the half-ruined bulk of the ancient castle sat before her, dead but for its lights.

She flew straight over it, across the breadth of the small mountainous island, to the landing strip on the sandy southwest spur. Laus was not populous enough to maintain a flyers' lodge, and for once Maris was thankful of that. There would be no lodge men to greet her or ask her questions. She landed alone and unnoticed in a shower of dry sand, and struggled out of her wings.

At the end of the landing strip, up against the base of the flyers' cliff, Dorrel's simple cabin was dark and empty. When he did not answer her knock, Maris opened the unlatched door and entered, calling his name. But the house was silent. She felt a rush of disappointment that quickly changed to nervousness. Where was he? How long would he be gone? What if Corm figured out where she had come and trapped her here, before Dorrel's return?

She set a rush against the banked and dimly glowing coals in the hearth and lit a sand-candle. Then she looked around the small, neat cabin, seeking some clue as to where and how long Dorrel had been gone.

There: tidy Dorrel had left some crumbs of fish cake on his otherwise clean table. She glanced toward a far corner and, yes, the house was truly empty, Anitra gone from her perch. So that was it; Dorrel was out hunting with his nighthawk.

Hoping they had not gone far, Maris took to the air again in search. She found him resting on a rock in the treacherous shallows of far western Laus, his wings strapped on but folded, Anitra perched on his wrist, enjoying a piece of the fish she had just caught. Dorrel was talking to the bird and did not see Maris until she swept above him, her wings eclipsing the stars.

Then he stared at her while she circled and dipped dangerously low, and for a moment there was no recognition at all on his blank face.

"Dorrel," she shouted, tension sharpening her voice.

"Maris?" Incredulity broke across his face.

She turned and caught an updraft. "Come onto shore. I have to talk to you."

Dorrel, nodding, stood suddenly and shook the nighthawk free. The bird surrendered her fish reluctantly and climbed into the sky on pale white wings, circling effortlessly and waiting for her master. Maris swung around in the direction she had come.

This time, when she came down in the landing strip, her descent was sudden and clumsy, and she scraped her knees badly. Maris was confused, in turmoil; the tension of the theft, the strain of the long flight after that stretch of days without the sky, the strange mixture of pain and fear and joy the sight of Dorrel had suddenly, unexpectedly given her—it all overwhelmed her, shook her, and she didn't know what to do. Before Dorrel could join her she set to work unstrapping her wings, forcing her mind through the motions with her hands. She wouldn't think yet, she wouldn't let herself think. Blood from her knees trickled maddeningly down her legs.

Dorrel landed beside her, neatly and smoothly. He was shaken by her sudden appearance, but he didn't let his emotions interfere with his flying. It was more than a matter of pride with him: it was almost bred into him, as much an inheritance as his wings were. Anitra found his shoulder as he unstrapped.

He moved toward her and put his arms out. The nighthawk made a bad-tempered noise, but he would still have embraced Maris, regardless of the bird, had she not suddenly thrust her wings into his outstretched hands.

"Here," Maris said. "I'm turning myself in. I stole these wings from Corm, and I'm giving them and myself over to you. I've come to ask you to call a Council for me, because you're a flyer and I'm not, and only a flyer can call one."

Dorrel stared at her, confused as someone awakened suddenly from a heavy sleep. Maris felt impatient with him, and overwhelmingly tired. "Oh, I'll explain," she said. "Let's go up to your place, where I can rest."

It was a long walk, but they went most of it in silence and without touching. Only once he said, "Maris—did you really *steal*—"

She cut him off. "Yes, I said." Then she suddenly sighed and moved as if to touch him, but stopped herself. "Forgive me, Dorrel, I didn't mean . . . I'm exhausted, and I suppose I'm frightened. I never thought I'd be seeing you again under such circumstances." Then she fell quiet again and he did not press her, and only Anitra broke the night with her grumbles and mutters at having her fishing ended so soon.

Once home, Maris sank into the one large chair, trying to force herself to relax, to make the tensions drain. She watched Dorrel and felt herself grow calmer as he went through his familiar rituals. He put Anitra on her perch and drew the curtains that hung around her (other folks might hood their birds to keep them quiet, but he disapproved of that), built up a fire, and hung a kettle to boil.

"Tea?"

"Yes."

"I'll put kerri blossoms in, instead of honey," he said. "That should relax you."

She felt a sudden flooding of warmth for him. "Thanks."

"Do you want to get out of those clothes? You can slip on my robe."

She shook her head—it would be too much effort to move now—and then she saw that he was gazing at her legs, bare below the short kilt she wore, and frowning with concern.

"You've hurt yourself." He poured warm water from the kettle into a dish, took a rag and some salve and knelt before her. The damp cloth cleaning away the dried blood was gentle as a soft tongue. "Ah, it's not as bad as it looked," he murmured as he worked. "Just your knees—just shallow scrapes. A clumsy landing, dear."

His nearness and his soft touch stirred her, and all tension, fear, and weariness were suddenly gone. One of his hands moved to her thigh and lingered there.

"Dorr," she said softly, almost too transfixed by the moment to speak, and he raised his head and their eyes met, and finally she had come back to him.

"It will work," Dorrel said. "They'll have to see. They can't deny you." They were sitting at breakfast. While Dorrel made eggs and tea, Maris had explained her plan in detail.

Now she smiled and spooned out more of the soft egg. She felt happy and full of hope. "Who'll go first to call Council?"

"Garth, I thought," Dorrel said eagerly. "I'll catch him at home and we'll divide up the nearby islands and branch out. Others will want to help—I just wish you could come, too," he said, and his eyes grew wistful. "It would be nice, flying together again."

"We'll have lots of that, Dorr. *If*—"

"Yes, yes, we'll have lots of time to fly together, but—it would be nice this morning, especially. It would be nice."

"Yes. It'd be nice." She went on smiling and finally he had to smile too. He was just reaching across the table to take her hand, or touch her face, when a sudden knock at the door, loud and author-itative, made them freeze.

Dorrel rose to answer it. Maris in her chair was in full view of the doorway, but there was no point in trying to hide, and there was no second door.

Helmer stood outside, folded wings strapped to his back. He looked straight at Dorrel, but not past him into the cabin at Maris. "Corm has invoked the flyer's right to call a Council," he said, his voice flat and strained and overly formal. "To concern the once-flyer Maris of Lesser Amberly who stole the wings of another. Your presence is requested."

"*What?*" Maris stood quickly. "Helmer—*Corm* has called a Council? Why?"

Dorrel tossed a glance over his shoulder at her, then looked at Helmer, who was plainly if uncomfortably ignoring Maris.

"Why, Helmer?" he asked, more quietly than Maris had.

"I've told you. And I don't have time to stand here moving the wind with my mouth. I have other flyers to inform, and it's a thick day for flying."

"Wait for me," Dorrel said. "Give me some names, some islands to go to. It will make your task easier."

The corner of Helmer's mouth twitched. "I wouldn't've thought you'd want to go on such a mission, for such a reason. I hadn't intended to ask for your help. But since you offer . . ."

Helmer gave Dorrel terse instructions while the younger flyer rapidly winged himself. Maris paced, feeling restless, awkward, and confused again. Helmer was obviously determined to ignore her, and to save them both embarrassment Maris did not question him again.

Dorrel kissed her and squeezed her tightly before he left. "Feed Anitra for me, and try not to worry. I'll be back before it's been dark too long, I hope."

When the flyers were gone, the house felt stifling. Outside was not much better, Maris discovered as she stood against the door. Helmer had been right, it was not a good day for flying. It was a day to make one think of still air. She shuddered, fearing for Dorrel. But he was too skilled and too smart to need her worry, she thought, trying to reassure herself. And she would go crazy if she sat inside all day imagining possible dangers for him. It was frustrating enough to have to wait here, denied the sky. She looked up at the cloudy-bright overcast. If, after the Council, she should be made a land-bound forever—

But there was plenty of time for sorrow in the future, so she resolved not to think about it now. She went back inside the house.

Anitra, a nocturnal flyer, was asleep behind her curtain; the cabin was still and very empty. She wished briefly for Dorrel, to ease her thoughts by sharing them, to speculate with her on why Corm had called the Council. Alone, her thoughts went around and around in her head, birds in a trap.

A geechi game sat on top of Dorrel's wardrobe. Maris took it down, and arranged the smooth black and white pebbles in a simple opening pattern, one her mind was comfortable with. Idly she began to move them, playing both sides, shoving the pebbles unthinkingly into new configurations, each suggested by the last, each as inevitable as chance. And she thought:

Corm is a proud man, and I injured his pride. He is known as a good flyer and I, a fisherman's daughter, stole his wings and outflew him when he pursued me. Now, to regain his pride, he must humble me in some very public, very grand way. Getting the wings back would not be enough for him. No, everyone, every flyer, must be present to see me humbled and declared an outlaw.

Maris sighed. That was it. This was the Council to outlaw the land-bound flyer who stole wings—oh, yes, songs would be written about it. But perhaps it made no difference. Even though Corm had stolen a flight on her, the Council could still be turned against him. She, the accused, would have the right to speak, to defend herself, to attack senseless tradition. And her chance was the same, Maris knew, the same in Corm's Council as it would have been in the one that Dorrel would have summoned. Only now she knew the full extent of Corm's hurt and his anger.

She looked down at the geechi board. The pebbles, white and black, were arrayed across the center of the board, facing each other. Both armies had committed themselves to attacking formations; it was clear that this would be no waiting game. With her next move, the captures would begin.

Maris smiled, and swept the pebbles from the table.

It took a full month for the Council to assemble.

Dorrel brought the call to four flyers that first day, and five others the next, and each of those contacted others, and those still others, and so the word went out in ever-widening ripples across the seas of Windhaven. A special flyer was sent off to the Outer Islands, another to desolate Artellia, the great frozen island to the north. Soon, all had heard, and one by one they flew to the meeting.

The site was Greater Amberly. By rights, the Council should have been held on Lesser Amberly, home to both Maris and Corm. But the smaller island had no building large enough for such a gathering as this would be, and Greater Amberly did: a huge, dank hall, seldom used.

To it came the flyers of Windhaven. Not all of them, no, for there were always emergencies, and a few still had not received the word, and others were missing on long, dangerous flights; but most of them, the vast majority, and that was enough. In no one's lifetime had there ever been such a gathering. Even the annual competitions at the Eyrie were small compared to this, mere local contests between Eastern and Western. Or so it seemed to Maris then, during the month she waited and watched while the streets of Ambertown filled with laughing flyers.

There was an air of holiday about it all. The early arrivals held drinking bouts each night, to the delight of the local wine merchants, and traded stories and songs, and gossiped endlessly about the Council and its outcome. Barrion and other singers kept them entertained by night, while by day they raced and frolicked in the air. The latecomers were greeted riotously as they straggled in. Maris, who had flown back from Laus after getting special leave to use the wings once more, ached to join them. Her friends were all there, and Corm's, and indeed all the wings of Western. The Easterners had come too, many in suits of fur and metal that reminded her irresistibly of the way Raven had dressed on that day so long ago. There were three pale-skinned Artellians, each wearing a silver circlet on his brow, aristocrats from a dark frigid land where flyers were kings as well as messengers. They mingled, brothers and equals, with the red-uniformed flyers of Big Shotan, and the twenty tall representatives of the Outer Islands, and the squadron of sunburned winged priests from the lush Southern Archipelago who served the Sky God as well as their Landsmen. Seeing them, meeting them, walking among them, the size and breadth and cultural diversity of Windhaven struck Maris as seldom before. She had flown, if only for a short time; she had been one of the privileged few. Yet there were still so many places she had not been. If only she could have her wings again . . .

Finally all those who were coming had arrived. The Council was set for dusk; there would be no crowds in the inns of Ambertown tonight.

"You have a chance," Barrion told Maris on the steps of the great hall just before the meeting. Coll was with her too, and Dorrel.

"Most of them are in a good mood, after weeks of wine and song. I drift, I talk, I sing, and I know this: they *will* listen to you." He grinned his wolfish grin. "For flyers, that is *quite* unusual."

Dorrel nodded. "Garth and I have talked to many of them. There is a lot of sympathy for you, particularly among the younger flyers. The older delegates, most of them, tend to side with Corm and tradition, but even they do not have their minds completely made up."

Maris shook her head. "The older flyers outnumber the younger ones, Dorr."

Barrion put a fatherly hand on her shoulder. "Then you will have to win them to your side also. After the things I've seen you do already, it should be easy enough." He smiled.

The delegates had all filed inside, and now, from the door behind her, Maris heard the Landsman of Greater Amberly sound the ceremonial drumbeats that signaled the beginning of the Council. "We must go," Maris said. Barrion nodded. As a non-flyer, he was barred from the assembly. He squeezed her shoulder once, for luck, then took his guitar and walked slowly down the steps. Maris, Coll, and Dorrel hurried inside.

The hall was an immense stone pit, ringed by torches. In the center of the sunken floor, a long table had been set up. The flyers sat around it in a semicircle, on rough stone seats that ascended, tier after tier after tier, to the place where wall met ceiling. Jamis the Senior, his thin face lined by age, sat in the center of the long table. Though a land-bound for several years now, his experience and character were still widely esteemed, and he had come by boat to preside. On either side of him sat the only two non-flyers admitted: the swarthy Landsman of Greater Amberly and the portly ruler of Lesser. Corm had the fourth seat, at the right-hand end of the table. A fifth chair was empty on the left.

Maris went to it, while Dorrel and Coll climbed the stairs to their places. The drumbeats sounded again, a call for silence. Maris sat and looked around as the room began to quieten. Coll had found a seat, high up among the unwinged youths. Many of them had come by boat from nearby islands, to see history be made; but like Coll, they were expected to play no part in the decision. Now they ignored Coll, as might be expected; children eager for the sky could scarcely understand a boy who had willingly given up his wings. He looked dreadfully out of place and lonely, much as Maris felt.

The drums stopped. Jamis the Senior stood, and his deep voice rang over the hall. "This is the first flyers' Council in the memory of any here," he said. "Most of you already know the circumstances under which it has been called. My rules will be simple. Corm shall speak first, since he invoked this meeting. Then Maris, whom he accuses, shall have her chance to answer him. Then any flyer or former flyer here may have his or her say. I ask only that you speak loudly, and name yourself before you talk. Many of us here are strangers to each other." He sat down.

And now Corm stood and spoke into the silence. "I invoked this Council by flyer's right," he said, his voice assured and resonant. "A crime has been committed, and its nature and implications are such that it must be answered by us all, by all flyers acting as one. Our decision shall determine our future, as have the decisions of Councils past. Imagine what our world should be now if our fathers and mothers before us had decided to bring warfare into the air. The kinship of all flyers would not be—we would be torn apart by petty regional rivalries instead of being properly airborne above the quarrels of the land."

He went on, painting a picture of the desolation that could have followed, had that long ago Council voted wrongly. He was a good speaker, Maris thought; he spoke like Barrion sang. She shook herself out of the spell Corm was creating, and wondered how she could possibly counter him.

"The problem today is equally grave," Corm continued, "and your decision will not simply affect one person, for whom you may feel sympathy, but rather all our children for generations to come. Mind you remember that as you listen to the arguments tonight." He looked around, and although his burning eyes did not fall on her, Maris nevertheless felt intimidated.

"Maris of Lesser Amberly has stolen a pair of wings," he said. "The story, I think, is known to all of you—" But Corm told it, nonetheless, from the facts of her birth to the scene on the beach.

". . . and a new bearer was found. But before Devin of Gavora, who is among us now, could arrive to claim his wings, Maris stole them, and fled.

"But this is not the whole of it. Stealing is shameful, but even the theft of wings might not be grounds for a flyers' Council. Maris knew she could not hope to keep the wings. She took them not to flee, but rather with the thought of revolting against our most vital traditions. She questions the very foundations of our society. She would open the ownership of the wings to dispute, threaten us with anarchy. Unless we make our disapproval plain, pass judgment on her in Council that will go down in history, the facts could easily become distorted. Maris could be remembered as a brave rebel, and not the thief she is."

A twinge went through Maris at that word. Thief. Was that truly what she was?

"She has friends among the singers who would delight in mocking us," Corm was saying, "in singing songs in praise of her daring." And Maris heard in memory Barrion's voice: *I'd rather make us all into heroes.* Her eyes sought out Coll and she saw that he was sitting straighter, with a slight smile on his lips. Singers did indeed have power, if they were good.

"So we must speak out plainly, for all of history, in denouncing what she has done," Corm said. He faced Maris and looked down at her. "Maris, I accuse you of the theft of wings. And I call upon the flyers of Windhaven, met in Council, to name you outlaw, and pledge that none will land on any island you call home."

He sat, and in the awful silence that followed Maris knew just how much she had offended him. She had never dreamed he would ask so much. Not content merely to take her wings, he would deny her life itself, force her into friendless exile on some distant empty rock.

"Maris," Jamis said gently. She had not risen. "It is your turn. Will you answer Corm?"

Slowly she got to her feet, wishing for the power of a singer, wishing that even once she could speak with the assurance Corm had in his voice. "I cannot deny the theft," she said, looking up at the rows of blank faces, the sea of strangers. Her voice was steadier than she had thought it would be. "I stole the wings out of desperation, because they were my only chance. A boat would have been far too slow, and no one on Lesser Amberly was willing to help. I needed to reach a flyer who would call Council for me. Once I did that, I surrendered my wings. I can prove this, if—" She looked over at Jamis; he nodded.

Dorrel picked up his cue. Halfway up in the tiered hall, he rose. "Dorrel of Laus," he said loudly. "I vouch for Maris. As soon as she reached me, she gave her wings into my safekeeping, and would not wear them again. I do not call this theft." From around him, there was a chorus of approving murmurs; his family was known and esteemed, his word good.

Maris had scored a point, and now she continued, feeling more confident with every word. "I wanted a Council for something I consider very important to us all, and to our future. But Corm beat me to it." She grimaced slightly, unconsciously. And out in the audience she noticed a few smiles on the faces of flyers who were strangers to her. Skepticism? Contempt? Or support, agreement? She had to will her hands to part and lie still by her sides. It would not do to be wringing her hands before them all.

"Corm says I am fighting tradition," Maris continued, "and that's true. He has told you this is a terrible thing, but he hasn't said why. He hasn't explained why tradition needs to be defended against me. Just because something has always been done in one way doesn't mean that change is impossible, or undesirable. Did people fly on the home worlds of the star sailors? If not, does that mean it was better *not* to fly? Well, after all, we aren't dauberbirds, that if our beaks get pushed to the ground we keep on walking that way until we fall over and die—we don't have to walk the same path every day—it wasn't bred into *us*."

She heard a laugh from her listeners, and felt elated. She could paint pictures with words even as Corm could! Those silly waddling cave birds had gone from her mind to someone else's and drawn a laugh; she had mentioned breaking tradition, and still they listened. Inspired, she went on.

"We are people, and if we have an instinct for anything, it is the instinct—the will—toward change. Things have always been changing and if we're smart we'll make the changes for ourselves, and for the better, before we're forced into them.

"The tradition of passing the wings on from parent to child has worked fairly well for a long time—certainly, it is better than anarchy, or the older tradition of trial by combat that sprang up in Eastern during the Days of Sorrow. But it is not the only way, nor is it the perfect way."

"Enough talk!" someone growled. Maris looked around for the source and was startled to see Helmer rise from his seat in the second tier front. The flyer's face was bitter, and he stood with folded arms.

"Helmer," Jamis said firmly, "Maris has the floor."

"I don't care," he said. "She attacks our ways, but she offers us nothing better. And for good reason. This way has worked for so many years because there *is* none better. It may be hard, yes. It's hard for you because you weren't born to a flyer. Sure, it's hard. But have you another way?"

Helmer, she thought as he sat. Of course, his anger made sense, he was one whom this tradition would soon hurt—was hurting. Still young, he would be a land-bound in less than a year, when his daughter came of age and took his wings. He had accepted the loss as inevitable, perhaps, as a rightful part of an honored tradition. But now Maris attacked the tradition, the only thing that gave nobility to Helmer's sacrifice-to-come. If things remained unchanged, Maris wondered briefly, would Helmer in time hate his own daughter for her wings? And Russ . . . if he had not been injured . . . if Coll had not been born . . .

"Yes," Maris said loudly, suddenly realizing that the room was silently awaiting her reply. "Yes, I do have a way; I would never have presumed to call a Council if—"

"You didn't!" someone shouted, and others laughed. Maris felt herself grow hot and hoped she was not blushing.

Jamis slapped the table, hard. "Maris of Lesser Amberly is speaking," he said, loudly. "The next one who interrupts her will be ejected!"

Maris gave him a grateful smile. "I propose a new way, a better way," she said. "I propose that the right to wear wings be *earned.*

Not by birth or by age, but by the one measure that truly counts—by skill!" And as she spoke, the idea sprang suddenly into her head, more elaborate, more complex, more *right* than her vague concept of a free-for-all. "I propose a flying academy, open to all, to every child who dreams of wings. The standards would be very high, of course, and many would be sent away. But all would have the right to try—the son of a fisherman, the daughter of a singer, or a weaver—everyone could dream, hope. And for those who passed all the tests, there would be a final test. At our annual competition, they could challenge any flyer of their choice. And, if they were good enough, good enough to outfly him or her, then they would win the wings!

"The best flyers would always keep the wings, this way. And a defeated flyer, well, could wait for next year and try to win back the wings from the one who had taken them. Or he or she could challenge someone else, some poorer flyer. No flyer could afford to be lazy, no one who did not love the sky would have to fly, and . . ." She looked at Helmer, whose face was unreadable. "And more, even the children of flyers would have to challenge to win the sky. They would claim their parents' wings only when they were ready, when they could actually fly better than their father or their mother. No flyer would become a land-bound just because he'd married young and had a child come of age while he should, by all that is just and right, still be in the sky. Only skill would be important, not birth, not age—the *person*, not tradition!"

She paused, on the verge of blurting out her own story, of what it was like to be a fisherman's daughter and know the sky could never be hers—the pain, the longing. But why waste her breath? These were all born flyers, and she would not wring sympathy from them for the land-bounds they held in contempt. No, it was important that the next Woodwings born on Windhaven have a chance to fly, but it was no good as an argument. She had said enough. She had set it all before them, and the choice was theirs. She glanced briefly at Helmer, at the odd smile flickering over his face, and she knew with dead certainty that his vote was hers. She had just given him a chance to reclaim his life, without being cruel to his daughter. Satisfied, smiling, Maris sat.

Jamis the Senior looked over at Corm.

"That sounds very nice," he said. Smiling, in control, Corm did not even bother to stand. At the sight of his calm, Maris felt all her painfully piled-up hope slip away. "A nice dream for a fisherman's daughter, and it's understandable. Perhaps you don't understand about the wings, Maris. How do you expect families who have flown since—since *forever*—to put their wings up for grabs, to pass them on to strangers. Strangers who without tradition or family pride may not care for them properly, may not respect them. Do you truly think any of us would hand over our heritage to an impudent land-bound? Instead of our own children?"

Maris' temper flared. "You expected me to give *my* wings to Coll, who could not fly as well as I."

"They were never your wings," Corm said.

Her lips tightened; she said nothing.

"If you thought they were, that was your folly," Corm said. "Think: If wings are passed from person to person like a cloak, if they are held for only a year or two, what sort of pride would their owners have in them? They would be—borrowed—not owned, and everyone knows a flyer must own his wings, or he is not a flyer at all. Only a land-bound would wish such a life on us!"

Maris felt the sentiments of the audience shifting with each of Corm's words. He piled his arguments on top of each other so glibly that they all slipped away from her before she'd had a chance to get at them. She had to answer him, but how, *how?* The attachment of a flyer to his wings was nearly as strong as his attachment to his feet; she couldn't deny that, she couldn't fight it. She remembered her own anger when she felt Corm had not cared for her wings properly, and yet they were never hers at all, only her father's, her brother's.

"The wings are a trust," she blurted out. "Even now a flyer knows he must pass them on, in time, to his child."

"That is quite different," Corm said tolerantly. "Family is not the same as strangers, and a flyer's child is not a land-bound."

"This is something too important to be silly about blood ties!" Maris flashed at him, her voice rising. "Listen to yourself, Corm!

Listen to the snobbery that has been allowed to grow in you, in other flyers; listen to your contempt for the land-bound, as if they could help what they are with the laws of inheritance as they now stand!" Her words were angry, and the audience grew perceptibly more hostile; she would lose it all if she championed the land-bound against the flyers, she suddenly realized.

Maris willed herself to be calm. "We *do* have pride in our wings," she said, consciously returning to her strongest arguments. "And that pride, if it is strong enough, should make sure we keep them. Good flyers will keep the sky. If challenged, they will not be defeated easily. If defeated, they will come back. And they will have the satisfaction of knowing that the flyer who takes their wings is good, of knowing that their replacement will bring honor to the wings and use them well, regardless of parentage."

"The wings are meant to be—" Corm began, but Maris would not let him finish.

"The wings are *not* meant to be lost in the sea," she said, "and clumsy flyers, flyers who have taken no care to be really good because they've never had to, *these* are the flyers who have lost wings for us all. Some hardly deserved the name of flyer. And what of the children who are really too young for the sky, though they may be of age technically? They panic, fly foolishly, and die, taking their wings with them." She glanced quickly at Coll. "Or how about the ones who were not meant to fly at all? Being born of a flyer doesn't mean you'll have the skill. My own—Coll, whom I love as a brother and a son, *he* was never meant to be a flyer. The wings were his, yet I couldn't give them to him—didn't want to give them to him—oh, even if he *had* wanted them, I wouldn't have wanted to give them up—"

"Your system won't change that," someone shouted.

Maris shook her head. "No, it wouldn't. I still wouldn't be *happy* about losing my wings, but if I were bested, well, I could stay on at the academy, train, wait for next year and try to get them back. Oh, nothing is going to be *perfect*, don't you see, because there aren't enough wings, and that's going to get worse, not better. But we must try to stop it, stop all the wings that are lost each year, stop sending out unqualified flyers, stop losing so many. There will still be accidents, we'll still have dangers, but we won't lose wings and flyers because of poor judgment and fear and lack of skill."

Exhausted, Maris ran out of words, but her speech had stirred the audience, moved it back toward her. A dozen hands were up. Jamis pointed, and a solidly built Shotaner rose from the mass.

"Dirk of Big Shotan," he said, in a low voice, and then he repeated it again when the flyers in the back shouted "Louder! Louder!" His speech was awkward and self-conscious. "I just wanted to say—I've been sitting here, and listening—I've been—I never expected—all this, just to vote on an outlawing—" He shook his head, clearly having difficulty getting the words out. "Oh, be damned," he said finally. "Maris is right. I'm half ashamed to say it, but I shouldn't be. It's the truth—I don't *want* my son to have my wings. I'm afraid to. He's a good boy, mind you, and I love him, but he has attacks now and again, you know, the shaking sickness. He can't fly like that—he *shouldn't* fly—but he's grown up thinking of nothing else, and next year when he's thirteen he'll expect my wings, and with things like they are I'll have to give them to him, and he'll fly off and die, and then I won't have my son and I won't have my wings and I might as well die too. No!" He sat down, a dark red color and out of breath.

Several people shouted support. Maris, heartened, looked over at Corm, and saw that his smile was flickering. Suddenly he had doubts.

A familiar friend rose then, and smiled at her from above. "I'm Garth of Skulny," he said. "I'm with Maris, too!" Another speaker backed her, then another, and Maris smiled. Dorrel had scattered friends all over the audience and now they were trying to stampede the assembly her way. And it seemed to be working! For, in between the endorsements from flyers she had known for years, total strangers stood to voice their support. Had they won, then? Corm clearly looked worried.

"You recognize what is wrong with our way, but I think your academy is not the answer." The words jolted Maris out of her complacent optimism. The speaker was a tall, blond woman, a leading flyer from the Outer Islands. "There is a reason for our tradition and we should not weaken it, or our children may go back to the idiocy of trial by combat. What we must do is teach our children better. We must teach them to have *more* pride, and we must build the needed skills in them from the time they are very small. This is as my mother taught me, and as I am teaching my son. Perhaps a test of some sort is necessary—your idea of a challenge is good." Her mouth twisted wryly. "I admit, I do not look forward to the day, which comes too quickly, when I must give up my wings to Vard. Both of us will be too young, I think, when that day comes. That he should have to compete with me, to prove himself as good—no, a *better* flyer—than I am, yes, that is an excellent idea."

Other flyers in the hall were nodding in agreement. Yes, yes, of course, why hadn't they seen what a good idea some sort of testing would be? Everyone knew that the coming-of-age was rather arbitrary, that some were still children when they took on wings, others full adults. Yes, let the youngsters prove themselves as flyers first . . . the tide swept the assembly.

"But this academy," the speaker said gently. "That is not necessary. We birth enough new flyers among ourselves. I know your background and I can understand your feelings, but I cannot share them. It would not be wise." She sat down, and Maris felt her heart sink with her. That had done it, she thought. Now they will vote for a test, but the sky will still be closed to those born of the wrong parents; the flyers would reject the most important part. So close, she had almost done it, but not close enough.

A gaunt man in silk and silver stood. "Arris, flyer and Prince of Artellia," he said, his eyes ice blue beneath his silver crown. "I vote with my sister from the Outer Islands. My children are of royal blood, born and bred to wings. It would be a joke to force them to fly in races with commoners. But a test, to see when they are worthy, now *that* is an idea worthy of a flyer."

He was followed by a dark woman all in leather. "Zeva-kul of Deeth in Southern Archipelago," she began. "Each year I fly messages for my Landsman, but I also serve the Sky God, like all of the upper castes. The concept of passing wings to a lower one, a soil-child, possibly an unbeliever—*no!*"

Other echoes came, and rolled across the hall:

"Joi, of Stormhammer-the-Outermost. I say yes, make us fly to earn our wings, but only against the children of flyers."

"Tomas, of Little Shotan. Children of the land-born could never learn to love the sky as we do. It would be a waste of time and money to build this academy Maris speaks of. But I'm for a test."

"Crain of Poweet, and I'm with these others. Why should we have to compete with the children of fisherpeople? They don't let us compete for their boats, do they?" The hall rocked with laughter, and the older flyer grinned. "Yes, a joke, a good one. Well, brothers, we would be a joke, this academy would be a joke if it let in riff-raff of any birth at all. Wings belong to flyers and over the years it has remained that way because it is the way it is. The other people are content, and very few of them *really* want to fly. For most it is only a passing whim, or too frightening to think about. Why should we encourage idle dreams? They are not flyers, were never meant to be, and they can lead worthwhile lives in some other . . ."

Maris listened in disbelief and rising anger, infuriated by the smug self-righteousness of his tone . . . and then she saw with horror that other flyers, including some of the younger ones, were bobbing their heads complacently in time with his words. Yes, they were better because they were born of flyers, yes, they were superior and did not wish to mix, yes, yes. Suddenly it did not matter that in times past, *she* had felt much the same way about the land-bound. Suddenly all she could think of was her father, her blood-father, the dead fisherman she scarcely remembered. Memories she had thought gone came back: sensory impressions, chiefly—stiff clothes that reeked of salt and fish; warm hands, rough but gentle, that smoothed her hair and wiped tears off her cheeks after her mother had scolded her—and stories he had told, in his low voice, tales of things he had seen that day in his little skiff—what the birds had looked like, racing away from a sudden storm, how the moonfish leaped toward the night sky, how the wind felt and the waves sounded against the boat. Her father had been an observant man and a brave one, daring the ocean every day in his frail boat, and Maris knew in her hot rage that he was the inferior of no one here, of no one on Windhaven.

"You snobs," she said sharply, not caring anymore whether it would help or hurt the vote. "All of you. Thinking how superior you are, just because you were born of a flyer and inherited wings through no goodness of your own. You think you inherited your parents' skill? Well, how about the other half of your heritage? Or were all of you born of flyer marriages?" She jabbed an accusing finger at a familiar face on the third tier. "You, Sar, you were nodding just then. Your father was a flyer, yes, but your mother was a trader, and born of fisherfolk. Do you look down on them? What if your mother confessed that her husband was not your real father—what if she told you that you could blame your birth on a trader she met in the East? What then? Would you feel obliged to give up your wings and seek some other life?"

Moon-faced Sar only gaped at her; never a quick man, he couldn't understand why she had singled him out. Maris withdrew her finger and launched her anger against them all.

"My true father was a fisherman, a fine, brave, honest man who never wore wings and never wanted them. But if, *if* he had been chosen to be a flyer, he would have been the best of all! Songs would be sung of him, celebrating him! If we inherit our talent from our parents, look at me. My mother can spin and gather oysters. I cannot. My father could not fly. I can. And some of you know how good I am—better than some who were born to it." She turned and glanced down the length of the table. "Better than you, Corm," she said in a voice that carried all through the great hall. "Or have you forgotten?"

Corm glared up at her, his face flushed with anger, a thick vein bulging in his neck. He said nothing. Maris turned back to the hall. Her voice softened, and she looked out on them with false solicitude. "Are you afraid?" she asked them. "Have you hung onto your wings only on the strength of a pretense? Are you afraid that all the grubby little fisherchildren will come and snatch them away from you, prove themselves better flyers than you and make you all look fools?"

Then all her words were gone, and her anger. And Maris sat back in her chair, and silence hung heavy in the great stone hall.

Finally a hand went up, and then another, but Jamis only stared blankly ahead, his face thoughtful. No one moved until at last he stirred himself, as if from sleep, and gestured at someone in the crowd.

High up against the wall, an old man with one dead arm stood alone in the flickering yellow torchlight. The assembly turned to watch him.

"Russ, of Lesser Amberly," he began. His tone was gentle. "My friends, Maris is right. We have been fools. And none of us has been so big a fool as I.

"Not long ago, I stood on a beach and said I had no daughter. Tonight, I wish I could have back those words, I wish I still had the right to call Maris my daughter. She has made me very proud. But she isn't mine. No, as she said, she was born of a fisherman, a better man than I. All I did was love her for a bit, and teach her how to fly. It didn't take much teaching, you know. She was always so eager. My little Woodwings. There was nothing could stop her, nothing. Not even me, when like a fool I tried to, after Coll was born.

"Maris is the finest flyer on Amberly, and my blood has nothing to do with it. Only her desire matters, only her dream. And if you, my flyer brothers, if you have such disdain for the children of the land-bound, then it is a shaming thing for you to fear them. Have you so little faith in your own children? Are you so certain that they could not keep their wings, against a fisherchild's hungry challenge?"

Russ shook his head. "I don't know. I'm an old man, and things have been confused lately. But I know this much: If I still had use of my arm, no one would take *my* wings from me, not even if his father was a nighthawk. And no one will ever take Maris' wings until she is ready to set them down. No. If you truly teach your children to fly well, they will keep the sky. If you have the pride you boast of, you'll live up to it, and prove it, by letting the wings be worn only by those who have earned them, only by those who have proven themselves in the air."

Russ sat down again, and the darkness at the top of the hall swallowed him up. Corm began to say something, but Jamis the Senior silenced him. "We have had enough from you," he said. Corm blinked in surprise.

"I think *I* will say something," Jamis said. "And then we will vote. Russ has spoken wisdom for all of us, but one thought I must add. Are we not, each of us, descended from the star sailors? All of Windhaven is family, really. And there is none among us who cannot find a flyer in his or her family tree, if we go back far enough. Think of that, my friends. And remember that while your eldest child may wear your wings and fly, his younger brother and sisters and all their children for generations after will be land-bound. Should we really deny them the wind forever, simply because their ancestors were second-born, instead of first?" Jamis smiled. "Perhaps I should add that I was my mother's second son. My elder brother died in a storm six months before he was to take his wings. A small thing, that. Don't you think?"

He looked around, at the two Landsmen who flanked him, who had sat silently through all the proceedings, quieted by flyers' law. He whispered first to one, then to the other, and nodded.

"We find that Corm's proposal, to name Maris of Lesser Amberly an outlaw, is out of order," Jamis said. "We will now vote on Maris' proposal, to establish a flyers' academy open to all. I vote in favor."

After that, there was no more doubt.

Afterward, Maris felt slightly in shock, giddy with victory, yet somehow not able to believe that it was really over, that she did not have to fight anymore. The air outside the hall was clean and wet, the wind blowing steadily from the east. She stood on the steps and savored it, while friends and strangers crowded about her, wanting to talk. Dorrel kept his arm around her, and did not ask questions nor express amazement; he was restful to lean against. What now? she wondered. Home again? Where was Coll? Perhaps he'd gone to fetch Barrion and bring the boat.

The crowd around her parted. Russ stood there, Jamis at his side. Her stepfather was holding a pair of wings. "Maris," he said.

"*Father?*" Her voice was trembling.

"This is how it should have been all along," he said, smiling at her. "I would be proud if you would let me call you daughter again, after all that I have done. I would be even prouder if you would wear my wings."

"You've won them," Jamis said. "The old rules don't apply, and you're certainly qualified. Until we get the academy going, there's no one to wear them except you and Devin. And you took better care of these than Devin ever did of his."

Her hands went out to take the wings from Russ. They were hers again. She was smiling, no longer tired, buoyed by the weight of them in her hands, the familiarity of them. "Oh, Father," she said, and then, weeping, she and Russ embraced each other.

When the tears were gone, they all went to the flyers' cliff, quite a crowd of them. "Let's fly to the Eyrie," she said to Dorrel. Then there was Garth, just beyond—she had not noticed him in the crowd before. "Garth! You come too. We'll have a party!"

"Yes," Dorrel said, "but is the Eyrie the place for it?"

Maris flushed. "Oh, of course not!" She glanced around at the crowd. "No, we'll go back to our house, on Lesser, and *everyone* can come, us and Father and the Landsman and Jamis, and Barrion will sing for us, if we can find him, and—" and then she saw Coll, running toward her, his face alight.

"Maris! Maris!" He ran to her and hugged her enthusiastically, then broke away, grinning.

"Where did you go to?"

"Off with Barrion, I had to, I'm making a song. Just got the start of it now, but it will be good, I can feel it, it really will be. It's about you."

"Me?"

He was obviously proud of himself. "Yes. You'll be famous. Everyone will sing it and everyone will know about you."

"They already do," Dorrel said. "Believe me."

"Oh, but I mean forever. For as long as this song is sung they'll know about you—the girl who wanted wings so much she changed the world."

And perhaps it was true, Maris thought later, as she strapped on her wings and rose into the wind with Dorrel and Garth by her side. But to have changed the world didn't seem half so important nor half so real as the wind in her hair, the familiar pull of muscles as she rose, riding the beloved currents she had thought might be lost to her forever. She had her wings again, she had the sky; she was whole now and she was happy.

PART TWO

One~Wing

THE ODDEST THING about dying was how easy it was, how calm and beautiful.

The still air had come upon Maris without warning. An instant before, the storm had raged all around her. Rain stung her eyes and ran down her cheeks and *ting*'d against the silver metal of her wings, and the winds were full of tumult, pushing her this way and that, slapping her contemptuously from side to side as if she were a child new to the air. Beneath the wing struts, her arms ached from the struggle. Dark clouds obscured the horizon, while the sea below was frothing and troubled; land was nowhere in sight. Maris cursed and hurt and flew.

Then peace enveloped her, and calm, and death.

The winds quieted and the rains stopped. The sea ceased its wild heaving. The clouds themselves seemed to draw back, until they were infinitely far away. A silence fell, an eerie hush, as if time had paused to catch its breath.

In the still air, with her bright wings spread wide, Maris began to descend.

It was a slow, gradual descent, a thing of beauty, graceful and inevitable. Without a breeze to push or lift, she could only glide forward and down. It was not a fall. It seemed to last forever. Far ahead she could see the spot where she would hit the water.

Briefly her flyer's instincts bid her struggle. She banked this way and that, tried to tack, searched vainly for an updraft or a current in the quiet sky. Her wings, twenty feet across, lifted and fell, and a sudden shaft of wan sunlight gleamed on the silver metal. But her descent continued.

Then she was calm, as calm as the air, her inner turmoil as still as the sea below. She felt the deep peace of surrender, the relief of ending her long battle with the winds. She had always been at their mercy, she thought, never truly in control. They were wild and she was weak, and she was foolish to have dreamed otherwise. She looked up, wondering if she would see the ghost flyers who were said to haunt still air.

The tips of her boots brushed the water first, and then her body shattered the gray, smooth mirror of the ocean. The impact of the cold water seared her like a flame, and she sank . . .

. . . and woke, wet and gasping for breath.

Silence pounded in her ears. The sweat on her body dried in the cool air, and she sat up, disoriented and blind. Across the room she could see a thin red line of banked coals, but they were at the wrong side of the bed to be the Eyrie, and too far away for her fire-place at home. The air smelled faintly of damp and sea mold.

The smell gave it away. She was at the academy, she thought with relief, at Woodwings; suddenly all the shadows resolved themselves into the mundane and familiar. The tension drained slowly from her body, and now Maris was fully awake. Pulling a roughly woven shift over her head, she moved carefully across the dark room to the fireplace, where she took a woven taper from the pile and lit a sand candle.

In the light she saw the little stone jug beside her low bed, and smiled. Just the thing to wash away the nightmares.

She sat cross-legged on the bed as she sipped the cool, woody wine, staring at the flickering candle flame all the while. The dream disturbed her. Like all flyers, Maris feared still air, but until now she had not had nightmares about it. And the peace of it all, the sense of surrender and acceptance—those were the worst parts. I am a flyer, she thought, and that was not a true flyer's dream.

Someone knocked on her door.

"Enter," Maris said, setting the wine jug aside.

S'Rella stood in the doorway, a slight, dark girl with her hair cropped short in the Southern fashion. "Breakfast soon, Maris," she said, the slight slurring of her speech reflecting her origins. "Sena wants to see you before, though. Up in her room."

"Thanks," Maris said, smiling. She liked S'Rella, perhaps best of all the students at the Woodwings academy. The island in the Southern Archipelago where S'Rella had been born was a world away from Maris' own Lesser Amberly, but despite their differences Maris saw a lot of herself in the younger girl. S'Rella was small but determined, with a stamina that belied her size. At the moment she was still graceless in the sky, but she was stubborn enough to give hope of quick improvement. Maris had been working with Sena's flock of would-be flyers for nearly ten days now, and she had come to regard S'Rella as one of the three or four most promising.

"Shall I wait and show you the way?" the girl asked when Maris climbed off the bed to wash at the basin of water in the far corner of the room.

"No," Maris said. "Off to breakfast now. I can find Sena well enough myself." She smiled to soften the dismissal, and S'Rella smiled back, a little shyly, before she left.

A few minutes later Maris was having second thoughts as she groped along a narrow, dank corridor in search of Sena's cubbyhole. Woodwings academy was an ancient structure, a huge rock shot through with tunnels and caves, some natural, others hollowed out by human hands. Its lower chambers were perpetually flooded, and even in the upper, inhabited portions, many of the rooms and all of the halls were windowless, cut off from sun and stars. The sea smell was everywhere. In the old days it had been a fortress, built during Seatooth's bitter revolt against Big Shotan and afterward unoccupied until the Landsman of Seatooth had offered it to the flyers as a site for a training academy. In the seven years since, Sena and her charges had restored much of it, but it was still easy to take a wrong turning and get lost in the abandoned sections.

Time passed without a trace in the corridors of Woodwings. Torches burned down in wall-sockets and lamps ran short of oil, and days often passed before anyone noticed. Maris felt her way carefully along one such dark stretch of corridor, nervous and a bit oppressed by the weight of the old fortress on her. She did not like being underground and enclosed; it quarreled with all her flyer's instincts.

With relief Maris saw the dim glow of a light ahead. One last, sharp corner and she found herself back in familiar territory. Unless she had gotten turned around completely, Sena's room was the first to the left.

"Maris." Sena looked up and smiled. She was sitting in a wicker chair, carving a soft block of wood with a bone knife, but now she set it aside and motioned Maris to enter. "I was about to call for S'Rella again and send her looking for you. Did you get lost in our maze?"

"Almost," Maris said, shaking her head. "I should have thought to carry a light. I can get from my room to the kitchen or the common room or the outside, but beyond that it is a less certain proposition."

Sena laughed, but it was only polite laughter, masking a mood that was far from light. The teacher was a former flyer, three times Maris' age, made land-bound a decade ago in the sort of accident all too common among flyers. Normally her vigor and enthusiasm cloaked her age, but this morning she looked old and tired. Her bad eye, like a piece of milky sea-glass, seemed to weigh down the left side of her face. It sagged and trembled beneath its burden.

"You sent S'Rella to me for a reason," Maris said. "News?"

"News," Sena said, "and not good. I thought it best not to talk about it at breakfast until I had discussed it with you."

"Yes?"

"Eastern has closed Airhome," Sena said.

Maris sighed and leaned back in her chair. Suddenly she too felt weary. The news was no great surprise, but it was still disheartening. "Why now?" she asked. "I spoke to Nord three months ago, when they sent me out with a message to Far Hunderlin. He thought they would keep the doors open at least through the next competition. He even told me that he had several promising students."

"There was a death," Sena said. "One of those promising students made a misjudgment, and struck a cliffside with her wing. Nord could only watch helplessly as she fell to the rocks below. Worse, her parents were there too. Wealthy, powerful people—traders from Cheslin with more than a dozen ships. The girl had been showing off for them. The parents went to the Landsman, of course, asking for justice. They said Nord was negligent."

"Was he?" Maris said.

Sena shrugged. "He was a mediocre flyer even when he had his wings, and I cannot believe he was better than that as a teacher. Always too eager to impress. And he constantly overpraised and overestimated his students. Last year, in the competition, he sponsored nine in challenges. They all failed, and most had no business trying. I sponsored only three. This girl that died, I'm told, had been at Airhome only a year. A *year*, Maris! She had talent perhaps, but it was like Nord to let her go too far too soon. Well, it is too late now. You know the academies have been a drain, a useless drain to hear some Landsmen talk. All they needed was an excuse. They dismissed Nord and closed the school. End. And all the children of Eastern can give up their dreams now, and content themselves with their lot in life." Her voice was bitter.

"Then we are the last," Maris said glumly.

"We are the last," Sena echoed. "And for how long? The Landsman sent a runner to me last night, and I hobbled up to get this joyous news, and afterward we talked. She is not happy with us, Maris. She says that she has given us meat and hearth and iron coin for seven years, but we have given her no flyer in return. She is impatient."

"So I gather," Maris said. She knew the Landsman of Seatooth only by reputation, but that was enough. Seatooth lay close by Big Shotan but had a long, fierce history of independence. Its present ruler was a proud, ambitious woman who was deeply resentful that her island had never had a flyer of its own. She had campaigned hard to make Seatooth the home of the training academy for the Western Archipelago, and once she had been lavish in her support. But now she expected results. "She doesn't understand," Maris said. "None of the land-bound understand, really. The Woodwingers come to the competitions almost raw, to vie with seasoned flyers and flyer-children who have been bred and reared to wings. If only they would give you *time* . . ."

"Time, time, time," said Sena, a hint of anger in her voice. "Yes, I said as much to the Landsman. She said that seven years was enough time. You, Maris, you are a flyer. I was a flyer once. We know the difficulties, the need for training year after year, for practice until your arms tremble with the effort and your palms come away bloody from the wing grips. The land-bound know none of that. Too many of them thought the fight was over seven years ago. They thought that next week the sky would be full of fisherfolk and cobblers and glassblowers, and they were dismayed when the first competition came and went and the flyers and flyer-children defeated all land-bound challengers.

"At least *then* they cared. Now they are only resigned, I fear. In the seven years since your great Council, the seven years of the academies, only once has a land-bound taken wings. And *he* lost them back again a year later, at the very next competition. These days I think the island folk come to the meets only to see flyer siblings compete for the family wings. The challenges from my Woodwingers are talked about as a kind of a comic interlude, a brief performance by some jesters to lighten up the moments between the serious races."

"Sena, Sena," Maris said with concern. The older woman had poured all of the passion of her own broken life into the dreams of the young people who came to Woodwings asking for the sky. Now she was clearly upset, her voice trembling despite herself. "I understand your distress," Maris said, taking Sena's hand, "but it isn't as bad as you say."

Sena's good eye regarded Maris skeptically, and she pulled her hand away. "It is," she insisted. "Of course they don't tell *you*. No one wants to bring bad news, and they all know what the academies mean to you. But it's true." Maris tried to interrupt, but Sena waved her quiet. "No, enough, and not another word about my distress. I did not call you here to comfort me, or to make us late for breakfast. I wanted to tell you the news privately, before I told the others. And I wanted to ask you to fly to Big Shotan for me."

"Today?"

"Yes," Sena said. "You have been doing good work with the children. It is a real benefit to them to have an actual flyer in their midst. But we can spare you for one day. It should only take a few hours."

"Certainly," Maris said. "What is this about?"

"The flyer who brought the news about Airhome to the Landsman also brought another message. A private message for me. One of Nord's students wishes to continue his studies here, and hopes that I will sponsor him in the next competition. He asks for permission to travel here."

"Here?" Maris said, incredulous. "From Eastern? Without wings?"

"He has word of a trader bold enough to try the open seas, I am told," Sena said. "The voyage is hazardous, to be sure, but if he is willing to make it I will not begrudge him admission. Take my agreement to the Landsman of Big Shotan, if you would. He sends three flyers to Eastern every month, and one is due to leave on the morrow. Speed is important. The ships will take a month getting here even if the winds are kind, and the competition is only two months away."

"I could take the message direct to Eastern myself," Maris suggested.

"No," said Sena. "We need you here. Simply relay my word to Big Shotan and then return to fly guard on my clumsy young birds." She rose unsteadily from her wicker chair, and Maris stood up quickly to help her. "And now we should see about breakfast," Sena continued. "You need to eat before your flight, and with all the time we have spent talking, I fear the others have probably eaten our share."

But breakfast was still waiting when they reached the common room. Two blazing hearths kept the large hall warm and bright in the damp morning. Gently curving walls of stone rose to become an arched and blackened ceiling. The furniture was rough and sparse: three long wooden tables with benches running the length of each side. The benches were crowded with students now, talking and joking and laughing, most at least half finished with their meals. Nearly twenty would-be flyers were currently in residence, ranging in age from a woman only two years younger than Maris to a boy just shy of ten.

The hall quieted only a little when Maris and Sena entered, and Sena had to shout to be heard above the din and clatter. But after she had finished speaking, it was very quiet indeed.

Maris accepted a chunk of black bread and a bowl of porridge and honey from Kerr, a chubby youth who was taking his turn as cook today, and found a place on one of the benches. As she ate, she conversed politely with the students on either side of her, but she could sense that neither had her heart in it, and after a short time both of them excused themselves and left. Maris could not blame them. She remembered how she had felt, years earlier, when her own dream of being a flyer had been imperiled, as their dreams were imperiled now. Airhome was not the first academy to shut its doors. The desolate island-continent of Artellia had given up first, after three years of failure, and the academies in the Southern Archipelago and the Outer Islands had followed it into oblivion. Eastern's Airhome was the fourth closing, leaving only Woodwings. No wonder the students were sullen.

Maris mopped her plate with the last of the bread, swallowed it, and pushed back from the table. "Sena, I will not be back until tomorrow morning," she said as she rose. "I'm going to fly to the Eyrie after Big Shotan."

Sena looked up from her own plate and nodded. "Very well. I plan to let Leya and Kurt try the air today. The rest will exercise. Be back as early as you can." She returned to her food.

Maris sensed someone behind her, and turned to see S'Rella. "May I help you with your wings, Maris?"

"Of course you may. Thank you."

The girl smiled. They walked together down the short corridor to the little room where the wings were kept. Three pair of wings hung on the wall now; Maris' own and two owned by the academy, dying bequests from flyers who had left no heirs. It was hardly surprising that the Woodwingers fared so poorly in competition, Maris thought bitterly as she contemplated the wings. A flyer sends his child into the sky almost daily during the years of training, but at the academies—with so many students and so few wings—practice time was not so easily come by. There was only so much you could learn on the ground.

She pushed the thought away and lifted her wings from the rack. They made a compact package, the struts folded neatly back on themselves, the tissue-metal hanging limply between and drooping toward the floor like a silver cape. S'Rella held them up easily with one hand while Maris partially unfolded them, checking each strut and joint carefully with fingers and eyes for any wear or defect that might become evident, too late, as a danger in the air.

"It's bad about them closing Airhome," S'Rella said as Maris worked. "It happened just the same way in Southern, you know. That was why I had to come here, to Woodwings. Our own school was closed."

Maris paused and looked at her. She had almost forgotten that the shy Southern girl had been a victim of a previous closing. "One of the students from Airhome is coming here, as you did," Maris said. "So you won't be alone among the savage Westerners anymore." She smiled.

"Do you miss your home?" S'Rella asked suddenly.

Maris thought a moment. "Truthfully, I don't know that I really have a home," she said. "Wherever I am is my home."

S'Rella digested that calmly. "I suppose that's a good way to feel, if you're a flyer. Do most flyers feel that way?"

"Maybe a little bit," Maris said. She glanced back to her wings and set her hands to work again. "But not so much as me. Most flyers have more ties to their home islands than I do, though never so many as the land-bound. Could you help me stretch that taut? Thanks. No, I didn't mean that particularly because I'm a flyer, but just because my old home is gone and I haven't made a new one yet. My father—my stepfather, really—died three years ago. His wife died long before that, and my own natural parents are both dead as well. I have a stepbrother, Coll, but he's been off adventuring and singing in the Outer Islands for a long time now. The little house on Lesser Amberly seemed awfully big and empty with Coll and Russ both gone. And since I had no one to go home to, I went there less and less. The island survives. The Landsman would like his third flyer to be in residence more often, no doubt, but he makes do with the two at hand." She shrugged. "My friends are flyers, mostly."

"I see."

Maris looked at S'Rella, who was staring at the wing she still held with more concentration than it warranted. "You miss your home," Maris said gently.

S'Rella nodded slowly. "It's different here. The others are different from the people I knew."

"A flyer has to get used to that," Maris said.

"Yes. But there was someone I loved. We talked of marrying, but I knew we never would. I loved him—I still love him—but I wanted to be a flyer even more. You know."

"I know," Maris said, trying to be encouraging. "Perhaps, after you win your wings, he could—"

"No. He'll never leave his land. He can't. He's a farmer, and his land has always been in his family. He—well, he never asked me to give up the idea of flying, and I never asked him to give up his land."

"Flyers have married farmers before," Maris said. "You could go back."

"Not without wings," S'Rella said fiercely. Her eyes met Maris'. "No matter how long it takes. And if—when—I win my wings, well, he'll have married by then. He's bound to. Farming isn't a job for a single person. He'll want a wife who loves the land, and a lot of children."

Maris said nothing.

"Well, I have made my choice," S'Rella said. "It's just that sometimes I get . . . homesick. Lonely, maybe."

"Yes," Maris said. She put a hand on S'Rella's shoulder. "Come, I have a message to deliver."

S'Rella led the way. Maris slung her wings over a shoulder and followed down a dark passageway that led to a well-fortified exit. It opened on what had once been an observation platform, a wide stone ledge eighty feet above where the sea crested and broke against the rocks of Seatooth. The sky was gray and overcast, but the wild salt smell of the ocean and the strong, eager hands of the wind filled Maris with exhilaration.

S'Rella held the wings while Maris fastened the restraining straps around her body. When they were secure, S'Rella began to unfold them, strut by strut, locking each into place so the silver tissue pulled tight and strong. Maris waited patiently, aware of her role as teacher, although she was anxious to be off. Only when the wings were fully extended did she smile at S'Rella, slide her arms through the loops, and wrap her hands around the worn, familiar leather of the wing grips.

Then, with four quick steps, she was off.

For a second, or less than a second, she fell, but then the winds took her, *thrumming* against her wings, lifting her, turning her plunge into flight, and the feel of it was like a shock running through her, a shock that left her flushed and breathless and set her skin to tingling. That instant, that little space of less than a second, made it all worthwhile. It was better and more thrilling than any sensation Maris had ever known, better than love, better than everything. Alive and aloft, she joined the strong western wind in a lover's embrace.

Big Shotan lay to the north, but for the moment Maris let the prevailing wind carry her, luxuriating in the fine freedom of an effortless soar before beginning her game with the winds, when she would have to tack and turn, test and tease them into taking her where she chose to go. A flight of rainbirds darted past her, each a different bright color, their haste an omen of a coming storm. Maris followed them, climbing higher and higher, rising until Seatooth was only a green and gray area off to her left, smaller than her hand. She could see Eggland as well, and off in the distance the fog banks that shrouded the southernmost coast of Big Shotan.

Maris began to circle, deliberately slowing her progress, aware of how easy it would be to overshoot her destination. Conflicting air currents whispered past her ears, taunting her with promises of a northbound gale somewhere above, and she rose again, seeking it in the colder air far above the sea. Now Big Shotan's coast and Seatooth and Eggland were all spread out before her on the metallic gray ocean like toys on a table. She saw the tiny shapes of fishing boats bobbing in the harbors and bays of Shotan and Seatooth, and gulls and scavenger kites by the hundreds wheeling around the sharp crags of Eggland.

She had lied to S'Rella, Maris realized suddenly. She *did* have a home, and it was here, in the sky, with the wind strong and cold behind her and her wings on her back. The world below, with its worries about trade and politics and food and war and money, was alien to her, and even at the best of times she always felt a bit apart from it. She was a flyer, and like all flyers, she was less than whole when she took off her wings.

Smiling a small, secret smile, Maris went to deliver her message.

The Landsman of Big Shotan was a busy man, occupied by the endless task of ruling the oldest, richest, and most densely populated island on Windhaven. He was in conference when Maris arrived—some sort of fishing dispute with Little Shotan and Skulny—but he came out to see her. Flyers were the equals of the Landsmen, and it was dangerous even for one as powerful as he to slight them. He heard Sena's message dispassionately, and promised that word would travel back to Eastern the next morning, on the wings of one of his flyers.

Maris left her wings on the wall of the conference room in the Old Captain's House, as the Landsman's ancient sprawling residence was named, and wandered into the streets of the city beyond. It was the only real city on Windhaven; oldest, largest, and first. Stormtown, it was called; the town the star sailors built. Maris found it endlessly fascinating. There were windmills everywhere, their great blades churning against the gray sky. There were more people here than on Lesser and Greater Amberly together. There were shops and stalls of a hundred different sorts, selling every useful good and worthless trinket imaginable.

She spent several hours in the market, browsing happily and listening to the talk, although she bought very little. Afterward she ate a light dinner of smoked moonfish and black bread, washed down with a mug of kivas, the hot spice wine that Shotan prided itself on. The inn where she took her meal had a singer and Maris listened to him politely enough, though she thought him much inferior to Coll and other singers she had known on Amberly.

It was close to dusk when she flew from Stormtown, in the wake of a brief squall that had washed the city streets with rain. She had good winds at her back all the way, and it had just turned dark when she reached the Eyrie.

It hulked out of the sea at her, black in the bright starlight, a weathered column of ancient stone whose sheer walls rose six hundred feet straight up from the foaming waters.

Maris saw lights within the windows. She circled once and came down skillfully in the landing pit, full of damp sand. Alone, it took her several minutes to remove and fold her wings. She hung them on a hook just inside the door.

A small fire was blazing in the hearth of the common room. In front of it, two flyers she knew only by sight were engrossed in a game of geechi, shoving the black and white pebbles around a board. One of them waved at her. She nodded in reply, but by then his glance had already gone back to his game.

There was one other present, slumped in an armchair near the fire with an earthenware mug in his hand, studying the flames. But he looked up when she entered. "Maris!" he said, rising suddenly and grinning. He set his mug aside and started across the room. "I hadn't expected to see you here."

"Dorrel," she said, but then he was there, and he put his arms around her and they kissed, briefly but with intensity. One of the geechi players watched them in a distracted sort of way, but his gaze fell quickly when his opponent moved a stone.

"Did you fly all the way from Amberly?" Dorrel asked her. "You must be hungry. Sit by the fire and I'll fetch you a snack. There's cheese and smoked ham and some sort of fruitbread in the kitchen."

Maris took his hand and squeezed it and led him back toward the fire, choosing two chairs well away from the geechi players. "I ate not too long ago," she said, "but thanks. And I flew from Big Shotan, not Amberly. An easy flight. The winds are friendly tonight. I haven't been to Amberly in almost a month, I'm afraid. The Landsman is going to be angry."

Dorrel did not look too happy himself. His lean face wrinkled in a frown. "Flying? Or gone to Seatooth again?" He released her hand and found his mug once more, sipping from it carefully. Steam rose from within.

"Seatooth. Sena asked me to come spend some time with the students. I've been working with them for about ten days. Before that I was on a long mission, to Deeth in the Southern Archipelago."

Dorrel set down his mug and sighed. "You don't want to hear my opinion," he said cheerfully, "but I'm going to tell it to you anyway. You spend too much time away from Amberly, working at the academy. Sena is teacher there, not you. She is paid good metal for doing what she does. I don't see her pressing any iron into your palm."

"I have enough iron," Maris said. "Russ left me well-off. Sena's lot is harder. And the Woodwingers need my help—they see precious few flyers on Seatooth." Her voice became warmer, coaxing. "Why don't you come spend a few days yourself? Laus would survive a week without you. We could share a room. I'd like to have you with me."

"No." His cheerful tone vanished abruptly, and he looked vaguely irritated. "I'd love to spend a week with you, Maris, in my cabin on Laus, or your home on Amberly, or even here in the Eyrie. But not at Woodwings. I've told you before: I won't train a group of land-bounds to take the wings of my friends."

His words wounded her. She pulled back in her chair and looked away from him, into the fire. "You sound like Corm, seven years ago," she said.

"I don't deserve that, Maris."

She turned back to look at him. "Then why won't you help? Why are you so contemptuous of the Woodwingers? You sneer at them like the most tradition-bound old flyer—but seven years ago you were with me. You fought for this, believed in it with me. I could never have done it without you—they would have taken my wings and named me outlaw. You risked the same fate by helping me. What has changed you so?"

Dorrel shook his head violently. "I haven't changed, Maris. Listen. Seven years ago, I fought for *you*. I didn't care about those precious academies you dreamed up—I fought for your right to keep your wings and be a flyer. Because I loved you, Maris, and I would have done anything for you. And," he went on, his tone a little cooler, "you were the best damn flyer I'd ever seen. It was a crime, madness, to give your wings to your brother and ground you. Now, don't look at me like that. Of course the principle mattered to me, too."

"Did it?" Maris asked. It was an old argument, but it still upset her.

"Of course it did. I wouldn't fly in the face of all I believed just to please you. The system as it existed was unfair. The traditions had to be changed—you were right about that. I believed that then, and I believe it now."

"You believe it," Maris said bitterly. "You say that, but words are easy. You won't do anything for your belief—you won't help me now, although we're on the verge of losing all we fought for."

"We aren't going to lose it. We won. We changed the rules—we changed the world."

"But without the academies, what does that mean?"

"The academies! I didn't fight for the academies. Changing bad tradition was what I fought for. I'll agree that if a land-bound can outfly me, I must give him my wings. But I will not agree to teach him to outfly me. And that's what you're asking of me. You, of all people, should understand what it means to a flyer to lose the sky."

"I also understand what it is to want to fly but to know that there's no chance of ever being allowed to," Maris said. "There's a student at the academy—S'Rella. You should have heard her this morning, Dorrel. She wants to fly more than anything. She's a lot like I was, when Russ first began to teach me how to fly. Come help her, Dorr."

"If she really is like you, she'll be flying soon enough, whether I choose to help her or not. So I choose not. Then if she defeats a friend of mine, takes his wings in competition, I won't have to feel guilty." He drained his mug and stood up.

Maris scowled and was seeking another argument when he said, "Have some tea with me?" She nodded, watching him go to the kettle on the fire where the fragrant spiced tea steamed. His stance, his walk, the way he bent to pour the tea—all so familiar to her. She knew him probably better than she had ever known anyone, she thought.

When Dorrel returned with the hot, sweetened drinks and took his place close to her again, the anger was gone, her thoughts having taken another direction.

"What happened to us, Dorr? A few years ago we planned to marry. Now we glare at each other from our separate islands and squabble like two Landsmen arguing fishing rights. What happened to our plans to live together and have children—what happened to our love?" She smiled ruefully. "I don't understand what happened."

"Yes you do," Dorrel said, his voice gentle. "This argument happened. Your loves and your loyalties are divided between the flyers and the land-bound. Mine aren't. Life isn't simple anymore—not for you. We don't want the same things, and it's hard for us to understand each other. We loved each other so much once . . ." He took a sip of the hot tea, his eyes cast down. Maris watched him, waiting, feeling sad. She wished for a moment that they could return to that earlier time, when their love had been so single-minded and strong that it had seemed certain to weather all storms.

Dorrel looked up at her again. "But I still love you, Maris. Things have changed, but the love's still there. Maybe we can't join our lives, but when we *are* together we can love each other and try not to fight, hmm?"

She smiled at him, a bit tremulously, and put her hand out. He grasped it strongly and smiled.

"Now. No more arguing, and no more sad talk of what might have been. We have the present—let's enjoy it. Do you realize it's been nearly two months since we were together last? Where have you been? What have you seen? Tell me some news, love. Some good gossip to cheer me up," he said.

"My news isn't very cheerful," Maris said, thinking about the messages she'd heard and carried recently. "Eastern has closed Airhome. One of the students there died in an accident. Another one is taking ship to Seatooth. The others have given up and gone home, I suppose. Don't know what Nord will do." She disengaged her hand and reached for her tea.

Dorrel shook his head, a small smile on his face. "Even your news is of nothing but the academies. Mine's more interesting. The Landsman of Scylla's Point died, and his youngest daughter was chosen to succeed him. Rumor has it that Kreel—d'you know him? Fair-haired boy missing a finger on his left hand? You might have noticed him at the last competition, he did a lot of fancy double-loops—anyway, that he's going to become Scylla Point's second flyer because the new Landsman's in love with him! Can you imagine—a Landsman and a flyer married?"

Maris smiled slightly. "It's happened before."

"Not in *our* time. Did you hear about the fishing fleet off Greater Amberly? Destroyed by a scylla, though they managed to kill it, and most got away with their lives, even if without their boats. Another scylla, dead, washed up on the shores of Culhall—I saw the carcass." He raised his brows and held his nose. "Even against the wind I could smell it! And up in Artellia, word is that two flyer-princes are warring for control of the Iron Islands." Dorrel stopped speaking, his head turning as a violent gust of wind from outside rattled the heavy lodge door.

"Ah," he said, turning back and sipping his tea. "Just the wind."

"What is it?" Maris asked. "You're so restless. Are you expecting someone?"

"I thought Garth might come." He hesitated. "We were supposed to meet here this afternoon, but he hasn't shown up. Nothing important, but he was flying a message out to Culhall and said he'd meet me here on the way back and we'd get drunk together."

"So maybe he got drunk alone. You know Garth." She spoke

lightly, but she saw that he was truly worried. "A lot of things could have delayed him—perhaps he had to fly an answer back. Or he might have decided to stay on Culhall for a party. I'm sure he's all right."

Despite her words, Maris, too, was worried. The last time she had seen Garth he had obviously put on weight—always dangerous for a flyer. And he was too fond of parties, particularly the wine and the food. She hoped he was safe and well. He'd never been a reckless flyer—that was comforting to remember—but he'd also never been more than solid and competent in the air. As he grew older, heavier, and slower in his responses, the steady skills of his youth were becoming less certain.

"You're right," Dorrel said. "Garth can take care of himself. He probably met up with some good companions on Culhall and forgot about me. He likes to drink, but he'd never fly drunk." He drained his mug and forced a smile. "We might as well return the favor and forget about him. At least for tonight."

Their eyes met, and they moved to a low, cushioned bench closer to the fire. There they managed, at least for a time, to put aside their conflicts and fears as they drank more tea and, later, wine, and talked of good times from the past, and exchanged gossip about the flyers they both knew. The evening passed in a pleasant haze, and much later that night they shared a bed and something more than memories. It was good to hold someone she cared about, Maris thought, and to be held in turn, after so many nights in her narrow bed alone. His head against her shoulder, his body a solid comfort against hers, Maris fell asleep at last, warm and contented.

But that night she dreamed again of falling.

The next day Maris rose early, cold and frightened from her dream. She left Dorrel sleeping and ate a lonely breakfast of hard cheese and bread in the deserted common room. As the sun brushed the horizon she donned her wings and gave herself to the morning wind. By midday she was back at Seatooth, flying guard for S'Rella and a boy named Jan while they tried their fledgling wings.

She stayed and worked with the Woodwingers for another week, watching their unsteady progress in the air, helping them through their exercises, and telling them stories of famous flyers each night around the fire.

But increasingly she felt guilty over her prolonged absence from Lesser Amberly, and finally she took her leave, promising Sena she would return in time to help prepare the students for their challenges.

It was a full day's flight to Lesser Amberly. She was exhausted when she finally saw the fire burning in its familiar light tower, and very glad to collapse into her own long-empty bed. But the sheets were cold and the room was dusty, and Maris found it hard to sleep. Her own familiar house seemed cramped and strange to her now. She rose and went in search of a snack, but she had been gone too long—the little food left in the kitchen was stale or spoiled. Hungry and unhappy, she returned to a cold bed and a fitful sleep.

The Landsman's greeting was polite but aloof when she went to him the next morning. "The times have been busy," he said simply. "I've sent for you several times, only to find you gone. Corm and Shalli have flown the missions instead, Maris. They grow weary. And now Shalli is with child. Are we to content ourselves with a single flyer, like a poor island half our size?"

"If you have flying for me to do, give it to me," Maris replied. She could not deny the justice of his complaint, yet neither would she promise to stay away from Seatooth.

The Landsman frowned, but there was nothing else he could do. He recited a message to her, a long, involved message to the traders on Poweet, seed grain in return for canvas sails, but only if they would send the ships to get it, and an iron bribe for their support in some dispute between the Amberlys and Kesselar. Maris memorized it word for word without letting it fully touch her conscious mind, as flyers often did. And then she was off to the flyers' cliff and the sky.

Anxious not to let her get away again, the Landsman kept her occupied. No sooner would she return from one mission than up she went again on another; back and forth to Poweet four times, twice to Little Shotan, twice to Greater Amberly, once to Kesselar, once each to Culhall and Stonebowl and Laus (Dorrel was not at home, off on some mission himself), once on a long flight to Kite's Landing in Eastern.

When at last she found herself free to escape to Seatooth again, barely three weeks remained before the competition.

"How many do you intend to sponsor in challenges?" Maris asked. Somewhere outside rain and wind lashed the island, but the thick stone walls that enclosed them kept the weather far away. Sena sat on a low stool, a torn shirt in her hands, and Maris stood before her, warming her back by the fire. They were in Sena's room.

"I had hoped to ask your advice on that," Sena said, looking up from her clumsy job of mending. "I think four this year, perhaps five."

"S'Rella certainly," Maris said, thoughtfully. Her opinions might influence Sena, and Sena's sponsorship was all-important to the would-be flyers. Only those who won her approval were allowed to issue challenge. "Damen as well. They are your best. After them— Sher and Leya, perhaps? Or Liane?"

"Sher and Leya," Sena said, stitching. "They would be impossible if I sponsored one and not the other. It will be chore enough to convince them that they cannot challenge the same person and race as a team."

Maris laughed. Sher and Leya were two of the younger aspirants, inseparable friends. They were talented and enthusiastic, although they tired too easily and could be rattled by the unexpected. She had often wondered if their constant companionship gave them strength, or simply reinforced their similar faults. "Do you think they can win?"

"No," Sena said, without looking up. "But they are old enough to try, and lose. The experience will do them good. Temper them. If their dreams cannot withstand a loss, they will never be flyers."

Maris nodded. "And Liane is the one in doubt?"

"I will not sponsor Liane," Sena said. "He is not ready. I wonder if he will ever be ready."

Maris was surprised. "I've watched him fly," she said. "He is strong, and at times he flies brilliantly. I grant you that he is moody and erratic, but when he is good he is better than S'Rella and Damen together. He might be your best hope."

"He might," Sena said, "but I will not sponsor him. One week he soars like a nighthawk, and the next he stumbles and tumbles like a child thrown into the air for the first time. No, Maris. I want to win, but a victory by Liane would be the worst thing that could happen to him. I would venture to bet that he would be dead within the year. The sky is no safe haven for one whose skills come and go with his moods."

Reluctantly, Maris nodded. "Perhaps you are wise," she said. "But who is your possible fifth, then?"

"Kerr," Sena said. Setting her bone needle aside, she inspected the shirt she had been working on, then spread it across her table and sat back to regard Maris evenly with her one good eye.

"Kerr? He is nice enough, but he is nervous and overweight and uncoordinated, and his arms are not half as strong as they need to be. Kerr is hopeless, at least for the present. In a few years, perhaps . . ."

"His parents want him to race this year," Sena said wearily. "He has wasted two years already, they say. They own a copper mine on Little Shotan, and are most anxious for Kerr to have his wings. They support the academy handsomely."

"I see," said Maris.

"Last year I told them no," Sena continued. "This year I am less certain of myself. Without a victory in this competition, the academy may lose its support from the Landsmen. Then only wealthy patrons will stand between us and closing. Perhaps it is best for everyone to keep them happy."

"I understand," Maris said. "Though I do not entirely approve. Still, I suppose it cannot be helped. And it will do Kerr little enough harm to lose. At times he seems to enjoy playing the clown."

Sena snorted. "I think I must do it. Yet I hate it. I had hoped you could talk me out of it."

"No," said Maris. "You overestimate my eloquence. I will give some advice, however. During these last weeks, reserve your wings solely for those who will challenge. They will need the seasoning. Occupy the others with exercises and lessons."

"I have done so in past years," Sena said. "They also race mock contests against each other. I would have you contest with them too, if only to teach them how to lose. S'Rella challenged last year, and Damen has lost twice, but the others need the experience. Sher . . ."

"*Sena, Maris, come quick!*" The shout came from the hall, and a breathless Kerr suddenly appeared in the doorway. "The Landsman sent someone, they need a flyer, they . . ." He panted, struggling with the words.

"Go with him, quickly," Sena told Maris. "I will hurry behind as fast as I am able."

The stranger who waited in the common room among the students was also panting; he had run all the way from the Landsman's tower. Yet speech seemed to burst from him. "You're the flyer?" He was young and obviously distraught, glancing about like a wild bird trapped in a cage.

Maris nodded.

"You must fly to Shotan. Please. And fetch their healer. The Landsman said to come to you. My brother is ill. Wandering in the head. His leg is broken—badly, I can see the bone—and he won't tell me how to fix it, or what to give him for his fever. Please, hurry."

"Doesn't Seatooth have its own healer?" Maris asked.

"His brother is the healer," volunteered Damen, a lean youth native to the island.

"What's the name of the healer on Big Shotan?" Maris asked, just as Sena came limping into the room.

The old woman immediately grasped the situation and took command. "There are several," she said.

"Hurry," the stranger implored. "My brother might *die.*"

"I don't think he'll die of a broken leg," Maris began, but Sena silenced her with a gesture.

"Then you're a fool," the youth said. "He has a fever. He raves.

He fell down the cliff face climbing after kite eggs, and he lay alone for almost a day before I found him. Please."

"There's a healer on the near end named Fila," Sena said. "She's old and crotchety and doesn't care for sea travel, but her daughter lives with her and knows her arts. If she can't come, she'll tell you the name of another who can. Don't waste your time in Stormtown. The healers there will all want to weigh your metal before they gather their herbs. And stop at the South Landing and tell the ferry captain to wait for an important passenger."

"I'll go at once," Maris said, with only the briefest of glances for the stew pot that was steaming over the fire. She was hungry, but it could wait. "S'Rella, Kerr, come help me with my wings."

"Thank you," the stranger muttered, but Maris and the students were already gone.

The storm had finally broken outside. Maris thanked her luck, and flew straight across the salt channel, skimming a few feet above the waves. There were dangers in flying so low, but she had no time to try for altitude, and scyllas rarely came so close to land anyway. The flight was short enough. Fila was easy to find but—as Sena had predicted—reluctant to come. "The waters make me sick," she muttered sourly. "And that boy on Seatooth, he thinks he's better than me anyway. Always has, the young fool, and now he comes crying to me for help." But her daughter apologized for her, and soon after left for the ferry.

On the way back, Maris indulged herself, enjoying the sensuous feel of the winds as if to make up for the brusque way that she had used them to travel to Big Shotan. The stormclouds were gone now; the sun was shining brightly on the waters, and a rainbow arched across the eastern sky. Maris went in search of it, soaring up on a warm current of air that rose from Shotan, frightening a flock of summerfowl when she joined them from below. She laughed as they scattered in confusion, banking at the same time, her body responding out of habit to the subtle, shifting demands of the winds. They went in all directions, some toward Seatooth, some toward Eggland or Big Shotan, some out toward the open sea. And farther out she saw—she narrowed her eyes, trying to be sure. A scylla, its long neck rearing out of the water to snap some unwary bird from the sky? No, there were several shapes. A hunting pack of seacats, then. Or ships.

She circled and glided out over the ocean, leaving the islands behind her, and very shortly she was sure. Ships all right, five of them sailing together, and when the wind had brought her closer she could see the colors as well, the faded paint on the canvas sails, the ragged streamers flapping and fluttering above, the hulls all black. Local ships were less gaudy; these had come a long way. A trading fleet from Eastern.

She swooped low enough to see the crew hard at work replacing sails, pulling in lines and shifting desperately to stay on the good side of the wind. A few looked up and shouted and waved at her, but most concentrated on their labors. Sailing the open seas of Windhaven was always a dangerous business, and there were many months in the year when travel between distant island groupings was made flatly impossible by the raging storms. To Maris the wind was a lover, but to the sailors it was a smiling assassin, pretending friendship only to gain the chance to slash a sail or drive a ship to splinters against an unseen rock. A ship was too large to play the games the flyers played; a ship at sea was always in a state of battle.

But these ships were safe enough now; the storm was past, and it would be sunset at least before another one would be upon them. There would be celebration in Stormtown tonight; arrival of an Eastern trade fleet this size was always an occasion. Fully a third of the ships that tried the hazardous crossing between archipelagos were lost at sea. Maris guessed the fleet would make port in less than an hour, judging from their position and the strength of the winds. She wheeled above them once more, made very aware of her grace and freedom in the sky by their struggles below, and decided to carry the news to Big Shotan instead of returning immediately to Seatooth. She might even wait for them, she thought, curious about their cargo and their news.

Maris drank too much wine in the boisterous tavern on the waterfront; it was pressed on her by the delighted customers, for she had been the first to bring word of the approaching fleet. Now everyone was at the docks, drinking and carousing and speculating about what the traders might be bringing.

When the cry went up—first one voice, then many—that the ships were docking, Maris stood up, only to lurch forward as she lost her balance, made dizzy by the wine. She would have fallen, but the crush of bodies around her, rushing toward the door, kept her upright and bore her along.

The scene outside was wild and noisy and for a moment Maris wondered whether she had been right to stay; she could see nothing, learn nothing in this excited, milling crowd. Shrugging, she slowly fought her way free of the mob, and sat down on an overturned barrel. She might as well stay out of it and keep her eyes open for anyone from the ship who could supply her with news. She leaned back against a smooth stone wall and folded her arms to wait.

She woke unwillingly, annoyed by someone who would not stop pushing at her shoulder. She blinked her eyes several times, looking up into the face of a stranger.

"You are Maris," he said. "Maris the flyer? Maris of Lesser Amberly?" He was a very young man, with the severe, sculpted face of an ascetic: a closed, guarded face that gave away nothing. Set in such a face, his eyes were startling—large, dark, and liquid. His rust-colored hair was pulled back sharply from a high forehead, and knotted at the back of his skull.

"Yes," she said, straightening. "I'm Maris. Why? What happened? I must have fallen asleep."

"You must have," he said flatly. "I came in on the ship. You were pointed out to me. I thought perhaps you had come to meet me."

"Oh!" Maris looked quickly around. The crowds had thinned and all but vanished. The docks were empty except for a group of traders standing on a gangplank, and a work-crew of stevedores unloading chests of cloth. "I sat down to wait," she muttered. "I must have closed my eyes. I didn't get much sleep last night."

There was something naggingly familiar about him, Maris thought groggily. She looked at him more closely. His clothing was Eastern in cut, but simple: gray fabric without ornamentation, thick and warm, a hood hanging down behind him. He had a canvas bag under one arm and wore a knife in a leather sheath at his waist.

"You said you were from the ship?" she asked. "Pardon, I'm still only half awake. Where are the other sailors?"

"The sailors are drinking or eating, the traders off haggling, I would say," he answered. "The voyage was difficult. We lost one ship to a storm, though all but two of the crew were pulled from the water safely. Conditions afterward were crowded and uncomfortable. The sailors were glad to come ashore." He paused. "I am no sailor, however. My apologies. I made a mistake. I do not think you were sent to meet me." He turned to go.

Suddenly Maris realized who he must be. "Of course," she blurted. "You're the student, the one from Airhome." He had turned back to her. "I'm sorry," she said. "I'd forgotten all about you." She jumped down from the barrel.

"My name is Val," he said, as if he expected it to mean something to her. "Val of South Arren."

"Fine," Maris said. "You know my name. I'm sure—"

He shifted his bag uneasily. The muscles around his mouth were tense. "They also call me One-Wing."

Maris said nothing. But her face gave her away.

"I see you know me after all," he said, a bit sharply.

"I've heard of you," Maris admitted. "You intend to compete?"

"I intend to fly," Val said. "I have worked for this for four years."

"I see," Maris said coolly. She looked up at the sky, dismissing him. It was nearly dusk. "I've got to get back to Seatooth," she said. "They'll be thinking I fell into the ocean. I'll tell them you arrived."

"Aren't you even going to speak to the captain?" he asked sardonically. "She's in the tavern across the way, telling stories to a gullible crowd." He canted his head at one of the dockside buildings.

"No," Maris said, too quickly. "But thanks." She turned away, but stopped when he called after her.

"Can I hire a boat to take me to Seatooth?"

"You can hire anything in Stormtown," Maris answered, "but it will cost you. There's a regular ferry from South Landing. You'd probably do best to stay the night here and take the ferry in the morning." She turned again and moved off down the cobbled street, toward the flyers' quarters where she had stored her wings. She felt a bit ashamed of leaving him so abruptly when he had come so far in his desire to be a flyer, but she did not feel ashamed enough to turn back. One-Wing, she thought furiously. She was surprised he admitted to the name, and even more surprised that he would come to try again at a competition. He must know how he would be met.

"You *knew!*" Maris shouted, angry enough not to care if the students heard her. "You knew and you didn't tell me."

"Of course I knew," Sena said. Her own voice was even, and her good eye was as impassive and fixed as her bad one. "I did not tell you earlier because I expected you would react like this."

"Sena, how could you?" Maris demanded. "Do you really intend to sponsor his challenge?"

"If he is good enough," Sena replied. "I have every reason to think he will be. I have serious qualms about sponsoring Kerr, but none whatsoever about Val."

"Don't you know how we feel about him?"

"We?"

"The flyers," Maris said impatiently. She paced back and forth before the fire, then paused to face Sena again. "He can't possibly win again. And if he did, do you think it would keep Woodwings open? The academies are still living down his first win. If he won again, the Landsman of Seatooth would—"

"The Landsman of Seatooth would be proud and pleased," Sena said, interrupting. "Val intends to take up residence here if he wins, I believe. It's not the land-bound who call him One-Wing—only you flyers do that."

"He calls *himself* One-Wing," Maris said, her voice rising once more. "And you know why he got the name. Even during the year he wore his wings, he was never more than half a flyer." She resumed her pacing.

"I'm less than half a flyer myself," the older woman said quietly, looking into the flames. "A flyer without wings. Val has a chance to fly again, and I can help him."

"You'd do anything to have a Woodwinger win in the competition, wouldn't you?" Maris said accusingly.

Sena turned up her wrinkled face, her good eye bright and sharp on Maris. "What did he do to make you hate him so?"

"You know what he did," Maris said.

"He won a pair of wings," Sena said.

She seemed suddenly a stranger. Maris spun away from her, turning her back on the older woman to avoid the blind stare of that white and hideous eye. "He drove a friend of mine to suicide," she said in a low, intense voice. "Mocked her grief, took her wings, and all but pushed her off that cliff with his own hands."

"Nonsense," Sena said. "Ari took her own life."

"I knew Ari," Maris said softly, still facing the fire. "She hadn't had her wings very long, but she was a true flyer, one of the best. Everyone liked her. Val could never have defeated her in fair flight."

"Val did defeat her."

"She talked to me at the Eyrie, just after her brother died," Maris said. "She had seen it all. He was out in his boat, the lines out for moonfish, and she was flying above, keeping an eye on him. She saw the scylla coming, but she was too far away, the winds tore the warning from her mouth. She tried to fly closer, but not in time. She saw the boat smashed to splinters, and the scylla's neck came craning up out of the water with her brother's body in its jaws. Then it dove."

"She should not have gone to the competition," Sena said simply.

"It was only a week off," Maris said. "She didn't intend to go, that day she was at the Eyrie, but she was so forlorn. Everyone thought it would help cheer her up. The games, the races, the singing and the drinking. We all urged her to go, never dreaming that anyone would challenge her. Not in her condition."

"She knew the rules the Council set," Sena insisted. "*Your* Council, Maris. Any flyer who appears at the competition is subject to challenge, and no healthy flyer may absent himself more than two years running."

Maris turned back to face the teacher once again, scowling. "You talk of law. What of humanity? Yes, Ari should have stayed away. But she desperately wanted to go on with her life, and she needed to be among her friends and forget her pain for a while. We watched over her. She was clumsy then, as if she often forgot where she was and what she was doing, but we kept her safe. She was enjoying the competition. No one could believe it when that boy challenged her."

"Boy," Sena repeated. "You used the right word, Maris. He was fifteen."

"He knew what he was doing. The judges tried to explain things to him, but he would not withdraw his challenge. He flew well and Ari flew badly, and that was it. One-Wing had her wings. It was only a month later that she killed herself."

"Val was half an ocean away at the time," Sena said. "The flyers had no cause to blame him, and shun him so. And no cause to do what they did the year after, at the competition on Culhall. Challenge after challenge after challenge, from retired flyers and flyer-children just come of age, and the best and the most talented at that."

"There was no rule against multiple challenges then," Maris said defensively.

"I notice that there is such a rule now, though. Where was the fairness in that?"

"It didn't matter. He lost to the second challenger."

"Yes. A girl who had been practicing with wings since she was seven, whose father was the senior flyer on Little Shotan, was able to defeat him *after* he had already outflown one other challenger," Sena said. She made an angry noise and rose slowly from her chair. "And what incentive did he have to fly well against her? There was another waiting to challenge next, a dozen more after him. And you all told him he was only half a flyer anyway." She moved toward the door.

"Where are you going?" Maris demanded.

"To dinner," Sena said gruffly. "I have news to tell my students."

• • •

Val arrived the next morning during breakfast. Sena sat spooning up her eggs in a grim silence while the students glanced at her curiously. Maris was seated well away from the teacher, listening to S'Rella and brawny young Liane try to convince a third student—a plain, quiet woman named Dana, the oldest of the Woodwingers—to remain at the academy. Last night at dinner, Sena had announced the names of the five she would sponsor in challenge. Dana, discouraged, was planning to return home and resume the life she had abandoned. S'Rella and Liane were not doing very well in their attempts to reconvert her. From time to time Maris would add a few words about the importance of desire, but she found it hard to care. Truth was that Dana had begun much too late and had never had real talent anyway.

All conversation ended when Val entered.

He took off his heavy woolen traveling cape and lowered his bag to the floor. If he took note of the sudden silence or the way the others stared at him, he gave no sign. "I'm hungry," he said. "Have you any extra food?"

That shattered the spell. Everyone began talking at once. Leya fetched him a platter of eggs and a mug of tea, and Sena rose and went to him, smiling, and led him back to her table, to sit and eat at her side. Maris watched in silence, staring and feeling uneasy, until S'Rella tugged at the sleeve of her shirt.

"I said, do you think he will win again?" S'Rella asked.

"No," Maris said, too loudly. She rose abruptly. "No one has lost a brother lately. How could he possibly win?"

That afternoon, he made her regret her words.

Sher and Leya had been up all morning, flying practice circuits while Sena yelled instructions from below and Maris observed them from the air. In the afternoon, S'Rella and Damen were supposed to have use of the academy wings, but Sena had asked one of them to yield to Val, since he had been grounded for a month and needed the feel of the wind again. S'Rella had quickly volunteered.

It was crowded on the observation platform when he emerged, wings strapped to his back and folded. Most of the students had come to see him fly. Maris, still winged, waited among them.

"Damen," Sena was saying, "I want you to practice skimming today. Fly as low over the water as you can. Keep your wings stiff and even. You wobble too much. You must improve, or someday you will fall in." She looked at her other student. "Val, you'd be best to just unlimber now. Later there will be time for other exercises."

"No," Val said. He was standing stiffly while two of the younger students unfolded and locked his wings. "I fly better when I *must* fly well. Set me a difficulty." He looked at Damen, who was flexing in preparation for flight. "Or give me a race."

Sena shook her head. "You are premature, Val. I will say when the time has come for racing."

But Maris pushed forward, possessed of a sudden urge to see how good the infamous Val One-Wing really was. "Let them race, Sena," she said. "Damen has had exercise enough. He needs a competition."

Damen looked from Maris to Sena and back again, clearly eager to race but unwilling to defy his teacher. "I don't know," he said.

Val shrugged. "As you will. I doubt you could give me much of a race in any case."

That was too much for Damen, who was fiercely proud of his status as one of Woodwings' best. "Don't flatter yourself, One-Wing," he snapped. He lifted an arm and pointed across the waters, to where the waves broke and foamed against a ridge of half-submerged stone. "When we are both aloft and Maris gives the word, three times there and three times back. Agreed?"

"Agreed," Val said, studying the distant rocks.

Sena pursed her lips but said nothing. Hearing no further objections, Damen grinned and ran and leapt. The wind took him and lifted. He soared upward, did a stately circle over the shoreline, and passed above them, his shadow rippling across the stone. Val moved to the edge, his wings fully extended now.

"Your knife, Val," S'Rella said suddenly. The rest of them looked. His ornate blade, obsidian with beaten silver edges, was still in its sheath at his hip.

Val reached down and pulled it free, looking at it curiously. "What of it?"

"Flyer tradition," Sena said. "No blade may be carried into the sky. S'Rella, take it. We will keep it safe for you."

S'Rella moved to obey, but Val gestured her away. "This was my father's knife, the only decent thing he ever owned. I carry it everywhere." He slid it back into its sheath.

"It's flyer tradition," S'Rella said, her voice puzzled.

Val smiled sardonically. "Ah. But I am only half a flyer. Move back, S'Rella." And when she moved back, he threw himself into the air.

Maris walked to the outer edge of the platform, to stand beside Sena and S'Rella, all of them watching Val as he spiraled upward to join Damen. Behind her, she could hear the others talking about him. "One-Wing," a voice said, Liane perhaps. Damen had called him that too, after Val had mocked him. The Easterner wasted no time making enemies, Maris thought. She said as much to Sena.

"The flyers wasted no time making an enemy of him," Sena replied. Even her bad eye was turned upward, toward the sky, where Damen and Val now wheeled in great circles around each other, like two birds of prey searching for a weakness. "You are to say the word, Maris," Sena reminded her.

Maris cupped her hands. "*Fly*," she shouted, as loud as she could shout it. The wind took it and carried it up to them.

Damen came out of his circle first, sweeping around and over the water in a slow, leisurely manner, as if he had all the time in the world. Val One-Wing came just behind him, wide silver wings weathervaning a bit, tilting first one way and then the other, as if he were not quite balanced. Both flyers kept low. Maris put a hand up to shade her eyes against the sunlight flashing from their wings.

Halfway to the first turn, Damen was widening his lead and Val began to rise. "The wind is picking up," Sena commented. Maris nodded. It felt like a crosswind as well. They'd have to fly; it would be no simple matter of letting the breeze carry them where they wished to go.

Damen reached the rocks well ahead of his competition, and began his turn. A ragged shout went up from the Woodwingers; Damen was winning. But he lost time on his turn; he came around slow and too wide, faltering at one point when he faced head on into the wind, before he took command of it again. He seemed less steady coming back.

Val began to tack well before the turn, changing his course as he climbed, not all at once but in a series of small increments. He was much higher than Damen now, but substantially behind. When he came around at last, Damen was already halfway back. But Val's turn was sharper and cleaner than his rival's.

"Damen's beating him," Liane called out. Damen swept by above them. "Hey, Damen!" Liane bellowed, hands cupped around his mouth. "Go!" Damen came around slowly—again the turn was too wide—and dipped his wing to acknowledge the cheers, but the gesture cost him. He lost the wind for an instant and slid down sharply and dangerously and when he passed in front of them, suddenly the bulk of the great rock fortress was between him and the prevailing wind. He drifted lazily, losing speed, and had to struggle to pull himself back up again.

Val made no such mistake. He turned tightly, keeping high enough above them so he lost no portion of the wind, however small. And suddenly he seemed to be moving much faster as well.

"Val has won it," Maris said suddenly. She hadn't meant to speak aloud, but no sooner had it come to her than the words were out.

Sena was smiling. S'Rella looked baffled. "But, Maris, look. Damen is well ahead."

"Damen is just riding on the winds," Maris said. "Val is using them. He was searching for the right wind, and now he's found it. Watch, S'Rella."

It didn't take long. Damen's lead shrank steadily as the two flyers moved out toward the rocks once more, and the Woodwinger slid badly off course when he tried to come around more sharply than before. By the time he'd corrected himself, Val had reached the turnaround point. A few moments later, Damen seemed visibly startled as the shadow of Val's wings fell upon his own. Then the shadow moved in front of him.

The students were quiet, even Liane.

"Give him my congratulations," Maris said. She turned and went back inside.

Her room was cold and damp. Maris built a fire in the hearth, and decided to heat the kivas she had bought in Stormtown. She was on her third cup, relaxing at last, when Sena entered unasked, and took a seat.

"How do the practices go?" Maris said.

"He has them all racing," Sena said. "Damen took it well enough, but he had no taste for another race, so he gave up his wings for the afternoon. They were all eager to try him." She smiled, clearly proud of their eagerness. "He defeated Sher and Jan handily, humiliated Kerr and Egon. Egon almost fell into the ocean. S'Rella flew him a close race, though. Stole all the tricks he used to defeat Damen. She's a clever girl, S'Rella."

"He flew six races?" Maris said.

"Seven," Sena said, smiling. "Liane almost beat him. The wind is gusting now, very turbulent. It knocked Val around a bit. He's lean, not as strong as he could be. I'll have him work on that. Pullups, pushups. And of course he was tired by then, but Liane insisted. Liane can handle rough winds. He's muscled like a scylla. Sometimes, the way he wrenches his wings around, I think he's yanking himself through the sky on sheer brawn. Val beat him anyway, though. Very close. Then Leya wanted to race, but the storm was about to break and I chased them all inside. What do you think of One-Wing now, Maris?"

Maris poured the teacher a mug of kivas while she thought.

"I think he can fly," Maris said at last. "I still don't like what he did to Ari. And I didn't like that business with his knife today, either. Yet I can't deny his skill."

"Will he win?"

Maris tasted her drink, let the sweet warmth flow down and into her. She closed her eyes briefly and leaned back. "Perhaps," she said. "I can think of a dozen flyers who don't handle themselves as well as he did today. I can also think of a dozen who are better than he, who know all his tricks and more. Tell me whom he's to challenge and I'll tell you his chances. Beyond that—well, speed is only one skill of a flyer. The competition will judge grace and precision as well."

"Fair enough," Sena said. "Will you help me ready him?"

Maris stared down at the gray stone floor. "You place me in a difficult position," she said. "And for the sake of someone I don't even like."

"So only those you approve of deserve to fly?" Sena said. "Is that the principle you struggled for seven years ago?"

Maris raised her head, meeting Sena's gaze. "You know better. Those who fly best deserve the wings."

"And you admit Val is skilled," Sena said. She sipped at her kivas while she waited for an answer.

Maris nodded reluctantly. "But if he *should* win, the others will not forget the past. You call him Val, but he'll always be One-Wing to them."

"I am not asking you to fly guard on him for the rest of his career," Sena said tartly. "I ask only that you help me now, help Val to get his wings."

"What do you want me to do?"

"Nothing more than you have already done for the others. Show him his mistakes. Teach him the things your years as a flyer have taught you, as you would teach a child of your own. Advise him. Push him. Challenge him. He is too skilled to gain much by pitting himself against my Woodwingers, and you saw today how little he is willing to listen to me. I am old and crippled, and I fly only in my dreams. But you are an active flyer, and reputed one of the best. He will heed you."

"I wonder," Maris said. She drained the last inch of kivas from her mug and set it aside. "Well, I suppose I must give him my advice, if he will take it."

"Good," Sena said. She nodded briskly and stood up. "I thank you. Now, if you'll excuse me, I have work to tend to." At the door she paused and half-turned. "I know this is hard for you, Maris.

Perhaps if you knew Val better, you might feel some sympathy between you. He admires you, I know."

Maris was startled by that, but tried not to show it. "I can't admire him," she said. "And the more I see of him, the less I see to sympathize with or like."

"He is young," Sena said. "His life has not been easy, and he is obsessed with winning back his wings—not so very different from you, some years back."

Maris choked down her anger to keep from launching into a tirade about just how different Val One-Wing was from her younger self; she would only sound spiteful.

The silence lengthened, and then Maris heard Sena's soft, uncertain footsteps taking her away.

The next day the final training began.

From sun-up until sundown the six challengers flew. Of those who would not compete this year, some went home to visit families on Seatooth or the Shotans or other nearby islands. The others, whose homes lay long, dangerous distances away, sat perched on bare rock to watch their fortunate companions and dream of the day when they, too, would have a chance to win their own wings.

Sena stood below on the launching deck, shouting up advice and encouragement to her fledglings, sometimes leaning on a wooden cane, more often using it to gesture and command. Maris, winged, flew guard; circling, watching, yelling cautions. She put S'Rella, Damen, Sher, Leya, and Kerr through their paces, racing against them two at a time, calling upon them to perform the sort of aerial acrobatics that might impress the judges.

Val was given a chance to use a pair of wings as often as any of the others, but Maris found herself observing him in silence. He had been in competition twice before, she reasoned; he knew what would be expected. To treat him as she did the other Woodwingers would be to condescend. But, mindful of her promise to Sena, she studied his flying closely, and that night at dinner she sought him out.

Only one hearth was lit in the common room, and the benches seemed strangely empty. When Maris arrived, one table was crowded with the students who would not be competing, and Sena sat at a second, talking in an animated fashion with Sher, Leya, and Kerr. S'Rella and Val were alone at the third table.

Maris let Damen fill her platter with his fish stew, then drew herself a glass of white wine and went to join them.

"How is the food?" she asked, as she sat down across from Val.

He looked at her evenly, but she could read nothing in his large, dark eyes. "Excellent," he said. "But even at Airhome, we never had cause to complain about the meals. Flyers eat well. Even those with wooden wings."

S'Rella, seated next to him, pushed a chunk of hookfin across her plate with marked indifference. "This isn't that good," she said. "Damen always makes everything so bland. You should be here when *I'm* cook, Val. Southern food has a lot of spices."

Maris laughed. "Too many, if you want my opinion."

"I'm not talking about spices," Val said. "I'm talking about food. This stew has four or five different kinds of fish in it, and chunks of vegetables, and I think there's wine in the sauce. There's plenty of it, and not a bit of it is rotten. Only flyers and Landsmen and rich traders would quibble about food like this."

S'Rella looked wounded. Maris frowned and put down her knife. "Most flyers eat simply, Val. We can't afford to get fat."

"I've been served fish that stank, and I've eaten fish stew that was entirely fishless," Val said coolly. "I grew up on scraps and leavings from flyer plates. I will be happy to spend the rest of my life eating as *simply* as a flyer." There was an infinite amount of sarcasm in the way he said *simply*.

Maris flushed. Her own true parents had not been wealthy, but her father had fished the sea off Amberly and they had always had enough to eat. After his death, when she had been adopted by the flyer Russ, she had always had enough of everything. She drank some of her wine and changed the subject. "I wanted to talk to you about your turns, Val."

"Oh?" He swallowed his last piece of fish and shoved the empty plate away. "Am I doing anything wrong, flyer?" His voice was so flat that Maris found it difficult to tell if the sarcasm was still there or not.

"Not wrong, not exactly. But given a choice, I notice that you always turn downwind. Why?"

Val shrugged. "It's easier."

"Yes," Maris said. "But not better. You'll come out of a downwind turn with more speed, but it will also take more room. And you tend to roll more on a downwind turn, particularly in high winds."

"An upwind turn is difficult in high winds," Val said.

"It requires more strength," Maris agreed. "But you need to work on your strength. You should not avoid difficulty. A habit like always turning downwind may seem harmless, but the time will come when you *have* to turn upwind, and you should be able to do it well."

Val's expression was as guarded as ever. "I see," he said.

Emboldened, Maris raised a touchier subject. "Something else. I saw that you wore your knife again today during practice."

"Yes."

"Next time, don't," Maris said. "I don't think you understand. No matter what the knife means to you, this is a matter of flyer law. No blades may be worn in the sky."

"Flyer law," Val said icily. "Tell me, who gave the flyers the right to make laws? Do we have farmers' law? Glassblowers' law? The Landsmen make the law. The only law. When my father gave me that knife, he told me never to put it aside. But I did put it aside, during the year I had my wings. I obeyed your flyer law. It did nothing but shame me. I was still One-Wing. Well, I was a boy then, and cowed by flyer law, but I am not a boy now. I choose to wear my knife."

S'Rella looked at him wonderingly. "But, Val—how can you disregard flyer law, if you're going to be a flyer?"

"I never said I was going to be a flyer," Val replied. "Only that I intend to win wings, and fly." His eyes moved from Maris to S'Rella. "And, S'Rella, you are not going to be a flyer either, even if you should win. Remember that, if it comes to pass. You'll be as I was—a One-Wing."

"*That's not true!*" Maris said angrily. "I was not born of flyers, but they've accepted me all the same."

"Have they?" Val said. He smiled a thin, ironic smile, and rose from the bench. "You'll excuse me. I have to rest. Tomorrow I must practice my upwind turns, and I'll need all my strength for that."

When he was gone, Maris reached across the table to take S'Rella by the hand, but the girl gave her a troubled look and pulled away. "I have to go too," she said, and Maris was left alone.

She sat for a long time, thinking, and it was not until Damen approached her that she remembered the half-eaten meal on her plate. "Everyone else is gone," he said softly. "Are you going to finish, Maris?"

"Oh," she said, "no, I'm sorry. I'm afraid I got distracted and let it get cold." She smiled and helped Damen with the plates, then left him to clean up the common room and set off down the dank stone corridors in search of Val's room.

She found it after only one wrong turning, and her anger grew as she walked; she was determined to have it out with Val. But it was S'Rella who answered her impatient knocking.

"What are you doing here?" Maris said, startled.

S'Rella hesitated, shy and uncertain. But Val's voice came from within the room. "She doesn't have to answer that," he said.

"No, of course not," Maris said, abashed. She had no right even asking, she realized. She touched S'Rella on the shoulder. "I'm sorry. Can I come in? I want to talk to Val."

"Let her in," Val said, and S'Rella smiled at Maris tentatively and opened the door.

Like all the rooms in the academy, Val's was small, damp, and cold. He'd lit a fire in the hearth to drive some of the chill away, but so far it had been only partially successful. Maris noticed how bare the room was, completely lacking in the personal touches and trinkets that would tell a visitor something about the person who lived here.

Val was on the floor before the fire, doing push-ups. He'd thrown his shirt over the bed and was exercising barechested. "Well?" he said, without slackening his pace.

Maris was staring, sickened by what she saw. The whole of Val's back was crisscrossed by lines and thin white scars, mementoes of long-ago beatings. She had to force her eyes away from them to remember why she had come. "We need to talk, Val," she said.

He came bounding to his feet, smiling at her and breathing hard. "Hand me my shirt, S'Rella," he said. Then, after he had pulled it on, "What do you want to talk about?" His hair, unbound now, fell to his shoulders in a rust-colored waterfall, softening the severity of his face and giving him an oddly vulnerable look.

"May I sit?" Maris asked. Val gestured toward the only chair in the room, and when Maris sat on it, lowered himself onto the backless stool near the fire. S'Rella sat on the edge of the narrow bed. "I don't want to play games with you, Val," Maris resumed. "We have a lot of work to do together."

"What makes you think I am playing games?" he asked.

"Listen to me," she said. "I realize that you are bitter toward the flyers. They made you an outcast, branded you with a mocking, insulting name, and stripped you of your wings, perhaps unfairly, with multiple challenges. But if you let that poison your feelings toward all flyers, forever, you will be the loser for it. Win your wings back in the competition, and you will be living with, competing with, and associating with flyers for much of the rest of your life. If you refuse to allow them to be your friends, then you will have no friends. Is that what you want?"

Val was unmoved. "Windhaven is full of people, and only a few of them are flyers. Or don't you count the land-bound?"

"Why are you so determined to be hateful? You waste no time making enemies. Maybe you feel the flyers have wronged you, and maybe you are right. But quarrels are seldom one-sided. Try to understand that. What you did to Ari was not without wrong, either. If you want to be forgiven for that, then forgive the flyers for what they did. Accept and you may be accepted."

Val smiled his thin-lipped smile. "What makes you think I want to be accepted? Or forgiven? I've done nothing that requires forgiving. I'd challenge Ari again. Unfortunately, she isn't available this year."

Maris was suddenly speechless with rage.

"*Val*," S'Rella said in a small, shocked voice. "How can you say that? She *killed* herself."

"Land-bound die every day," Val told her, his voice softening a bit. "Some of them kill themselves too. No one makes a cause out of that, or sings about it, or avenges their squalid little suicides. You have to shield your own flank, S'Rella. My parents taught me that. No one else will do it for you." His eyes went back to Maris. "I've met your brother, you know," he said suddenly.

"Coll?" she said, surprised.

"He visited South Arren seven years ago, on his way to the Outer Islands. There was another singer with him, an older man."

"Barrion," Maris said. "Coll's mentor."

"They stayed a week or two, singing in the dockside taverns, waiting for a ship to take them farther east. That was the first time I heard about you, Maris of Lesser Amberly. You were my hero for a time. Your brother sings a pretty little song about you."

"Seven years ago," Maris said. "That must have been right after the Council."

Val smiled. "It was the first we had heard of it. I was around twelve, just short of the age when a flyer child would be taking up his wings, but of course I had no hope of that. Until your brother came to my island and sang about you and your Council and your academies. When Airhome opened a few months later, I was one of the first students. I still loved you then, for making it all possible."

"And what happened?"

Val half-turned on his stool, stretching his hands out toward the fire. "I grew disillusioned. I thought that you'd opened the world to everyone, where once it had belonged only to flyers. I felt such a kinship with you. I was naive."

He turned back again, and Maris shifted uncomfortably under his intense, accusing gaze. "I thought we were alike," he continued. "I thought you wanted to break open the rotten flyer society. I found out I was wrong. All you ever wanted was to be a part of the whole thing. You wanted the fame and the status and the wealth and the freedom, you wanted to party on the Eyrie with the rest of them and look down on the dirt-digging land-bound. You embrace what I despise.

"The irony of it, though, is that you can't be a flyer, no matter how much you want to. No more than I can be a flyer, or S'Rella here, or Damen, or any of the rest of them."

"I *am* a flyer," Maris said quietly.

"They let you play at it," Val said, "because you try so very hard to fit in, to be *just like them*. But both of us know that they don't really trust you, or accept you as they'd accept one of their own. You have your wings, but you're still suspect, aren't you? Whether you admit it or not, you were the first One-Wing, Maris."

Maris stood up. His words had made her furious, but she didn't want to lash out at him, or lose her dignity by quarreling with him in front of S'Rella. "You're wrong," she said as calmly and quietly as she could manage. But then she found she had no words to refute him with. "I feel sorry for you, Val," she continued. "You hate the flyers and you have contempt for the land-bound. For everyone who is not yourself. I don't want your respect or your gratitude. It's not just the privileges of flyer society you're rejecting, it's the re-sponsibilities as well. You're totally selfish and self-absorbed. If I hadn't promised Sena, I'd have nothing more to do with helping you get your wings. Good night."

She left the room. Val didn't move or call her back. But as the door swung shut behind her, she heard him speaking to S'Rella. "You see," he said flatly.

And that night the dream came to Maris again, and she twisted and fought and woke with the bedclothes wrapped about her, soaked with sweat. It had been worse than before. She had been falling, falling endlessly through still air, and all around were other flyers, soaring on their silver wings and watching, and not one of them moved to help.

Day after day the practice continued.

Sena grew hoarse and intense and short-tempered, and presided over all like a tyrannical Landsman. Damen sharpened his turns and heard long lectures every day on flying with his head and not just his arms. S'Rella worked on launchings and landings and acrobatics, looking for grace to match her stamina. Sher and Leya, already graceful, stayed in the air for hours at a time in high winds, trying to build endurance. Kerr worked on everything.

And Val One-Wing did what he would. Maris watched him from afar, as she watched all of them, and said little. She answered what questions he had, gave advice on the rare occasions that he asked for it, and treated him always with careful, distant courtesy.

Sena, absorbed entirely in the flying of her protégés, noticed none of it, but the Woodwingers picked up their cues from Maris, and carefully kept their distance from Val. He aided the process himself; he had a sharp tongue and no compunction about making enemies. He told Kerr to his face that he was hopeless, sending the boy into a fit of sulking, and he mocked proud, stubborn Damen endlessly, defeating him again and again in informal races. The students, led by Damen and Liane and a few others, soon began calling Val "One-Wing" openly. But if that bothered him, he gave no sign.

Val's isolation was not quite total. If the others shunned him, he at least had S'Rella. She was more than merely polite to Val; she sought him out, asking for his advice, ate with him, and always, when Sena paired students off to race, S'Rella was the first to challenge Val.

Maris saw sense in her actions; pitting her skills against those of a stronger flyer would help her learn and overcome her weaknesses faster than anything else. And S'Rella, Maris knew, was determined to win her wings this year. There were other, less practical, reasons why S'Rella might be drawn to Val as well. The shy Southern girl had always been a bit out of place among the Woodwingers, all of whom were Westerners; she cooked differently, dressed differently, wore her hair differently, spoke with a slight accent, even told different tales when the students gathered together for storytelling. Val One-Wing, from Eastern, was similarly displaced, and it was natural, Maris told herself, that the two odd birds would fly together.

Still, it made Maris uneasy to see the two talking together. S'Rella was young and impressionable, and Maris did not want her picking up Val's ideas. Besides, too close an association with One-Wing would make her unpopular among the other flyers, and S'Rella was vulnerable enough to be hurt by that.

But Maris pushed those worries to the back of her mind and did not interfere. There was no time now for personal fretting; she had to train these Woodwingers for the real thing.

At the end of every day of training Maris raced each student individually. On the second day before the scheduled departure for the competition, the wind was strong from the north, and its cold edge seemed to slice through the shivering students. It grew colder by the minute.

"You don't need to wait," Maris told them. "It's too cold for standing around. After I race you, help the next student with the wings, and then you can go on inside."

The exertion of flying kept Maris warm, but it also tired her. Finally, bone weary and beginning to really feel the cold, Maris saw that she was alone on the flyers' cliff with Val.

Her shoulders slumped. She had not expected him to wait. And to race him now, when he was fresh and she was so tired . . . She looked up at the swirling purple sky and licked dried salt from the corners of her mouth.

"It's late for flying," she said. "The winds are wild and it's getting dark. We can race another time."

"The winds will make it that much more of a challenge," Val said. His eyes rested coolly on hers, and Maris knew, with a sinking heart, that he'd been waiting a long time for this moment.

"Sena may worry," she began weakly.

"Of course, if flying against the Woodwingers has worn you out . . ."

"I once flew thirty hours without a rest," she said, stung. "An afternoon of play doesn't wear me out."

His smile mocked her; she saw that she had fallen into his trap.

"Get your wings on," she said.

She did not offer to help him, but it was obvious that he was accustomed to putting on his wings unaided. Maris tried unobtrusively to flex some resilience back into her muscles, telling herself that a victory for him, with her as tired as she was and the winds so capricious, would mean nothing. And he must know that.

"The usual? Twice out and back?"

Maris nodded, glancing across the gray, churning waves to the distant spire of rock they all used as a marker. How many times had she flown out there today? Thirty? More? It didn't matter. She would fly the last two laps as if they were the first; her pride insisted.

"Who will judge us?" she asked.

Val snapped the last two joints of his wings into place. "We'll know," he said. "That's all that matters. I'll launch first. You call ready. Agreed?"

"Yes." She watched as, with a few swift steps, Val moved to the edge of the cliff and leapt outward. His body bobbed on the conflicting winds like a small boat on rough water until he took command, veered off to the right, and began to climb.

Maris took a breath and let her mind clear. She ran lightly forward and pushed off. For one brief moment she fell; then her wings caught the winds and she was buoyed upward. She took her time coming to Val's level, climbing in a ragged spiral, needing those few moments to get the feel back, so her tired body would know how best to use the winds.

When she came up to him, the two of them circled warily, around and around each other, struggling to hold position amid the restless winds. Her eyes met his, and then she looked away, straight ahead, toward the rock that was their marker.

"Ready . . . go," she shouted, and they were off.

The winds were strong but turbulent, the prevailing north wind interrupted by gusts from one direction, then from another. The whole eastern sky was a mass of darkening clouds, towering shapes that threatened a storm. Maris gave them an uneasy glance and started to climb again, looking for a steadier, faster wind in the heights. She fought constantly to keep on course; the gusts pushed her first one way, then another, demanding constant attention and frequent half-turns and corrections. She could not afford any detours.

Although she did not look for him, she often caught sight of Val. He sometimes flew below her, but more often he was beside her, disconcertingly close. He flew well, and it did not help Maris to re- flect that he was using the advice she had given him. There would be nothing easy or simple about defeating him, she thought.

Then Val surged ahead.

A shock of adrenaline coursed through Maris and she flung her body to the left to catch the changing wind that had given him his push. They might call him One-Wing, but he knew how to use both wings in the air. Flying races against Woodwingers had made her soft, Maris thought. Her responses were dulled.

Ahead of her, just barely out of reach, Val's wings swept around the spike of rock. He turned downwind, Maris noted, coming around wide and rocking just a little, but picking up speed as he did so. Then he was headed back toward the cliff.

Determined to overtake him, Maris flew dangerously close to the rock. Her wingtip grazed the spire and that slight scraping threw her sideways, off balance for a crucial moment. She sheared down- ward crookedly, the wind lost to her, stalling, her heart pounding in her throat, before she finally gained control again. Val had put more distance between them. She was only grateful that he hadn't seen her blunder.

She had lost altitude, but she caught a strong updraft above the rocks, and suddenly Maris was rising again. She flew recklessly, thinking only of the immediate need for speed, searching and shift- ing until she found a steady current she could use.

It moved her close to Val, but she was so intent on passing him that she barely noticed the approach of land, and abruptly she was clutched by a sinker, a cold pocket of air that yanked her down like an icy hand from below. Val somehow flew clear of it, found some impossible lift that shoved him up and further ahead while Maris checked her abrupt descent and banked to free herself from the downdraft. He circled above the fortress, gauging the winds by the thin smoke rising from the academy's chimneys, and was on his way back out again, higher and higher, before Maris had finished her re- covery.

It was as if the sky itself favored Val this evening, Maris thought resentfully as she came around. The winds toyed with her and stalled her, gusting unpredictably every time she tried to ride them, but let Val fly them freely. He seemed almost unaware of the dangerous uncertainty of the gales, somehow finding, amid the constant shifting, the sure and fluid wind on which to glide.

Maris knew then that she had lost the race. Val was high above her, knowing that altitude often meant speed, and it would take her too long to reach his height, even if she should find the winds she needed to take her there. She tried to make up the distance between them, but the struggle against the ragged gusts wore her out, and the awareness that already it was too late took the heart out of her efforts. Val lost some time descending for his landing, but still passed above the cliff the second, final time more than a full wingspan ahead of her. Clearly, he had won.

Maris was too drained by the flight to smile at him when they had both come down in the soft sand of the landing pit, too depressed to pretend that it didn't matter. In silence, she removed her wings as hastily as she could, her numbed fingers often slipping and fumbling uselessly at the straps. At last, still without a word having passed between them, Maris slung her wings over her shoulder and turned toward the weathered fortress.

Val blocked her way.

"I won't tell anyone," he said.

Her head jerked up, and she felt a hot flush of embarrassment rise in her cheeks. "I don't care what you say—about anything—to anyone!"

"Oh?" His faint smile taunted her, made her realize how hollow her words rang. Obviously she *did* care.

"It wasn't a fair trial," she snapped, and instantly regretted the feeble, childish complaint.

"No," Val agreed, his tone flat enough so Maris had no clue as to whether irony was intended. "You were flying all day, while I was well-rested. I could never have beaten you if we were both fresh. We all know that."

"I've lost before," Maris said, trying hard to control her emotions. "It doesn't bother me."

"I see," said Val. "Good." He smiled again.

Maris shrugged irritably, feeling the wings scrape her back. "I'm very tired," she said. "Please excuse me."

"Certainly." Val moved out of her way and she trudged past him, crossed the sand wearily, and began climbing the flight of worn, moss-covered steps that led to the fortress's seaward entrance. But at the top, some impulse made her hesitate and turn before ducking inside.

Val had not followed her. He still stood out on the sand, a gaunt solitary figure in the gathering dusk, his folded wings propped lightly on one shoulder. He was looking off over the sea, where a lone scavenger kite sailed in ragged circles against the clouds of sunset.

Maris shivered and went inside.

The yearly competition was a festive three-day affair. Once it had been only games and drinking, with nothing at stake except pride. In those days it was smaller, and traditionally held on the Eyrie. But since the challenge system had been instituted seven years ago, flyer participation had grown dramatically, and it had been necessary to move the competition to the islands.

The Landsmen competed for it eagerly, donating facilities and labor. It was a holiday for their own people, and brought crowds of visitors with good metal coin from other islands. The land-bound had few spectacles like it, and the flyers were still figures of romance and adventure to many of them.

This year the contests were to be held on Skulny, a mid-sized island to the northeast of Little Shotan. Seatooth's Landsman had chartered a ship for Sena and the Woodwingers, and a runner had just brought word that it was waiting at the small island's only port. They would sail on the evening tide.

"Setting out in the dark," Sena grumbled, taking a seat beside Maris at breakfast. "Asking for trouble."

Kerr looked up from his porridge. "Oh, but we have to leave on the tide," he said earnestly. "That's why we leave in the evening."

Sena regarded him sourly with her good eye. "Know a lot about sailing, do you?"

"Yes, ma'am. My brother Rac captains a trading ship, one of the big three-masters, and my other brother is a sailor too, though he's only a hand on a channel ferry. I thought that I—well, before I came to Woodwings, I thought I'd be a sailor too. It's about the closest thing there is to flying."

Sena shuddered. "Like flying without control, like flying with weights dragging you into the sea, like flying blind, yes, that's sailing."

She'd been speaking loud enough for everyone to hear, and there was widespread laughter around the room. Kerr blushed and concentrated on his bowl.

Maris looked at Sena with sympathy, trying not to laugh for Kerr's sake. Sena, although grounded for years, had never lost the flyer's almost superstitious fear of traveling by sea.

"How long will it take?" Maris asked.

"Oh, they say, winds willing, three days, with a stop in Stormtown. What does it matter? Either we'll get there, or we'll all drown." The teacher looked at Maris. "You fly to Skulny today?"

"Yes."

"Good," Sena said, reaching across to take Maris by the arm. "Then everyone need not drown. We have two sets of wings we'll be needing in the competition. It would be insane to take them in the boat with us—"

"Ship," Kerr interrupted.

Sena looked at him. "Boat or ship, it would be insane. We might as well put them to use. Will you take two of the students with you? The long flight should be good practice."

Maris looked down the table and saw how everyone within hearing distance had suddenly become still. No spoons were raised, no jaws moved as they waited for her answer.

"That's a fine idea," Maris said, smiling. "I'll take S'Rella with me, and—" She hesitated, trying to decide who to choose.

Two tables down, Val set down his spoon and rose. "I'll go," he said.

Maris' eyes met his across the room. "S'Rella and Sher or Leya," she said stubbornly. "They need that kind of flight the most."

"I'll stay with Val, then," S'Rella said quietly.

"And I'd rather go with Leya," Sher added.

"It will be S'Rella and Val," Sena said irritably, "and I'll hear no more about it. If the rest of us die at sea, they have the best chance of becoming flyers and honoring our memory." She pushed aside her porridge bowl and turned on the bench. "Now I must go see our patron the Landsman and be obsequious to her for a while. I will see you again before you leave for Skulny."

Maris scarcely heard her; her eyes were still locked with Val's. He smiled at her thinly, then spun and followed Sena from the room. S'Rella left soon after.

Kerr was talking to her, Maris suddenly realized. She shook herself back to attention and smiled at him. "Sorry. I didn't hear you."

"It isn't so dangerous," he said quietly. "Not just to sail from here to Skulny. There's only a few miles of open ocean, when the ship crosses from Little Shotan to Skulny. Mostly we'll hug the shores of the Shotans, with land never out of sight. And the ships aren't as fragile as she thinks. I know about ships."

"I'm sure you do, Kerr," Maris said. "Sena is just thinking like a flyer. After the freedom of having your own wings, it's a hard thing to travel by sea and trust your life to those handling the sails and the tiller."

Kerr chewed his lip. "I guess I see," he said, without conviction. "But if the flyers all think that, they don't know much. It's not as dangerous as she says." Satisfied, he went back to his breakfast.

Maris grew thoughtful as she ate. He was right, she realized with a sense of vague unease; flyers were often too limited in the ways they thought, judging everything from their own perspective. But the idea that Val's sweeping condemnation of them might have some justice to it disturbed her more than she was willing to admit.

Afterward she went to look for S'Rella and Val. They were not in their rooms, nor in any of the other obvious places, and no one seemed to know where they had gone after leaving the common room. Maris wandered through the dark, cool corridors until she was thoroughly lost, making her choice of turning according to whether or not there were torches for her to light in the wall-sockets.

She was thinking of giving out a cry for help, and laughing at herself for being so helpless within the enclosure of walls, when she heard, very faintly, the sound of voices, and pressed on. One more turn to the right and she found them, together, sitting close in a small cul-de-sac with a window overlooking the sea. There was something in the way they leaned near to each other that spoke of intimacy, and it changed Maris' mood to one of annoyance.

"I've been looking all over for you," Maris said abruptly.

S'Rella half-turned away from Val and stood up. "What is it?" she asked eagerly.

"We're flying to Skulny, you know," Maris said. "Can you be ready to leave in an hour? Anything you wanted to take with you, you can pack up and give to Sena."

"I can be ready to leave in a minute," S'Rella said, and her smile put a damper on Maris' pique. "I was so happy when you named me, Maris. You don't know what this means to me." Her face alight, she leaped forward and embraced Maris.

Maris hugged her back. "I think I do," she said. "Now, go off and get ready."

S'Rella bid a brief goodbye to Val and then was off. Maris stood watching her go, then turned back to him, and hesitated.

Val was still looking down the tunnel where S'Rella had disappeared, smiling, but there was something about him—the smile was real, Maris realized. That was it. He was smiling with something like fondness, and it gave him a softer, more human look than she had ever seen him wear.

Then his eyes snapped back to her, and the smile changed, subtly, a small twist at the corners, and now he was smiling for Maris and the smile was full of derision and hostility. "I haven't thanked you for naming *me*," he said. "I was *so* happy when you said I could fly with you."

"Val," Maris said wearily, "we may not like each other, but we have a long flight to make together. You could at least try to be civil. Don't mock me. Are you going to pack?"

"I've never unpacked," he said. "I'll give my bag to Sena, and wear my knife. It's the only thing that matters. Don't worry, I'll be ready." He hesitated. "And I won't bother you on Skulny. When we land, I'll find my own quarters. Fair enough?"

"Val," Maris started. But he had turned away and was staring through the cell's small window at the moving, cloudy sky, his face cold and closed.

Sena brought the others out to the launching cliff to watch Maris, S'Rella, and Val depart. All of them were in the highest of spirits, laughing and joking, vying with each other for the privilege of helping Maris and S'Rella with their wings. There was a mood of wild and restless gaiety among them that was infectious; Maris felt her own spirits rise, and for the first time she was eager for the competitions.

"Let them be, let them be!" Sena cried, laughing. "They certainly can't fly with the lot of you hanging on their wings!"

"Wish they could," mumbled Kerr. He pushed at his nose, which had turned bright red in the wind.

"You'll have your chance," S'Rella said, sounding defensive.

"No one grudges you this," Leya said quickly.

"You're the best of us," Sher added.

"Save it," Sena said, putting one arm around Leya, the other around Sher. "Go now. We'll wave goodbye and meet you again on Skulny."

Maris turned to S'Rella and saw that the younger woman was watching her intently, her whole body tensed and ready for Maris' slightest signal. She remembered her own earliest flights, when she had still not quite believed that she could have wings of her own, and she touched S'Rella's shoulder and spoke to her kindly.

"We'll all stay close together and take it easy," she said. "The stunts are for the competitions—right now, we'll concentrate on steady flying. This will be a long trip for you, I know, but don't worry about it—you've got enough stamina for twice the distance. Just relax and trust yourself. I'll be there watching out for you, but you won't really need me."

"Thank you," S'Rella said. "I'll do my best."

Maris nodded and signaled, and Damen and Liane came out and unfolded her wings for her, strut by strut, pulling the bright silver fabric taut until her wings were spread twenty feet. Then she was off, leaping away from the cliff to a chorus of farewells and good wishes, into the cool, steady, faintly rain-scented flow of the wind. She circled and watched S'Rella's takeoff, trying to judge it as if S'Rella were in competition.

No doubt about it, S'Rella had improved greatly recently. The clumsiness was gone, and she did not hesitate at the edge, but sprang smoothly clear of the fortress and, having judged the wind nicely, began to rise almost at once.

"I don't believe your wings are of wood at all!" Maris called to her.

Then both of them swung through the sky in impatient, widening circles, waiting for Val.

He had been leaning against the door through all of the joking and the preparations, standing outside it all, his face blank and guarded. He was winged already, having strapped them on without help. Now he walked calmly through the group of students and would-be flyers, and stood perched on the brink of the precipice, his feet half-over the edge. Painstakingly he unfolded the first three struts, but he did not lock them into place. Then he slid his arms through the loops, flexed, knelt, and stood again.

Damen reached to help him unfold his wings, but Val turned and said something sharp to him—Maris, circling above, lost the words in the wind—and Damen fell back in confusion.

Then Val laughed, and jumped.

S'Rella trembled visibly in the air, her wings shaking with her shock. From below, Maris heard someone scream, and someone else was swearing.

Val fell, body straight like a diver's, twenty feet down, forty . . .

And suddenly he was falling no more—the wings came out of nowhere, flaring, flashing silver-white in the sun as they sprang open almost with their own volition. The air screamed past them, and Val caught it and turned it and rode on it, and all at once he was flying, skimming the breakers with impossible speed, then pulling up, climbing, soaring, the waves and the rocks and death all receding visibly beneath him, and Maris could hear dimly the peal of his triumphant wind-blown laughter.

S'Rella had locked into a stall, still watching Val. Maris shouted commands at her, and she broke out of it, twisting her wings at an angle and slanting off back over the land. Above the fortress, its bare rock heated in the sun, she found a strong riser and sailed back up to safety.

Below, Sena was cursing up at Val and shaking her cane in apoplectic fury. He paid no attention. He was rising, higher and higher, and from the Woodwingers on the cliff came the ragged, popping sound of applause.

Maris went after him, banking, breaking her circle, heading out over the sea. Val was already ahead of her. But flying easily this time, luxuriating in his stunt.

When she caught him, flying as near to him as she dared—above and a bit behind and to the right—she began to shout curses down at him, borrowing freely from Sena's more extensive vocabulary.

Val laughed at her.

"That was dangerous and useless and stupid," Maris shouted. "You could have killed yourself . . . a jammed strut . . . if you hadn't flung them hard enough . . ."

Val still laughed. "My risk," he shouted back. "And I didn't fling them . . . rigged springs . . . better than Raven."

"Raven was a fool," she shouted. "And long dead . . . what's Raven to you?"

"Your brother sang *that* song, too," Val yelled. Then he banked and dove, away from her, abruptly terminating the conversation.

Numb, and seeing no use in further pursuit of Val, Maris wheeled around and looked for S'Rella, who was following several hundred yards behind and below them. She drifted down to join her, trying to tell her pounding heart to relax, willing her stiff muscles to loosen and get the feel of the wind.

S'Rella was ghost-pale, and flying badly. "What *happened?*" she cried when Maris approached. "I could have *died.*"

"It was a stunt," Maris called to her. "Flyer named Raven used to do it. Val concocted his own version."

S'Rella flew silently for a moment, considering that, and then a little color came tentatively back into her face. "I thought someone had pushed him," she shouted. "A stunt—it was beautiful."

"It was *insane*," Maris called back. She was quietly horrified that

S'Rella could possibly have thought one of her fellow students capable of shoving Val to his death. He *has* been influencing her, she thought bitterly.

The rest of the flight, as Maris had predicted, was easy. Maris and S'Rella flew close together, Val ahead and much higher, preferring the company of rainbirds, it seemed. They kept him in sight throughout the afternoon, but only with an effort.

The winds were cooperative, blowing them so steadily toward Skulny that they hardly needed to do more than relax and glide. It was at times a dull flight, but Maris did not regret it. They skirted the coast of Big Shotan, fishing fleets everywhere beyond the little harbor towns, bringing in as big a catch as possible in the storm-free weather. And they saw Stormtown from the air, its great bay in the center of the city, windmills turning all along the shores, forty of them, or fifty—S'Rella tried to count them, but they were behind her before she was half done. And in the open sea between Little Shotan and Skulny, near sunset, they spied a scylla, its long neck craning up out of the blue-green water as its rows of powerful flippers churned just beneath the surface. S'Rella seemed delighted. She had heard about scyllas all her life, but this was the first she had actually seen.

They reached Skulny just ahead of the night. As they circled before landing, they could see figures below setting up lanterns on poles all along the beach, to guide in later flyers. Already the small flyers' lodge nearby was ablaze with lights and activity: the parties, thought Maris, began earlier every year.

Maris tried to make her landing an example to S'Rella, but even as she was on her hands and knees, shaking sand out of her hair, she heard S'Rella thump to the ground nearby, and realized the girl had surely been too busy with her own landing to notice how clumsy or adept her teacher was.

Whoops of pleasure and welcome surrounded them at once. Eager hands reached out to them. "Help you, flyer? Help you, please?"

Maris took hold of one strong hand, and looked up into the eager face of a young boy with wind-tangled hair. His face was alive with pleasure; he was here for the glory of being near flyers, and was probably thrilled by the thought of the coming competition on his own island.

But as he was helping her off with her wings—and another boy was helping S'Rella—suddenly there was the sound of wind-on-wings again, and another thump, and Maris glanced over to see that Val had come in. They had lost sight of him near dusk, and she had assumed he was already down.

He climbed awkwardly to his feet, the great silver wings bobbing on his back, and two young girls moved in on him. "Help you, flyer." The refrain was almost a chant. "Help you, flyer," and their hands were on him.

"*Get away*," he snapped, anger in his voice. The girls jumped back, startled, and even Maris looked up. Val was always so cool and controlled; the outburst was unlike him.

"We just want to help you with your wings, flyer," the bolder of the girls said.

"Don't you have any pride?" Val said. He was unstrapping himself, without help. "Don't you have anything better to do than fawn over flyers who treat you like dirt? What are your parents?"

The girl quailed. "Tanners, flyer."

"Then go and learn tanning," he said. "It's a cleaner trade than slaving for the flyers." He turned away from her, began to fold up his wings carefully.

Maris and S'Rella were free of their own wings now. "Here," said the boy who had been helping Maris, as he offered them to her, neatly folded. Suddenly abashed, she fumbled in her pocket and offered the boy an iron coin. She had always accepted the help without payment before, but something in what Val said had struck a chord.

But the boy just laughed and refused to take her money. "Don't you know?" he said. "It's good luck to touch a flyer's wings." And then he was off, and Maris saw as he darted toward his companions that the beach was full of children. They were everywhere, helping with the poles, playing in the sand, waiting for the chance to aid a flyer.

But looking at them, Maris thought of Val, and wondered if there were others on the island who were *not* so thrilled by the fly-

ers and the competition, others who stayed home to brood and sulk
and resent the privileged caste that flew the skies of Windhaven.

"Take your wings, flyer?" a voice said sharply, and Maris glanced
over. It was Val, mocking. "Here," he said, in his normal tone, and
he offered her the wings he'd worn on the flight. "I imagine you'll
want these for safekeeping."

She took the wings from him, holding one pair awkwardly in
each hand. "Where are you going?"

Val shrugged. "This is a fair-sized island. Somewhere there's a
town or two, and a tavern or two, and a bed to sleep in. I have a
few irons."

"You could come up to the lodge with S'Rella and me," Maris
said hesitantly.

"Could I?" Val said, his voice perfectly level. His smile flickered
at her. "That would be an interesting scene. More dramatic than
my launching today, I'd guess."

Maris frowned. "I haven't forgotten that," she said. "S'Rella
could have hurt herself, you know. She was badly startled by that
fool's leap of yours. I ought—"

"I believe I've heard this before," Val said. "Excuse me." He
turned and was gone, walking quickly up the beach with his hands
shoved deep in his pockets.

Behind her, Maris heard S'Rella laughing and talking with the
other young people, sharing with them her delight in her first long
flight. When Maris approached, she broke off and ran to take her
hand. "How was I?" she asked breathlessly. "How did I do?"

"You know how you did—you just want me to praise you," Maris
said, her tone a mock-scold. "All right, I will. You flew as if you'd
never done anything else in your life, as if you'd been born to it."

"I know," S'Rella said shyly. Then she laughed in sheer joy. "It
was marvelous. I never want to do anything but fly!"

"I know how you feel," Maris said. "But a rest will do us good
right now. Let's go in and sit by the fire and see who else has come
early."

But when she turned to go, S'Rella hung back. Maris looked
at her curiously, and then understood; S'Rella was worried about
the sort of reception she would find inside the lodge. She was an

outsider, after all, and no doubt Val had been filling her with tales of his own rejection.

"Well," Maris said, "you might as well come in, unless you feel like flying back tonight. They'll have to meet you sometime."

S'Rella nodded, still a bit timorous, and they started up the pebbled incline toward the lodge.

It was a small two-room building built of soft, weathered white rock. The main room, well-lit and overheated by a roaring fire, was noisy, crowded, and unappealing after the clean solitude of the open air. The faces of the flyers seemed to blur together as Maris looked around in search of special friends, S'Rella standing nervously behind her. They hung the wings on hooks along the walls, and began to fight their way across the room.

A heavy-set, middle-aged man with a full beard was pouring some liquid into the huge, fragrant stewpot hung over the fire, and roaring insults at someone demanding nourishment. Something about him drew Maris' eyes back after they had passed over him, and with a strange little shock she recognized the overweight cook. When had Garth grown so old and fat?

She started toward him when thin arms went around her from behind, hugging her fiercely, and she caught the faint whisper of a flowery scent.

"Shalli!" she said, turning. She noticed the rounded stomach. "I didn't expect to see you here—heard you were preg—"

Shalli stopped her lips with a finger. "Hush. I get enough of that from Corm. And I tell him that our little flyer has to learn about flying from the very beginning. But I am careful, truly. I took the flight slow and easy. I couldn't miss this! Corm wanted me to take a boat. Can you imagine?" Shalli's beautiful, mobile face went from one comic expression to another as she spoke.

"You're not going to compete?"

"Oh, no. It wouldn't be fair, me with the extra ballast!" She patted the small mound and laughed. "I'm to judge. And I've promised Corm that after this I'll stay home and be a good little mother 'til the baby comes, unless there's an emergency."

Maris felt a pang of guilt, knowing that the "emergencies" Shalli had to fly were caused by her own absence from Amberly. But after the competition, she swore to herself, she'd stay home and tend to her duties.

"Shalli, I'd like you to meet a friend of mine," Maris said. S'Rella was hanging back shyly, so Maris pulled her gently forward. "This is S'Rella, our most promising student. She flew here from Woodwings with me today, her longest flight so far."

"Ooh." Shalli arched her brows.

"S'Rella, this is Shalli. From Lesser Amberly, like me. She used to fly guard on me, when I was just learning how to use the wings."

They exchanged polite greetings. Then Shalli, giving S'Rella a measuring look, said, "Good luck in the competitions. You'd better not beat Corm, though. I think I'd go mad if he was around the house every day for a year."

Shalli smiled, but S'Rella seemed to take the jest in earnest. "I don't want to hurt anyone," she said, "but someone has to lose. I want to win as much as any flyer."

"Mmm, well, it's not quite the same," Shalli murmured. "But I was only joking, child. You wouldn't want to challenge Corm, really. You wouldn't have a very good chance." She glanced across the room. "Excuse me, please—I see that Corm has found a cushion for me, and now I suppose I must go and sit on it if I'm not to hurt his feelings. I'll talk to you later, Maris. S'Rella, it was nice to meet you."

They watched her moving easily through the crowded room, away from them.

"Would I?" S'Rella asked, her tone troubled.

"Would you what?"

"Have a chance against Corm."

Maris looked at her unhappily, not knowing what to say. "He's very good," she managed finally. "He's been flying for almost twenty years now, and he's won prizes in lots of these competitions. No, you're probably not his match. But that's no disgrace, S'Rella."

"Which one is he?" S'Rella said, frowning.

"Over by Shalli—see—the dark-haired one in black and gray."

"He's handsome," S'Rella said.

Maris laughed. "Ah, yes. Half the land-bound girls on Amberly were in love with him when he was younger. They were all heart-broken when he and Shalli wed."

That drew a small smile back to S'Rella's face. "On my home island, all the boys used to dream about S'Landra, our flyer. Were you in love with Corm too?"

"Never. I knew him too well."

"MARIS!" The bellow rang from the rafters, attracting attention all over the lodge. Garth was yelling at her from across the room, gesturing her closer.

She grinned. "Come," she said, pulling S'Rella after her through the press, nodding polite hellos at old acquaintances as she went.

Garth crushed her in a formidable hug when she reached him, then pushed her back to look at her. "You look tired, Maris," he told her. "Flying too much."

"And you," she said, "have been eating too much." She jabbed a finger into his stomach where it hung over his belt. "What's this? Are you and Shalli going to give birth together?"

Garth snorted with laughter. "Ah," he growled, "my sister's fault. She brews her own ale, you know. Got a right little business going. I have to help her out, of course, buy a little now and again."

"You're probably her best customer," Maris said. "When did you grow the beard?"

"Oh, a month ago, two, something like that. I haven't seen you in a half-year, it seems."

Maris nodded. "Dorrel was fretting over you the last time we were at the Eyrie together. Something about a date to get drunk, and you didn't make it."

He frowned. "Ah," he said, "yes, I know all about it. Dorrel goes on endlessly. I was ill, that's all, no great mystery." He turned back to the fire and gave his stew a stir. "There'll be food soon. Hungry? I made this myself, Southern style, with lots of spices and wine."

Maris turned. "You hear that, S'Rella? You'll get some decent food, it sounds like." She ushered the girl forward to face Garth. "S'Rella's a Woodwinger, and one of the best. She'll be taking some poor soul's wings this year. S'Rella, this is Garth of Skulny, one of our hosts here and an old friend."

"Not *that* old," Garth protested. He smiled at S'Rella. "Why, you're as beautiful as Maris used to be, before she got thin and tired. Do you fly as well?"

"I try to," S'Rella said.

"Modest, too," he said. "Well, Skulny knows how to treat flyers, even fledglings. Anything you want, you tell me about it. Are you hungry? This will be ready soon. In fact, maybe you can help me with the spices. I'm not really from Southern, you know, maybe I didn't get it right." He took her by the hand and drew her closer to the fire, then forced a spoonful of stew at her. "Here, try this, tell me what you think."

As S'Rella tasted, Garth glanced at Maris and pointed. "Look, you're wanted," he said. Dorrel was standing in the doorway, still holding his folded wings, shouting to her above the din of the party. "Go on," Garth said gruffly. "I'll keep S'Rella occupied. I'm the host, after all." He pushed her toward the door.

Maris smiled at him, then began to work her way back across the floor, which had grown even more crowded. Dorrel, after hanging up his wings, met her. He threw his arms around her and kissed her briefly. Maris found herself trembling as she leaned against him.

When they broke apart, there was concern in his eyes. "What's wrong?" he said. "You were shaking." He looked at her hard. "And you look worn out, exhausted."

Maris forced a smile. "Garth said the same thing. No, really, I'm fine."

"No, you're not. I know you too well, love." He put his hands on her shoulders, his gentle, familiar hands. "Really. Can't you tell me?"

Maris sighed. She *did* feel tired, she realized suddenly. "I guess I don't know myself," she muttered. "I haven't been sleeping well this past month. Nightmares."

Dorrel put an arm around her and led her through the press of flyers to a wide wooden table against the wall, covered with wines, liquors, and food. "What kind of nightmares?" he asked. He poured them each glasses of rich red wine, and carved out two wedges of a white, crumbly cheese.

"Only one. Falling. I fall through still air, hit the water, and die."

She bit off a mouthful of cheese and washed it down with a gulp of the wine. "Good," she said, smiling.

"Should be," Dorrel replied. "It's from Amberly. But you can't really be worried about this dream, can you? I didn't think you were superstitious."

"No," Maris said, "that's not it at all. I can't explain. It just— bothers me. And that's not all." She hesitated.

Dorrel watched her face, waiting.

"This competition," Maris said. "There could be trouble."

"What kind of trouble?"

"Remember when I saw you at Eyrie? I mentioned that one of the students from Airhome had taken ship for Woodwings?"

"Yes," Dorrel said. He sipped at his own wine. "What of it?"

"He's on Skulny now, and he's going to challenge, and it isn't just any student. It's Val."

Dorrel's face was blank. "Val?"

"One-Wing," Maris said quietly.

He frowned. "One-Wing," he repeated. "Well, I understand why you're upset. I would never have expected *him* to try again. Does he expect to be welcomed?"

"No," Maris said. "He knows better. And his opinion of flyers is no better than their opinion of him."

Dorrel shrugged. "Well, it will be unpleasant, but it needn't ruin the competition," he said. "He'll be easy enough to ignore, and I don't imagine we have to worry about him winning again. No one has lost a relative lately."

Maris drew back a little. Dorrel's voice abruptly seemed so hard, and the gibe sounded so cruel from his lips—and yet, it was almost identical to what she'd said at the academy on the day Val had arrived. "Dorr," she said, "he's *good*. He's been training for years. I think he's going to win. He has the skills. I know, I've flown against him."

"You've flown against him?" Dorrel said.

"In practice," Maris said. "At Woodwings. What—"

He drained his wine and set the glass aside. "Maris," he said, his voice low but strained. "You're not going to tell me you've been helping *him* too. One-Wing?"

"He was a student, and Sena asked me to work with him," Maris said stubbornly. "I'm not there to play favorites and help only those I like."

Dorrel swore and took her by the arm. "Come outside," he said. "I don't want to talk about this in here, where someone might hear."

It was cool outside the lodge, and the wind coming in off the sea had the tang of salt to it. Along the beach, the poles were up and the lanterns had been lit to welcome night-flying travelers. Maris and Dorrel walked away from the crowded lodge and sat together on the sand. Most of the children had gone now, and they were alone.

"Maybe this is what I feared," Maris said, with a tinge of bitterness in her tone. "I knew you'd balk at that. But I can't make exceptions—*we* can't make exceptions. Can't you understand that? Can't you try to understand?"

"I can try," he said. "I can't promise to succeed. *Why*, Maris? He's no ordinary land-bound, no little Woodwings dreaming of being a flyer. He's One-Wing, half a flyer even when he had his wings. He killed Ari. Have you forgotten that?"

"No," Maris said. "I'm not happy about Val. He's hard to like, and he hates flyers, and there's always the specter of Ari peering over his shoulder. But I *have* to help him, Dorr. Because of what we did seven years ago. The wings must go to those who can use them best, even if they are . . . well, like Val. Vindictive, and angry, and cold."

Dorrel shook his head. "I can't accept that," he said.

"I wish I knew him better," Maris said, "so I could understand what made him the way he is. I think he hated the flyers even before they named him One-Wing." She reached over and took Dorrel by the hand. "He's always accusing, making venomous little jests, when he isn't shielding himself in ice. According to Val, I'm a One-Wing too, even if I pretend that I'm not."

Dorrel looked at her and squeezed her hand tight within his own. "No," he said. "You are a flyer, Maris. Have no fear of that."

"Am I?" she said. "I'm not sure what it means to be a flyer. It's more than having wings, or flying well. Val had wings, and he flies well enough, but you yourself said he was only half a flyer. If it means . . . well, accepting everything the way it is, and looking down on the land-bound, and not offering help to the Woodwingers for fear they'll hurt a fellow flyer, a *real* flyer . . . if it means things like that, then I don't think I am a flyer. And sometimes I wonder if I'm not beginning to share Val's opinions of those who are."

Dorrel let go her hand but his eyes were still on her. Even in the dark she could feel the anguished intensity of his gaze. "Maris," he said softly. "*I'm* a flyer, born to my wings. Val One-Wing surely despises me for it. Do you?"

"Dorr," she said, hurt. "You know I don't. I've always loved and trusted you—you're my best friend, truly. But . . ."

"But," he echoed.

She could not look at him. "I wasn't proud of you when you refused to come to Woodwings," she said.

The distant sounds of the party and the melancholy wash of the waves against the beach seemed to fill the world. Finally Dorrel spoke.

"My mother was a flyer, and her mother before her, and on back for generations the pair of wings that I bear has been in my family. That means a great deal to me. My child, should I ever father one, will fly, too, someday.

"You weren't born to that tradition, and you've been the dearest person in the world to me. And you've always proved that you deserved wings at least as much as any flyer's child. It would have been a horrible injustice if you'd been denied them. I'm proud that I could help you.

"I'm proud that I fought with you in Council to open the sky, but now you seem to be telling me that we fought for different things. As I understood it, we were fighting for the right of anyone who dreamed hard enough and worked long enough to become a flyer. We weren't out to destroy the great tradition of the flyers, to throw the wings out and let land-bound and would-be flyers alike fight over them like scavenging gulls over a pile of fish.

"What we were trying to do, or so I thought, was to open the sky, to open the Eyrie, to open the ranks of the flyers to anyone who could prove worthy of bearing wings.

"Was I wrong? Were we actually fighting instead to give up everything that makes us special and different?"

"I don't know anymore," she said. "Seven years ago, I could think of nothing more wonderful than being a flyer. Neither could you. We never dreamed that there were people who might want to wear our wings, but reject everything else that makes up a flyer. We never dreamed of them, but they existed. And we opened the sky for them, too, Dorr. We changed more than we knew. And we can't turn our backs on them. The world has changed, and we have to accept it, and deal with it. We may not like all the results of what we've done, but we can't deny them. Val is one of those results."

Dorrel stood up and brushed the sand from his clothes. "I can't accept that result," he said, his voice more sorrowful than angry. "I've done a lot of things for the love of you, Maris, but I can see the limits. It's true that the world has changed—because of what we've done—but we *don't* have to accept the evil with the good. We don't have to embrace those, like Val One-Wing, who sneer at our traditions and seek to tear us apart. He'll destroy us in the end, Maris—with his selfishness and his hatred. And because you don't understand that, you'll help him. I won't. Do you understand that?"

She nodded without looking up at him.

A minute passed in silence. "Will you come with me, back to the lodge?"

"No," she said. "No, not just now."

"Good night, Maris." Dorrel turned and walked away from her, his boots crunching on the sand until the lodge door opened for him with a burst of party noise, then closed again.

It was quiet and peaceful on the beach. The lanterns, burning atop their poles, moved weakly in the breeze, and she heard their faint clattering and the never-ending sound of the sea rolling in and out, in and out.

Maris had never felt so alone.

Maris and S'Rella spent the night together in a roughly finished cabin for two not far from the shore, one of fifty such structures that the Landsman of Skulny had had erected to house the visiting flyers. The little village was only half full as yet, but Maris knew that the earliest arrivals had already appropriated the more comfortable accommodations in the lodge house and the guest wing of the Landsman's own High Hall.

S'Rella didn't mind the austerity of their lodgings. She was in high spirits when Maris retrieved her at last from the dying party. Garth had stayed close to her throughout the evening, introducing her to almost everybody, forcing her to eat three portions of his stew after she had praised it incautiously, and regaling her with embarrassing anecdotes about half of the flyers present. "He's nice," S'Rella said, "but he drinks too much." Maris could only agree with that; though it had not always been so: when she'd come to find S'Rella, Garth had been red-eyed and close to staggering. Maris helped him to the back room and put him to bed while he carried on a slurred, unintelligible conversation.

The next day dawned gray and windy. They woke to the cries of a food vendor, and Maris slipped outside and bought two steaming hot sausages from his cart. After breakfast, they donned their wings and flew. Not many of the flyers were in the air; the holiday atmosphere was a contagion, and most were drinking and talking in the lodge, or paying their respects to the Landsman, or wandering about Skulny to see what there was to see. But Maris insisted that S'Rella practice, and they stayed aloft for close to five hours on steadily rising winds.

Below them, the beach was again choked with children eager to assist incoming flyers. Despite their numbers, they were kept busy. Arrivals were constant throughout the day. The most spectacular moment—S'Rella looked on with wondering, awe-struck eyes—was when the flyers of Big Shotan approached en masse, nearly forty strong, flying in a tight formation, gorgeous against the sun in their dark red uniforms and silver wings.

By the time the competition began, Maris knew, virtually all the flyers from the scattered reaches of Western would be here. Eastern would be heavily represented too, although not quite with the unanimity of Western. Southern, smaller and farther, would have fewer still, and there would be only a handful of competitors from the

Outer Islands, desolate Artellia, the volcanic Embers, and the other far-off places.

It was afternoon, and Maris and S'Rella were sitting outside the lodge with glasses of hot spiced milk in their hands, when Val made his appearance.

He gave Maris his mocking half-smile and sat down next to S'Rella. "I trust you enjoyed flyer hospitality," he said flatly.

"They were nice," S'Rella said, blushing. "Won't you come tonight? There's to be another party. Garth is going to roast a whole seacat, and his sister is providing ale."

"No," Val said. "They have ale enough and food enough where I'm staying, and it suits me better." He glanced at Maris. "No doubt it suits us all better."

Maris refused to be baited. "Where *are* you staying?"

"A tavern about two miles down the sea road. Not the sort of place you'd care to visit. They don't get many flyers there, just miners and landsguard and some less willing to talk about their professions. I doubt they'd know how to treat a flyer properly."

Maris frowned in annoyance. "Do you ever stop?"

"Stop?" He smiled.

All at once Maris was filled with a perverse determination to erase that smile, to prove Val wrong. "You don't even know the flyers," she said. "What right have you to hate them so? They're people, no different from you—no, that's wrong, they are different. They're warmer and more generous."

"The warmth and generosity of flyers is fabled," Val said. "No doubt that's why only flyers are welcome at flyer parties."

"They welcomed *me*," S'Rella said.

Val gave her a long look, cautious and measuring. Then he shrugged and the thin smile returned to his lips. "You've convinced me," he said. "I'll come to this party tonight, if they'll let a landbound through the door."

"Come as my guest, then," Maris said, "if you refuse to call yourself a flyer. And put aside your damned hostility for a few hours. Give them a chance."

"Please," S'Rella said. She took his hand and smiled hopefully at him.

"Oh, they'll have a chance to show their warmth and generosity," Val said. "But I won't beg for it, or polish their wings, or sing songs in their praise." He stood up abruptly. "Now, I would like to get some flying in. Is there a pair of wings I might use?"

Maris nodded and directed him to the cabin where his wings were hung. After he was gone, she turned to S'Rella. "You care for him a lot, don't you?" she said softly.

S'Rella lowered her eyes and blushed. "I know he's cruel at times, Maris, but he's not always like that."

"Maybe that's so," Maris admitted. "He hasn't let me get to know him very well. Just—just be careful, all right, S'Rella? Val has a lot of hurt in him and sometimes people like that, when they've been hurt a lot, get back by hurting others, even those who care for them."

"I know," S'Rella said. "Maris, you don't think—they won't hurt him tonight, will they? The flyers?"

"I think he wants them to," Maris said, "so you'll see that he's right about them—about us. But I'm hoping that we'll prove him wrong."

S'Rella said nothing. Maris finished her drink and rose. "Come," she said. "There's still time for more practice, and you need it. Let's get our wings back on."

By early evening it was common knowledge among the flyers that Val One-Wing was on Skulny and intended to challenge. How the word had gotten out Maris was unsure. Perhaps Dorrel had said something, or perhaps Val had been recognized, or perhaps the news had come in from Eastern with some flyer who knew that Val had taken ship from Airhome. It was out and flying in any case. Twice Maris heard the epithet "One-Wing" as she and S'Rella walked back to their cabin in the flyer village, and outside their door a young flyer Maris knew casually from the Eyrie stopped her and asked point-blank if the rumor was true. When Maris admitted that it was, the other woman whistled and shook her head.

It was not quite dark when Maris and S'Rella wandered up to the lodge, but the main room was already half-full of flyers, drinking and talking in small clusters. The promised seacat was roasting on a spit above the fire, but by the look of it still had several hours to go.

Garth's sister, a stout plain-faced woman named Riesa, drew Maris a mug of her ale from one of three huge wooden casks that had been set along one wall. "It's good," Maris said after tasting. "Although I confess I'm no expert. Wine and kivas are my usual drinks."

Riesa laughed. "Well, Garth swears by it, and he's drunk enough ale in his time to float a small trading fleet."

"Where is Garth?" S'Rella asked. "I thought he'd be here."

"He should be, later," Riesa said. "He wasn't feeling well, so he sent me on ahead. I think it was just an excuse to avoid helping with the barrels, actually."

"Wasn't feeling well?" Maris said. "Riesa, is everything all right? He's been ill frequently of late, hasn't he?"

Riesa's pleasant smile faded. "Has he told you, Maris? I wasn't sure. It's only been the past half-year. It's his joints. When it gets bad, they swell up on him something terrible, and even when they aren't swelling he's got pain." She leaned a little closer. "I'm worried about him, in truth. Dorrel is too. He's seen healers, here and in Stormtown too, but no one has been able to do much. And he's drinking more than he used to."

Maris was appalled. "I knew Dorrel was fretting over him, but I thought it was just his drinking." She hesitated. "Riesa, has Garth told the Landsman about his troubles?"

Riesa shook her head. "No, he's—" She interrupted herself to draw a mug for a craggy-looking Easterner and resumed only after he had drifted away. "He's afraid, Maris."

"Why is he afraid?" S'Rella asked quietly, looking from Maris to Riesa and back again. She had been standing silently by Maris' elbow, listening.

"If a flyer is sick," Maris said, "the Landsman can call together the island's other flyers, and if they agree, he can take the wings from the sick one, lest they be lost at sea." She looked back toward Riesa. "Then Garth is still flying missions as if he were well," she said, with concern in her voice. "The Landsman isn't sparing him."

"No," Riesa said, chewing on her lip. "I'm frightened for him,

Maris. The pain comes on so suddenly sometimes, and if it should come while he's flying—I've told him to speak to the Landsman, but he won't hear of it. His wings are everything to him, you know that. All you flyers are alike."

"I'll talk to him," Maris said firmly.

"Dorrel has spoken to him endlessly," Riesa said. "It does no good. You know how stubborn Garth can be."

"He should lay down his wings," S'Rella blurted suddenly.

Riesa gave her a hard look. "Child, you don't know what you are saying. You are the Woodwinger Garth met last night, are you not? Maris' friend?"

S'Rella nodded.

"Yes, Garth spoke of you," Riesa said. "You would understand better if you were a flyer. You and I, we can only watch from out-side, we can never feel as a flyer feels about his wings. At least Garth has told me so."

"I *will* be a flyer," S'Rella insisted.

"Certainly you will, child," Riesa said, "but you are not now, and that is why you talk so easily of laying down the wings."

But S'Rella looked offended. She stood very stiffly and said, "I'm not a child, and I *do* understand." She might have said more, but just then the door opened and she and Maris both glanced in that direction.

Val had arrived.

"Excuse me," Maris said, taking Riesa by the forearm and giving her a squeeze for reassurance. "We'll talk more later." She hurried to where Val stood, his dark eyes sweeping the room, one hand resting on the hilt of his ornate knife in a pose that was half ner-vousness and half challenge.

"A small party," he said noncommittally when Maris and S'Rella joined him.

"It's early," Maris replied. "Give it time. Come, let's get you a drink and a bit of food." She gestured to the far wall, where a lavish table had once again been spread with spiced eggs, fruit, cheese, bread, various shellfish, sweetmeats, and pastries. "The seacat is the main course, but we'll be waiting hours for that," she concluded.

Val took in the seacat on the spit and the table covered with other edibles. "I see the flyers are eating simply once again," he said. But he let himself be led across the room, where he ate two spiced eggs and a wedge of cheese before pausing to pour a goblet of wine.

Around them the party went on; Val had attracted no particular attention. But Maris did not know if that was because the others had accepted him, or simply failed to recognize him.

The three of them stood quietly for a few moments, S'Rella talking to Val in a low voice while he sipped at his wine and nibbled some more cheese, Maris quaffing her ale and watching the front door a bit apprehensively each time it opened. It had grown dark outside, and the lodge was filling up rapidly. A dozen Shotaners she knew only vaguely swept in all at once, still in their red uniforms, followed by a half-dozen Easterners she knew not at all. One of them climbed atop Riesa's ale casks; a companion tossed him up a guitar, and he began to sing flyers' songs in a passably mellow voice. Beneath him the crowd grew dense, and listeners began to shout up requests.

Maris, still glancing at the door whenever it opened, drifted a bit closer to Val and S'Rella, and tried to listen to them above the music.

Then the music stopped.

In mid-song, suddenly singer and guitar both grew silent, and the silence flowed across the room, as conversations ceased and all eyes turned curiously to the man perched atop the ale keg. In less than a minute, everyone in the lodge was looking at him.

And he was looking across the room at Val.

Val turned in his direction and raised his wine glass. "Greetings, Loren," he called, in his maddeningly flat tones. "I toast your *fine* singing." He drained his wine and set the glass aside.

Someone, taking Val's words for a veiled insult, snickered. Others took the toast in earnest, and raised their own glasses. The singer just sat and stared, his face darkening, and most of the flyers watched him, baffled, waiting for him to resume.

"Do the ballad of Aron and Jeni," someone called out.

The guitarist shook his head. "No," he said, "I've got a more ap-propriate song." He played a few opening bars and began to sing a song unfamiliar to Maris.

Val turned to her. "Don't you recognize it?" he said. "It's popular in Eastern. They call it the ballad of Ari and One-Wing." He poured himself more wine and raised the glass again in mocking tribute to the singer.

With a sinking feeling, Maris realized that she *had* heard the song before, years past, and what was worse had enjoyed it. It was a rousing, dramatic story of betrayal and revenge, with One-Wing the villain and the flyers the heroes.

S'Rella was biting her lip in anger, barely holding back her tears. She started forward impulsively, but Val restrained her with a hand on her arm and shook his head. Maris could only stand helplessly, listening to the cruel words, so very different from those of her own song, the one Coll had composed for her. She wished he were here now, to compose a song in answer to this. Singers had a strange power, even amateurs like the Easterner across the room.

When he was finished, everyone knew.

He tossed his guitar down to a friend, and jumped down after it. "I'll be singing on the beach, if anyone cares to hear," he said. Then he took his instrument and left, followed by all of the Easterners who had arrived with him and a good many others. The lodge was suddenly half-empty again.

"Loren was a neighbor," Val said. "From North Arren, just across the bay. I haven't seen him in years."

The Shotaners were talking softly among themselves, one or two of them giving Val, Maris, and S'Rella pointed looks from time to time. All of them left together.

"You haven't introduced me to your flyer friends," Val said to S'Rella. "Come." He took her hand and led her forcefully to where four men were clustered in a tight circle. Maris had no choice but to follow. "I'm Val of South Arren," he said loudly. "This is S'Rella. Fine flying weather today, wasn't it?"

One of the four, a huge, dark man with a massive jaw, frowned at him. "I admire your courage, One-Wing," he rumbled, "but nothing else about you. I knew Ari, though not well. Do you want me to make polite conversation with you?"

"This is a flyers' lodge and a flyers' party," one of his companions said sharply. "Do you two have business here?"

"They are *my* guests," Maris said furiously. "Or do you question my right to be here too?"

"No. Only your taste in guests." He clapped the big man on the shoulder. "Come. I have a sudden urge to hear some singing."

Val tried another group, two women and a man with ale mugs in their hands. Before he had quite reached them, they set down their mugs—still half-full—and left.

Only one party remained in the room, six flyers that Maris knew vaguely from the far reaches of Western, and a single blond youth from the Outer Islands. And suddenly they were leaving too, but on the way to the door one of them, a man well into his middle years, stopped to talk to Val. "You may not remember, but I was among the judges the year you took Ari's wings," the man said. "We judged fairly, but some have never forgiven us for the verdict we handed down. Perhaps you did not know what you were doing, perhaps you did. It makes no difference. If they were so reluctant to forgive me, they will never forgive *you*. I pity you, but we're helpless. You were wrong to come back, son. They will never let you be a flyer."

Val had been calm through everything else, but now his face contorted in rage. "I do not want your pity," he said. "I do not want to be one of you. *And I am not your son!* Get out of here, old man, or I will take *your* wings this year."

The gray-haired flyer shook his head, and a companion took him by his elbow. "Let's go, Cadon. You waste your concern on him."

When they left, only Riesa remained in the lodge room with Maris, Val, and S'Rella. She busied herself with her ale mugs, gathering them up to wash, and did not look at them.

"Warmth and generosity," Val said.

"They're not all—" Maris started, and found she could not go on. S'Rella looked as if she were about to cry.

Then the door crashed open, and it was Garth standing there, frowning, looking puzzled and angry. "What is going on?" he said. "I stumble up from home to host my party, and everyone is out on the beach. Maris? Riesa?" He slammed the door and started across the room. "If there was a fight, I'll break the neck of the fool who started it. Flyers have no business quarreling like land-bound."

Val faced him squarely. "I'm the cause of your empty party," he said.

"Do I know you?" Garth said.

"Val. Of South Arren." He waited.

"He didn't start anything," Maris said suddenly. "Believe that, Garth. He's my guest."

Garth looked baffled. "Then why—?"

"I'm also called One-Wing."

Comprehension broke across Garth's face, and Maris knew how she must have looked the day she had met Val on the Stormtown docks, and had a sickening realization of what it must have felt like to Val.

Whatever Garth felt, he struggled to control it. "I wish I could bid you welcome," he said, "but that would be a lie. Ari was a sweet, fine woman who never hurt anyone, and I knew her brother too. We all did." He sighed and looked to Maris. "He is your guest, you say? What would you have me do?"

"Ari was my friend as well," Maris said. "Garth, I don't ask you to forget her. But Val is not her killer. He took her wings, not her life."

"They are one and the same," Garth grumbled, but it was half-hearted. He looked back at Val. "You were a boy then, though, and none of us knew that Ari would kill herself. I've made my own share of mistakes, though none as big as yours, and I suppose—"

"I made no mistake," Val interrupted.

Garth blinked. "Your challenge was a mistake," he said. "Ari killed herself."

"I would challenge her again," Val said. "She was not fit to fly. Her death was *her* mistake, not mine."

Garth was always gentle and genial, even his infrequent angers full of bluff and bluster; Maris had never seen his face as cold and bitter as it looked now. "Out, One-Wing," he said, his voice low.

"Leave this lodge and do not enter it again, whether you wear wings or not. I will not have you."

"I won't be back," Val said evenly. "Nonetheless, I thank you for your warmth and generosity." He smiled and headed toward the door. S'Rella started after him.

"S'Rella," Garth said. "I don't—you can stay, girl, I have no—"

S'Rella whirled. "Everything Val says is true. I hate you all."

And she followed Val One-Wing out into night.

S'Rella did not return to their little cabin that night, but she was there just after dawn the next day, Val with her, both ready for practice. Maris gave them the wings and accompanied them up the steep, twisting stone stairs to the flyers' cliff. "Race," she told them. "Fly above the coastline, using the sea breeze and staying low. Circle the entire island."

It was not until they were out of sight that Maris took wing herself. They would take several hours to complete the circuit, and she was thankful for the time. She felt tired and irritable, in no mood for even the best of company, and Val was never that. She gave herself to the healing embrace of the wind and angled out to sea.

The morning was pale and quiet, the wind steady behind her. She rode it, letting it take her where it would; all directions were the same to her. She wanted only to fly, to feel the touch of the wind, to forget all the petty troubles below in the cold, clean air of the upper sky.

There was little enough to see: gulls and scavenger kites and a hawk or two near the shores of Skulny, a fishing boat here and there, and farther out only ocean, ocean everywhere, blue-green water with long bright streaks of sun upon it. Once she saw a pack of seacats, graceful silver shapes whose playful leaps took them twenty feet above the waves. An hour later, she caught a rare glimpse of a wind wraith, a vast strange bird with semi-translucent wings as wide and thin as the sails of a trading ship. Maris had never seen one before, though she had heard other flyers speak of them. They liked the higher altitudes where humans seldom flew, and almost never came within sight of land. This one was quite low, floating on the wind, its great wings scarcely seeming to move. She soon lost sight of it.

A deep sense of peace filled her, and she felt all the tensions and angers of the land drain away from her. *This* was what it meant to fly, she thought. The rest, the messages she flew, the honor paid to her, the ease of living, the friends and enemies in flyer society, the rules and laws and legends, the responsibility and the boundless freedom, all of it, all of it was secondary. This, for her, was the real reward; the simple feel of flying.

S'Rella felt it too, she thought. Perhaps that was why she was so drawn to the Southern girl, because of the way she looked when she came from flying, cheeks flushed, eyes glowing, smiling. Val had none of that look about him, Maris realized suddenly. The thought saddened her. Even if he should win his wings, he would miss so much; he took a fierce pride in his flying, came away from it with a sheen of satisfaction, but he was not capable of finding joy in the sky. Whether or not he ever won his wings, the peace and happiness of the true flyer would always be denied him. And that, thought Maris, was the cruelest truth about Val's life.

When she saw by the sun that it was nearly noon, Maris finally banked and swept around in a long, graceful arc to begin the flight back to Skulny.

Maris was resting alone in her cabin late that afternoon when she was startled by loud, insistent pounding at the door.

Her visitor was a stranger, a short, slight, hollow-cheeked man with graying hair pulled back hard and tied in a knot at the back of his head. An Easterner: his hairstyle and fur-trimmed clothes told her that. He wore an iron ring on one finger and silver on another, testimonials to his wealth.

"My name is Arak," he said. "I have flown for South Arren these past thirty years."

Maris opened the door wider and let him in, gesturing him toward the one chair. She sat on a bed. "You are from Val's home island."

He grimaced. "Indeed. It is Val One-Wing I would speak to you about. Some of us have been talking—"

"Us?"

"Flyers."

"Which flyers?" His self-centered intensity made her hostile; she did not like his presumption or his tone.

"That doesn't matter," Arak said. "I was sent to talk with you because it is generally felt that you are a flyer at heart, even if not flyer-born. You would not help Val One-Wing if you knew the sort of man he is."

"I know him," Maris said. "I do not like him, and I have not forgotten Ari's death, but still he deserves his chance."

"He has had more chances than he ever deserved," Arak said angrily. "Do you know the stock he springs from? His parents were vicious, dirty, ignorant. From Lomarron, not South Arren at all. Do you know Lomarron?"

Maris nodded, remembering the time she had flown to Lomarron three years before. A large, mountainous island, soil-poor but metal-rich. Because of that wealth, warfare was endemic. Most of the land-bound there worked in the mines. "His parents were miners," she guessed.

But Arak shook his head. "Landsguard," he said. "Professional killers. His father was a knife-fighter, his mother a sling."

"Many islands have landsguard forces," Maris said uneasily.

Arak seemed to be enjoying this. "On Lomarron they get more practice than on other islands," he said. "Too much, finally. His mother had her sling hand lopped off in an engagement, severed clean at the wrist. Not long after that there was a truce. But Val's family didn't take to truces. His father killed a man anyway, and then the three of them had to flee Lomarron in a fishing boat they stole. That was how they came to South Arren. The mother was a useless one-handed cripple, but the father joined the landsguard again. Only for a short time, though. One night he got too drunk and told a mate who he was, and word reached the Landsman, and then Lomarron. He was hanged as a thief and a murderer."

Maris sat silent, feeling numb.

"I know all this," Arak went on, "because I took pity on the poor widow. I took her in as housekeeper and cook, never mind that she was clumsy and slow with the one hand. I gave them a place to live, plenty to eat, and raised Val with my own son. With his father gone, he should have looked up to me. I set him a good example; I gave him the discipline he lacked. But it was wasted—his blood was bad. The kindness was wasted on both of them, and anything you do for him is going to be wasted as well. His mother was lazy and shiftless, always whining and complaining about how she felt, never getting her work done on time, but expecting to be paid for it all the same. Val used to play at being a knife-fighter, and killing people. Even tried to drag my own boy into his sick games, but I stopped that soon enough. He was a terrible influence. Both of them stole, you know, him and his mother. There was always something missing. I had to keep my iron under lock and key. I even caught him handling my wings once, in the middle of the night, when he thought I was asleep.

"Give him a chance to win wings fairly, and what does he do? Attacks poor Ari, who hadn't a chance, and as good as kills her. He has no morals, no code. I couldn't beat it into him when he was a boy, and now—"

Maris rose, suddenly remembering the scars on Val's back. "You beat him?"

"Eh?" Arak looked up at her in surprise. "Of course I beat him. The only way to lick some sense into him. A blackwood stick when he was small, a touch of the whip now and then when he was older. Same as I gave my own."

"Same as you gave your own. How about the other things you gave your own—did Val and his mother eat at table with you?"

Arak stood up, his sharp face twisted in dismay. Even standing, he was a small figure, and had to look up at Maris. "Of course not," he snapped. "They were help, hired land-bound. Servants don't eat with their masters. I gave them all they needed—don't you imply that I starved them."

"You gave them scraps," Maris said with angry certainty. "Scraps and refuse, the garbage you didn't want."

"I was a wealthy flyer when you were a land-bound brat digging for your dinner. Don't try to tell me how to feed my household."

Maris stepped closer, looming above him. "Raised him with your own son, did you? And what did you say when you were training your son, and Val asked if he might try on the wings?"

Arak gave a choking snort of laughter. "I whipped that idea out of him fast enough," he said. "That was before you came along with your damned academies and put notions in the heads of the land-bound."

She shoved him.

Maris had scarcely ever touched another person in anger, but now she shoved him hard, with both hands, wanting to hurt him, and Arak staggered backward, the laughter dying in his throat. She shoved him again and he stumbled and fell. She stood over him, seeing the nervous disbelief in his eyes. "Get up," she said. "Get up and get out, you filthy little man. If I could I'd rip the wings from your back. You foul the sky."

Arak rose and moved quickly to the door. Outside, he was brave again. "Blood will tell," he said, glaring through the doorway at Maris. "I knew it. I told them all. Land-bound is land-bound. The academies will close. We should have taken your wings early, but we'll take them late, just the same."

Maris, shaking, slammed the door.

Suddenly a terrible suspicion hit her, and she wrenched the door open again and ran out after him. Arak, seeing her coming, began to run, but she soon caught up with him, and knocked him flat on the sand. Several astonished flyers watched, but no one moved to interfere.

Arak cringed beneath her. "You're mad," he shouted. "Leave me alone!"

"Where was Val's father executed?" Maris demanded.

Arak got clumsily to his feet.

"On Lomarron or South Arren?"

"On Arren, of course. No sense shipping him back," he said, stepping away from her. "Our rope was just as good."

"But the crime was committed on Lomarron, so the Landsman of

Lomarron had to order the execution," Maris said. "How did that order get to your Landsman? You flew it, didn't you? *You flew the messages both ways!*"

Arak glared at her and broke and ran again. Maris did not go after him this time.

The look on his face had been all the admission she needed.

The wind off the sea was brisk and cold that night, but Maris walked slowly, not eager to leave the solitude of the sea road for a conference with Val. She wanted to speak with Val—she felt she had to—but she wasn't certain what she would say. For the first time, she felt she understood him. And her sympathy disturbed her.

She was angry with Arak; she had responded to him emotionally and, she now thought, irrationally. She had no right to that anger, even if Val did. A flyer could not be blamed for the message he or she flew—that was common sense, as well as the stuff of legend. Maris herself had never flown a message leading directly to anyone's death, but she had carried information once that had resulted in the imprisonment of a woman accused of theft—did that woman bear a grudge against Maris as well as against the Landsman who sentenced her?

Maris shoved her hands into her pockets and hunched her shoulders against the bite of the wind, scowling as she turned the problem over in her mind. Arak was an unpleasant person, and he might well have taken pleasure in the idea of being the instrument of revenge against a murderer, and there was no doubt that he had taken advantage of the situation. Val and his mother had been cheap labor to him, however sanctimoniously he might speak of his generosity.

As she neared the tavern where Val was lodged, Maris still argued with herself. Arak was a flyer, and flyers could not refuse to carry messages, no matter how unwelcome or unfair they might sound. She couldn't let her dislike of the man trick her into blaming him for the execution (deserved or not) of Val's father. And that was something that Val, if he was ever to be more than One-Wing, would have to understand, too.

The tavern was a shabby place, its interior dark and cold and smelling faintly of mold. The fire was too small to heat the main room properly, and the candles on the table burned smokily. Val was dicing with three dark-haired, heavy women in landsguard brown-and-green, but he came away when Maris asked him to, a wine glass in his hand.

He nursed his wine as she spoke, his face closed and silent. When she had finished, his smile was faint and fast-fading. "Warmth and generosity," he said. "Arak has them both in abundance." After that he said nothing.

The silence was lengthy and awkward. "Is that all you're going to say?" Maris asked finally.

Val's expression changed just a little, the lines around his mouth tightening, eyes narrowing; he looked harder than ever. "What did you expect me to say, flyer? Did you think I'd embrace you, bed you, sing a song in praise of your understanding? What?"

Maris was startled by the anger in his tone. "I—I don't know what I expected," she said. "But I wanted to let you know that I understood what you'd been through, that I was on your side."

"I don't want you on my side," Val said. "I don't *need* you, or your sympathy. And if you think I appreciate your prying into my past, you are wrong. What went on between Arak and myself is our business, not yours, and neither of us needs your judgments." He finished his wine, snapped his fingers, and the barkeep came across the room and set a bottle on the table between them.

"You wanted revenge on Arak, and rightly so," Maris said stubbornly, "but you've changed that into a desire for revenge against *all* flyers. You should have challenged Arak, not Ari."

Val poured himself a refill and tasted it. "There are several problems with that romantic notion," he said more calmly. "For one, Arak did not have wings the year Airhome sponsored me. His son had come of age; Arak was retired. Two years ago, the son picked up some Southern fever and died, and Arak took up the wings again."

"I see," Maris said. "And you didn't challenge the son because he was a friend."

Val's laugh was cruel. "Hardly. The son was an ill-bred bully who grew more like his father every day. I didn't shed a tear when they dropped him into the sea. Oh, we played together once, when he was still too young to comprehend how superior he was, and we were whipped together often enough, but that made no bond between us." He leaned forward. "I didn't challenge the son because he was good, the same reason I would not have challenged Arak. I am not interested in revenge, no matter what you might think. I am interested in wings, and the things that go with them. Your Ari was the feeblest flyer I saw, and I knew I could take her wings. Against Arak or his son I might have lost. It is that simple."

He sipped at his wine again, while Maris watched, dismayed. Whatever she had hoped to accomplish by coming here was not happening. And she realized that it would not happen, *could* not happen. She had been foolish to think otherwise. Val One-Wing was who he was, and that would not change simply because Maris understood the cruel forces that had shaped him. He sat regarding her with the same cool disdain as ever, and she knew then that they could never be friends, never, no matter what might come to pass.

She tried again. "Don't judge all flyers by Arak." As she heard her own words, she wondered why she had not said *us*, why she spoke of the flyers as if she were not one of them. "Arak is not typical, Val."

"Arak and I understand each other well enough," Val said. "I know exactly what he is, thank you. I know that he is crueler than most, flyer or land-bound, and less intelligent, and more easily angered. That does not make my opinion of other flyers any less true. His attitudes are shared by most of your friends, whether you care to admit it or not. Arak is only a bit less reticent about voicing those views, and a little more crude in his speech."

Maris rose. "We have nothing more to say to each other. I'll expect you and S'Rella tomorrow morning for practice," she said as she turned away.

Sena and the other Woodwingers arrived several hours ahead of schedule the day before the competition was to open, putting in at the nearest port and trekking twelve miles overland along the sea road.

Maris was up flying and did not know they had arrived for several hours. When she found them, Sena immediately asked after the academy wings, and sent Sher and Leya running for them. "We must take advantage of every hour of good wind we have left," she said. "We were trapped on that ship too long."

Her students gone, Sena beckoned Maris to be seated and looked at her keenly. "Tell me what is wrong."

"What do you mean?"

Sena shook her head impatiently. "I noticed it at once," she said. "In years past the flyers may have been cool to us, but they were always polite and patronizing. This year the hostility hangs in the air like a bad smell. Is it Val?"

Briefly, Maris told the older woman what had happened.

Sena frowned. "Well, it is unfortunate, but we will survive it. Adversity will toughen them. They need that."

"Do they? This is not the kind of toughness you get from wind and weather and hard landings. This is something else. Do they need their hearts toughened as well as their bodies?"

Sena put a hand on her shoulder. "Perhaps they do. You sound bitter, Maris, and I understand your disappointment. I too was a flyer, and I would have liked to believe better of my old friends. We'll survive, flyers and Woodwingers both."

That night the flyers enjoyed a boisterous party at the lodge, so noisy that even in the village Maris and the others could hear it. But Sena would not let her charges attend. They need rest tonight, she said, after one final meeting in her cabin.

She began by discussing the rules. The competition was to last three days, but the serious business, the formal challenges, would be restricted to the mornings.

"Tomorrow you name your opponent and race," Sena said. "The judges will rate you according to speed and endurance. The day after they will look for grace. On the third day, precision: you will fly the gates to show your control."

The evenings and afternoons would be filled with less serious contests, games, personal challenges, singing contests, drinking bouts and so on. "Leave those to flyers not involved in the real challenges," Sena warned. "You have no business with such foolery. They can only tire you, and waste your strength. Watch if you will, but take no part."

When she had finished talking about the rules, Sena answered questions for a time, until she was asked one she could not answer. It came from Kerr, who had lost some weight during the three days at sea, and looked surprisingly fit. "Sena," he said, "how do we decide who is best to challenge?"

Sena looked at Maris. "We have had this problem before," she said. "The children of flyer families know everything they need to when they come of an age to challenge, but we hear no flyer gossip, know little about who is strong or who is weak. What things I know myself are ten years out of date. Will you advise them, Maris?"

Maris nodded. "Well, obviously, you want to find someone you can beat. I'd say challenge those from Eastern or Western. The flyers from farther away are usually the best from their regions. When the competition is in Southern, then the weaker Southern flyers are on hand, but only the most skilled from Western make the flight.

"Also, you'd do best to avoid the flyers from Big Shotan. They are organized almost in a military fashion, and they practice and drill endlessly."

"I challenged a woman from Big Shotan last year," Damen put in glumly. "She hadn't seemed very good beforehand, but she beat me easily enough when it mattered."

"She was probably being deliberately clumsy earlier, trying to lure a challenge from someone," Maris said. "I've known some who did that."

"That still leaves a lot of people to choose from," Kerr said, unsatisfied. "I don't know any of them. Can't you tell me the name of someone I can beat?"

Val laughed. He was standing by the door, S'Rella close to him. "You can't beat anyone," he said, "unless it's Sena here. Challenge her."

"I'll beat you, One-Wing," Kerr snapped back.

Sena hushed him and glared at Val. "Quiet. I'll have no more of that, Val." She looked back to Maris. "Kerr is right. Can you tell us specific flyers who are vulnerable?"

"You know, Maris," Val said. "Like Ari." He was smiling.

Once, not so very long ago, the suggestion would have filled Maris with horror. Once she would have thought it betrayal of the worst kind. Now she was not so sure. The poorer flyers endangered themselves and their wings, and it was no secret who they were for one privy to Eyrie gossip.

"I—I suppose I can suggest a few names," she said hesitantly. "Jon of Culhall, for one. His eyes are said to be weak, and I've never been impressed by his abilities. Bari of Poweet would be another. She has gained a good thirty pounds this past year, a sure sign of a flyer whose will and body are failing." She named about a half-dozen more, all frequent subjects of flyer talk, reputed to be clumsy or careless or both, the old and the very young. Then, impulsively, she added one other name. "An Easterner I met yesterday might be worth a challenge. Arak of South Arren."

Val shook his head. "Arak is small but hardly frail," he said calmly. "He would outfly anyone here, except perhaps for me."

"Oh?" Damen, as ever, was annoyed by the implied slur. "We'll see about that. I'll trust Maris' judgment."

They talked for a few minutes more, the Woodwingers eagerly discussing the names Maris had tossed out. Finally Sena chased them all away and told them to get some rest.

In front of the cabin she had shared with Maris, S'Rella bid goodnight to Val. "Go on," she told him. "I'll stay here tonight."

He looked a bit nonplussed. "Oh? Well, suit yourself."

When Val was out of sight, Maris said, "S'Rella? You're welcome, of course, but why . . . ?"

S'Rella turned to her with a serious expression on her face. "You left out Garth," she said.

Maris was taken aback. She had thought of Garth, of course. He was ill, drinking too much, gaining weight; it might be best for him to lose his wings. But she knew he would never agree to that, and he had been close to her for a long time, and she could not bring herself to name his name when speaking to the Woodwingers. "I couldn't," she said. "He's my friend."

"Aren't we your friends too?"

"Of course."

"But not as close friends as Garth. You care more about protecting him than about whether we win our wings."

"Maybe I was wrong to omit him," Maris admitted. "But I care for him too much, and it isn't easy—S'Rella, you haven't said anything about Garth to Val, have you?" She was suddenly worried.

"Never mind," S'Rella said. She brushed past Maris into the cabin and began to undress. Maris could only follow helplessly, already regretting her question.

"I want you to understand," Maris said to S'Rella as the Southern girl slipped under the blankets.

"I understand," S'Rella replied. "You're a flyer." She rolled over on her side, her back to Maris, and said no more.

The first day dawned bright and still.

From where she stood outside the flyers' lodge, it seemed to Maris that half the population of Skulny had come to watch the competition. People were everywhere: wandering up and down the shores, climbing over the rugged cliff face to get better vantage points, sitting on grass and sand and stone alone or in groups. The beach was littered with children of all ages, running up and down kicking sand up in their wake, playing in the surf, shouting excitedly, running with their arms stretched out stiffly, playing at being flyers. Merchants moved among the crowds: one man decorated with sausages, another bearing wineskins, a woman wheeling a cart burdened with meat pies. Even the sea was full of spectators. Maris could see more than a dozen boats, laden with passengers, lying dead in the water just beyond the breakers, and she knew there must be even more beyond her sight.

Only the sky was empty.

Normally the sky would have been crowded with impatient flyers, full of the glint of silver wings wheeling and turning as they took some last-minute practice or simply tested the wind. But not today.

Today the air was still.

The dead calm was frightening. It was unnatural, impossible: along the coast the brisk seabreeze should have been constant. Yet a suffocating heaviness hung over everything. Even the clouds rested wearily in the sky.

Flyers paced the beach with their wings slung over their shoulders, glancing up uneasily from time to time, waiting for the wind to return, and talking among themselves about the calm in low, careful voices.

The land-bound were waiting eagerly for the competition to start, most of them unaware that anything was amiss. It was, after all, a beautiful, clear day. And, atop the cliffs, the judges were setting up their station and taking their seats. The competition could not wait on the weather; contests in this sluggish air might not be as exciting, but they would still be tests of skill and endurance.

Maris saw Sena leading the Woodwingers across the sands toward the stairs leading up the cliffs. She hurried to join them.

A line had already formed in front of the judges' table, behind which sat the Landsman of Skulny and four flyers, one each from the Eastern, Southern, Western and the Outer Islands.

The Landsman's crier, a massive woman with a chest like a barrel, stood on the edge of the cliff. As each of the challengers named an opponent to the judges, she would cup her hands and shout out the name for all to hear, and her apprentices would take up the cry all along the beach, shouting it over and over until the flyer challenged acknowledged and moved off toward the flyers' cliff. Then the challenger would go to meet his or her opponent, and the line would shuffle forward. Most of the names called were vaguely familiar to Maris, and she knew they were in-family challenges, parents testing children, or—in one case—a younger sibling disputing the right of her older brother to wear the family wings. But just before the Woodwingers reached the judges' table, a black-haired girl from Big Shotan, daughter to a prominent flyer, named Bari of Poweet, and Maris heard Kerr swear softly. That was one good target gone.

Then it was their turn.

It seemed to Maris to be quieter than it had been before. The Landsman was animated enough, but the four flyer judges all looked grave and nervous. The Easterner was toying with the wooden telescope that had been set before her on the table, the muscular blond from the Outer Islands was frowning, and even Shalli looked concerned.

Sher went first, followed by Leya. Both named flyers that Maris had suggested to them. The crier bellowed out the names, and Maris heard the shouts being repeated up and down the beach.

Damen named Arak of South Arren, and the judge from Eastern smiled slyly at that. "Arak will be *so* pleased," she said.

Kerr named Jon of Culhall. Maris was not happy with that. Jon was a weak flyer, a likely opponent, and she had been hoping that he would be challenged by one of the academy's better prospects— Val, S'Rella, or Damen. Kerr was the poorest of their six, and Jon would probably escape with his wings.

Val One-Wing moved to the table.

"Your choice?" rumbled the Outer Islander. He was tense, as were the other judges, even the Landsman. Maris realized she was on edge as well, afraid of what Val might do.

"Must I choose only one?" Val said sardonically. "The last time I competed, I had a dozen rivals."

Shalli replied sharply. "The rules have been changed, as you very well know. Multiple challenges have been disallowed."

"A pity," Val said. "I had hoped to win a whole collection of wings."

"It will be unfortunate if you win any wings at all, One-Wing," the Easterner said. "Others are waiting. Name your opponent and move on."

Val shrugged. "Then I name Corm of Lesser Amberly."

Silence. Shalli looked shocked at first; then she smiled. The Easterner chuckled softly to herself, and the Outer Islander laughed openly.

"*Corm of Lesser Amberly!*" the crier thundered. "*Corm of Lesser Amberly!*" A dozen lesser voices echoed the call.

"I shall have to disqualify myself from this judging," Shalli said quietly.

"No, Shalli," said the judge from Eastern. "We have confidence in your fairness."

"I do not ask you to step aside," Val said.

She looked at him, puzzled. "Very well. You contribute to your own fall, One-Wing. Corm is no grief-stricken child."

Val smiled at her enigmatically and moved off, and Maris and Sena accosted him instantly. "Why did you do that?" Sena demanded. She was furious. "I have wasted my time with you, clearly. Corm! Maris, tell him how good Corm is, tell this willful fool how he has just thrown away his wings."

Val was looking at her. "I think he knows how good Corm is," Maris said, meeting his eyes. "And he knows Shalli is his wife. I think that was why he chose him."

Val had no chance to disagree. Behind them, the line had moved on, and now the crier was shouting out another name. Maris heard it and whirled, her stomach twisting. "No," she said, though the word caught in her throat and no one heard. But the crier, as if in answer, shouted the name once again. "*Garth of Skulny! Garth of Skulny!*"

S'Rella was walking away from the judges, her eyes downcast. When she looked up at last to see Maris, her face was reddened, but defiant.

Two by two they flew off into the morning sun, struggling against the heavy air—the calm had broken, but the winds were still sluggish and erratic—with wings grown suddenly awkward. The flyers wore their own wings, the challengers pairs lent them by judges or friends or bystanders. The course would take them to a rocky little island named Lisle, where they would have to land and collect a marker from the waiting Landsman before proceeding back. It was a flight of some three hours under normal conditions; in this weather, Maris suspected, it would take longer.

The Woodwingers and their opponents launched in the order in which they had challenged. Sher and Leya got away well enough. Damen had more trouble; Arak abused him verbally while they were circling, waiting for the shout to start, and flew dangerously

close to him as they veered out over the ocean. Even from a distance, Maris thought Damen looked shaken.

Kerr did even worse. He botched his leap badly, almost seeming
to stumble from the cliff, and a cry went up from below as he
plunged down sharply toward the beach. Finally he regained some
control and pulled himself up, but by the time he sailed out over
the sea his opponent had opened up a substantial lead.

Corm was cheerful and smiling as he prepared for his match
against Val, joking and flirting with the two land-bound girls who
helped him open his wings, calling out comments to the spectators,
waving to Shalli. He even threw a grim smile in Maris' direction.
But he did not speak to Val, except once, before he launched.
"This is for Ari," he shouted, his tone deadly, and then he was running and the wind took him. Val said nothing. He unfolded his
own wings in silence, leaped from the cliff in silence, swept up and
around near Corm in silence. The crier gave the shout, and the two
of them broke in opposite directions, both coming around cleanly,
the shadow of their wings passing across the upturned faces of the
children on the beach. When they moved out of sight, Corm was
ahead, but only by a wingspan.

Lastly came S'Rella and Garth. Maris stood with Sena near the
judges. She could look down on the flyers' cliff and see them both,
and watching them she felt heartsick. Garth was somber and pale,
and from a distance he appeared far too stout and clumsy to have
much of a chance against the slim young challenger. Both of them
prepared quietly, Garth speaking only once or twice to his sister,
S'Rella saying nothing at all. Neither got off to a good start, Garth
having a bit more difficulty with the thick air because of his weight.
S'Rella moved in front of him quickly, but he had closed the gap by
the time they reached the horizon and vanished.

"I know you wanted to help your Woodwingers, but couldn't you
have stopped short of the betrayal of a friend?"

Dorrel's voice, deceptively calm. Feeling heartsick, Maris turned
to face him. She had not spoken to him since that night on the
beach.

"I didn't want it to happen, Dorr," she said. "But it may be for
the best. We both know he's sick."

"Sick, yes," he snapped. "But I wanted to protect him—this will kill him if he loses."

"It may kill him if he wins."

"I think he'd prefer that. But if that girl takes his wings from him—he liked her, did you know that? He mentioned her to me, how nice she was, that night after Val wrecked the party in the lodge."

Maris, too, had been sick and angry over S'Rella's choice of opponent, but Dorrel's cold fury turned her feelings another way.

"S'Rella hasn't done anything wrong," she said. "Her challenge was perfectly proper. And Val didn't wreck the party, as you say. How *dare* you say that: It was the flyers who insulted him and then walked out."

"I don't understand you," Dorrel said quietly. "I haven't wanted to believe how much you've changed. But it's true, it's as they say. You've turned against us. You prefer the company of the Woodwingers and the one-winged to that of true flyers. I don't know you anymore."

The unhappiness on his face hurt her as much as the harshness of his words. Maris forced herself to speak. "No," she said. "You don't know me anymore."

Dorrel waited a moment, waited for her to say something more, but Maris knew that if she opened her mouth again it could only be for a scream or a sob. She could see anger warring with sadness on Dorrel's face, and anger finally won. He turned without another word and stalked away.

She felt, as she watched him walk away from her, that she was bleeding to death, and she knew it was a self-inflicted wound.

"My choice," she whispered, and the tears ran down her face as she stared blindly out to sea.

They had flown away two by two; they returned, hours later, one by one.

Crowds of the land-bound waited on the beaches, their eager eyes scanning the horizon. They had engaged in their own games and contests as well as in eating and drinking as they waited for the results of the flyers' contest.

The judges watched the skies through telescopes made for them by the finest lensmakers in Stormtown. On the table before them were a number of wooden boxes, one for each match, and piles of small pebbles: white pebbles for the flyers, black pebbles for the challengers. When a race was completed, each judge tossed a pebble into the wooden box. In a particularly close match, a judge might choose to vote for a tie by putting one stone of each color into the box. Or—but this was rarely done—if the winner was especially obvious, two white pebbles or two black could be cast.

The first flyer was sighted from the boats before anyone on shore saw him, and the shout went rippling over the water. On the beach, people began to stand and raise their hands to shield their eyes from the sun. Shalli lifted her telescope.

"See anything?" another judge asked.

"A flyer," Shalli said, laughing. "There"—she tried to point—"below the cloud. Can't tell who it is yet."

The others looked. Maris could barely see the speck they were straining at; it might have been a kite or a rainbird to her, but they had their telescopes.

The Eastern woman recognized the flyer first. "That's Lane," she said, surprised. The others looked impressed as well. Lane had started in the third pair, Maris recalled, which meant that not only had he outflown his own son, but four others who had started ahead of him as well.

By the time he had landed, two other flyers had come surging out of the clouds, one several wingspans ahead of the other. The first pair to depart, the judges announced. One of the Landsman's attendants passed two of the wooden boxes down the table, and Maris heard the small clicks as the stones were dropped.

When the boxes were set aside, she drifted closer. In the first box, she counted five black pebbles and one white; four judges ruling for the challenger, one for a tie. The other, the box representing the race in which Lane had flown, had five whites in it, but as she watched the judges dropped in three more—two more flyers had appeared, far apart, but neither one was Lane's son. When he finally did appear, some twenty minutes later, five others had preceded him, and Lane's box had ten white pebbles in it. A formidable margin; the boy had probably lost already, Maris knew.

As each incoming flyer was recognized, the judges announced the name to the crier, who shouted it out for all to hear. Ragged cheers went up for some of the announcements from the land-bound thronging the beaches, and now and again Maris heard a loud groan as well. She suspected that most of the cheering was for financial reasons rather than personal. Most of the land-bound did not know flyers from other islands well enough to like or dislike them, but it was traditional to gamble on the outcome of the races, and she knew that a lot of money was changing hands below. It would be difficult, however, for S'Rella. This was Skulny, Garth's home island, and he was familiar and popular with many of the spectators.

"*Arak of South Arren!*" the crier yelled.

Sena swore softly. Maris borrowed a scope from Shalli. It was Arak, sure enough, flying alone, ahead of not only Damen but of Sher and Leya and their opponents as well.

One by one the Woodwingers and their rivals struggled in.

Arak came first, then the man Sher had challenged, then Damen, followed by Leya's rival. Minutes later, three flyers appeared bunched close together; Sher and Leya, inseparable as always, and close to them—moving ahead now—Jon of Culhall. Sena was swearing again, her face screwed up in disappointment. Maris tried to think of something reassuring to say, but nothing came to mind. The judges were dropping pebbles into the boxes. On the beach, Damen was down and getting out of his wings, while the others approached for a landing.

The sky was clear for a moment, with nothing to see. Kerr was losing badly too; Jon of Culhall had landed now, and Kerr was nowhere in sight. Maris took advantage of the free moment to see how the judges had scored her students.

She was not cheered. Sher's box had seven whites in it, Leya's had five, Damen's eight. Kerr had six against him at the moment, but the judges were dropping in more as minutes went by and he did not appear. "Come on," Maris mumbled under her breath.

"I see someone," the Southern judge said. "Very high, angling down now."

The others lifted their scopes. "Yes," one of them said. Now people on the beach had spotted the incoming flyer as well, and Maris could hear the buzz of speculation.

"Is it Kerr?" Sena said anxiously.

"I'm not sure," the Easterner answered. "Wait."

But it was Shalli who lowered her telescope first, looking stunned. "It's One-Wing," she said, in a small voice.

"Give me that," Sena said, snatching the telescope from her hands. "It *is* him." She passed the instrument over to Maris, beaming.

It was Val, all right. The wind had picked up quite a bit, and he was using it well, slipping from current to current, riding with a veteran's grace.

"Announce him," Shalli said numbly to the crier.

"Val One-Wing, Val of South Arren!"

The crowd was hushed for a moment, then erupted into noise; wild cheering, groans, cursing. No one was indifferent to Val One-Wing.

Another pair of silvered wings sliced into view from above. Corm, Maris guessed, and a glance through Shalli's telescope confirmed it. But he was behind, too far behind, with no chance of catching up. It was by no means a humiliation for him, but it was clearly a defeat.

"Maris," Shalli said, "I want you to see this, so everyone will know that my judging is fair." She opened her hand, and a single black pebble rested in the hollow of her palm, and as Maris watched she dropped it into the box. Four others followed it.

"Another one," someone said. "No, two."

Val had landed, and was calmly taking off his wings. As always he had refused the help of the land-bound children who crowded around him. Corm came sliding over the beach and cliffs, then swept around in an angry predatory circle, reluctant to come down and face the fact of his defeat. Corm did not take defeat well, Maris knew.

All eyes moved to the two new flyers. "Garth of Skulny," the Outer Islander said, "and his challenger. She's close behind him."

"Yes, it's Garth," the Landsman put in. He had not been happy when S'Rella challenged one of his flyers; the prospect of losing a pair of wings was something no Landsman relished. "Fly, Garth," he said now, openly partisan. "Hurry."

Sena grimaced at him. "She's doing well," she said to Maris.

"Not well enough," Maris said. She could see them clearly now. S'Rella was one, two wingspans behind. But with the beach in sight, she seemed to be faltering. Garth began his descent, cutting sharply in front of her, and the turbulence created by his passing seemed to shake her. Her wings seesawed for a moment before she regained stability, giving him a chance to open his lead a bit wider.

He passed over the beach about three wingspans ahead of her. The pebbles began to clatter into the box. Maris turned to see. It had been a close race, credible, spirited. Perhaps some of the judges would score it a tie.

One did, but only one. Maris counted. Five white pebbles for Garth, one lonely black for S'Rella.

"Let's go down to her," Maris said to Sena.

"Kerr hasn't come in yet," the teacher replied.

Maris had almost forgotten about Kerr. "Oh, I hope he's safe."

"I should never have sponsored him," Sena grumbled. "Damn his parents' iron."

They waited five minutes, ten, fifteen. Sher, Leya, and a very dispirited Damen all wandered up to join them. Other wings appeared on the horizon, but none of them was Kerr. Maris began to grow seriously afraid for him.

But finally he was there, the last of all those who had left that morning, and coming from the wrong direction too; he had been blown off course, he explained, and overshot Skulny. He was very sheepish about it.

By then, of course, ten white pebbles had been cast against him.

The crowds of land-bound were breaking up below, going off in search of food or drink or shade. Flyers were preparing for the afternoon games. Sena shook her head. "Come," she said, throwing an arm around Kerr. "Let's find the others and get some food into them."

●　　●　　●

The afternoon passed quickly. Some of the Woodwingers went off to watch the flying games—an Outer Islander and two Shotaners won the individual prizes, and Western came away with the medals in the team races—while the others rested, talked or played. Damen had brought a geechi set, and he and Sher spent hours bent over it, both of them trying to recoup some of their lost pride.

In the evening the parties started. The Woodwingers had a small party of their own outside Sena's cabin, in a halfhearted effort to lighten dampened spirits. Leya played the pipes and Kerr told sea stories, and all of them drank from the wineskin Maris had brought. Val was in his usual mood, cool and distant and invulnerable, but everyone else remained glum.

"No one has died," Sena said at last, her manner gruff. "When you lose an eye and shatter a leg as I did, then you will have a right to be morose. You don't have that right now. Get out of here, the lot of you, before you make me irritable." She waved her cane at them. "Off now, and to bed. We still have two more days of competition, and all of you can win your wings if you fly well enough. Tomorrow I expect more of you."

Maris and S'Rella walked along the beach for a while, talking and listening to the slow restless sound of the sea, before heading back to the cabin they shared. "Are you angry with me?" S'Rella asked quietly. "For naming Garth?"

"I was," Maris said wearily. She did not have the heart to speak of her break with Dorrel. "Maybe I had no right to be. If you beat him, you have a right to his wings. I'm not angry now."

"I'm glad," S'Rella said. "I was angry with you, but I'm not now. I'm sorry."

Maris put an arm around her shoulders. They walked in silence for a minute, and then S'Rella said, "I've lost, haven't I?"

"No," Maris said. "You can still win. You heard what Sena said."

"Yes," said S'Rella, "but tomorrow they'll be judging grace, and that's always been my weakest point. Even if I win at the gates, I'll be so far behind that I won't be able to catch up."

"Hush," Maris said. "Don't talk like that. Just fly as best you can, and leave the rest to the judges. It's all you can do. If you do lose, there's always next year."

S'Rella nodded. They had reached the cabin. She darted ahead to get the door, and then drew back. "Oh," she said. Her voice was suddenly frightened. "*Maris*," she whimpered.

Alarmed, Maris hurried to her side. S'Rella stood trembling and looking at their cabin door. Maris looked too, and felt sick.

Someone had nailed two dead rainbirds to the door. They hung limp and disheveled, bright feathers dark and stained, the nails driven through their small bodies, blood dripping slowly and steadily to the ground.

Maris went inside for a knife and came back to take the grisly warnings from the door. But when she pried loose the first nail and the dead rainbird thumped to the ground, Maris discovered to her horror that it had not only been slaughtered, but mutilated as well.

One wing had been ripped from its body.

The second day was chilly and overcast. It was raining at dawn, and although the rain stopped by the time the morning contests got under way, the day remained damp and cold, the sky heavily overcast. The land-bound spectators were fewer—sitting on the beach was not so pleasant now—and the choppy seas carried only a few boats of observers.

But all that mattered to the flyers was the wind, and the wind on the second day was strong and steady, promising the possibility of some excellent flying.

Maris pulled Sena apart from the Woodwingers on the beach below the cliff, and spoke to her quietly.

"Who would do a thing like that?" Sena demanded, her voice shocked.

Maris put her finger to her lips. She didn't want the others to overhear. S'Rella had been badly frightened by the incident, and there was no sense in alarming the others.

"A flyer, I would guess," Maris said grimly. "A sick, bitter flyer. But we have no proof of anything. It could have been done by a flyer who was challenged, or the friend of someone we challenged, or simply some stranger who hates Woodwingers. It might even be some local land-bound who lost money on a bet over Val One-Wing. My own suspicions fall on Arak, but I can't prove that."

Sena nodded. "You were right to keep it quiet. I only hope S'Rella wasn't too disturbed by it."

Maris glanced at where S'Rella stood among the other students, talking softly to Val. "She needs to do well today, or it is all over for her."

"They're starting," Damen called, pointing up at the cliffs.

The first pair of contestants had taken to the air and were moving quickly over the beach. They would circle over the water, Maris knew, and each would go into a sequence of stunts and maneuvers designed to demonstrate flying skills. The specific stunts were the choice of each individual flyer; some satisfied themselves with performing basics as flawlessly as possible, while others tried to be daring and ambitious. Seldom were there clear-cut winners or losers; it was in this event that the judges wielded the most power.

The first two pairs were nothing special, merely long sequences of launchings, landings, and graceful, sweeping turns, all done skillfully but not spectacularly. The third match was something else. The flyer Lane, who had raced so well yesterday, was a splendid stunter as well. Leaping from the cliff, he plunged down low over the beach, skimming so close to the sand that land-bound had to duck to be out of his way. Then he found a riser and swooped up, up, soaring through the overcast and out of sight before he came diving down again, with reckless speed, only to pull out at the last possible instant. He attempted vertical banks and a full loop, and only went into a stall once—he broke out quickly—and Maris found herself admiring his verve. His son was no match for him; the poor boy would be waiting a long time for wings, unless he challenged out-of-family next year. After they had finished, Maris counted eighteen white stones in the voting box, eight new ones added to the ten Lane had won yesterday.

Sher was the first Woodwinger to try the air. It was a good effort; a clean launch, almost perfect but for a slight wobble, followed by a standard sequence of turns, circles, dives, and climbs, all performed smoothly. Sher seemed lithe and buoyant in the air, compared to the stolid competency of the opposition. Maris would have given the judgment to Sher by a slight margin, but when she looked she found the judges had been more critical of the Woodwinger than she. Two had given the victory to the flyer, two had called it even, and only one had cast for Sher, who was now down eleven stones to three.

Sena sighed when Maris told her the count. "I've grown used to it. I always hate the stunting. Perhaps the judges try to be fair, but the bias creeps in nonetheless. Nothing can be done about it, except to have our Woodwingers fly so well that they can't be denied their victories."

Leya was next, with the same sequence Sher had flown, all basic, but with less luck. The wind shifted during the match, robbing Leya of the fluid grace that Maris had so often seen her display, giving her flight a ragged appearance. And several times gusts threw her sideways, breaking up what had been well-executed turns. Her rival had trouble as well, but less. Four judges gave him their stones, and only one made it a tie, leaving Leya behind ten to one.

Damen was more ambitious than either of them. Today, when Arak threw insults at him, Damen spat them right back, which brought a smile to Maris' lips. And he began with a passable imitation of the spectacular swoop-on-the-beach that the flyer Lane had used. Arak tried to shadow him, to fly so close that Damen would be forced to break off his glide clumsily, but Damen twisted away with a graceful bank and vanished into a cloud, losing the older flyer. One of the judges, the Outer Islander, grumbled about Arak's tactics, but the others only shrugged. "Whatever else he might be, he is still the better flyer," the Easterner insisted. "Note how tight his turns are. The boy is spirited, but slipshod." Maris had to admit that she was right; Damen habitually slid wide on turns, especially downwind turns.

When they scored it, four judges cast for Arak, only the Outer Islander for Damen.

"*Jon of Culhall, Kerr the Woodwinger!*" the crier bellowed. The wind was gusting, and Kerr was as clumsy as ever.

After a few minutes, Sena faced Maris. "Even with one eye, this is painful to watch," she said.

Jon of Culhall accumulated another eight white pebbles, and Maris felt sorry for Kerr.

"*Corm of Lesser Amberly*," announced the crier, "*Val One-Wing, Val of South Arren!*"

They stepped into view on the flyers' cliff, wings strapped in place but folded, and Maris could feel a ripple of excitement go through the onlookers. People along the beach were making noise, and even the landsguard and attendants who stood near the Landsman moved closer to watch.

Corm was not laughing or joking today. He stood as silently as Val, his dark hair tossing in the wind, while his wings were unfolded and locked by others. Val, as usual, waved away the help.

"Corm can be quite graceful," Maris warned Sena. "Val may have trouble today."

"Yes," Sena agreed, glancing at Shalli's seat among the judges.

The crowd was growing impatient; the two flyers still had not launched. Corm's helpers had stepped back from him, and he stood with his silver wings fully extended, but Val had made no move to unfold his own. Instead he kept examining the joints of one wing, as if looking for something wrong. Corm said something to him, sharply, and Val looked up from what he was doing and made a broad gesture.

"All right," Corm said clearly, and then he was running and an instant later he was aloft.

"There's Corm," Shalli said. "Where's One-Wing?"

"Doesn't he know that this will cost him?" Sena muttered.

Maris gripped Sena tightly by the elbow. "He's going to do it again," she said urgently.

"Do *what?*" Sena said, but even as she spoke a light broke over her face and Maris knew she understood.

Val jumped.

It was a long way down, and only sand and spectators below; trickier and more dangerous than the same stunt over water. But he was doing it, falling, his wings flapping behind him like a silver cape. Shalli and the Southern judge jumped to their feet, two of the landsguard rushed to the cliffside, even the crier gave a grunt of surprise. Maris heard people screaming, somewhere below.

Val's wings took flower.

For an instant it did not seem to be enough. He still fell, speed increasing, even with the wings fully extended. But then he yanked himself to one side and that did it; suddenly he was veering up sharply, angling over the beach and out toward sea. People were dropping to the sand, and someone was still screaming, but there was shouting as well.

Then silence, a hush, a long indrawn breath. Val skimmed the waves, gliding as if over ice, and smoothly began to rise. Serenely he flew out to where Corm, almost unnoticed, had just performed a difficult loop.

The applause began, and the cheering, and all along the shore land-bound began clapping and chanting the refrain, "One-Wing, One-Wing, One-Wing," over and over. Even Lane's spectacular plunge had not thrilled them as Val had.

The judge from Eastern was laughing. "I never thought I'd see that again," she exclaimed. "Damn, *damn*. Even Raven never did it better."

Shalli looked miserable. "A cheap trick," she said. "And dangerous as well."

"Probably," the Outer Islander agreed, "but I've never seen anything like it. How did he do it, anyway?"

The Easterner tried to explain, and the two of them fell to talking. In the distance, Val and Corm were going through their stunts. Val flew well, though Maris noted that his upwind turns were still not all they should be. Corm flew better, matching Val stunt-for-stunt and doing each of them just a little more gracefully, with the skill that comes with decades of flying. But he flew hopelessly, Maris thought; after Raven's Fall, no amount of finesse was going to redress the balance.

She was right. Shalli was the only exception. "Corm was much superior overall," she insisted. "One foolhardy stunt does not change that." She dropped a white stone into the box with an emphatic flick of her wrist.

But the other judges just smiled at her indulgently, and the four pebbles that followed hers were black.

"Garth of Skulny, S'Rella the Woodwinger!"

S'Rella and Garth, though totally different in appearance, looked almost alike this morning, Maris thought as she watched them prepare. Garth should have been elated by his victory yesterday, and the likelihood that his wings were safe, but if anything he seemed paler and more aged today. He hardly spoke to Riesa, and went about the motions of donning his wings with a wooden deliberateness. S'Rella bit her lip as she let the helpers unfold her wings, and looked as if she were holding back tears.

Neither of them attempted anything spectacular on launching. Garth banked right, S'Rella left, and they passed above the beach and the boats with approximately equal ease. A few of the locals waved to Garth and shouted his name as he sailed by overhead, but otherwise the crowd was silent, still breathless over Val's leap.

Sena shook her head. "S'Rella was never as pretty to watch as Sher or Leya, but she can fly better than that." She had just stalled and lost altitude on a rather routine upwind turn, and Maris had to agree with the teacher's assessment. S'Rella was not flying well.

"She's just going through the motions," Maris said. "I think she's still shaken by last night."

Garth was taking full advantage of his opponent's lassitude. He soared with his usual quiet competence, performed graceful, languorous turns, and slid into a loop. It was not an especially good loop, but S'Rella was attempting none at all.

"This one will be easy to judge," the Landsman of Skulny said with relief. He was already looking about for a white pebble. Maris could only hope that he would not drop two.

"Look at that," Sena snorted with disgust. "My best student, and she's wandering all over the sky like some eight-year-old on her first flight."

"What's Garth doing?" Maris wondered aloud. His wings were moving out to sea, tilting first one way and then the other, almost shaking. "That's an awful wobble."

"If the judges notice," Sena said sourly. "Look, he's righted it now."

He had; now the great silver wings had straightened, and Garth was sailing steadily away from them, riding on the wind, sinking slightly.

"He's just flying," Maris said, puzzled. "He isn't doing any stunts."

Garth continued to move off, toward the deep waters beyond the breakers. He flew gracefully, but so *straight*; it was no great task to be graceful when yielding to the wind. Gradually he was descending. Now he was about thirty feet above the water, and still he sank. His flight seemed so calm, so peaceful.

Maris gasped. "He's falling," she said. She turned to the judges. "Help him," she shouted. "He's *falling!*"

"What's she yelling about?" the Easterner asked.

Shalli put her telescope to her eye, found Garth in it. He was skimming the waves now. "She's right," she said, in a small voice.

Instantly there was chaos. The Landsman jumped to his feet and began to wave his arms and shout orders, and two of the landsguard went sprinting off down the stairs, and the others all started running somewhere. The crier cupped her huge hands and shouted, "*Help him! Help the flyer! People in the boats, help the flyer!*" Down on the beach other criers repeated the chant, and spectators ran for the shore, shouting and pointing.

Garth hit the water. His forward motion sent him skipping over the surface, once, twice, and sheets of spray fanned out from his wings, but he lost speed rapidly, slowed, stopped.

"It's all right, Maris," Sena was saying, "it's all right. Look, they'll get him." A small sailboat, alerted by the shouts of the criers, was moving in on him rapidly. Maris watched it apprehensively. It took them a minute to reach him, another minute to fish him out in a net they tossed over the side. But from this distance, she had no way of telling whether he was dead or alive.

The Landsman lowered his telescope. "They got him, and the wings too."

S'Rella was flying low above the sailboat that had rescued Garth. Too late she had realized what was happening, and started after him, but it was unlikely she would have been able to help in any event.

The Landsman, grim, ordered another of his landsguard down to find out Garth's condition, and walked back to his seat. The judges talked nervously among themselves and Maris and Sena shared an anxious silence until the man returned, ten minutes later. "He is alive and recovering, though he swallowed some water," the lands-guard announced. "They are taking him back to his house."

"What happened?" the Landsman demanded.

"His sister says he has been ill for some time," the man replied. "It seems he had an attack."

The Landsman swore. "He never told me any such thing." He glared at the four flyer judges. "Must we score this?"

"I'm afraid we must," Shalli said gently. She picked up a black pebble.

"Her?" the Landsman said. "Garth outflew her easily, until he was taken sick. You mean to give the *girl* the victory?"

"You can't be serious, sir," the big man from the Outer Islands said. "Your Garth fell into the ocean. He might have stunted as well as Lane and he'd still lose."

"I must agree," the Easterner said. "Landsman, you are not a flyer, you do not understand. Garth is fortunate to be alive. If he had fallen while flying a mission, with no ship to save him, he would have been food for a scylla."

"He was sick," the Landsman insisted, frantic not to lose the wings for Skulny.

"It does not matter," the quiet Southern judge put in, and she cast the first pebble into the voting box with a flick of her thumb. It was black. Three other black stones followed in quick succession, Shalli placing hers with obvious dismay, until the Landsman defi-antly added a white.

Garth's fall intensified the bitterness of flyers and Woodwingers both. The afternoon games, stunts conducted in an increasingly dark and stormy cloud, had little zest to them. An Easterner from Kite's Landing was the grand winner, but she had scant competi-tion, as many of the flyers decided to drop out at the last moment. A few of those not directly involved in challenges were even seen taking wing for their home islands. Kerr, the only Woodwinger who bothered to attend the games, reported that the spectators had grown sparse as well, and all their talk was of Garth.

Sena tried to encourage the students, but it was a formidable
task. Sher and Leya were philosophical about their chances, neither expecting to win, but Damen was in a dismal condition and
Kerr seemed ready to slink off and throw himself into the sea.
S'Rella was nearly as despondent. She was tired and withdrawn for
most of the afternoon, and that evening she quarreled with Val.

It was just after dinner. Damen was setting up his geechi board
and looking for an opponent, and Leya had gotten out her pipes
again. Val found S'Rella sitting with Maris on the beach, and
joined them uninvited. "Let's walk down to the tavern," he suggested to S'Rella, "and celebrate our victories. I want to get free of
these losers and hear what people are saying about us, maybe even
get down some bets for tomorrow."

"I've got no victory to celebrate," S'Rella replied sullenly. "I flew
horribly. Garth was much better than I was. I didn't deserve
to win."

"You win or you lose, S'Rella," Val said. "What you deserve has
nothing to do with it. Come on." He tried to take her by the hand
and pull her to her feet, but S'Rella yanked loose of him angrily.

"Don't you even *care* about what happened to Garth?"

"Not particularly. You shouldn't either. As I recall, the last thing
you said to him was how much you hated him. It would have gone
better for you if he'd drowned. Then they would have to give you
his wings. As it is, they'll try to find some way to cheat you out of
them."

Maris, listening, began to lose her temper. "Stop it, Val," she
said.

"Keep out of this, flyer," he snapped. "This is between us."

S'Rella jumped to her feet. "Why are you always so hateful?
You're cruel to Maris all the time, and she's only tried to help you.
And the things you've been saying about Garth—Garth was *nice* to
me, and what did I do, I challenged him, and now he almost died
and you're saying awful things about him. Don't you say another
word! *Don't you!*"

Val's face became an expressionless mask. "I see," he said flatly.
"Suit yourself. If you care so much for flyers, go visit Garth and tell

him to keep his wings. I'll celebrate by myself." He turned away and began to stride across the sand, toward the sea road that would take him to his tavern.

Maris took S'Rella's hand. "Would you like to visit Garth?" she said impulsively.

"Could we?"

Maris nodded. "He and Riesa share a big house a half mile up the hill road. He likes to stay close to the sea and the lodge. We could go see how he is."

S'Rella was eager, and they set off at once. Maris had been a bit afraid of the reception they might receive when they arrived, but her own concern about Garth's condition was great enough that she was willing to take the risk. She needn't have worried. Riesa beamed at them when she opened the door, and all at once began to cry, and Maris had to take her in her arms and comfort her. "Oh, come see him, come see him," Riesa kept saying through her tears. "He'll be so glad."

Garth was propped up in bed against a mountain of pillows, a shaggy woolen blanket thrown over his legs. His face was frighteningly pale and puffy, but when he saw them in the doorway his smile was real enough. "Ah," he boomed, his voice loud as ever, "Maris! And the little demon who's out to take my wings." He waved them to his side. "Come and sit and talk to me. Riesa does nothing but fuss and fret, and she won't even bring me any of her ale."

Maris smiled. "You don't need any ale," she said primly as she walked to his bedside and kissed him lightly on the brow.

S'Rella hung back by the door, however. When he saw that, Garth's face turned serious. "Ah, S'Rella," he said, "don't be frightened. I'm not angry with you."

She came forward to stand by Maris. "You're not?"

"No," Garth said firmly. "Riesa, bring them seats." His sister did as he asked, and when they were seated, Garth resumed. "Oh, I was furious when you challenged me—hurt, too—I can't deny that."

"I'm sorry," S'Rella blurted. "I didn't want to hurt you. I don't hate you—what I said that night at the lodge."

He waved her quiet. "I know that. And you needn't be sorry.

The water was terribly cold out there, but maybe it woke me up a bit, and I've had all afternoon to lie here and think. I've been a fool, and I'm lucky I have the breath to say so. I did wrong to keep it secret, the way that I was feeling, and you did right to name me when you knew." He shook his head. "I couldn't accept being land-bound, you know. I love the flying too much, all my friends, the travel. But it's over, my little swim proved that, the only question is whether I'm to be a live land-bound or a drowned flyer at the end of it all. Before today, I'd always managed to shrug off the pain, get where I was going. But this morning—ah, it was miserable, shoot-ing pains in my arms and legs. But I don't want to talk about that. Bad enough it happened." He reached across and took S'Rella by the hand. "What I mean to say, S'Rella, is that I can't compete to-morrow, and I wouldn't if I could. Riesa and the sea have brought me to my senses. The wings are yours."

S'Rella could hardly believe him. She stared at him wide-eyed, and a tremulous smile broke across her face.

"What will you do, Garth?" Maris asked.

He grimaced. "That depends on the healers," he said. "Seems to me I have three choices. Maybe I'll be a corpse, and maybe I'll be a cripple, but if I can find a healer who knows what he's about, I thought I might try my hand at trade. I've got enough iron put aside to buy myself a ship, and I could travel that way, see other is-lands—though I'm half scared out of my wits at the idea of travel-ing by sea." He chuckled. "You and Dorr used to kid me about being a trader. You remember, Maris? Said I'd trade my wings if the deal was good enough, just because I liked to swap a little now and again. Well, some trader I turned out to be. Here S'Rella gets my wings and doesn't give me anything." He laughed, and Maris found herself joining him.

They talked for over an hour, about traders and sailors and fi-nally flyers, relaxing as they laughed at Garth's jokes and ex-changed gossip. "Corm is livid about your friend Val," Garth said at one point, "and I can't say I blame him. He's a good enough flyer that he never considered that he might lose his wings, and here it seems he's lost them, and to One-Wing of all people. Did you have anything to do with that, Maris?"

She shook her head. "Hardly. All Val's idea. He'll never admit it, but I think he wanted to beat a flyer of the top rank to make them forget about Ari. The fact that Corm's wife sits among the judges just added an extra flair to the feat, and of course it gave him a convenient excuse if he lost. He could blame a defeat on flyer prejudice."

Garth nodded and made a rude joke about Corm, then turned to his sister. "Riesa, why don't you show S'Rella our house?"

Riesa took the hint. "Yes, do come see," she said. S'Rella followed her from the room.

"She's nice," Garth said when they were gone, "and she does remind me an awful lot of you, Maris. Do you remember when we first met?"

Maris smiled at him. "I remember. It was my first flight to the Eyrie and there was a party that night."

"Raven was there too. That was where he did his trick."

"I've never forgotten it," Maris said.

"Did you teach it to One-Wing?"

"No."

Garth laughed. "Everyone is certain you did. We all remember how impressed you were by Raven. Coll even made a song about him, didn't he?"

Maris smiled. "Yes."

Garth started to say something else, then thought better of it. For a long moment the room was filled with silence, and the smile slowly faded on Garth's face.

He began to cry, fighting it and losing; he reached out his big hands for her, and Maris came and sat on the edge of the bed and hugged him, and ran her hands across his brow. "I knew—I didn't want S'Rella to see me—ah, Maris, it's so damned rotten, so *damned*—"

"Oh, Garth," she whispered, kissing him lightly and fighting to hold back her own tears. She felt so helpless. Briefly she thought of what it would be like if she were in Garth's place. She trembled and pushed the thought away and hugged him again all the harder.

"Come and see me," he said. "I—you know how—when you

don't fly, you can't go to the Eyrie—you know—bad enough to lose your freedom, and the wind—but I don't want to lose you too, and my other friends, just because—oh, damn, *damn these tears*—visit me, Maris, promise, promise."

"I promise, Garth," she said, trying to keep her voice light. "Unless you gain so much weight that I can't stand to look at you."

Beneath his tears, he laughed. "Ah," he said. "Here—and just when I thought I could get fat in peace. You—"

Footsteps sounded outside, Riesa and S'Rella returning, and Garth quickly used the blanket to dry his tears. "Go," he said, smiling again, "go, I'm tired, you've exhausted me. But come back tomorrow when it's all over and tell me how the games went."

Maris nodded. And S'Rella came up to her side and bent to give Garth a quick, shy kiss before they left.

They walked the half-mile back to the village slowly, talking as they went and savoring the cool wind that moved through the night. They spoke of Garth, and a little bit of Val, and S'Rella mentioned the wings—*her* wings—with wonder in her voice. "I'm a flyer," she said happily. "It's really true."

But it was not that simple.

Sena was waiting for them inside their cabin, sitting on the edge of a bed and looking impatient. She rose when they entered. "Where have you been?"

"We went to see how Garth is," Maris answered. "Is anything wrong?"

"I don't know. We have been summoned up to the lodge house by the judges." She gave S'Rella a meaningful look with her good eye. "All three of us, and we're late."

They left at once. On the way, Maris told Sena what Garth had said about giving up the wings, but the old teacher did not seem pleased. "Well, we shall see about that," she said. "I would not go flying off with them just yet."

The flyers were not partying tonight. The main room of the lodge was sparsely populated, only a half-dozen Western flyers

Maris knew vaguely sitting and drinking, and the atmosphere was anything but festive. One of them stood up when Maris and the others entered. "In the back room," he said.

The five judges were squabbling around a circular table, but they broke off in mid-argument when the door opened. Shalli stood up. "Maris, Sena, S'Rella, do come in," she said. "And close the door."

They took seats around the table, and Shalli folded her hands neatly in front of her as she resumed. "We summoned you because we have a dispute, and it involves young S'Rella here, and you have a right to state your views. Garth has sent word that he will not fly tomorrow—"

"We know," Maris broke in. "We just came from him."

"Good," Shalli said. "Then perhaps you understand our problem. We must decide what to do with the wings."

S'Rella looked stricken. "They're mine," she said. "Garth said so."

The Landsman of Skulny was drumming his fingers on the table and frowning. "The wings are not Garth's to give," he said loudly. "Here, child, I will ask you a question. If you are given the wings, will you promise to make a home here, and fly for Skulny?"

S'Rella did not flinch under his intense gaze, Maris noted with approval. "No," she answered bluntly. "I couldn't. I mean, Skulny is nice, I'm sure, but—but this isn't my home. I'm going to return to Southern with the wings, to Veleth, the little island where I was born."

The Landsman shook his head violently. "No, no, *no*. You may return to this Southern rock if you wish, but if you do it will be without the wings." He looked at the other judges. "See. I gave her a chance. I insist."

Sena thumped a fist on the table. "What is this? What is going on? S'Rella has a right to the wings, more right than anyone else. She challenged Garth and he has failed the test. How can you speak of not giving her the wings?" She looked from judge to judge furiously.

Shalli, who seemed to be the spokesman, gave an apologetic shrug. "We have a disagreement," she said. "The question is how tomorrow's contest should be scored. Some of us feel that if Garth does not fly, S'Rella must be given the victory by forfeit. But the Landsman is of the opinion that we cannot vote on a contest in which only one flyer flies. He insists that the decision be made on the basis of the two legs already completed, and on them alone. If that is done, Garth is presently ahead six stones to five, and would retain the wings."

"But Garth has renounced the wings!" Maris said. "He can't fly, he is too ill."

"The law provides for that," the Landsman said. "If a flyer is sick, his wings are given over to the Landsman and the island's other flyers to dispose of, provided he or she has no heir. We will give the wings to someone worthy of them, someone who is willing to take up residence in Skulny. I offered that chance to the girl here and you all heard her answer. It must be someone else, then."

"We had hoped that S'Rella would consent to remain on Skulny," Shalli said. "That would have resolved our differences."

"No," S'Rella repeated stubbornly, but she looked miserable.

"What you propose is a cheat," Sena said bitterly to the Landsman.

"I am inclined to agree with that," put in the big man from the Outer Islands. He ran his fingers through unkempt blond hair. "The only reason Garth stands ahead now is because you cast a stone for him today, even after he fell into the ocean, Landsman. That was hardly fair."

"I judged it fair," the Landsman said angrily.

"Garth wants S'Rella to take his wings," Maris said. "Don't his wishes matter in this?"

"No," the Landsman said. "The wings were never his alone. They are a trust, they belong to all the people of Skulny." He looked around at his fellow judges, imploring. "It is not fair to give them away to this Southerner, to reduce Skulny to only two flyers without cause. Listen to me. If Garth had been well, he would have defended his wings ably against any challenge, and it never would have come to this. If he had been sick and had come to me and told me, as your own flyer law requires, then by now we would have found someone else to wear the wings, someone capable of retaining them for Skulny. It is only because Garth chose to conceal his condition that we are in this predicament. Will you punish all the folk of my island because a flyer kept a secret?"

Maris had to admit that there was some justice in the argument. The judges seemed swayed too. "What you say is true," said the small woman from Southern. "I would be glad to see a new set of wings come south, but your claim is hard to deny."

"S'Rella has rights too," Sena insisted. "You must be fair to her."

"If you give the wings to the Landsman," Maris added, "you will be taking away her right to challenge. She is only down one stone. She has an excellent chance."

Then S'Rella spoke up. "I didn't earn the wings," she said uncertainly. "I was ashamed of the way I flew today. But I could win them fairly, if I had another chance. I know I could. Garth wants me to."

Shalli sighed. "S'Rella, my dear, it isn't that simple. We can't start the whole competition over for your sake."

"She should get the wings," the Outer Islander grumbled. "Here, I cast tomorrow's pebble for her already. That makes it six to six. Will anyone join me?" He looked around.

"There are no pebbles here to cast," the Landsman snapped, "and you cannot have a contest with only one flyer." He crossed his arms and sat back, scowling.

"I fear I must vote with the Landsman," the Southerner said, "lest I be charged with unfairly favoring a neighbor."

That left Shalli and the woman from Eastern, both of whom looked hesitant. "Isn't there some way we can be fair to all?" Shalli said.

Maris looked at S'Rella and touched her on her arm. "Are you truly willing to fly again in contest, to try to earn the wings?"

"Yes," S'Rella said. "I want to win them right. I want to deserve them, no matter what Val says."

Maris nodded and turned back to the judges. "Then I have a proposition for you," she said. "Landsman, you have two other flyers on Skulny. Do you think them able enough?"

"Yes," he asked suspiciously. "What of it?"

"Only this—I propose that you resume the match. Keep the

score as it stands, with S'Rella down one stone. But since Garth cannot fly, name a proxy for him, another of your flyers to bear wings in his place. If your proxy wins, then Skulny retains the wings and you can award them to whomever you choose. If S'Rella wins, well, then no one can dispute her right to go south as a flyer. What do you say?"

The Landsman thought it over for a minute. "Well," he said, "I could accept that. Jirel can fly in Garth's stead. If this girl can outfly her, then she has earned her place, though it will not make me happy."

Shalli looked immensely relieved. "An excellent suggestion," she said, smiling. "I knew we could count on Maris for good sense."

"Are we agreed, then?" the Easterner said quickly.

All of the judges nodded except the Outer Islander, who shook his head again and muttered, "The girl should get the wings. The man fell into the ocean." But he did not dissent too loudly.

Outside the lodge in the cool night air, a thin rain had begun to fall. But Sena stopped them anyway, looking troubled. "S'Rella," she said, leaning on her cane, "are you certain this is what you want? You might lose the wings this way. Jirel is said to be a good flyer. And perhaps we could have won the judges to our side, if we had argued longer."

"No," S'Rella said gravely. "No, I want it this way."

Sena looked her in the eye for a long time, and finally nodded. "Good," she said, satisfied. "Let's get you home, then. Tomorrow there is flying to be done."

On the third day of the competition, Maris woke before dawn, confused by the dark and the cold and aware that something was wrong. Someone was pounding on the door.

"Maris," S'Rella said from the next bed. "Should I get it?" Maris could not see her; it was well before dawn, and none of their candles were lit.

"No," Maris whispered. "Quiet." She was afraid. The pounding went on and on, without letup, and Maris remembered the dead rainbirds that had been left for them and wondered who was on the other side of the door at this hour, trying so angrily to get them to open it. She climbed out of bed and padded across the room, and in the dark she managed to locate the blade she had used to pry free the birds. It was nothing, a little metal table knife, not a fighting blade at all, but it gave her confidence. Only then did she go to the door. "Who's there?" she demanded. "Who is it?"

The pounding stopped. "Raggin," said a deep voice she did not recognize.

"Raggin? I know no Raggin. What do you want?"

"I'm from the Iron Axe," the voice said. "You know Val? The one who's been staying with me?"

Maris felt her fears drain away, and she hurried to open the door. The man standing in the starlight was gaunt and stooped, with a hook nose and a dirty beard, but he was suddenly familiar to her: the barkeep from Val's tavern. "What is it? Is something wrong?"

"I was closing up, and your friend hadn't been in yet. Thought he'd just found some pretty to sleep with, but then I found him outside, lying in the back. Somebody hurt him bad."

"*Val*," S'Rella said. She rushed to the door. "Where is he? Is he all right?"

"He's up in his room," Raggin said. "I dragged him up the stairs, and it wasn't easy. But I remembered he knew people up here so I thought I better come and ask around, and they sent me here. You gonna come down? *I* don't know what to do for him."

"Right away," Maris said urgently. "S'Rella, get dressed." She hurried to collect her own clothes and slipped into them, and shortly they were hurrying down the sea road. Maris had a lantern in one hand. The road ran along the seaside cliffs for part of its length, and a misstep in the dark could be fatal.

The tavern was dark and shuttered, the front door braced from inside with a heavy wooden beam. Raggin left them standing in front of it and vanished around back to enter by what he called his "secret way." When he opened the door from the inside, he said, "Got to lock up good, lots of hard types around here. I got customers you wouldn't believe, flyers."

They hardly listened. S'Rella ran up the stairs to the room she had sometimes shared with Val, and Maris came close behind.

S'Rella was lighting a candle by Val's bedside when Maris caught up with her.

Flickering ruddy light filled the small room, and the shape huddled beneath the blankets moved with a small animal whimper. S'Rella set down the candle and pulled off the blankets.

Val's eyes found her, and he seemed to recognize her—his left arm clutched at her hand desperately. But when he tried to speak, the only sounds he could make were choking, pain-wracked sobs.

Maris felt sick. He had been beaten savagely about the head and shoulders, and his face was an unrecognizable mass of swelling and bruises. A gash along one cheek was still bleeding, and he had dried blood all over his shirt and jaw. His mouth was bloody too, when he opened it and tried to speak.

"*Val!*" S'Rella cried, weeping. She touched his brow and he shrank away from her hand, trying to say something.

Maris came closer. Val was holding S'Rella tight with his left hand, clutching at her, pulling. But his right arm just lay still along his side, and there was something wrong, blood on the sheet beneath it. The angle at which it lay was impossible, and his jacket was ripped, bloody. She knelt by the right side of the bed and touched his arm gingerly, and Val shrieked so loudly that S'Rella jumped away, terrified. It was only then that Maris saw the jagged edge of bone peeking through his skin and clothing.

Raggin was observing them from the doorway. "His arm's broke, don't touch it," he said helpfully. "He screams when you do. You shoulda heard the noise he made when I carried him up here. I think his leg's broke too, but I'm not sure."

Val had quieted, but his breath came in painful gasps. Maris was on her feet. "Why didn't you call a healer?" she demanded of Raggin. "Why didn't you give him something for the pain?"

Raggin drew back, shocked, as if those ideas had never occurred to him. "I got you, didn't I? Who's gonna pay a healer? He's not, that's for sure. Don't have near enough. I went through his things."

Maris balled her fists and tried to control her fury. "You're going to go and fetch a healer right now," she said. "And I don't care if you have to run ten miles, you're going to do it *fast*. If you don't, I swear I'll talk to the Landsman and have this place closed."

"Flyers." The barkeep spat. "Throwing your weight around, eh? Well, I'll go, but who's gonna pay this healer? That's what I want to know, and he'll want to know too."

"Damn you," Maris said. "I'll pay, damn you, *I'll* pay. He's a flyer, and if his bones don't heal right, if they aren't taken care of, *he'll never fly again.* Now *hurry!*"

Raggin gave her a last sour look and turned for the stairs. Maris went back to Val's bedside. He was making whimpering noises and trying to move, but every motion seemed to wrack him with pain.

"Can't we help him?" S'Rella said, glancing up at Maris.

"Yes," Maris said. "This is a tavern, after all. Go downstairs and find the stock, bring up a few bottles. That should help a little with the pain, until the healer arrives."

S'Rella nodded and started for the door. "What should I bring?" she asked. "Wine?"

"No, we need something stronger. Look for some brandy. Or— that liquor from Poweet, what do they call it?—they make it from grain and potatoes—"

S'Rella nodded and was gone. Shortly she returned with three bottles of local brandy and an unmarked flask that gave off a pungent, potent smell. "Strong stuff," Maris said. She tasted it herself, then had S'Rella hold up Val's head while she dribbled it into his mouth. He seemed anxious to cooperate, sucking down the drink eagerly as they took turns pouring it into him.

When Raggin finally returned with a healer more than an hour later, Val had passed out. "Here's your healer," the barkeep said. He took one look at the empty bottles on the floor and added, "You'll pay for those too, flyer."

When the healer had set Val's arm and leg—Raggin had been right, it was broken as well, though not as badly—and splinted them, and treated his swollen face, he gave Maris a small bottle full of a dark green liquid. "This is better than brandy," he said. "It will numb the pain and let him sleep." He departed, leaving Maris and S'Rella alone with Val.

"It was flyers, wasn't it?" S'Rella asked tearfully as they sat together in the smoky, candle-lit room.

"One arm and one leg broken, and the other side not touched," Maris said angrily. "Yes, that says flyer to me. I don't think any flyer could have done this personally, but I suspect it was a flyer who had it done." On a sudden impulse Maris moved to where Val's blood-stained, torn clothing had been piled, and rummaged through it. "Hmm. Just as I thought. His knife is gone. Maybe they took it, or maybe he just had it in his hand and dropped it."

"I hope he cut them, whoever it was," S'Rella said. "Do you think it was Corm? Because Val was going to take his wings tomorrow?"

"Today," Maris said ruefully, glancing toward the window. The first blush of dawn was visible against the eastern sky. "But, no, it wasn't Corm. Not that Corm wouldn't gladly destroy Val if he could, but he'd do it legally, not like this. Corm is too proud to resort to beatings."

"Who, then?"

Maris shook her head. "I don't know, S'Rella. Some sick person, obviously. Maybe a friend of Corm's, or a friend of Ari's. Maybe Arak or one of *his* friends. Val made a lot of enemies."

"He wanted me to go with him," S'Rella said guiltily, "but I went to see Garth instead. If I had gone with him like he wanted, this wouldn't have happened."

"If you had gone with him," Maris said, "you'd probably be lying there broken and bleeding as well. S'Rella, love, remember those rainbirds they left for us. They wanted to tell us something. You're a one-wing too." She glanced out toward the dawn. "And so am I. Maybe it's time I admitted it. I'm half-a-flyer and that's all I'll ever be." She smiled for S'Rella. "But I guess what matters is what half."

S'Rella seemed puzzled, but Maris said, "No more talk. You still have a few hours before the competition opens, and I want you to try to get some sleep. You have to win your wings today, remember?"

"I can't," S'Rella protested. "Not now."

"Especially now," Maris said. "Whoever had this done to Val

would be delighted to know that it lost you your wings as well as his. Do you want that?"

"No," S'Rella said.

"Then sleep."

Later, while S'Rella slept, Maris looked up again at the window. The sun was half-risen, its reddened face streaked with heavy dark clouds. It was going to be a good, windy day. A fine day for flying.

The competition was already well under way when Maris and S'Rella arrived. They had been delayed in the tavern when Raggin demanded immediate payment of Val's bill, and it had taken a long argument to convince him that he would get everything due him. Maris made him promise to tend to Val's needs, and allow no one else up those stairs.

Sena was at her usual station by the judges, watching the early contestants fly the gates. Maris sent S'Rella off to join the other Woodwingers, and hurried up the cliff. Sena was relieved to see her. "Maris!" she exclaimed. "I was worried something was wrong. No one knew where you had gone. Are S'Rella and Val with you? It will be time soon. Sher is next up, in fact."

"S'Rella is ready to fly," Maris said. She told Sena about Val.

All the strength and vitality seemed to drain from the teacher as she listened. Her good eye clouded over with tears and she leaned more heavily on her cane, and suddenly she was very old indeed. "I did not believe," she muttered weakly. "I did not—even when that terrible thing happened with the birds, even then—I could not think they would do such a thing." Her face was the color of ash. "Help me, child. I must sit down."

Maris put an arm about her for support and led her to the judges' table, where Shalli looked up, concerned. "Is everything all right?"

"No," said Maris, easing Sena into a seat. "Val will not fly today," she continued, swinging around to face the judges. "Last night he was attacked and beaten at the tavern where he had a room. An arm and a leg were broken."

All of the judges looked shocked. "How terrible," Shalli said. The Easterner swore, the Outer Islander shook his head, and the

Landsman of Skulny rose. "This is dreadful. I won't allow this on my island. We'll find whoever did it, you have my promise on that."

"A flyer did it," Maris said, "or paid for it, anyway. They broke his right arm and his right leg. One-Wing. You understand."

Shalli frowned. "Maris, this is a horrid thing, but no flyer would do such a thing. And if you mean to imply that *Corm* would—"

"Do you have proof a flyer was involved?" the Easterner interrupted.

"I know the tavern where Val One-Wing was staying," the Landsman said. "The Iron Axe, was it not? That is a very bad place, with the worst sort of patrons, rough people. It could have been anyone. A drunken fight, a jealous lover, a gambling quarrel. I've seen many beatings come before me from that place."

Maris stared at him. "You'll never find who did it, no matter what you promise," she said. "That isn't what concerns me. I want to take Val's wings back to him tonight."

"Val's—*wings?*"

"I'm afraid," the Southerner said, "he must wait and try again next year. I am sorry he was hurt when he was so close to winning."

"Close?" Maris looked the length of the table, found the box she sought, picked it up and rattled it at them. "Nine black stones to one white. That is more than close. Val had won. Even if he lost five to nothing today, he had *won.*"

"No," Shalli said stubbornly. "Corm deserves his chance. I won't have you cheat him of it for One-Wing, no matter how sorry I feel for him. Corm is very good at the gates. He might have won ten to nothing, two stones from each of us, and then he would have kept his wings."

"Ten to nothing," Maris said. "How likely is that?"

"It is possible," Shalli said.

"It is," echoed the Easterner. "We can't give the victory to One-Wing. It would not be fair to Corm, who has flown well for many years. I think we must declare Val forfeit."

Heads were bobbing up and down the table, but Maris only smiled. "I was afraid you might take this position." She put her hands on her hips and defied them. "But Val will have his wings.

Luckily there is a precedent. You set it yourselves last night, with S'Rella and Garth. Let the score stand and the match continue. Summon Corm.

"I will fly proxy for Val."

And she knew they would not deny her.

Maris got her wings and joined the mill of contestants, impatient and increasingly nervous.

The gates had been erected during the night, nine flimsy wooden constructions planted firmly in the sand, in a course demanding a series of difficult turns and tacking maneuvers. The first gate, straight out from the flyers' cliff, consisted of two tall black-wood poles, each some forty feet high, set fifty feet apart in the sand. A rope had been tied from the top of one pole to the top of the other. To score, the flyer had to glide through that gate. Easy enough, but the next gate was only a few yards farther down the beach, not straight ahead but off to one side, so the flyer had to angle quickly before shooting past it. And the second gate was smaller, the poles just a little bit shorter and set just a little bit closer together. So it went, the course wandering out into the shallows and then veering sharply back onto land, a twisting, wing-snapping course, with each of the nine gates smaller than the one before, until the ninth and final gate, two poles barely eight feet off the ground, set exactly twenty-one feet apart. A flyer's wingspan was twenty feet. No one had ever flown more than seven gates. Even that was no mean task; of all the flyers to try the gates this morning, the best score was six, and that had been flown by the phenomenal Lane.

Challengers traditionally flew first in this test; the flyer was given the courtesy of knowing what score he had to beat. Wings on her shoulders, Maris watched the Woodwingers make their attempts.

Sher dove straight from the cliff through the first gate, coming in barely under the rope, banked sharply toward the second but continued to descend, fast, too fast. Panicking, the young Wood-winger leveled off quickly to avoid hitting the ground, and suddenly started to rise, passing over the second gate instead of through it. The flyer that Sher challenged managed only two gates, but that was enough for the victory.

Leya, watching Sher, chose a different strategy. She leapt from the cliff to circle widely above the beach, dropping down gradually so that she'd pass through the first gate level instead of in a descent. She began her turn well before she entered the gate proper, so that she actually swung *around* one pole gracefully, already heading for the second gate. She sailed smoothly through that as well, again beginning her turn early, but this time it was a sharper turn, more demanding, upwind. Leya made it well enough, and the third gate with it, but had nothing left to wrench herself around afterward. She flew peacefully out to sea, missing the fourth gate by a wide margin. A few of the spectators applauded her anyway, and her flyer rival could only manage two gates before he landed roughly in the sand. So Leya had her first triumph, though it was not enough to win a pair of wings.

Damen and Arak were announced by the crier. Both of them had trouble. Damen took the gates too fast, and couldn't recover after the second in time to turn for the third. Arak passed through the second gate too high; the upper edge of a wing grazed the rope, and it was enough to send him off balance and far off course. But even with the two-gate tie, Arak easily retained his wings.

Kerr, surprisingly, also managed a tie. Imitating Leya, he entered the first gate leveled and starting his turn, and handled the second easily enough. But like Leya he had trouble veering upwind into the third, and unlike Leya, he did not manage it. He thumped to a halt in the sand a few yards short of the gate, and the land-bound children rushed in from all sides to help him out of his wings. Jon of Culhall tried to avoid Kerr's fate by maintaining a higher altitude, but passed over and to the right of the third gate.

"*Corm of Lesser Amberly,*" the crier was announcing, "*Val One-Wing, Val of South Arren.*" Then a brief pause. "*Maris of Lesser Amberly, flying proxy for Val, Maris of Lesser Amberly.*"

She stood on the flyers' cliff, helpers unfolding her wings, locking each strut in place. A few dozen yards away, Corm too stood and let them work. She looked over at him, and his eyes met hers, dark, intense. "Maris One-Wing," he called bitterly. "Is this what you've come to? I'm glad Russ is not alive to see you."

"Russ would be proud," she threw back, angry, and knowing Corm had wanted to make her angry. Anger brought carelessness, and that was his only hope. Seven years ago she had outflown him, in a much fiercer contest. She was confident she could outfly him today as well. Precision, control, reflexes, a feel for the wind; that was all it required, and she had them in full measure.

Her wings were wide and tight, metal humming softly in the wind, and she felt utterly serene and sure of herself. She reached up, wrapped her hands around the grips, ran, jumped, soared. Up she flew, up and up, and she did a loop for the sheer joy of it and then dove, sliding down and down through the air, riding and shifting with the little eddies and currents, angling toward the gates. She was banked sharply and wheeling as she went through the first gate, her wings drawing a silver line from the top of one pole to the bottom of the other, but she stabilized gracefully and swayed the other way for the approach to the second, slid through it fluidly. It was the feel of it, the love of it, not the thought; it was instinct and reflex and knowing the wind, and Maris *was* the wind. The third gate was next, the difficult upwind turn, but she snapped around easily, quickly, cleanly, then looped above the water to correct her angle on the fourth gate, and she was through that too, and the fifth was a wide lazy downwind turn, and the sixth was almost straight ahead, not a difficult angle at all, but small, so she dropped a little and skimmed low over the sand, her wings taut and full, and the spectators were shouting and cheering.

In a heartbeat it was over.

Just as the sixth gate loomed ahead of her, she hit a sink, a sudden cold downdraft that had no right being there. It pushed at her, clutched at her, just for an instant, but that was long enough for her wings to brush the ground, and then her legs were trailing through the wet sand and she slid along bumpily before finally jolting to a halt in the shadow of the gate.

A small blond girl ran up to her and helped her to her feet, then began folding up her wings. Maris stood breathless and exhilarated. Five, then, five it was. Not the best score of the day, but a good score, and it was enough. Corm trailed Val by such a margin that it would not be enough for him to beat her. He had to humiliate her, crush her, collect two pebbles from each of the judges. And that he could not do.

He knew it too. Disheartened by her flight, he did not even come close. He failed on the fourth gate, a decisive victory for her, for Val. She felt elated as she trudged across the beach, wings folded on her back.

Criers' calls ran up and down the shore. S'Rella stood poised on the precipice, the sun shining off the bright metal of her wings, and behind her Maris glimpsed wiry, black-haired Jirel of Skulny.

S'Rella leaped, and Maris stood to watch, her heart flying with her, hoping, hoping. S'Rella banked and circled, a leisurely approach instead of the wild rush Maris had employed, and came gliding down smoothly on the same tack Leya and Kerr had used in their turns. Through the first gate, turning, leveling, wheeling now in the opposite direction—Maris felt her breath stop for a minute—and through the second gate, and now a *very* sharp turn upwind, a clean knife-thrust of a turn as if the wind itself had changed direction at her command, and through the third gate, still in control, and another hard veer and she was through the fourth gate—people began to rise and cheer—and the fifth was as easy for her as it had been for Maris, and now it was the sixth that she was moving in on, the sixth on which Maris had failed, and her wings were swaying a bit but then they stilled and she came in higher than Maris, and the sink shook her but didn't ground her, and then she was through the *sixth* gate too—shouts everywhere— and the seventh demanded a split-second bank at just the right angle, and S'Rella did that as well, and she came around toward the eighth—

—and it was too narrow, the poles set too close together, and S'Rella was just a bit too far to one side. Her left wing hit the pole with a snap, and the wing-struts shattered even as the pole did, and S'Rella went sprawling on the ground.

And Maris was only one of dozens running toward her.

When she got there, S'Rella was sitting up, laughing and breathing hard, surrounded by land-bound who were shouting at her, yelling hoarse-voiced congratulations. The children pressed close to touch her wings. But S'Rella, her face reddened by the wind, couldn't seem to stop laughing.

Maris pushed her way through the crowd and hugged her, and S'Rella giggled through it all. "Are you all right?" Maris asked, pushing her away and holding her at arm's length. S'Rella nodded furiously, still giggling. "Then what . . . ?"

S'Rella pointed at her wing, the wing that had struck the gate. The fabric, virtually indestructible, was undamaged, but a support strut had broken. "That's easily fixed," Maris said after she'd looked it over. "No problem."

"Don't you *see?*" S'Rella said, jumping to her feet. Her right wing bobbed with the motion, taut and vibrant, but her left hung limp and broken, silver tissue dragging on the sand.

Maris looked and began to laugh. "One-Wing," she said helplessly, and they collapsed into each other's arms again, laughing.

"Jirel didn't disgrace you," Maris said to Garth that night, as she sat with him by his fire. He was up and about again, looking better, and drinking ale once more. "She was an admirable proxy, flew five gates, as good as I'd done. But five isn't seven, of course, and it wasn't enough. Even the Landsman couldn't call it a tie."

"Good," Garth said. "S'Rella deserves the wings. I like S'Rella. Make her promise to come visit me too."

Maris smiled. "I will," she said. "She's sorry she couldn't come tonight, but she wanted to go straight down to Val. I'm to join her after I leave here. I don't relish it, but . . ." She sighed.

Garth took a healthy swig of ale and stared into the fire for a long moment. "I feel sorry for Corm," he said. "Never liked him, but he knew how to fly."

"Don't fret," Maris said. "He's bitter but he'll recover. Shalli's pregnancy will soon be too advanced for her to fly, so Corm will have the use of her wings for a few months, and if I know him he'll bully her into sharing even after the baby comes. Next year he can challenge. It won't be Val, either. Corm is cleverer than that. I'll wager he names someone like Jon of Culhall."

"Ah," Garth said, "if the damned healers ever cure me, I may name Jon myself."

"He'll be a popular choice next year," Maris agreed. "Even Kerr wants another chance at him, though I doubt Sena will sponsor him again until he's a lot more seasoned. She'll have better prospects to choose from next year. With the double victory by S'Rella and Val, Woodwings is suddenly thriving again. She'll soon have more students than she knows what to do with." Maris chuckled. "You and Corm weren't the only flyers grounded, either. Bari of Poweet lost her wings in an out-of-family challenge, and Big Hara went down to her own daughter."

"A flock of ex-flyers," Garth grumbled.

"And a lot of one-wings," Maris added, smiling. "The world is changing, Garth. Once we had only flyers and land-bound."

"Yes," Garth said, gulping down some more ale. "Then you confused everything. Flying land-bounds and grounded flyers. Where will it end?"

"I don't know," Maris said. She stood up. "I'd stay longer, but I must go talk to Val, and I'm long overdue on Amberly. With Shalli pregnant and Corm wingless, the Landsman will no doubt work me to death. But I'll find time to visit, I promise."

"Good." He grinned up at her. "Fly well, now."

When she left, he was shouting to Riesa for another ale.

Val was propped up awkwardly in bed; his head raised just enough so that he could eat, he was spooning soup into his mouth with his left hand. S'Rella sat by his side, holding the bowl. They both looked up when Maris entered, and Val's hand trembled, spilling hot soup on his bare chest. He cursed and S'Rella helped him mop it up.

"Val," Maris said evenly, nodding. On the floor by the door she set the wings she had carried, once belonging to Corm of Lesser Amberly. "Your wings."

The swelling in his face had subsided enough so that Val was beginning to look like himself again, although his puffed lip gave him an atypical sneer. "S'Rella told me what you did," he said with difficulty. "Now I suppose you want me to thank you."

Maris folded her arms and waited.

"Your friends the flyers did this to me, you know," he said. "If the bones mend crooked, I'll never use those damn wings you got me. Even if they heal properly, I'll never be as good as I was."

"I know that," Maris said, "and I'm sorry. But it wasn't my friends who did this, Val. Not all flyers are my friends. And they aren't all your enemies."

"You were at the party," Val said.

Maris nodded. "It won't be easy, and most of the burden is on you. Reject them if you like, hate all of them. Or find the ones worth knowing. It's up to you."

"I'll tell you who I'm going to find," Val said. "I'm going to find the ones who did this to me, and then I'm going to find whoever sent them."

"Yes," Maris said. "And then?"

"S'Rella found my knife," Val said simply. "I dropped it in the bushes last night. But I cut one of them, well enough so I'll know her by the scar."

"Where are you going, when you heal?" Maris said.

Val seemed thrown off-stride by the sudden change of subject. "I had thought Seatooth. I've heard the stories, about how much the Landsman there wants a flyer. But S'Rella tells me that the Landsman of Skulny is anxious as well. I'll talk to them both, see what they offer."

"Val of Seatooth," Maris said. "It has a nice sound to it."

"It will always be One-Wing," he said. "Maybe for you too."

"A half-flyer," she agreed. "Both of us. But which half? Val, you can make the Landsmen bid for your services. The flyers will despise you for it, most of them, and maybe some of the younger and greedier will imitate you, and I'd hate to see that. And you can wear that knife your father gave you when you fly, even though you break one of the oldest and wisest flyer laws by doing so. It is a small point, a tradition, and the flyers again will despise you, but no one will do anything. But I tell you now, if you find who ordered you beaten, and kill them with that same knife, you'll be One-Wing no longer. The flyers will name you outlaw and strip your wings away, and not a Landsman on Windhaven will take your side or give you landing, no matter how much they need flyers."

"You want me to forget," Val said. "Forget *this?*"

"No," said Maris. "Find them, and take them to a Landsman, or call a flyer court. Let your enemy be the one who loses wings and home and life, and not you. Is that such a bad alternative?"

Val smiled crookedly, and Maris saw he had lost some teeth as well. "No," he said. "I almost like it."

"It's your choice," Maris said. "You won't be flying for a good while, so you'll have time to think about it. I think you're intelligent enough to use that time." She looked to S'Rella. "I must return to Lesser Amberly. It's on your way, if you're going back to Southern. Will you fly with me, and spend a day in my home?"

S'Rella nodded eagerly. "Yes, I'd love—that is, if Val will be all right."

"Flyers have unlimited credit," Val said. "If I promise Raggin enough iron, he'll nurse me better than my own parent."

"I'll go, then," S'Rella said. "But I'll see you again, Val, won't I? We both have wings now."

"Yes," Val said. "Go fly with yours. I'll look at mine."

S'Rella kissed him and crossed the room to where Maris stood. They started out the door.

"*Maris!*" Val called sharply.

She turned at the sound of his voice, in time to see his left hand reach awkwardly behind his head, under the pillow, and come whipping out with frightening speed. The long blade sliced through the air and struck the doorframe not a foot from Maris' head. But the knife was ornamental obsidian, bright and black and sharp, but not resilient, and it shattered when it struck.

Maris must have looked terrified; Val was smiling. "It was never my father's," he said. "My father never owned anything. I stole it from Arak." Across the room their eyes met, and Val laughed painfully. "Get rid of it for me, will you, One-Wing?"

Maris smiled and bent to pick up the pieces.

PART THREE

The Fall

SHE GREW OLD in less than a minute.

When Maris left the side of the Landsman of Thayos she was still young. She took the underground way from his spare rocky keep to the sea, a damp, gloomy tunnel through the mountain. She walked quickly, with a taper in her hand, her folded wings on her back, surrounded by echoes and the slow drip of water. There were puddles on the floor of the tunnel, and the water soaked through her boots. Maris was anxious to be off.

It was not until she emerged into the twilight on the far side of the mountain that Maris saw the sky. It was a dim threatening purple, a violet so dark it was almost black; the color of a bad bruise, full of blood and pain. The wind was cold and unruly. Maris could taste the fury that was about to break, could see it in the clouds. She stood at the foot of the time-worn stairs that led up the sea cliff, and briefly she considered turning back, resting overnight at the lodge house and postponing her flight until dawn.

The thought of the long walk back through the tunnel dismayed her, however, and Maris took no joy in this place. Thayos seemed to her a dark and bitter land, and its Landsman rude, his brutality barely hidden beneath the civilities required between Landsman and flyer. The message he had given her to fly weighed heavily upon her. The words were angry, greedy, full of the threat of war, and Maris was eager to deliver and forget them, to free herself of the burden as quickly as she could.

So she extinguished her taper and started up the stairs, climbing easily with long, impatient strides. There were lines on her face and gray in her hair, but Maris was still as graceful and vigorous as she had been at twenty.

Where the steps opened onto a broad stone platform above the sea, Maris unfolded her wings. They caught the wind and tugged at her as she snapped the last struts into place. The purple gloom of the storm gave a dark cast to the silver metal, and the rays of the setting sun left red streaks of light upon it, like fresh wounds welling full of blood. Maris hurried. She wanted to get ahead of the storm, to use the front for added speed. She tightened the straps around herself, checked the wings a final time, and wrapped her hands about the familiar grips. With two quick steps she flung herself from the cliff, as she had uncounted times before. The wind was her old and true lover. She folded herself into its embrace and flew.

She saw lightning on the horizon, a lingering three-pronged bolt in the eastern sky. Then the wind slackened and went soft on her, and she fell, and banked, and turned, searching for a stronger current until the storm hit her, sudden as the crack of a whip. The wind gusted out of nowhere with terrible force, and as she struggled to ride with it, it changed direction. Then a second time, then a third. Rain stung her face, lightning blinded her, and there was a pounding in her ears.

The storm pushed her backward, then head over heels, as if she were a toy. She had no more choice, no more chance, than a leaf in a gale. She was buffeted this way and that until she was sick and dizzy and aware that she was falling. And she looked over her shoulder and saw the mountain rushing at her, a sheer wall of slick wet stone. She tried to pull away, and managed only to turn herself in the fierce embrace of the wind. Her left wing brushed the rock, collapsed, and Maris fell sideways, screaming, her left wing limp; though she tried to fly one-winged, she knew that it was useless, and was blinded by the rain; the storm had her in its killing teeth, and with her last clear thought, Maris knew this was her death.

The sea took her, and broke her, and spit her out. They found her late the next day, broken and unconscious, but alive, on a rocky beach three miles from Thayos' flyers' cliff.

When Maris woke, days later, she was old.

She was seldom more than semi-conscious during that first week, and afterward she remembered little. Pain, when she moved and when she did not; waking and sleeping. She slept most of the time, and her dreams were as real to her as the constant pain. She walked through long tunnels beneath the earth, walked until her legs ached horribly, but she never found the steps that would lead her out to the sky. She fell through still air endlessly, her strength and skill useless in a windless sky. She stood before hundreds in Council and argued, but her words were slurred and too soft, and the people there would not listen. She was hot, terribly hot, and she could not move. Someone had taken her wings and tied her legs and arms. She struggled to move, to speak. She had to fly somewhere with an urgent message. She couldn't move, she couldn't speak, she didn't know if there were tears or rain on her cheeks. Someone wiped her face and made her drink a thick, bitter liquid.

At some point Maris knew she was lying in a big bed, a hearth nearby that always had a blazing fire in it, and she was covered with heavy layers of furs and blankets. She was hot, terribly hot, and she struggled to push off the blankets but could not.

There seemed to be people in the room, coming and going. She recognized some of them—they were her friends—but although she asked them to remove the blankets, they never did. They didn't seem to hear her, but they would often sit at the foot of the bed and talk to her. They spoke of things gone by as if they were present still, which confused her, but everything was confused, and she was glad to have her friends with her.

Coll came, singing his songs, and Barrion was with him, Barrion of the quick grin and the deep, rumbly voice. Old, crippled Sena sat on the edge of the bed and said nothing. Raven appeared once, dressed all in black and looking so bold and beautiful that her heart ached with unspoken love for him all over again. Garth brought her steaming hot kivas, then told her jokes so that she laughed and forgot to drink. Val One-Wing stood in the doorway, watching, cold-faced as ever. S'Rella, her dear friend, came often, speaking of old times. And Dorrel, her first love and still a trusted friend, came again and again, his presence a familiar comfort to her through the pain and confusion. Others came as well: old lovers she had never thought to see again appeared before her to speak, to plead, to accuse, and then vanished, leaving all her questions unanswered. There was chubby blond T'mar, bringing her gifts he'd carved from stone, and Halland the singer, strong, black-bearded, looking just as he had when they had lived together on Lesser Amberly. She remembered then that he had been lost at sea, and she wept, her tears blotting out the sight of him.

There was another visitor, a man strange to Maris. And yet he was not a stranger: She knew the touch of his gentle, sure hands, and the sound of his almost musical voice speaking her name. Unlike her other visitors, he came close to her and held up her head and fed her hot milky soups and spice tea and a thick, bitter potion that made her sleep. She could not think how or when she had met him, but she felt glad to see him. He was thin and small but sinewy. Pale skin was stretched taut over the bones and planes of his face, freckled with age. Fine white hair grew well back from a high forehead. His eyes, beneath prominent brows and in a webwork of tiny wrinkles, were brilliantly blue. But although he came so often, and knew her, Maris could not bring his name to mind.

Once, as he stood beside her and watched her, Maris struggled out of her half-sleep and told him how hot it was, and asked him to take away the blankets.

He shook his head. "You're feverish," he said. "The room is chilly and you are very sick. You need the warmth of the blankets."

Startled by this phantom who had finally answered her, Maris struggled to sit up and get a better look at him. Her body responded sluggishly, and a sickening pain seared her left side.

"Easy," said the man. His cool fingers were on her brow. "Your bones must knit before you can move. Here, drink this." He lifted her head and pressed the smooth, thick rim of a cup to her lips. She tasted familiar bitterness, swallowed obediently. The tension and pain drained out of her as her head sank back on the pillow.

"Sleep and don't worry," said the man.

With difficulty she managed to speak: "Who . . . ?"

"My name is Evan," he said. "I'm a healer. You've been in my care for weeks now. You are healing, but still very weak. You must sleep now, and conserve your strength."

"Weeks." The word frightened her. She must be terribly sick, horribly injured, to spend weeks in the house of a healer. "Wh— where?"

He put his strong, thin fingers against her mouth to hush her. "On Thayos. No more questions now. I'll tell you everything later, when you are stronger. Now sleep. Let your body heal itself."

Maris stopped fighting the coming sleep. He had said she was mending and must conserve her strength. She wished only, as she sank into sleep, that she would not dream again about that brief, terrible flight through the storm, and the awful crushing of her body.

Later, when she awoke, the world was dark, with only dim embers alive in the hearth to give shape to the shadows. As soon as she stirred, Evan was there. He prodded the fire into new life, felt her brow, and then sat lightly on the bed.

"The fever has broken," he said, "but you are not well yet. I know you want to move—it will be hard to keep still. But you must. You are still very weak, and your body will mend better if you do not tax it. If you cannot keep still by yourself I must give you more tesis."

"Tesis?" Her own voice sounded strange in her ears. She coughed, trying to clear her throat.

"The bitter drink that quiets the body and mind, brings sleep and relaxation to stop the pain. It's a very helpful drink, full of healing herbs, but too much of it can be a poison. I had to give you more than I liked to, to keep you still. Physical restraints were no good for you—you thrashed and struggled and strained to be free. You wouldn't let the broken parts of your body rest and heal. When you drank the tesis you fell into the quiet, healing, painless sleep you needed. But I don't want to give you any more. There will be pain, but I think you can bear it. If you cannot, then I will give you tesis. Do you understand me, Maris?"

She looked into his bright blue eyes. "Yes," she said. "I understand. I'll try to be still. Remind me."

He smiled. It made his face suddenly young. "I'll remind you," he said. "You're accustomed to a life of activity, motion, always going and doing. But you can't go somewhere to get your strength back— you must wait for it, lying here, as patiently as you can."

Maris began to nod her head, checking it as she felt a dull, straining pain on her left side. "I've never been a patient person," she said.

"No, but I've heard that you are strong. Use that strength to be still, and you may recover."

"You must tell me the truth," Maris said. She watched his face, trying to read the answer there. She felt fear like a cold poison moving throughout her body. She longed for the strength to sit up, to check her arms and legs.

"I'll tell you what I know," said Evan.

She felt the fear in her throat and could scarcely speak. The words came in a whisper. "How . . . how badly was I hurt?" She closed her eyes, afraid now to read his face.

"You were terribly battered, but you lived." He stroked her cheek and she opened her eyes. "Both your legs were broken in the fall, the left one in four places. I set them, and they seem to be mending well—not as quickly as they would if you were younger, but I think you will walk without a limp again. Your left arm was shattered, with bone protruding through the flesh. I thought I would have to amputate. But I did not." He pressed his fingers against her lips and withdrew them—it was like a kiss. "I cleaned it and used the fireflower essence and other herbs. You'll have stiffness there a long time, but I don't think there was any nerve damage, so that with time and exercise I think your left arm will be strong and useful again. You broke two ribs when you fell, and you hit your head on the rock. You were unconscious for three days in my care—I didn't know if you would ever return."

"Only three broken limbs," Maris said. "An easy landing, after all." Then she frowned. "The message . . ."

Evan nodded. "You repeated it again and again in your delirium like a chant, determined to deliver it. But you needn't worry. The Landsman was informed of your accident, and by now he has sent the same message to the Landsman of Thrane by another flyer."

"Of course," Maris murmured. She felt a burden she had not even known she carried lifted from her.

"Such an urgent message," Evan said, his voice bitter. "It couldn't wait for better flying weather. It sent you out into the storm, to injury. It might have meant your death. The war hasn't come yet, but already they start, disregarding human lives."

His bitterness distressed her even more than his talk of war, which merely puzzled her. "Evan," she said gently, "the flyer chooses when to fly. The Landsmen have no power over us, war or no. It was my eagerness to leave your bleak little island that made me start out despite the weather."

"And now my bleak little island is your home for a time."

"How long?" she asked. "How long before I can fly again?"

He looked at her without replying.

Maris suddenly feared the worst. "My wings!" She struggled to rise. "Are they lost?"

Evan was quick, with hands on her shoulders. "Be still!" His blue eyes blazed.

"I forgot," she whispered. "I'll be still." Her whole body throbbed painfully in response to the mild exertion. "Please . . . my wings?"

"I have them," he said. He shook his head. "Flyers. I should have known—I've healed other flyers. I should have hung them over your bed so they would be the first thing you saw. The Landsman wanted to take them for repair, but I insisted on keeping them. I'll get them for you." He vanished into the next room. A few minutes later he returned, carrying her wings in his arms.

They were mangled and broken and did not fold properly. The

metallic fabric of the wings themselves was virtually indestructible, but the supporting struts were ordinary metal, and Maris could see that several of them had shattered, while others were bent and twisted grotesquely. The bright silver was crusted with dirt and stained black in places. In Evan's uncertain grasp they seemed a hopeless ruin.

But Maris knew better. They were not lost to the sea. They could be made whole again. Her heart soared to see them. They meant life to her; she would fly again.

"Thank you," she said to Evan. She tried not to weep.

Evan hung the wings on the wall beyond the foot of the bed, where Maris could see them. Then he turned to her.

"It will be longer and harder to repair your body than your wings," he said. "Much longer than you will like. It won't be a matter of weeks, but of months, many months, and even then I can't promise you anything. Your bones were shattered, and the muscles torn—you aren't likely, at your age, to regain all the strength you once had. You'll walk again, but as for flying—"

"I will fly. My legs and my ribs and my arm will mend," Maris said quietly.

"Yes, given time, I hope they will mend. But that may not be enough." He came close, and she saw the concern in his face. "The head injury—it may have affected your vision, or your sense of balance."

"Stop it," Maris said. "Please." Tears leaked from her eyes.

"It's too soon," Evan said. "I'm sorry." He stroked her cheeks, wiping away the tears. "You need rest and hope, not worry. You need time to grow strong again. You'll put on your wings again, but not before you are really ready—not before *I* say you are ready."

"A land-bound healer—telling a flyer when to fly," Maris muttered with a mock scowl.

Although she might suffer it, a time of forced inactivity was not something Maris could enjoy. As the days passed and she began to spend more time awake, she grew restless. Evan was beside her much of the time, coaxing her to eat, reminding her to lie still, and talking to her, always talking, to give her restless mind something to exercise itself on, even though her body must stay motionless.

And Evan proved to be a gifted storyteller. He considered himself more an observer of life than a participant, and he had a rather detached outlook and a sharp eye for detail. He made Maris laugh, often; he made her think; and he even managed to make her forget, for minutes at a time, that she was trapped in bed with a broken body.

At first Evan told stories of Thayos society, his descriptions so vivid that she could almost see the people. But after a time his talk turned to himself, and he offered her his own life, as if in exchange for the confidences she had made to him during her delirium.

He had been born in the deep woods of Thayos, an island on the northern fringe of Eastern, sixty years before. His parents were foresters.

There had been other families in the forest, other children to play with, but from his earliest years Evan had preferred the time he spent alone. He liked to hide in the brush to watch the shy, brown dirt diggers; to hunt out the places where the most beautifully scented flowers and tastiest roots grew; to sit quietly in a small clearing with a chunk of stale bread, and tame the birds to come to his hand.

When Evan was sixteen, he fell in love with a traveling midwife. Jani, the midwife, was a small, brown woman with a ready wit and a sharp tongue. In order to be near her, Evan appointed himself Jani's assistant. She seemed amused by his interest at first, but soon accepted him, and Evan, his interest sharpened by love, learned a great deal from her.

On the eve of her departure, he confessed his love for her. She wouldn't stay, and she wouldn't take him with her—not as lover, not as friend, not even as assistant, although she admitted he had learned well and had a skillful touch. She traveled alone always, and that was that.

Evan continued to practice his new healing skills when Jani had gone. Since the nearest healer lived in Thossi village, a full day's walk from the forest, Evan was soon much in demand. Eventually he apprenticed himself to the healer in Thossi. He might have attended a college of healers, but that would have meant a sea-voyage, and the idea of traveling on the dangerous water frightened him as nothing else ever had.

When he had learned all she could teach him, Evan returned to the forest to live and work. Although he never married, he did not always live alone. Women sought him out—wives seeking an undemanding lover, traveling women who paused a few days or months in his company, patients who stayed until their passion for him was cured.

Maris, listening to his soft, mellow voice and gazing at his face for so many hours that she knew it as well as that of any lover in her past, understood the attraction. The bright blue eyes, the skillful, gentle hands, the high cheekbones and imposing beak of a nose. She wondered, though, what he had felt—was he as self-contained as he seemed?

One day Maris interrupted his story of a family of tree-kits he'd recently found to ask, "Didn't you ever fall in love? After Jani, I mean."

He looked surprised. "Yes, of course I did. I told you about . . ."

"But not enough to want to marry someone."

"Sometimes I did. With S'Rai—she lived here with me for almost a year, and we were very happy together. I loved her very much. I wanted her to stay. But she had her own life elsewhere. She wouldn't stay in the forest with me; she left."

"Why didn't you go away with her? Didn't she ask you to?"

Evan looked unhappy. "Yes, she did. She wanted me to go with her; somehow it just didn't seem possible."

"You've never been anywhere else?"

"I've traveled all over Thayos, whenever there has been need," Evan said, rather defensively. "And I lived in Thossi for nearly two years when I was younger."

"All Thayos is much the same," Maris said, shrugging her good shoulder. There was a twinge in her left, which she ignored. She was allowed to sit up now, and she was afraid Evan would revoke the privilege if she ever admitted to pain. "Some parts have more trees, some parts have more rocks."

Evan laughed. "A very superficial view! To you, all parts of the forest would seem identical."

This was so obvious as to require no comment. Maris persisted. "You've never been off Thayos?"

Evan grimaced. "Once," he said. "There'd been an accident, a boat cracked up against the rocks, and the woman in it had been badly injured. I was taken out in a fishing boat to see to her. I got so sick on the journey out that I could scarcely help her."

Maris smiled sympathetically, but she shook her head. "How can you know that this is the only place you ever want to live if you've never been anywhere else?"

"I don't claim to know that, Maris. I might have left, I might have had a very different life. But this is what I've chosen. I know this life—it's mine, for better or worse. It's rather late now to mourn all the opportunities I've missed. I'm happy with my life." He rose then, ending the conversation. "Now it's time for your nap."

"May I . . ."

"You may do whatever you like, as long as you do it lying flat on your back without moving."

Maris laughed, and let him help her back down on the bed. She wouldn't admit it, but sitting up had tired her, and it was a welcome relief to rest. The slowness of her body to mend frustrated her. And she didn't understand why, just because a few bones were broken, she should tire so easily. She closed her eyes, listening to the sounds Evan made as he tended the fire and tidied the room.

She thought about Evan. She was attracted to him, and of course the circumstances had made for an easy intimacy between them. She had imagined that, once she mended, she and Evan might become lovers. She thought better of it now, knowing more of his life. Evan had loved, and been left, too many times. She liked him too well to want to hurt him, and she knew that she would leave Thayos, and Evan, just as soon as she could fly again. It was better, she decided sleepily, that she and Evan remain only friends. She would have to ignore how much she liked that bright sparkle in his blue eyes, and forget her fantasies about his slim, wiry body and skilled hands.

She smiled and yawned and fell asleep, to dream that she was teaching Evan how to fly.

The next day S'Rella arrived.

Maris was drowsy and half asleep, and at first she thought she was dreaming. The stuffy room suddenly became fresher, full of the clean, sharp scent of sea winds, and when Maris looked up S'Rella was standing in the doorway, wings slung over one arm. For an instant she looked like the shy, slight girl she had been more than twenty years ago, when Maris had helped teach her to fly. But she smiled then, a self-assured smile that lit her dark, thin face and emphasized the lines that time had left there. And when she came forward, spraying salt water from her wings and wet clothes, the phantom of S'Rella the Woodwinger dissolved entirely, and she was S'Rella of Veleth, a seasoned flyer and the mother of two grown daughters. The two women embraced, awkwardly because of the huge cast protecting Maris' left arm, but with fierce emotion.

"I came as soon as I heard, Maris," S'Rella said. "I'm sorry you had to be here alone for so long, but communication among flyers isn't what it once was, especially for one-wings. I might not be here now, but I had to fly a message to Big Shotan, and afterward I decided to visit the Eyrie. A strange whim, now that I think about it—it must have been four, five years since the last time. Corina was there, fresh from Amberly, and she told me that an Eastern flyer had just brought word of your accident. I left at once. I was so worried . . ." And she bent down to hug her friend again, the wings almost slipping from her grasp.

"Let me hang them for you," Evan said quietly, stepping forward. S'Rella handed them to him with hardly a glance, her attention all for Maris.

"How . . . how are you?" she asked.

Maris smiled. With her good arm she threw back the blanket, revealing two cast-bound legs. "Broken, as you can see, but mending. Or so Evan assures me. My ribs hardly pain me at all now. And I'm sure the casts on these legs are ready to be removed—they itch abominably!" She scowled and pulled a long straw from a vase of flowers on the bedside table. Frowning with concentration, she poked the straw down between flesh and cast. "This helps sometimes, but other times it just makes it worse, by tickling."

"And your arm?"

Maris looked to Evan for the answer.

"Don't put me on the spot, Maris," he said. "You know as much as I do about it. I think your arm is healing properly, and there hasn't been any more infection. As for your legs—you'll be able to scratch them to your heart's content in a day or two."

Maris gave a small bounce of joy, then caught her breath. She turned pale and swallowed hard.

Frowning, Evan stepped toward the bed. "What happened? What hurt you?"

"Nothing," Maris said quickly. "Nothing. I just felt a . . . a little sick, that's all. I must have jarred my arm."

Evan nodded, but he did not look satisfied. "I'll make tea," he said, and left the two women alone together.

"Now I want your news," Maris said. "You know mine. Evan has been wonderful, but healing takes so much time, and I've felt so dreadfully cut off here."

"It is a distant place," S'Rella agreed. "And cold." Southerners thought the whole of the world was cold, outside their own archipelago. Maris grinned—it was an old joke between them—and clasped S'Rella's hand.

"Where shall I begin?" S'Rella asked. "Good news or bad? Gossip or politics? You're the one who's bed-bound, Maris. What would you like to know?"

"Everything," Maris said, "but you can begin by telling me about your daughters."

S'Rella smiled. "S'Rena has decided to marry Arno, the boy who has the meat-pie concession on the docks of Garr. She has the only fruit-pie stand, of course, and they've decided to combine their businesses and corner the waterfront pie market."

Maris laughed. "It seems a very sensible arrangement."

S'Rella sighed. "Oh, yes, a marriage of convenience, all very businesslike. There's not a speck of romance in her soul—sometimes I can hardly believe S'Rena is my daughter."

"Marissa has enough romanticism for two. How is she?"

"Oh, wandering. In love with a singer. I haven't heard from her in a month."

Evan brought in two steaming mugs of tea, his own special brew, fragrant with white blossoms, and then discreetly vanished.

"Any news from the Eyrie?" Maris asked.

"A little, but none of it good. Jamis vanished on a flight from Geer to Little Shotan. The flyers fear him lost at sea."

"Oh," Maris said, "I'm sorry. I never knew him well, but he was said to be a good flyer. His father presided over the flyers' Council, back when we adopted the academy system."

S'Rella nodded. "Lori of Varon gave birth," she continued, "but the child was sickly, and died within the week. She's distraught; Garret too, of course. And T'katin's brother was killed in a storm. He captained a trading ship, you know. They say the storm took the whole fleet. These are hard times, Maris. I've heard they are warring again on Lomarron."

"They may be warring on Thayos too, before very long," Maris said gloomily. "Don't you have any cheerful news?"

S'Rella shook her head. "The Eyrie was not a cheerful place. I got the feeling I was not terribly welcome. One-wings never go there, but there I was, violating the last sanctuary of the flyer-born. It made them all uneasy, though Corina and a few others tried to be polite."

Maris nodded. It was an old story. Tensions between the flyers born to wings and the one-wings who had taken theirs in competition had been growing for years. Each year saw more land-bound take to the air, and the old flyer families felt more threatened. "How is Val?" she asked.

"Val is Val," S'Rella said. "Richer than ever, but otherwise he doesn't change. The last time I visited Seatooth, he was wearing a belt of linked metal. I can't imagine what it cost. He works with the Woodwingers a lot. They all look up to him. The rest of the time he spends partying in Stormtown with Athen and Damen and Ro and the rest of his one-wing cronies. I hear he's taken up with a land-bound woman on Poweet, but I don't think he's bothered to tell Cara. I tried to scold him about it, but you know how self-righteous Val can get . . ."

Maris smiled. "Ah, yes," she said. She sipped at her tea as S'Rella continued, the talk ranging all over Windhaven. They gossiped about other flyers, spoke of friends and family and places where they both had been, continuing a long-running, far-ranging conversation. Maris felt comfortable, happy and relaxed. Her captivity would not last much longer—she would be walking again in a matter of days, and then she could begin to exercise and work out, to get back in flying trim—and S'Rella, her closest friend, was now beside her to remind her of her real life that waited beyond these thick walls, and to help her back into it.

A few hours later Evan joined them with plates of cheese and fruit, freshly baked herb bread and eggs scrambled with wild onions and peppers. They all sat on the big bed and ate hungrily. Conversation, or new hope, had given Maris a ravenous appetite.

The conversation turned to politics. "Will there really be war here?" S'Rella asked. "What's the cause?"

"A rock," Evan grumbled. "A rock barely a half-mile across and two miles long. It doesn't even have a name. It sits square in the Tharin Strait between Thayos and Thrane, and everyone thought it was worthless. Only now they've found iron on it. It was a party from Thrane that found the ore and began working it, and they aren't about to give up their claim, but the rock is marginally closer to Thayos than it is to Thrane, so our Landsman is trying to grab it. He sent a dozen landsguard to seize the mine, but they were beaten off, and now Thrane is fortifying the rock."

"Thayos doesn't seem to have a strong claim," S'Rella said. "Will your Landsman really go to war over it?"

Evan sighed. "I wish I thought otherwise. But the Landsman of Thayos is a belligerent man, and a greedy one. He beat Thrane once before, in a fishing dispute, and he's certain he can do it again. He'd rather kill any number of people than compromise."

"The message I was to fly to Thrane was full of threats," Maris offered. "I'm surprised war hasn't broken out already."

"Both islands are gathering allies, arms, and promises," Evan said. "I am told flyers come and go from the keep every day. No doubt the Landsman will press a threat or two on you, S'Rella, when you leave. Our own flyers, Tya and Jem, haven't had a day's rest for the past month. Jem has carried most of the messages back and forth across the Strait, and Tya has carried offers and promises to dozens of potential allies. Luckily, none of them seem interested. Time after time she has come back with refusals. I think it is only that keeping the war at bay." He sighed again. "But it is only a matter of time," he said, his voice weary. "And there will be much killing before it is all over. I'll be called in to patch up those who can be patched up. It's a mockery—a healer in wartime treats the symptoms without being allowed to talk about healing the actual cause, the war itself, unless he wants to be locked up as a traitor."

"I suppose I should be relieved to be out of it," Maris said. But her voice was reluctant. She didn't feel as Evan did about war; flyers stayed above such conflicts, just as they skimmed above the treacherous sea. They were neutrals, never to be harmed. Objectively war was a thing to be regretted, but war had never touched Maris or any of those she had loved, and she could not feel the horror of it deeply. "When I was younger, I could learn a message without ever hearing it, really. I seem to have lost the talent. Some of the words I've carried have taken the joy out of flight."

"I know," S'Rella agreed. "I've seen the results of some messages I've flown, and sometimes I feel very guilty."

"Don't," Maris said. "You are a flyer. You aren't responsible."

"Val disagrees, you know," S'Rella said. "I argued it with him once. He thinks we are responsible."

"That's understandable," Maris said.

S'Rella frowned at her, uncomprehending. "Why?"

"I'm surprised he never told you," Maris said. "His father was hanged. A flyer carried the order for the execution from Lomarron to South Arren. Arak, in fact. You remember Arak?"

"Too well," S'Rella said. "Val always suspected Arak was behind that beating he got. I remember how angry he was when he couldn't find his assailants to prove anything." She smiled wryly. "I also remember the party he threw on Seatooth when Arak died, black cake and all."

Evan was looking at the two women thoughtfully. "Why do you carry messages if you feel guilty about them?" he asked S'Rella.

"Why, because I'm a flyer," S'Rella said. "It's my job. It's what I do. The responsibility comes with the wings."

"I suppose," Evan said. He stood and began collecting the empty plates. "I don't think I could take that attitude, frankly. But I'm a land-bound, not a flyer. I wasn't born to wings."

"Nor were we," Maris started to say, but Evan left the room. She felt a flash of annoyance, but S'Rella began to talk again; Maris was drawn back into the conversation, and it wasn't very long until she had forgotten what she was annoyed about.

At last it was time for the casts to be cut off. Her legs were to be freed, and Evan promised that it would not be much longer for her arm.

Maris cried out at the sight of her legs. They were so thin and pale, so odd-looking. Evan began to massage them gently, washing them with a warm, herb-scented solution, and gently, skillfully kneading the long-unused muscles. Maris sighed with pleasure and relaxed.

When at last Evan had done, and he rose and put away the bowl and cloth, Maris thought she would burst with impatience. "Can I walk?" she asked.

Evan looked at her, grinning. "Can you?"

Her heart lifted at the challenge, and she sat up and slipped her legs over the edge of the bed. S'Rella offered her support, but Maris shook her head slightly, motioning her friend away.

Then she stood. On her own two feet, without support. But there was something wrong. She felt dizzy and sick. She said nothing but her face gave her away.

Evan and S'Rella moved closer. "What's wrong?" Evan asked.

"I, I must have stood up too fast." She was sweating, and afraid to move, afraid she would fall or faint or throw up.

"Take it easy," Evan said. "There's no rush." His voice was warm and soothing, and he took her good arm. S'Rella offered support on her left side. This time Maris did not shake them off or try to move alone.

"One step at a time," said Evan.

Leaning on them, guided by them, Maris took her first few steps. She felt mildly nauseated still, and strangely disoriented. But she also felt triumphant. Her legs were working again!

"Can I walk by myself now?"

"I don't know why not."

Maris took her first unsupported step, and then her second. Her spirits lifted. It was easy! Her legs were as good as ever. Trying to ignore the uneasiness in her stomach, Maris took her third step, and the room tilted sideways.

Her arms flailed and she stumbled, seeking level ground in the suddenly shifting room, and then Evan caught hold of her.

"NO!" she cried. "I can do it—"

He helped her back on her feet and steadied her.

"Let me go, please." Maris drew a shaky hand across her face and looked around. The room was calm and still, the floor as flat as it had ever been. Her legs held up firmly. She took a deep breath and began to walk again.

The floor suddenly slipped out from under her feet, and would have hit her in the face had not Evan caught her again.

"S'Rella—hand me the basin," he said.

"I'm fine—I can walk—let me do it—" But then she couldn't speak, because she had to throw up, and blessedly S'Rella was holding a basin before her face.

Afterward, shaky but feeling better, Maris walked back to the bed with Evan's guidance.

"What's wrong?" Maris asked him.

He shook his head, but he looked uneasy. "Maybe just too much exertion too soon," he said. He turned away. "I have to go now and tend a colicky baby. I'll be back in an hour or so—don't try to get up until I return."

•   •   •

She was elated when Evan removed the cast from her arm; over-joyed that the arm proved whole and strong, with no permanent damage. She knew she would have to work hard at building up the muscles before she could fly again, but the idea of long, hard hours of exercise excited rather than dismayed her after so much time spent doing nothing.

Too soon, S'Rella announced that she had to leave. A runner had come from the Landsman of Thayos. "He has an urgent mes-sage for North Arren," she told Maris and Evan, making a disgusted face, "and his own flyers are off on other missions. But it is time I left anyway. I must get back to Veleth."

They were gathered around the rough wooden table in Evan's kitchen, drinking tea and eating bread and butter as a farewell breakfast. Maris reached across the table and took S'Rella by the hand. "I'll miss you," she said, "but I'm glad you came."

"I'll return as soon as I can," S'Rella said, "though I expect they'll keep me busy. Anyway, I'll spread the word about your re-covery. Your friends will be relieved to hear."

"Maris hasn't entirely recovered," Evan said quietly.

"Oh, that's only a matter of time," Maris said cheerfully. "By the time everyone hears from S'Rella, I'll probably be flying again." She didn't understand Evan's gloom; she had expected his spirits to lighten with her own when her arm came out of the cast. "I may meet you in the sky before you get back here!"

Evan looked at S'Rella. "I'll walk you to the road," he volun-teered.

"You needn't bother," she said. "I know my way."

"I'd like to see you off."

Maris stiffened at something undefined in his tone. "Say it here," she said quietly. "Whatever it is, you may as well tell me."

"I've never lied to you, Maris," Evan said. He sighed, and his shoulders slumped, and Maris suddenly saw him as an old man.

Evan leaned back in his chair, but looked steadily into Maris' eyes. "Haven't you wondered about the dizziness you feel when you stand or sit or turn too suddenly?"

"I'm still weak. I have to be careful. That's all," Maris said, al-ready defensive. "My limbs are sound."

"Yes, yes, we need have no worries about your legs, or your arm. But there is something else wrong with you, something that can't be reset, splinted and allowed to heal. I think something happened when you hit your head on the rock. There was some damage inside, to your brain. It affected your sense of balance, your depth perception, perhaps your vision. I'm not sure what exactly. I know so little—no one knows much . . ."

"There's nothing wrong with me," Maris said in a reasonable tone of voice. "I was dizzy and weak at first, but I'm getting better. I can walk now—you have to admit that—and I'll be able to fly again."

"You are learning to adjust, to compensate, that's all," Evan said. "But your sense of balance was affected. You will probably learn to adjust to life on the ground. But in the air—an ability you need in the air may be gone now. I don't think you can learn to fly without it. So much depends on your sense of balance—"

"What do you know about flying? How can you tell me what I need to fly?" Her voice was as hard and cold as ice.

"Maris," whispered S'Rella. She tried to catch Maris' hand, but the injured woman pulled away.

"I don't believe you," Maris said. "There's nothing wrong with me that won't heal. I will fly again. I am just a little sick, that's all. Why should you assume the worst? Why should I?"

Evan sat still, thinking. Then he rose and went to the corner by the back door, where the firewood was kept. Separate from the logs and kindling were some long, flat boards, leftover lumber that Evan cut up to use as splints. He selected one about six feet long, seven inches wide, and two inches thick, and laid it down on the bare boards of the kitchen floor.

He straightened up and looked at Maris. "Can you walk along this?"

Maris raised her eyebrows in mocking surprise. Absurdly, her stomach was tight with nerves. Of course she could do it; she couldn't imagine failing such a test.

She rose from her chair slowly, one hand gripping the table edge. She walked across the floor smoothly, not too slowly. The floor did not slip or buckle beneath her as it had that first day. Absurd to say there was anything wrong with her sense of balance; she wouldn't fall on level ground, and she wouldn't fall from a two-inch height.

"Shall I hop on one foot?" she asked Evan.

"Just walk along it normally."

Maris stepped upon the plank. It wasn't quite wide enough to stand normally, feet side by side, so she had to take a second step at once, with no time for consideration. She remembered high cliff ledges she had skipped along as a child, some with paths narrower than this board.

The board wobbled and shifted beneath her feet. Despite herself, Maris cried out as she felt herself falling to one side. Evan caught her.

"You made the board move!" she said in sudden fury. But the words sounded petulant and childish in her ears. Evan only looked at her. Maris tried to calm herself. "I'm sorry," she said. "I didn't mean that. Let me try again."

Silently, he let go of her and stepped back.

Tense now, Maris stepped up again and walked three steps. She began to waver. One foot went over the side onto the floor. She cursed and pulled it back, and took another step, and felt the board shift again. Again she missed it. She lifted her foot back onto the board and took another step forward, and lurched to one side, falling.

Evan did not catch her that time. She hit the floor on hands and knees and jumped up, her head spinning from the exertion.

"Maris, enough." Evan's firm, gentle hands were on her, pulling her away from the treacherous plank. Maris could hear S'Rella weeping softly.

"All right," Maris said. She tried to keep the anguish out of her voice. "There's something wrong. All right. I admit it. But I'm still healing. Give me time. I will get well. I will fly again."

In the morning, Maris began exercising in earnest. Evan brought her a set of stone weights, and she began working out regularly. She was dismayed to find that both her arms, not merely the injured one, were sadly weakened by her time of enforced idleness.

Determined to test the air again as soon as possible, Maris had her wings taken to the keep, to the Landsman's own metalsmith, for repair. The woman was busy with preparations for the impending war, but a flyer's request was never to be ignored, and she promised to have the damaged struts straightened and restored within a week. She was true to her word.

Maris checked out her wings carefully on the day they were returned, folding and unfolding each strut in turn, scanning the fabric to make sure it was taut and firmly mounted. Her hands fell to the task as if they had never stopped doing it; they were a flyer's hands, and there was nothing in all the world they knew how to do better than tend a pair of wings. Almost Maris was tempted to strap on the wings and make the long walk to the flyers' cliff. Almost, but not quite. Her balance had not yet come to her, she thought, though she was steadier on her feet now. Every night, surreptitiously, she gave herself the plank test. She had not yet passed it, but she was improving. She was not yet ready for wings, but soon, soon.

When she was not working, sometimes she walked with Evan in the forest, when he went abroad to gather herbs or tend to other patients. He taught her the names of the plants he used in his work, and explained what each herb was good for, and when and how to use it. He showed her all manner of animals as well; the beasts of the chilly Eastern forests were not at all like the familiar denizens of Lesser Amberly's tame woods, and Maris found them fascinating. Evan seemed so at home in the forest that the creatures did not fear him. Strange white crows with scarlet eyes accepted breadcrumbs from his fingers, and he knew the hidden entrances to the tunnel-monkey lairs that honeycombed the wild, and once he caught her arm and pointed out a hooded torturer, gliding sensuously from limb to limb in pursuit of some unseen prey.

Maris told him stories of her adventures in the sky and on other islands. She had been flying for more than forty years, and her head was full of wonders. She told him of life on Lesser Amberly, of Stormtown with its windmills and its wharves, of the vast blue-white glaciers of Artellia and the fire mountains of the Embers. She talked of the loneliness of the Outer Islands, hard up against the

Endless Ocean to the east, and the fellowship that had once thrived on the Eyrie before flyers had divided into factions.

Neither ever spoke of what lay between them, dividing them. Evan did not contradict Maris when she spoke of flying, nor did he mention any invisible damage to her head. The subject was like a patch of dangerous ground, no wider than a wooden plank, upon which neither was willing to step. Maris kept her occasional dizzy spells to herself.

One day as they stepped outside Evan's house, Maris stopped him from turning deeper into the forest. "All those trees make me feel like I'm still inside," she complained. "I need to see the sky, to smell clean, open air. How far away is the sea?"

Evan gestured to the north. "About two miles that way. You can see where the trees begin to thin."

Maris grinned at him. "You sound reluctant. Do you feel sad when there aren't any trees around? You don't have to come if you can't bear it—but I don't understand how you can breathe in that forest. It's too dim and close. Nothing to smell but dirt and rot and leaf-mold."

"Wonderful smells," Evan said, smiling back. They began to walk toward the north. "The sea is too cold and empty and big for my tastes. I feel comfortable and at home in my forest."

"Ah, Evan, we're so different, you and I!" She touched his arm and grinned at him, somehow pleased by the contrast. She threw her head back and sniffed the air. "Yes, I can smell the sea already!"

"You could smell it on my doorstep—you can smell the sea all over Thayos," Evan pointed out.

"The forest disguised it." Maris felt her heart lightening with the thinning of the forest. All her life had been spent beside the sea, or over it. She had felt the lack every morning waking in Evan's house, missing the pounding of the waves and the sharp salt smell, but most of all missing the sight of that vast, gray immensity, beneath an equally immense and turbulent sky.

The tree line ended abruptly, and the rocky cliffs began. Maris broke into a run. She stopped on the cliff's edge, breathing hard, and gazed out over the sea and the sky.

The sky was indigo, filled with rapidly scudding gray clouds. The wind was relatively gentle at this height, but Maris could tell from the patient circling of a pair of scavenger kites that up higher the flying was still good. Not a day for rushing urgent messages, perhaps, but a good day for playing, for swooping and diving and laughing in the cool air.

She heard Evan approaching. "You can't tell me that's not beautiful," she said, without turning. She took another step closer to the edge of the cliff and looked down . . . and felt the world drop beneath her.

She gasped for breath and her arms flailed, seeking some solidity, and she was falling, falling, falling, and even Evan's arms wrapped tight around her could not draw her back to safety.

It stormed all the next day. Maris spent the day inside, lost in depression, thinking of what had happened on the cliffs. She did not exercise. She ate listlessly, and had to force herself to tend to her wings. Evan watched her in silence, frowning often.

The rain continued the following day, but the worst of the storm was past, and the downpour grew more gentle. Evan announced that he was going out. "There are some things I need from Port Thayos," he said, "herbs that do not grow here. A trader came in last week, I understand. Perhaps I will be able to replenish my stores."

"Perhaps," Maris said evenly. She was tired, though she had done nothing this morning except eat breakfast. She felt old.

"Would you like to walk with me? You have never seen Port Thayos."

"No," Maris said. "I don't feel up to it just now. I'll spend the day here."

Evan frowned, but reached for his heavy raincloak nonetheless. "Very well," he said. "I will be back before dark."

But it was well after dark when the healer finally returned, carrying a basket full of bottled herbs. The rain had finally stopped. Maris had begun to worry about him when the sun went down. "You're late," she said when he entered, and shook the rain from his cloak. "Are you all right?"

He was smiling; Maris had never seen him quite so happy. "News, good news," he said. "The port is full of it. There will be no war. The Landsmen of Thayos and Thrane have agreed to a personal meeting on that accursed rock, to work out a compromise about mining rights!"

"No war," Maris said, a little dully. "Good, good. Odd, though. How did it happen?"

Evan started a fire and began to make some tea. "Oh, it was all happenstance," he said. "Tya returned from another mission, bearing nothing. Our Landsman was rebuffed on all sides. Without allies, he did not feel strong enough to press his claims. He is furious, I'm told, but what can he do? Nothing. So he sent Jem to Thrane to set up a meeting, to haggle out whatever settlement he can. Anything is better than nothing. I would have thought he'd find support on Cheslin or Thrynel, particularly if he offered them a large enough share of the iron. And certainly there is no love lost between Thrane and the Arrens." Evan laughed. "Ah, what does it matter? The war is off. Port Thayos is giddy with relief, except for a few landsguard who'd hoped to weigh down their pockets with iron. Everyone is celebrating, and we should celebrate too."

Evan went to his basket and rummaged among the herbs, pulling out a large moonfish. "I thought perhaps seafood would cheer you up," he said. "I know a way of cooking this with dandyweed and bitternuts that will make your tongue sing." He found a long bone knife, and began to scale the fish, whistling happily as he worked, and his mood was so infectious that Maris found herself smiling too.

There was a loud knocking at the door.

Evan looked up, scowling. "An emergency, no doubt," he said, cursing. "Answer it if you would, Maris. My hands are full of fish."

The girl standing in the door wore a dark green uniform, trimmed with gray fur; a landsguard, and one of the Landsman's runners. "Maris of Lesser Amberly?" she asked.

"Yes," Maris said.

The girl nodded. "The Landsman of Thayos sends his greetings, and invites you and the healer Evan to honor him at dinner tomorrow night. If your health permits it."

"My health permits it," Maris snapped. "Why are we suddenly so honored, child?"

The runner had a seriousness beyond her years. "The Landsman honors all flyers, and your injury in his service has weighed heavily on him. He wishes to show his gratitude to all the flyers who have flown for Thayos, however briefly, in the emergency just past."

"Oh," Maris said. She still was not satisfied. The Landsman of Thayos had not struck her as the type who cared much about expressing gratitude. "Is that all?"

The girl hesitated. Briefly her detachment left her, and Maris saw that she was indeed very young. "It is not part of the message, flyer, but . . ."

"Yes?" Maris prompted. Evan had stopped his work to stand behind her.

"Late this afternoon, a flyer arrived, with a message for the Landsman's ears only. He received her in private chambers. She was from Western, I think. She dressed funny, and her hair was too short."

"Describe her, if you can," Maris said. She took a copper coin from a pocket and let her fingers play with it.

The girl looked at the coin and smiled. "Oh, she was a Westerner, young—twenty or twenty-five. Her hair was black, cut just like yours. She was very pretty. I don't think I've ever seen anyone as pretty. She had a nice smile, I thought, but the lodge men didn't like her. They said she didn't even bother thanking them for their help. Green eyes. She was wearing a choker. Three strands of colored sea-glass. Is that enough?"

"Yes," Maris said. "You're very observant." She gave the girl the coin.

"You know her?" Evan asked. "This flyer?"

Maris nodded. "I've known her since the day she was born. I know her parents as well."

"Who is she?" he demanded, impatiently.

"Corina," said Maris, "of Lesser Amberly."

The runner remained at the door. Maris glanced back at her. "Yes?" she asked. "Is there more? We accept the invitation, of course. You may give the Landsman our thanks."

"There's more," the girl blurted. "I forgot. The Landsman said, most respectfully, that you are requested to bring your wings, if that would not put too great a burden on your health."

"Of course," Maris said numbly. "Of course."

She closed the door.

The keep of the Landsman of Thayos was a grim, martial place that lay well away from the island's towns and villages in a narrow, secluded valley of its own. It was close to the sea, but shielded from it by a solid wall of mountains. By land, only two roads gave approach, and both were fortified by landsguard. A stone watchtower stood atop the tallest peak, a high sentinel for all the paths leading to the keep.

The fortress itself was old and stern, built of great blocks of weathered black stone. Its back was to the mountain, and Maris knew from her last visit that much of it lay underground, in chambers chiseled from solid rock. Its exterior face showed a double set of wide walls—landsguard armed with longbows walked patrol on the parapets—ringing a cluster of wooden buildings and two black towers, the taller of which was almost fifty feet high. Stout wooden bars closed off the tower windows. The valley, so close to the sea, was damp and cold. The only ground cover was a tenacious violet lichen, and a blue-green moss that clung to the underside of boulders and half-covered the walls of the keep.

Coming up the road from Thossi, Maris and Evan were stopped once at the valley checkpoint, passed, stopped again at the outer wall, and finally admitted to the keep. They might have been detained longer, but Maris was carrying her bright silver wings, and landsguard did not trifle with flyers. The inner courtyard was full of activity—children playing with great shaggy dogs, fierce-looking pigs running everywhere, landsguard drilling with bow and club. A gibbet had been built against one wall, its wood cracked and well-weathered. The children played all about it, and one of them was using a noose as a swing. The other two nooses hung empty, twisting ominously in the chill wind of evening.

"This place oppresses me," Maris told Evan. "The Landsman of

Lesser Amberly lives in a huge wooden manor on a hill overlooking the town. It has twenty guest rooms, and a tremendous banquet hall, and wonderful windows of colored glass, and a beacon tower for summoning flyers—but it has no walls, and no guards, and no gibbets."

"The Landsman of Lesser Amberly is chosen by the people," Evan said. "The Landsman of Thayos is from a line that has ruled here since the days of the star sailors. And you forget, Maris, that Eastern is not as gentle a land as Western. Winter lasts longer here. Our storms are colder and fiercer. Our soil has more metal, but it is not so good for growing things as the soil in the West. Famine and war are never very far away on Thayos."

They passed through a massive gate, down into the interior of the keep, and Maris fell silent.

The Landsman met them in his private reception chamber, seated on a plain wooden throne and flanked by two sour-faced landsguard. But he rose when they entered; Landsmen and flyers were equal. "I'm pleased you could accept my invitation, flyer," he said. "There was some concern about your health."

Despite the polite words, Maris did not like him. The Landsman was a tall, well-proportioned man with regular, almost handsome, features, his gray hair worn long and knotted behind his head in the Eastern fashion. But there was something disturbing about his manner, and he had a puffiness around his eyes, and a twitch at the corner of his mouth that his full beard did not quite conceal. His dress was rich and somber; thick blue-gray cloth trimmed with black fur, thigh-high boots, a wide leather belt inlaid with iron and silver and gemstones. And he wore a small metal dagger.

"I appreciate your concern," Maris replied. "I was badly injured, but I have recovered my health now. You have a great treasure here on Thayos in Evan. I have met many healers, but few as skilled as he."

The Landsman sank back into his chair. "He will be well rewarded," he said, as if Evan was not even present. "Good work deserves a good reward, eh?"

"I will pay Evan myself," Maris said. "I have sufficient iron."

"No," the Landsman insisted. "Your near-death in my service gave me great distress. Let me show my gratitude."

"I pay my own debts," Maris said.

The Landsman's face grew cold. "Very well," he said. "There is another matter we must discuss, then. But let it wait for dinner. Your walk must have left you hungry." He stood up abruptly. "Come, then. You'll find I set a good table, flyer. I doubt you've ever had better."

As it turned out, Maris had eaten better on countless occasions. The food was plentiful, but badly prepared. The fish soup was far too salty, the bread was hard and dry, and the meat courses had all been boiled until even the memory of taste had fled. Even the beer tasted sour to her.

They ate in a dim, damp banquet hall, at a long table set for twenty. Evan, looking desperately uncomfortable, was placed well down the table, among several landsguard officers and the Landsman's younger children. Maris occupied a position of honor at the Landsman's side next to his heir, a sharp-faced, sullen woman who did not speak three words during the entire meal. Across from her the other flyers were seated. Closest to the Landsman was a weary gray-faced man with a bulbous nose; Maris recognized him vaguely from past encounters as the flyer Jem. Third down was Corina of Lesser Amberly. She smiled at Maris across the table. Corina *was* terribly pretty, Maris thought, remembering what the runner had said. But then her father, Corm, had always been handsome.

"You look well, Maris," Corina said. "I'm glad. We were very worried about you."

"I am well," Maris said. "I hope to be flying again soon."

A shadow passed across Corina's pretty face. "Maris . . . ," she started. Then she thought better. "I hope so," she finished weakly. "Everyone asks about you. We'd like you home again." She looked down and occupied herself with her meal.

Between Jem and Corina sat the third flyer, a young woman strange to Maris. After an abortive attempt to start a conversation with the Landsman's daughter, Maris fell to studying the stranger over her food. She was the same age as Corina, but the contrast between the two women was marked. Corina was vibrant and beautiful; dark hair, clean healthy skin, green eyes sparkling and alive, and an air of confidence and easy sophistication. A flyer, daughter of two flyers, born and raised to the privileges and traditions that went with the wings.

The woman next to her was thin, though she had a look of stubborn strength about her. Pockmarks covered her hollow cheeks, and her pale blond hair was knotted in an awkward lump behind her head and pulled back in such a way as to make her forehead seem abnormally high. When she smiled, Maris saw that her teeth were crooked and discolored.

"You're Tya, aren't you?" she said.

The woman regarded her with shrewd black eyes. "I am." Her voice was startlingly pleasant; cool and soft, with a faint ironic undertone.

"I don't think we've ever met," Maris said. "Have you been flying long?"

"I won my wings two years ago, on North Arren."

Maris nodded. "I missed that one. I think I was on a mission to Artellia. Have you ever flown to Western?"

"Three times," Tya replied. "Twice to Big Shotan and once to Culhall. Never to the Amberlys. Most of my flying has been in Eastern, especially these days." She gave her Landsman a quick sharp glance from the corner of her eyes, and smiled a conspiratorial smile at Maris.

Corina, who had been listening, tried to be polite. "What did you think of Stormtown?" she asked. "And the Eyrie? Did you visit the Eyrie?"

Tya smiled tolerantly. "I'm a one-wing," she said. "I trained at Airhome. We don't go to your Eyrie, flyer. As to Stormtown, it was impressive. There's no city like it in Eastern."

Corina flushed. Maris was briefly annoyed. The friction between flyers born to wings and the upstart one-wings depressed her; the skies of Windhaven were not the friendly place they had once been, and much of that was her doing. "The Eyrie isn't such a bad place, Tya," she said. "I've made a lot of friends there."

"You're not a one-wing," Tya said.

"Oh? Val One-Wing himself once told me I was the *first* one-wing, whether I admitted it or not."

Tya looked at her speculatively. "No," she said finally. "No, that isn't right. You're different, Maris. Not one of the old flyers, but not a one-wing either. I don't know what you are. It must be lonely, though."

They finished the meal in a strained, awkward silence.

When the dessert cups had been cleared away, the Landsman dismissed family, counselors, and landsguard, so only the four flyers and Evan remained. He tried to dismiss Evan as well, but the healer would not go. "Maris is still in my care," he said. "I stay with my patient." The Landsman gave him an angry stare, but elected not to press the point.

"Very well," he snapped. "We have business to discuss. Flyer business." He turned his hot eyes on Maris. "I will be direct. I have received a message from my colleague, the Landsman of Lesser Amberly. He inquires after your health. Your wings are needed. When will you be well enough to return to Amberly?"

"I don't know," Maris said. "You can see that I've recovered. But the flight from Thayos to Amberly is taxing for any flyer, and I do not have my full strength back yet. I will depart Thayos as soon as I can."

"A long flight," the flyer Jem agreed, "especially for one who does not make even short flights."

"Yes," the Landsman said. "You and the healer have done a lot of walking. You seem healthy again. Your wings are repaired, I am told. Yet you do not fly. You have never come to the flyers' cliff. You do not practice. Why?"

"I am not ready," Maris said.

"Landsman," said Jem, "it is as I told you. She has not recovered, no matter how it seems. If she were able, she would be flying." He shifted his gaze to her. "I'm sorry if I hurt you," he said, "but you know I speak the truth. I am a flyer too. I know. A flyer *flies*. There is no way to keep a healthy flyer on the ground. And you, you are no ordinary flyer—they used to tell me that you loved flying above all else."

"I did," said Maris. "I do."

"Landsman . . ." Evan began.

Maris turned her head to look at him. "No, Evan," she said, "the burden isn't yours. I will tell them." She faced the Landsman again. "I am not entirely recovered," she admitted. "My balance . . . there is something wrong with my balance. But it is healing. It is not so bad as it once was."

"I'm sorry," Tya said quickly. Jem nodded.

"Oh, *Maris*," Corina said. She looked grief-stricken, suddenly close to tears. Corina had none of her father's malice, and she knew what balance meant to a flyer.

"Can you fly?" the Landsman said.

"I don't know," Maris admitted. "I need more time."

"You have had time enough," he said. He turned to Evan. "Healer, can you tell me that she will recover?"

"No," Evan said sadly. "I cannot tell you that. I do not know."

The Landsman scowled. "This affair belongs to the Landsman of Lesser Amberly, but the burden is on me. And I say that a flyer who cannot fly is no flyer at all, and has no need of wings. If your recovery is that uncertain, only a fool would wait for it. I ask you again, Maris—can you fly?"

His eyes were fixed on her, and the corner of his mouth moved in a malicious little twitch, and Maris knew she had run out of time. "I can fly," she said.

"Good," the Landsman said. "Tonight is as good as any other time. You say you can fly. Very well. Get your wings. Show us."

The walk through the damp, dripping tunnel was as long as Maris remembered it, and as lonely, though this time she had company. No one talked. The only sound was the echo of their footsteps. Two landsguard walked ahead of the party with torches. The flyers wore their wings.

It was a cold, starry night on the far side of the mountain. The sea moved restlessly below them, a vast, dark, melancholy presence. Maris climbed the stairs to the flyers' cliff. She climbed slowly, and when she reached the top her thighs ached and her breathing was labored.

Evan took her hand briefly. "Can I persuade you not to fly?"

"No," she said.

He nodded. "I thought not. Fly well, then." He kissed her, and stepped away.

The Landsman stood against the cliff, flanked by his landsguard. Tya and Jem unfolded her wings. Corina hung back until Maris called to her. "I'm not angry," Maris said. "This is not your doing. A flyer isn't responsible for the messages she bears."

"Thank you," Corina said. Her small, pretty face was pale in the starlight.

"If I fail, you are to bring my wings back to Amberly, yes?"

Corina nodded reluctantly.

"Do you know what the Landsman intends to do with them?"

"He will find a new flyer, perhaps someone who has lost his wings by challenge. Until someone is found . . . well, Mother is ill, but Father is still fit enough to fly."

Maris laughed lightly. "There's a wonderful irony in that. Corm has always wanted my wings—but I'm going to do my best to keep them from him once again."

Corina smiled.

Her wings were fully extended; Maris could feel the familiar, insistent push of the wind against them. She checked her straps and struts, motioned Corina out of her way, and walked to the brink of the precipice. There she steadied herself and looked down.

The world reeled dizzily, drunkenly. Far below, breakers crashed against black rocks, sea and stone locked in eternal war. She swallowed hard, and tried to keep from lurching off the cliff. Slowly the world grew solid and steady again. No motion. It was just a cliff, like any other cliff, and below the endless ocean. The sky was her friend, her lover.

Maris flexed her arms, and took the wing-grips in hand. Then she took a deep breath and leaped.

Her kick sent her clean away from the cliff, and the wind grabbed her, supporting her. It was a cold, strong wind; a wind that cut through to the bone, but not an angry wind, no, an easy wind to fly. She relaxed and gave herself to it, and she glided down and around in a long graceful curve.

But the current pushed around again toward the mountain, and Maris glimpsed the Landsman and the other flyers waiting there—Jem had unfolded his own wings and was preparing to launch—before she decided to turn away from them. She twisted her body, tried to bank.

The sky lurched and turned fluid on her. She banked too far, stalled, and when she tried to correct by throwing her weight and strength back in the other direction, she tilted wildly. Her breath caught in her throat.

The feel was gone. Maris closed her eyes for an instant, and felt sick. She was falling, her body screamed at her. She was falling, her ears rang, and the feel was gone from her. She had always *known*: subtle changes in the wind, shifts she had to react to before she was half-aware of them, the taste of a building storm, the omens of still air. Now it was all gone. She flew through an endless empty ocean of air, feeling nothing, dizzy, and this strange savage wind she could not understand had her in its grasp.

Her great silver wings tilted back and forth wildly as her body shook, and Maris opened her eyes again, suddenly desperate. She steadied herself and tried to fly on vision alone. But the rocks *moved*, and it was too dark, and even the bright cold stars above seemed to dance and shift and mock her.

Vertigo reached up and swallowed her whole, and Maris released her wing-grips—she had never done that before, never—and now she was not flying, but only hanging beneath her wings. She doubled over in the straps, retching, and sent the Landsman's dinner down into the ocean. She was trembling violently.

Jem and Corina were both airborne and coming after her, Maris saw, but she did not care. She was weak, drained, old. There were boats below her, gliding across the black ocean. She took her wing-grips in hand again, tried to pull up, but all she accomplished was a sharp downwind turn that sheered into a plunge. She tried to correct, and couldn't.

She was crying.

The sea came up at her. Shimmering. Shifting.

Her ears hurt.

She could not fly. She was a flyer, had always been a flyer, windlover, Woodwinger, skychild, alone, home in the sky, flyer, flyer, *flyer*—and she could not fly.

She closed her eyes again, so the world would stand still.

With a slap and a spray of salt water, the sea took her. It has been waiting, she thought. All those years.

"Leave me alone," she said that night, when they finally returned to his home. Evan took her at her word.

Maris slept most of the next day.

The following day Maris woke early, when the ruddy light of dawn first broke across the room. She felt terrible, cold and sweaty, and a great weight pressed across her chest. For a moment, she could not think what was wrong. Then she remembered. Her wings were gone. She tried to think about it, and the despair welled up inside her, and the anger, and the self-pity, and soon she curled up under the blankets once again and tried to go back to sleep. When she slept, she did not have to face it.

But sleep would not take her. Finally she rose and dressed. Evan was in the next room, cooking eggs. "Hungry?" he asked her.

"No," Maris said dully.

Evan nodded, and cracked two more eggs. Maris sat at the table and, when he set a plate of eggs before her, she picked at them listlessly.

It was a wet, windy day, marked by frequent violent storms. When he had finished his breakfast, Evan went about his business. Near noon he left her, and Maris wandered aimlessly through the empty house. Finally she sat by the window and watched the rain.

Well after dark Evan returned, wet and dispirited. Maris was still sitting by the window, in a cold and darkened house. "You might at least have started a fire," Evan grumbled. His tone was disgusted.

"Oh," she said. She looked at him blankly. "I'm sorry. I didn't think."

Evan built the fire. Maris moved to help him, but he snapped at her and chased her out of the way. They ate in silence, but the food seemed to restore Evan's mood. Afterward he brewed some of his special tea, set a mug down in front of her, and settled into his favorite chair.

Maris tasted the steaming tea, conscious of Evan's eyes on her. Finally she looked up at him.

"How do you feel?" he asked her.

She thought about it. "I feel dead," she said, finally.

"Talk about it."

"I can't," she said. She began to weep. "I can't."

When the weeping would not stop, Evan fixed her a sleeping draught, and put her to bed.

The next day Maris went out.

She took a road that Evan had shown her, a well-worn path that led not to the cliffs but down to the sea itself, and she spent the day walking alone on a cold pebble beach that seemed endless. When she wearied, she rested at the water's edge and flung pebbles into the waves, taking a small, melancholy pleasure in the way they skipped, then sank.

Even the sea was different here, she thought. It was gray and cold, without highlights. She missed the flashing blues and greens of the waters around Amberly.

Tears ran down her cheeks and she did not bother to wipe them away. At times she became aware that she was sobbing, without remembering just when or why she had started to cry.

The sea was vast and lonely, the empty beach went on forever, and the wild, cloudy sky was all around, but Maris felt hemmed in, suffocated. She thought of all the places in the world that she would never see again, the memory of each one a fresh pain to her. She thought of the impressive ruins of the Old Fortress on Laus. She remembered Woodwings Academy, vast and dark, carved into the rock of Seatooth. The Temple of the Sky God on Deeth. The drafty castles of the flyer-princes of Artellia. The windmills of Stormtown, and the Old Captain's House, ancient beyond telling. The tree-towns of Setheen and Alessy, the boneyards and battlegrounds of Lomarron, the vineyards of the Amberlys, and Riesa's warm, smoky alehouse on Skulny. All lost to her now. And the Eyrie—ships might take her elsewhere, but the Eyrie was a flyer's place, now closed to her forever.

She thought of her friends, scattered over Windhaven like the many islands. Some of them might visit her, but so many others had been snatched out of her world as if they no longer existed. The last time she had seen him, T'mar had been fat and happy in his little stone house on Hethen, teaching his granddaughter to draw the beauty out of a lump of rock. Now he was as dead to her as Halland; a memory, nothing more. She would never see Reid again, nor his beautiful, laughing wife. Never again could she pass the night away drinking Riesa's ale and sharing memories of Garth. She'd buy no more wooden trinkets from S'mael, nor joke with the cook in that little inn on Poweet.

Never again would she watch the flying at the great annual competitions, or sit, gossiping and singing, among flyers at a party.

The memories cut her like a thousand knives, and Maris cried out her pain, sobbing until she could scarcely breathe. She knew how she must look: a ridiculous old woman, weeping and moaning alone on a beach. But she could not stop.

She could hardly bear to think of flying itself, of that great joy and freedom she had lost forever. The memories came of themselves, though: the world spread out beneath her, the joy of being winged, the thrill of running before a storm, the myriad colors of the sky, the magnificent solitude of the heights. All the things she could never see or feel again, except in memory. Once she had found a riser that took her halfway to infinity, up to the realms where the star sailors had moved, where the sea itself vanished below and nothing flew but the strange, ethereal wind wraiths. She would always remember that day, always.

The world grew dark around her, and the stars began to appear. The sound of the sea was everywhere. She was numb, chilled to the bone, emptied of tears, as she faced the emptiness of her life. Finally she began the long walk back to the cabin, turning her back on the sea and the sky.

The house was warm and filled with the rich aroma of stew. The sight of Evan standing by the fire made her heart beat faster. His blue eyes were infinitely tender when he spoke her name. She ran to him and flung her arms around him, holding tight, holding on for dear life. She closed her eyes against the dizziness.

"Maris," he said again. "Maris." He sounded pleased and surprised. His arms came up and held her even more closely, protectively. At last he led her to the table and set her dinner before her.

He spoke as they ate, telling her the events of his day. An adventure chasing the goat. Finding a bush of ripe silverberries. A special dessert he'd made for her.

She nodded, scarcely taking in the sense of what he said, but comforted by the sound of his voice, wanting it to continue. His words, his presence, told her the world had not utterly ended.

At last she interrupted him. "Evan, I have to know. This . . . injury I have. Is there any chance that it will ever heal? That I will be able . . . that I will recover?"

He set down his spoon, the animation gone out of his face at once. "Maris, I don't know. I don't think anyone could tell you if your condition is a passing thing, or permanent. I can't be sure."

"Your guess, then. Your best guess."

There was pain in his face. "No," he said quietly. "I don't think you'll recover fully. I don't think you can regain what you have lost."

She nodded, externally calm. "I understand." She pushed her food aside. "Thank you. I had to ask. Somewhere, I was still hoping." She stood up.

"Maris . . ."

She motioned him back. "I'm tired. It's been a hard day for me and I have to think, Evan. There are decisions I must make now, and I need to be alone. I'm sorry." She forced a smile. "The stew was fine. I'm sorry to miss the dessert you made, but I'm not hungry."

The room was black and cold when Maris woke. The fire she had started had gone out. She sat up in bed and stared into the darkness. No more tears, she thought. That's over.

When she threw back the covers and stood up, the floor shifted under her feet and she lurched dizzily for an instant. She steadied herself, slipped into a short robe, and then walked to the kitchen where she lit a candle from the embers still smoldering in the hearth. The wooden floor was cold beneath her bare feet as she walked down the hall, past the workroom where Evan prepared his brews and ointments, past the empty bedrooms he kept for those who came to him.

When she opened his door Evan stirred, rolled over, and blinked at her.

"Maris?" he said, his voice thick with sleep. "What's wrong?"

"I don't want to be dead," she said.

Maris walked across the room and set the candle on the bedside table. Evan sat up and caught her hand. "I've done all I can for you as a healer," he said. "If you want my love . . . if you want me . . ."

She stopped his words with a kiss. "Yes," she said.

"My dear," he said, looking at her in the candlelight. The shadows made his face strange, and for a moment she felt awkward and frightened.

But the moment passed. He threw back his blankets, and she shrugged off her robe and climbed into bed with him. His arms went around her, and his hands were gentle, loving, and familiar, and his body was warm and full of life.

"Teach me to heal," Maris said the next morning. "I'd like to work with you."

Evan smiled. "Thank you very much," he said. "It's not that easy, you know. Why this sudden interest in the healing arts?"

She frowned. "I must do something, Evan. I have only one skill, flying, and that's lost to me now. I've never done anything else. I could take a ship back to Amberly, and live out the rest of my days in the house I inherited from my stepfather, doing nothing. I'd be provided for—even if I had nothing, the people of Amberly don't let their retired flyers end as paupers." She moved away from the breakfast table and began to pace.

"Or I could stay here, if there is something for me to do. If I don't find something to fill my days, something useful, my memories will drive me mad, Evan. I'm past my childbearing years—I decided against motherhood years ago. I can't sail a ship or carry a tune or build a house. The gardens I began always died, I'm hopeless at mending, and being cooped up in a shop, selling things all day, would drive me to drink."

"I see you've considered all the options," Evan said, the ghost of a smile about his lips.

"Yes, I have," Maris said seriously. "I don't know that I would have any skills as a healer—there is no reason for me to think so. But I'm willing to work hard, and I've got a flyer's memory. I wouldn't be likely to confuse poisons with healing potions. I can help you gather herbs, mix remedies, hold down your victims while you cut them up, or whatever. I've assisted at two births—I would do whatever you told me, whatever you needed another pair of hands for."

"I've worked alone for a long time, Maris. I have no patience with clumsiness, or ignorance, or mistakes."

Maris smiled at him. "Or opinions that contradict your own."

He laughed. "Yes. I suppose I could teach you, and I could use your help. But I don't know if I believe this 'I'll do whatever you say' of yours. You're starting a bit late in life to be a humble servant."

She looked at him, trying not to show the sudden panic she felt. If he refused her, what could she do? She felt like begging him to let her stay.

He must have seen something of this in her face, for he caught hold of her hand and held it tightly. "We'll try it," he said. "If you are willing to try to learn, I am surely willing to teach. It is time I passed some of my learning on to someone else, so that if I am bitten by a blue tick or seized with liar's fever, everything will not be lost by my death."

Maris smiled her relief. "How do we start?"

Evan thought a moment. "There are small villages and encampments in the forest that I haven't visited in half a year. We'll travel for a week or two, making the rounds, and you'll gain some idea of what I do, and we'll learn if you have the stomach for it." He released her hand and stood up, walking toward the storeroom. "Come help me pack."

Maris learned many things during her travels with Evan through the forest, few of them pleasant.

It was hard work. Evan, so patient a healer, was a demanding teacher. But Maris was glad of it. It was good to be pushed to her limits, to work until she could work no longer. She had no time to think of her own loss, and she slept deeply every night.

But while she was pleased to be of use and gladly performed the tasks Evan set her, other requirements of this new life were harder for Maris to fulfill. It was difficult enough to comfort strangers, more difficult still when there was no comfort to be offered. Maris had nightmares about one woman whose child died. It was Evan who told her, of course; but it was to Maris the woman turned in her sorrow and her rage, refusing to believe, demanding a miracle that no one could give. Maris marveled that Evan could give of himself so steadily, and absorb so much pain, fear, and grief, year after year, without breaking. She tried to copy his calm, and his firm, gentle manner, reminding herself that he had called *her* strong.

Maris wondered if she would gain more skill and inner certainty with time. Evan at times seemed to know what to do by instinct, Maris thought, just as some Woodwingers took to the air as if born to it, while others struggled hopelessly, lacking that special feel for the air. Evan's very touch could soothe an ailing person, but Maris had no such gift.

As night began to fall on the nineteenth day of their travels, Maris and Evan did not stop to make camp, but only walked more quickly. Even Maris, to whom all trees looked alike, recognized this part of the forest. Soon Evan's house came into sight.

Suddenly Evan caught her wrist, stopping her. He was staring ahead, at the house. There was a light shining in the window, and smoke rising from the chimney.

"A friend?" she hazarded. "Someone who needs your help?"

"Perhaps," Evan said quietly. "But there are others . . . the home-less, people driven from their villages because of some crime or madness. They attack travelers, or break into houses, and wait. . . ."

They approached the house quietly, Evan in the lead, going for the lighted window rather than the door.

"A man and a child . . . doesn't look bad," murmured Evan. It was a high window. Standing on the tips of her toes, leaning on Evan for support, Maris could just see in.

She saw a large, ruddy, bearded man sitting on a stool before the fire. At his feet sat a child, looking up into his face.

The man turned his head slightly, and the firelight brought out a glint of red in his dark hair. She saw his face in the light.

"Coll!" she cried, joyful. She tottered and nearly fell, but Evan caught her.

"Your brother?"

"Yes!" She ran around the side of the house, and as she laid her hand on the doorpull, it opened from within, and Coll caught her up in a big bear-hug.

Maris was always surprised by the size of her stepbrother. She saw him usually at intervals of years, and in between thought of him as young Coll, her little brother, thin, awkward and undeveloped, at ease only with a guitar in his hand when he could transcend himself by singing.

But her little brother had filled out, and grown into his height. Years of travel, earning passage to other islands by working as a sailor and laboring at whatever task came to hand when his audience was too poor to pay for his songs, had strengthened him. His hair, once red-gold, had darkened mostly to brown—the red showed only in his beard now, and in fire-lit glints.

"You are Evan, the healer?" Coll asked, turning to Evan. He held Maris in the crook of one arm. At Evan's nod, he went on, "I'm sorry to seem so rude, but we were told in Port Thayos that Maris was living here with you. We've been waiting these past four days for you. I broke a shutter to get in, but I've repaired it—I think you'll find it even better now." He looked down at Maris and hugged her again. "I was afraid we'd missed you—that you had flown away again!"

Maris stiffened. She saw the quick concern on Evan's face and shook her head at him very slightly.

"We'll talk," she said. "Let's sit by the fire—my legs are nearly worn off from walking. Evan, will you make your wonderful tea?"

"I've brought kivas," Coll said quickly. "Three bottles, traded for a song. Shall I heat one?"

"That would be lovely," Maris said. As she moved toward the cupboard where the heavy pottery mugs were kept, she caught sight of the child again, half-hiding in the shadows, and stopped short.

"Bari?" she asked, wonderingly.

The little girl came forward shyly, head hanging, looking up with a sideways glance.

"Bari," Maris said again, warmth in her tone. "It *is* you! I'm your Aunt Maris!" She bent to hug the child, then drew back again to take a better look. "You couldn't remember me, of course. You were no bigger than a burrow bird when I last saw you."

"My father sings about you," Bari said. Her voice rang clearly, bell-like.

"And do you sing, too?" Maris asked.

Bari shrugged awkwardly and looked at the floor. "Sometimes," she muttered.

Bari was a thin, fine-boned child of about eight years. Her light brown hair was cropped short, lying like a sleek cap on her head, framing a freckled, heart-shaped face with wide gray eyes. She was dressed like a smaller version of her father in a belted woolen tunic over leather pants. A piece of hardened resin, a clear, golden color, hung on a thong around her neck.

"Why don't you bring some cushions and blankets near the fire so we can all be comfortable," Maris suggested. "They're kept in that wooden chest in the far corner."

She got the mugs and returned to the fireside. Coll caught her hand and pulled her down beside him.

"It's so good to see you walking, healed," he said in his deep, warm voice. "When I heard of your fall, I was afraid you'd be crippled, like Father. All the long journey here from Poweet I kept hoping for more news, better news, and hearing none. They said that it was a terrible fall, onto rock; that both your legs and arms were broken. But now, better than any report, I see you're whole. How long before you fly back to Amberly?"

Maris looked into the eyes of the man who, although not blood-kin, she had loved as a brother for more than forty years.

"I'll never go back to Amberly, Coll," she said. Her voice was even. "I'll never fly again. I was hurt more badly than I knew in that fall. My arm and my legs mended, but something else stayed broken. When I hit my head . . . My sense of balance has gone wrong. I can't fly."

He stared at her, the happiness draining out of his face. He shook his head. "Maris . . . no . . ."

"There's no use saying no anymore," she said. "I've had to accept it."

"Isn't there something . . ."

To Maris' relief, Evan interrupted. "There's nothing. We've done all we can, Maris and I. Injuries to the head are mysterious. We don't even know what exactly happened, and there's no healer anywhere on Windhaven, I'd wager, who would know what to do to fix it."

Coll nodded, looking dazed. "I didn't mean to imply . . . It's just so hard for me to accept. Maris, I can't imagine you grounded!"

He meant well, Maris knew, but his grief and incomprehension grated against her, tore her wounds open again.

"You don't have to imagine it," she said rather sharply. "This is my life now, for anyone to see. The wings have already been taken back to Amberly."

Coll said nothing. Maris didn't want to see the pain on his face, so she stared into the fire, and let the silence grow. She heard the sound of a stone bottle being unstoppered, and then Evan was pouring the steaming kivas into three mugs.

"Can I taste?" Bari crouched beside her father, looking up, hopeful. Coll smiled down at her and shook his head teasingly.

Watching the father and daughter together, Maris felt the tension suddenly dissolve. She met Evan's eyes as he put a mug filled with the hot, spiced wine into her hands, and smiled.

She turned back to Coll and was about to speak to him when her eyes fell on his guitar, which lay as always close to hand. The sight of it released a torrent of memories, and suddenly Maris felt that Barrion, dead now for many years, was again in the room with them. The guitar had been his, and he had claimed it had been in his family for generations, passed down from the days of the star sailors. She had never known whether or not to believe him—exaggerations and beautiful lies came from him as easily as breathing—but certainly the instrument was very old. He had entrusted it to Coll, who had been his protégé and the son he'd never had. Maris reached out to feel the smooth wood, dark with many varnishings and constant handling.

"Sing for us, Coll," she suggested. "Sing us something new."

The guitar was in his arms, cradled against his chest, almost before the words were out of her mouth. The soft chords sounded.

"I call this 'The Singer's Lament,'" he said, a wry smile on his face. And he began to sing a song, melancholy and ironic in turns, about a singer whose wife leaves him because he loves his music too well. Maris suspected it was his own marriage he was singing of, although he had never told her why it had ended, and she had not been around to see much of it first-hand.

The recurring refrain of the song was: "A singer should not marry/A singer should not wed/Just kiss the music as she flies/And take a song to bed."

Next he sang a song about the turbulent love affair between a proud Landsman and an even prouder one-wing—Maris recognized one of the names, but had not heard the story.

"Is that true?" she asked when the song had ended.

Coll laughed. "I remember you used to ask that same question of Barrion! I'll give you his answer: I can't tell you when or where or if it happened, but it's a true story all the same!"

"Now sing my song," Bari said.

Coll dropped a kiss on his daughter's nose and sang a tuneful fantasy about a little girl named Bari who makes friends with a scylla who takes her to find treasure in a cave beneath the sea.

Later, he sang older songs: the ballad of Aron and Jeni, the song about the ghost flyers, the one about the mad Landsman of Kennehut, his own version of the Woodwings song.

Later still, when Bari had been put to bed and the three adults were working on the third bottle of kivas, they spoke about their lives. More calmly now, Maris could talk to Coll about her decision to stay with Evan.

The first shock past, Coll knew better than to express pity for her, but he let her know he did not understand the choice she had made.

"But why stay here, in Eastern, far from all your friends?" Then with drunken courtesy he added, "I don't mean to slight you, Evan."

"Anywhere I chose to live would be far from someone," Maris said. "You know how widely my friends are scattered." She sipped the hot, intoxicating drink, feeling detached.

"Come with me back to Amberly," he coaxed. "Live in the house we grew up in. We might wait awhile, for spring when the sea is calmer, but the voyage is not so bad between here and there, truly."

"You can have the house," she said. "You and Bari can live there. Or sell it if you like. I can't go live there again—there are too many memories there. Here on Thayos I can start a new life. It will be hard, but Evan helps me." She took his hand. "I can't stand idleness; it's good to be useful."

"But as a healer?" Coll shook his head. "It's odd, to think of you doing that." He looked to Evan. "Is she any good? Truthfully."

Evan held Maris' hand between his own, stroking it.

"She learns quickly," he said after a few moments' thought. "She has a strong desire to help, and does not balk at dull or difficult tasks. I don't know yet whether she has it in her to be a healer—if she will ever be truly skilled.

"But I must admit, quite selfishly, I am glad she is here. I hope she'll never want to leave me."

A flush rose to her cheeks, and Maris bent her head and drank. She was startled, yet gratified, by his last words. There had been very little in the way of love-talk between her and Evan—no romantic promises or extravagant claims or compliments. And, although she had tried to put it out of her mind, somewhere within she feared that she had given Evan no choice in their relationship—that she had installed herself in his life before he could have any second thoughts. But there had been love in his voice.

There was a silence. To fill it, Maris asked Coll about Bari. "When did she start traveling with you?"

"It's been about six months," he said. He set his mug down, drained, and picked up his guitar. He stroked the strings, producing faint chords as he spoke. "Her mother's new husband is a violent man—he beat Bari once. Her mother wouldn't say no to him, but she had no objections to my taking her away. She told me he might be jealous of Bari—he's been trying to get a child of his own."

"How does Bari feel?"

"She's glad to be with me, I think. She's a quiet little thing. She misses her mother, I know, but she's glad to be out of that household, where nothing she did was right."

"Are you making a singer of her, then?" Evan asked.

"If she wants to be. I knew when I was younger than she, but Bari doesn't know yet what she wants to do with her life. She sings like a little chime-bird, but there's more to being a singer than singing other people's songs, and she's shown no talent yet for making up her own."

"She's very young," said Maris.

Coll shrugged and set his guitar aside again. "Yes. There's time. I don't press her." He blinked and yawned hugely. "It must be past my bedtime."

"I'll show you to a room," Evan said.

Coll laughed and shook his head. "No need," he said. "After four days, I feel quite at home here."

He stood, and Maris also rose, gathering up the empty mugs. She kissed Coll goodnight and then lingered as Evan banked the fire and straightened the furniture, waiting to walk hand in hand with him to the bed they shared.

For the next few days Coll kept Maris' spirits high. They were together constantly and he told her stories of his adventures and sang to her. In all the years since Coll had first gone wandering with Barrion, and Maris had become a full-fledged flyer, they had not spent much time together. Now, as the days passed and Coll and Bari lingered, they grew closer than they had been since Coll's boyhood. He spoke for the first time of his failed marriage and his feeling that it was his fault for being so much away from home. Maris did not speak of her accident, or her unhappiness, but there was no need. Coll knew all too well what the wings had meant to her.

As the days merged almost imperceptibly into weeks, Coll and Bari stayed on. Coll traveled abroad to sing at the inns in Thossi and Port Thayos, while Bari began trailing after Evan. She was quiet, unobtrusive, and attentive, and Evan was pleased by her interest. The four of them lived comfortably together, taking turns with the chores and gathering together in the evenings for stories or games before the fire. Maris told Evan, told Coll, told herself, that she was contented. She thought of no other life.

Then, one day, S'Rella arrived.

Maris was alone in the house that afternoon, and she answered the knocking on the door. Her first response was one of pleasure at the sight of her old friend, but even as she opened her arms to embrace, Maris felt her eyes drawn to the wings S'Rella carried slung over one arm, and her heart lurched painfully. As she led S'Rella to a chair near the fire, and put the kettle on for tea, she was thinking dully, soon she'll fly away again and leave me.

It required a great effort for her to seat herself beside S'Rella and ask, with a show of interest, for news.

S'Rella's face was shining with barely repressed excitement. "I've come here on business," she said. "I've come with a message for *you*. I've come to ask you, to invite you, to make the voyage to Seatooth, and live there as the new head of the Academy. They need a strong, permanent teacher at Woodwings, not like the ones who have come and gone over the past six years. Someone committed, someone knowledgeable. A leader. You, Maris. Everyone looks up to you—there could be no one better than you for the job. We all want you there."

Maris thought of Sena, dead nearly fifteen years now, as she had been in the last years of her very long life. The fallen, crippled flyer, standing on the cliff at Woodwings, shouting herself hoarse as she tried to convey her knowledge of flight to the young Woodwingers circling in the air above her. Never to fly again herself, permanently grounded with one almost useless leg and one blind, milk-white eye. Forever standing below, staring fiercely into the storm-winds, watching the Woodwingers fly away from her, year after year. All those years until she finally died. How had she borne it?

A deep shudder went through Maris, and she shook her head wildly.

"Maris?" S'Rella sounded bewildered. "You've always been the staunchest supporter of Woodwings—of the whole system. There's still so much you could do. . . . What's wrong?"

Maris stared at her, goaded, wanting to scream. She said, very softly, "How can you ask that?"

"But . . ." S'Rella spread her hands. "What can you do here? Maris, I know how you feel—believe me. But your life isn't over. I remember that once you told me that we, we flyers, were your family. We still are. It's foolish to exile yourself like this. Come back. You need us now, and we still need you. Woodwings is your place—without you, it could never have existed. Don't turn your back on it now."

"You don't understand," Maris said. "How could you? You can still fly."

S'Rella reached out and took Maris' hand, and held it even though it remained limp, not answering her pressure.

"I'm trying to understand," she said. "I know how you must be suffering. Believe me, ever since I heard the news I've thought about what my life would be if I were injured. I have been grounded for a year at times, you know, so I have some idea, even though I've never had to come to terms with the idea of its being permanent. Everyone has to think about it. The end comes for all flyers, you know. Sometimes it comes in competition, sometimes in injury, often just in age."

"I always thought I would die," Maris said quietly. "I never thought about going on living and being unable to fly."

S'Rella nodded. "I know," she said. "But now it has happened, and you have to adjust to it."

"I am," Maris said. "I was." She pulled her hand away. "I've made a new life for myself here. If you hadn't come—if I could just forget—" She saw by the quick flash of pain in S'Rella's face that she had wounded her friend.

But S'Rella shook her head and looked determined. "You can't forget," she said. "That's hopeless. You have to go on, to do the things you can do. Come and teach at Woodwings. Stay close to your friends. Hiding here—you're just pretending . . ."

"All right, it's pretense," Maris said harshly. She stood up and walked to the window where she looked blindly out at the wet blur of brown and green that was the forest. "It's a pretense I need, in order to go on living. I can't bear the constant reminder of what I've lost. When I saw you standing in the doorway all I could think of was your wings, and how I wished I could strap them on and fly away from here. I thought I'd stopped thinking about that. I thought I had settled down here. I love Evan, and I'm learning a lot as his assistant. I'm doing something useful. I've been enjoying having Coll around, and getting to know his daughter. And the sight of one pair of wings sweeps it all away, turns my life to dust."

Silence filled the cabin. Finally Maris turned away from the window to look at S'Rella. She saw the tears on her friend's face, but also the look of stubborn disapproval.

"All right," Maris said, sighing. "Tell me I'm wrong. Tell me what you think."

"I think," said S'Rella, "that what you are doing is wrong. I think you are making things harder for yourself in the long run. You can't wipe out your life as if it never was; you don't live in a world without flyers. You may hide here and pretend to be an assistant healer, but you can never really forget that you were, that you *are* a flyer. We still need you—there's still a life for you. You haven't come to terms with your life yet—you're still avoiding it. Come to Woodwings, Maris."

"No. No. No. S'Rella—I couldn't bear it. You may be right, and what I am doing may be wrong, but I've thought about it, and it's the only thing I can do. I can't bear the pain. I have to go on living, and to do that I *must* forget what I've lost, or I'll go mad. You don't know—I couldn't bear to see them all flying around me, rejoicing in the air, and to know that I could never again join them. Forever to be reminded of what I've lost. I can't. Woodwings will survive without me. I can't go back there." She stopped, shaking with intensity, with fear, with the renewed reminder of her loss.

S'Rella rose and held her until the shaking passed.

"All right," S'Rella said softly. "I won't press you. I have no right to tell you what you should do. But . . . if you should change your mind, if you think about it again when more time has passed, I know the position would always be open to you. It's your decision. I won't mention it again."

The next day she and Evan rose early, and spent the morning humoring a sick, querulous old man in his lonely forest hut. Bari, who had been up and playing at first light, tagged along after them, since her father was still asleep. She had better luck than either of them in bringing a smile to the old man's thin lips. Maris was glad. She herself was depressed and out of sorts, and the ancient's whining complaints only made her more irritable. She had to suppress the urge to snap at him.

"You'd think he was dying, the way he carried on," Maris said as they started the walk back home.

Little Bari looked at her strangely. "He *is*," she said in a small voice. She looked at Evan for support.

The healer nodded. "The child's right," he said grumpily. "The signs are clear enough, Maris. Haven't you listened to anything I've taught you? Bari is more attentive than you've been of late. I doubt that he'll last three months. Why do you think I made him the tesis?"

"Signs?" Maris felt confused and embarrassed. She could memorize the things Evan told her easily enough, but applying the knowledge was so much harder. "He was complaining about aches in his bones," she said. "I thought—he was old, after all, and old people often—"

Evan made an impatient noise. "Bari," he said, "how did you know he was dying?"

"I felt in his elbows and knees, like you showed me," she said eagerly, proud of the things she learned from Evan. "They were lumpy, getting hard. Under his chin, too. Behind the whiskers. And his skin felt cold. Did he have the puff?"

"The puff," Evan said, pleased. "Children often recover from it, but not adults, never."

"I—I didn't notice," Maris said.

"No," Evan said. "You didn't."

They walked on in silence, Bari skipping along happily, Maris feeling inordinately tired.

There was the faintest breath of spring in the air.

Maris felt her spirits lift as she walked through the clean dawn air with Evan. The Landsman's grim keep waited at the end of the journey, but the sun was out, the air was fresh, and the breeze felt almost caressing through the cloak she wore. Red, blue, and yellow flowers gleamed like jewels amid the gray-green moss and dark humus alongside the road. Birds, like quick glimpses of flame or sky, flew through the trees and sang. It was a day when being alive and moving was a pleasure in itself.

Beside her, Evan was silent. Maris knew he was puzzling over the message that had brought them out. They had been awakened before it was light by a pounding at the door. One of the Landsman's runners, out of breath, had blurted out the need for a healer at the keep. He could say no more, knew no more—just that someone was injured and needed aid.

Evan, warm and bemused from bed, his white hair standing up like a bird's ruffled feathers, was not eager to go anywhere.

"Everyone knows the Landsman keeps his own healer by him for his family and servants," he objected. "Why can't he deal with this emergency?"

The runner, who obviously knew no more than he had been told, looked confused. "The healer, Reni, has lately been confined for treason, suspected treason," he said in his soft, breathless voice.

Evan swore. "Treason! That's madness. Reni would not—oh, very well, stop chewing your lip, boy. We'll come, my assistant and I, and see about this injury."

All too soon they reached the narrow valley and saw the Landsman's massive stone keep looming ahead of them. Maris pulled her cloak, which she had worn loosely open, more tightly around her. The air was colder here: spring had not ventured past the mountain wall. There were no flowers or bright tendrils of ivy to relieve the dull-colored rock and lichen, and the only birds that sounded were the harsh-voiced scavenger gulls.

An elderly, scar-faced landsguard with a knife in her belt and a bow strapped to her back met them before they had advanced more than a few feet into the valley. She questioned them closely, searched them, and took charge of Evan's surgical kit, before escorting them past two checkpoints and through the gate into the keep. Maris noticed that there were even more landsguard patrolling the high, wide walls than on her last visit, and saw a new fierceness, a repressed excitement, in the drilling troops within the courtyard.

The Landsman met them in an outer hall, alone except for his omnipresent guards five steps behind him. His face darkened when he saw Maris, and he addressed Evan harshly.

"I sent for you, healer, and not for this wingless flyer."

"Maris is my assistant now," Evan said calmly. "As you yourself should know very well, she is not a flyer."

"Once a flyer, always a flyer," growled the Landsman. "She has flyer friends, and we do not need her here. The security—"

"She is a healer's apprentice," Evan said, interrupting. "I vouch for her. The code that binds me will also bind her. We will not gossip of anything we learn here."

The Landsman still frowned. Maris was rigid with fury—how could he speak of her like that, ignoring her as if she were not even present?

Finally the Landsman said, grudgingly, "I do not trust this 'apprenticeship,' but I will take your word on her behalf, healer. But bear in mind, if she should carry tales of what she sees here today, both of you will hang."

"We made haste to get here," Evan said coldly. "But I judge by your manner that there is no cause for hurry."

The Landsman turned aside without replying and sent for

another brace of landsguard. Then, without a backward glance, he left them.

The landsguard, both young and heavily armed, escorted Evan and Maris down steep stone steps into a tunnel carved out of the solid rock of the mountain, far below the living quarters of the fortress. Tapers burned smokily on the walls at wide intervals, providing a shifting, uncertain light. The air in the narrow, low-ceilinged tunnel smelled of mold and of acrid smoke. Maris felt a sudden wave of claustrophobia and clutched Evan's hand.

At last they came to a branching corridor, set with heavy wooden doors. At one of these doors they stopped, and the guards removed the heavy bars that locked it. Inside was a small stone cell with a rough pallet on the floor and one high, round window. Leaning against the wall was a young woman with long, pale blond hair. Her lips were swollen, one eye blackened, and there were bloodstains on her clothes. It took Maris a few moments to recognize her.

"Tya," she said, wondering.

The landsguard left them, bolting the door behind them, with the assurance they would be right outside if anything was needed.

While Maris still stared, uncomprehending, Evan went to Tya's side. "What happened?" he asked.

"The Landsman's bullies were none too gentle about arresting me," Tya said in her cool, ironic voice. She might have been speaking about someone else. "Or maybe it was my mistake to fight them."

"Where are you hurt?" Evan asked.

Tya grimaced. "From the feel of it, they broke my collarbone. And chipped a tooth. That's all—just bruises, otherwise. All that blood came from my lips."

"Maris, my kit," said Evan.

Maris carried it to his side. She looked at Tya. "How could he arrest a flyer? Why?"

"The charge is treason," Tya said. Then she gasped as Evan's fingers probed around her neck.

"Sit," said Evan, helping her down. "It will be better."

"He must be mad," Maris said. The word called up the ghost of the Mad Landsman of Kennehut. In grief, hearing of his son's death in a far-off land, he had murdered the messenger who flew the unwelcome news. The flyers had shunned him afterward, until proud, rich Kennehut became a desolation, ruined and empty, its very name a synonym for madness and despair. No Landsman since would dream of harming a flyer. Until now.

Maris shook her head, gazing at Tya but not really seeing her. "Has he lost his reason so far as to imagine that the messages you carry from his enemies come from your own heart? To call it *treason* is wrong in itself. The man *must* be mad. You aren't subject to him—he knows that flyers are above petty local laws. As his equal, how could you do anything treasonous? What does he say you did?"

"Oh, he knows what I did," Tya said. "I don't claim I was arrested on false pretenses. I simply didn't expect him to find out. I'm still not sure how he knew, when I thought I'd been so careful." She winced. "But now it's all for nothing. There will be war, just as fierce and bloody as if I'd stayed out of it."

"I don't understand."

Tya grinned at her. Her black eyes were still sharp and aware despite her bruises and her obvious pain. "No? I've heard that some old-time flyers could carry messages without knowing what they said. But I always knew—each belligerent threat, each tempting promise, each potential alliance for war. I learned things I had no intention of saying. I changed the messages. Slightly, at first, making them a little more diplomatic. And returned with responses that would delay or sidestep the war he was after. It was working—until he found out about my deception."

"All right, Tya," Evan said. "No more talking just now. I'm going to set your collarbone, and it will hurt. Can you hold still, or do you want Maris to help hold you down?"

"I'll be good, healer," Tya said. She took a deep breath.

Maris stared blankly at Tya, hardly believing what she had just heard. Tya had done the unthinkable—she had altered a message entrusted to her. She had meddled in land-bound politics, instead of staying above them as a flyer always did. The mad act of jailing a flyer no longer seemed so mad—what else could the Landsman have done? No wonder he had been so disturbed by Maris' presence. When word reached other flyers . . .

"What does the Landsman plan to do with you?" Maris asked.

For the first time, Tya looked somber. "The usual punishment for treason is death."

"He wouldn't dare!"

"I wonder. I was afraid that he planned to bury me here, kill me secretly and silence the landsguard who had arrested me. Then I would simply vanish, and be presumed lost at sea. But now that you have been here, Maris, I don't think he can. You would denounce him."

"And then we would both hang, as treasonous liars," said Evan. His tone was light. More seriously, he added, "No, I think you are right, Tya. The Landsman would not have sent for me if he meant to kill you in secret. Much easier just to let you die. The more people who know of your arrest, the greater the danger to himself."

"There's flyer's law—the Landsman has no right to judge a flyer," Maris said. "He'll simply have to turn you over to the flyers. A court will be called, and you'll be stripped of your wings. Oh, Tya. I never heard of a flyer doing such a thing."

"I've shocked you, Maris, haven't I?" Tya smiled. "You can't see beyond the horror of breaking tradition—not even you? I told you you were no one-wing."

"Do you think it makes a difference?" Maris asked quietly. "Do you expect that the one-wings will flock to your side, and applaud this crime? That somehow you'll be allowed to keep your wings? What Landsman would have you?"

"The Landsmen won't like it," Tya said, "but perhaps it is time for them to learn they can't control us. I have friends among the one-wings who agree with me. The Landsmen have too much power, particularly here in Eastern. And by what right? By birth? Birth used to determine who wore wings, but your Council changed that. Why should it determine who rules?

"You don't realize the things a Landsman can do, Maris. It's different in Western. And you were above it all, like all the old flyers. But it is different for a one-wing.

"We grow up like all the other land-bound, nothing special about us. And after we win our wings, the Landsmen still see us as subjects. The wings we bear command their respect for us as their equals, but it's a fragile thing, that respect. At any competition we might lose the wings and again be weak, lowly citizens.

"In Eastern, in the Embers, in most of Southern and even a few islands in Western—wherever the Landsmen inherit their power—they look with respect upon the flyers who were born to wings. They may disguise it, but they feel a sort of contempt for those of us who had to work and struggle to win a pair of wings. They treat us only superficially as their equals. All the time they are trying to control us, trying to buy and sell us, commanding us, feeding us messages to fly as if we were no more than a flock of trained birds. Well, what I've done will shake them, make them look again. We're not their servants, and we won't submit anymore to flying messages we despise, carrying death-warrants and ultimatums to ignite wars that might destroy our families, friends, and other innocents!"

"You can't pick and choose like that," Maris interrupted. "You can't—the messenger isn't responsible for the content of the message."

"That's what the flyers told themselves for centuries," Tya said. Her eyes glittered with anger. "But of *course* the messenger is responsible! I have brains, a heart, a conscience—I won't pretend I don't."

Abruptly, like a sluice of cold water, the thought "This has nothing to do with me" doused Maris' passion. She was left feeling angry and bitter. What was she doing arguing flyer business? She was no flyer. She looked at Evan. "If you are through here, we had better leave," she said dully.

He rested a hand on her shoulder and nodded to her, then looked to Tya. "It's only a minor fracture," he said. "There should be no problem with its healing. Just rest—don't do anything violent that might dislodge the brace."

Tya grinned crookedly, showing her discolored teeth. "Like trying to escape? I have no activities planned. But you'd better tell the Landsman, so his guards don't forget themselves and massage me with their clubs."

Evan knocked on the door for the guards, and almost immediately came the noise of the heavy bolts being drawn back.

"Goodbye, Maris," Tya called.

Maris hesitated, about to walk through the door. Then she turned back. "I don't think the Landsman will dare to try you himself," she said earnestly. "He will have to let your peers judge you. But I don't think they will be kind, Tya. What you have done is too dangerous. It affects too many people—it affects everyone."

Tya stared at her. "So was what you did, Maris. But the world is ready for another change, I think. I know what I did was right, even if I failed."

"Maybe the world is ready for another change," Maris said steadily. "But is this the way we should change it? You've only replaced threats with lies. Do you really think flyers as a whole are wiser and more noble than Landsmen? That they should bear the whole responsibility for choosing what messages to fly, and which to alter, and which to refuse?"

Tya looked back at her, unmoved. "I'd do it again," she said.

The trip through the tunnels seemed shorter on their return. The Landsman was again waiting for them in the drafty outer hall, and he looked at them both sharply, as if seeking signs of anger or fear. "A most unfortunate accident," he said.

Evan said, "She suffered only a fractured collarbone and a few bruises. She should recover quickly if she is given good food and allowed to rest."

"She will have the best of care during her detention here," said the Landsman. He looked at Maris, although he directed his words to Evan. "I've sent Jem to spread word of her arrest. A thankless task—the flyers have no leaders, no rational organization—that would make things too easy. Instead word must be spread among as many of them as possible, and that takes time. But it will be done. Jem has flown for me for many years, and his mother flew for my father. He at least I can count on."

"Then you intend to hand Tya over to the flyers for trial?" said Maris.

The Landsman's mouth twitched spasmodically. He looked at Evan, making an elaborate charade of ignoring Maris. "It occurred to me that the flyers might wish to send someone to represent their viewpoint. To formally condemn Tya's actions, to plead for mercy, to present any mitigating factors. But the crime was committed against me—against Thayos—and only the Landsman of Thayos can hold trial and mete out punishment in such a case. You agree?"

"I know nothing of the law, nor of what Landsmen must do," Evan said quietly. "The ways of healing are what I know."

Maris felt the warning pressure of Evan's hand on her arm, and said nothing. It was a hard silence. For years, she had always said what she thought.

The Landsman smiled at Evan. It was a gloating, unpleasant expression. "Perhaps you would like to learn? You and your assistant are welcome to stay and sup with me, and afterward I can promise you a most edifying entertainment. A traitor, Reni the healer, is to be hanged at sunset."

"For what crime?"

"Treason, as I said. This Reni had family on Thrane. And he was often seen in the company of the traitorous flyer—was known, in fact, to cohabit with her. He was her accomplice. Won't you stay and observe the fate of those who betray me?"

Maris felt sick.

"I think not," said Evan. "Now, if you will excuse us, we must be on our way."

Evan and Maris did not speak again until the landsguard had left them at the mouth of the valley and they were on the road toward home, presumably safely away from unfriendly ears.

"Poor Reni," Evan said then.

"Poor Tya," said Maris. "He means to hang her, too. Oh, what she did was wrong, no doubt, but what a fate! I don't know what the flyers will do, but they can't tolerate this. A flyer can't be tried and executed by a Landsman!"

"It may not happen," Evan said. "Poor Reni will die, no doubt, but that may be enough to appease the Landsman. He's a man who must have blood, but he is not totally mad. He surely realizes that he will have to give Tya over to the flyers, eventually; that her punishment must come from them."

"Whatever happens to Tya is none of my business anyway,"

Maris said with a sigh. "It's a hard habit to break, after more than forty years of thinking of myself as a flyer. But I'm a land-bound now, like any other, and what happens to Tya shouldn't mean anything to me."

Evan put his arm around her and hugged her close as they walked. "Maris, no one expects you to forget your life as a flyer, or to stop feeling those ties."

"I know," said Maris. "No one except me. But it's no good, Evan. I have to. I don't know how else to go on. When I was younger I thought the story of Woodwings was romantic. I thought that dreams were the most important things of all, and that if you wanted something strongly and surely enough, you would eventually have it, even if it meant dying to attain it. It never occurred to me to wonder what might have happened to Woodwings if he had been rescued from the ocean, if his legendary fall had not killed him. If he'd been picked up floating on those ridiculous wooden wings of his, and given back to his land-bound friends. How he would have lived with the failure, with his dreams shattered. What compromises he would have made." She sighed and rested her head on Evan's shoulder. "I've had a long life as a flyer—longer than many. I should be content. I wish I could be. In some ways I'm still a child, Evan. I never learned how to deal with disappointment—I thought there was always a way to get what I wanted, without giving up or compromising. It's hard, Evan."

"Growth can be painful," Evan said. "And healing takes time. Give it time, Maris."

Coll and Bari were gone. They planned to tour Thayos one last time before taking ship to other Eastern islands. They would come back before very long, Coll assured Maris and Evan, but Maris suspected that one thing would lead to another, and that it would be a matter of years, rather than months, before she saw either Coll or his daughter again.

In fact, it was only a matter of days.

Coll was raging. "Permission of the Landsman is required to leave this godforsaken rock," he said in response to Maris' surprised greeting. He was almost shouting. "A time of crisis, when singers might be spies!"

Bari peeked shyly around her father's bulk, then rushed forward to hug first Maris and then Evan.

"I'm glad we came back," she murmured.

"Has war with Thrane been declared, then?" asked Evan. Despite the quick flash of a smile for Bari, his face was grim.

Coll threw himself into the large chair near the fireplace. "I don't know if it is called war yet or not," he said. "But the story abroad in the streets was that the Landsman had just sent three warships crammed with landsguard to wrest control of that iron mine." He fiddled with his guitar as he spoke, his restless fingers striking soft discords. "And while we wait for the outcome of this little venture, no one is to land on or leave Thayos without the Landsman's express, personal permission. The traders are furious, but afraid to protest." Coll scowled. "Wait until I'm decently away from here! I'll make a lyric that will blister the Landsman's ears when it gets back to him. And it will, it will."

Maris laughed. "Now you sound like Barrion. He always said you singers were the ones who really ruled."

That finally drew a smile from Coll, but Evan remained grim. "No song will heal the wounded, or bring the dead back to life," he said. "If war is at hand, we must leave the forest for Port Thayos. That is where they will bring the wounded, those that survive the crossing. I'll be needed there."

"The streets are mad just now," said Coll. "Rumors and wild stories of all sorts. The town has an ugly feel to it. The Landsman has hanged his healer, and people are afraid to go to the keep. There will be trouble soon, and not just with Thrane." His eyes found Maris. "Something is going on with the flyers as well. I must have counted a dozen pair of wings coming and going over the Strait. War messages, I assumed, but I drank with a tanner in the Scylla's Head who said more. She has a sister in the landsguard, she told me, and she said her sister bragged of arresting a flyer not long ago. The Landsman has taken it upon himself to try a flyer for treason! Can you believe that?"

"Yes," Maris said. "It's true."

"Ah," said Coll. He looked surprised, and distracted from his speech. "Well. Could I have some tea?"

"I'll get it," said Evan.

"Go on," said Maris. "What other rumors?"

"You may know more than I. What of this arrest? I hardly believed it. How much do you know?"

Maris hesitated. "We were warned not to speak of it."

Coll made an impatient thrumming noise with his guitar. "I'm your brother, damn it. Singer or no, I can keep silent. Out with it!"

So Maris told him about their summons to the keep, and what they had learned there. "That would explain a lot," he said when she had finished. "Oh, I'd heard of it anyway—people talk, even landsguard, and the Landsman's secrets aren't as well kept as he imagines. But I never dreamed it was true. No wonder so many flyers have been about. Let the Landsman try to keep flyers in or out!" He grinned.

"The other rumors," Maris prompted.

"Yes," Coll said. "Well, did you know that Val One-Wing has been on Thayos?"

"Val? Here?"

"He has left again now. They told me he arrived only a few days ago, looking very worn, as from a long flight. He wasn't alone, either. Five or six others were with him. Flyers, all of them."

"Did you hear any names?"

"Only Val's. He's notorious. But some of the others were described to me. A stocky Southern woman with white hair. A huge man with a black beard and a scylla-tooth necklace. Several Westerners, including two enough alike to be brothers."

"Damen and Athen," Maris said. "I'm not sure of the others."

Evan returned with cups of steaming tea and a platter of thick sliced bread. "I am," he said. "Of one, at least. The man with the necklace is Katinn of Lomarron. He comes to Thayos frequently."

"Of course," Maris said. "Katinn. A leader among Eastern one-wings."

"Was there more?" Evan asked.

Coll set aside his guitar and blew on his tea to cool it. "I was told that Val came representing the flyers, to try to talk the Landsman into releasing this woman he's imprisoned, this Tya."

"A bluff," Maris said. "Val doesn't represent the flyers. All those you named are one-wings. The old families, the traditionalists, still hate Val. They'd never let him speak for them."

"Yes, I heard that too," Coll said. "Anyway, it was claimed that Val offered to summon a flyer's court to judge Tya. He was willing enough to let the Landsman keep Tya imprisoned until—"

Maris nodded impatiently. "Yes, yes. But what did the Landsman say?"

Coll shrugged. "Some say he was very cool, some say he and Val One-Wing quarreled loudly. In any case, he insisted that the flyer would be tried in the Landsman's own court, and that he would do the judging and sentencing himself. The word on the streets is that the verdict has already been reached."

"So poor Reni wasn't enough for him," Evan murmured. "The Landsman must have another death to avenge his pride."

"What did Val say to that?" Maris asked.

Coll sipped his tea. "I gather Val left after his meeting with the Landsman. Some say the one-wings are going to raid the keep and rescue Tya. There's talk of a flyer's Council too, summoned by Val. To invoke a sanction against Thayos, and shun it."

"No wonder the people are frightened," Evan said.

"Flyers should be frightened, too," Coll said. "Feeling among the locals is running against them. In a tavern near the northside cliffs I overheard a conversation about how the flyers have always secretly ruled Windhaven, deciding the fate of islands and of individuals by the messages they bear and the lies they tell."

"That's absurd!" Maris said, shocked. "How can they believe that?"

"The point is that they do," Coll replied. "I am a flyer's son. Never a flyer, although I was raised to be. I understand the traditions of the flyers, the bonds that link them, the feeling they have of being a society apart from all others. But I also know the people the flyers call 'land-bound,' as if they were all the same, joined together in one large family like the flyers are."

He set down his mug of tea and again picked up his guitar, as if holding it gave him some special eloquence.

"You know how scornful the flyers can be of land-bound, Maris," he said. "I don't think you realize how resentful the land-bound can be of the flyers."

"I have land-bound friends," Maris said. "And the one-wings all began as land-bound."

Coll sighed. "Yes, there *are* those who worship the flyers. Lodge men who devote their lives to caring for them, children who want to touch a flyer's wings, hangers-on who get a special thrill and a special status from coaxing a flyer into bed. But there are others as well. The land-bound who resent flyers seldom seek them out as friends, Maris."

"I know there are problems. I haven't forgotten the hostility we faced when Val got his wings, the threats, the beating, the coolness. But surely things are changing, now that the society of flyers is no longer limited by birth."

Coll shook his head. "It's grown worse," he said. "In the old days, when it was a matter of birth, a lot of people felt flyers were special. In many of the Southern islands the flyers are priests, a special caste blessed by their Sky God. In Artellia they are princes. Just as the Landsmen of Eastern inherited their offices from their parents, so did the flyers inherit their wings.

"But no one now could make the mistake of thinking flyers divinely chosen. Suddenly there are new questions. How did this grubby farm-child I grew up with suddenly become so high and mighty? What sets this former neighbor apart, and gives him the freedom, power, and wealth of a flyer? These one-wings aren't as aloof as the traditional flyers—they lord over their old companions sometimes, or meddle in local affairs. They don't withdraw entirely from island politics—they still have local interests. It makes for bad feelings."

"Twenty years ago no Landsman would have dared seize a flyer," said Evan thoughtfully. "But twenty years ago, would any flyer have dared to misrepresent a message?"

"Of course not," said Maris.

"I wonder, though, how many will believe that?" Coll added.

"Now that it's happened, it's clear that it might have happened before. Those farmers I overheard were convinced that the flyers have been manipulating messages all along. From what I heard, the Landsman of Thayos is becoming rather a hero for being the one to flush out the truth."

"A *hero?*" Evan was disgusted.

"It can't all change because of one well-meaning lie," Maris said stubbornly.

"No," said Coll. "It's been changing all along. And it's all your fault."

"*Me?* I've nothing to do with this."

"No?" Coll grinned at her. "Think again. Barrion used to tell me a story, big sister. About how he and you floated in a boat together, waiting to steal back your wings from Corm, so that you could call your Council. Do you remember?"

"Of course I remember!"

"Well, he said you floated there quite a while, waiting for Corm to leave his house, and all that waiting gave Barrion a chance to think over what you and he were doing. At one point, he said, he sat cleaning his nails with his dagger, and it occurred to him that maybe the best thing he could do was to use that dagger on you. It would have saved Windhaven a lot of chaos, he said. Because if you won, there were going to be more changes than you imagined, and several generations worth of pain. Barrion thought the world of you, Maris, but he also thought you were naive. *You can't change one note in the middle of a song,* he told me. Once you make the first change, others have to follow, until you've redone the whole song. Everything relates, you see."

"So why did he help me?"

"Barrion was always a troublemaker," Coll said. "I guess he wanted to redo the whole song, make something better out of it." Her stepbrother grinned wickedly. "Besides," he added, "he never liked Corm."

After a week without news, Coll decided to return to Port Thayos, to hear what he could. The docks and taverns where he plied his trade were always a rich source of news. "Maybe I'll even visit the Landsman's keep," he said jauntily. "I've been making up a song about our Landsman here, and I'd love to see his face when he hears it!"

"Don't you dare, Coll," Maris said.

He grinned. "I'm not mad yet, big sister. But if the Landsman likes good singing, a visit might be worthwhile. I might learn something. Just keep Bari safe for me."

Two days later a wineseller brought Evan a patient: a huge, shaggy black dog, one of two such monstrous hounds that pulled his wooden cart from village to village. A hooded torturer had mauled the animal and now it lay among the wineskins, crusted with blood and filth.

Evan could do nothing to save the beast, but for his efforts he was offered a skin of sour red wine. "They tried that traitor flyer," the wineseller reported as they drank together by the fire. "She's to hang."

"When?" Maris asked.

"Who's to say? Flyers are everywhere, and the Landsman's afraid of them, I think. She's locked up now in his keep. Think he's waiting to see what those flyers do. If it was me, I'd kill her and have done with it. But I wasn't born Landsman."

Maris stood in the doorway when he departed, watching the man and the surviving dog straining together in the traces. Evan came up behind her and put his arms around her. "How do you feel?"

"Confused," Maris said, without turning. "And afraid. Your Landsman has challenged the flyers directly. Do you realize how serious that is, Evan? They have to do something—they can't let this pass." She touched his hand. "I wonder what they're saying on the Eyrie tonight? I know I can't let myself be drawn into flyer affairs, but it's hard . . ."

"They are your friends," Evan said. "Your concern is natural."

"My concern will bring me more pain," Maris said. "Still . . ."

She shook her head and turned to face him, still within the circle of his arms. "It makes me realize how small my own problems are," she said. "I wouldn't want to trade places with Tya tonight, though she's still a flyer and I'm not."

"Good," Evan said. He kissed her lightly. "For it's you I want here by my side, not Tya."

Maris smiled at him, and together they went inside.

They came in the middle of the night, four strangers dressed as fisherfolk, in heavy boots and sweaters and dark caps trimmed with seacat fur, and they brought the strong, salt smell of the sea with them. Three of them wore long bone knives, and had eyes the color of ice on a winter lake. The fourth one spoke. "You don't remember me," he said, "but we've met before, Maris. I'm Arrilan, of the Broken Ring."

Maris studied him, remembering a pretty youth she had met once or twice. Beneath three days' growth of blond beard, his face was unrecognizable, but his piercing blue eyes seemed familiar. "I believe you are," she said. "You're a long way from home, flyer. Where are your wings? And your manners?"

Arrilan smiled a humorless smile. "My manners? Forgive my rudeness, but I come in haste, and at considerable risk. We made the crossing from Thrynel to see you, and the seas were choppy and dangerous for a boat as small as ours. When this old man tried to send us away, I ran out of patience."

"If you call Evan an old man again, *I'm* going to run out of patience," Maris said coldly. "Why are you here? Why didn't you fly in?"

"My wings are safe on Thrynel. It was thought best to send someone to you in secret, someone whose face is not known on Thayos. Being from the Embers, and new among the flyers, I was chosen. My parents were fisherfolk, and I was raised to the life." He removed his cap, shook out his fine blond hair. "May we sit?" he asked. "We have important business to discuss."

"Evan?" Maris asked.

"Sit," Evan said. "I will make tea."

"Ah." Arrilan smiled. "That would be most welcome. The seas are cold. I'm sorry if I spoke too harshly. These are hard times."

"Yes," Evan agreed. He went outside to draw water for the kettle.

"Why are you here?" Maris asked when Arrilan and his three silent companions were seated. "What's all this about?"

"I was sent to bring you out of here. You can hardly take ship from Port Thayos, you know. You'd not be permitted to leave. We have a small fishing boat hidden not far from here. It will be safe. If the landsguard seize us, we are simple fisherfolk from Thrynel blown northeast by a storm."

"My escape seems well-planned," Maris said. "A pity no one thought to consult me about it." She gazed at the disguised flyer, frowning. "Whose idea was this? Who sent you?"

"Val One-Wing."

Maris smiled. "Of course. Who else? But why does Val want me taken from Thayos?"

"For your own safety," Arrilan said. "As an ex-flyer living here, helpless, your life might be in danger."

"I'm no threat to the Landsman," Maris said. "He'd have no cause to—"

The young flyer shook his head vehemently. "Not the Landsman. The people. Don't you know what's going on?"

"It seems I don't," Maris said. "Perhaps you should tell me."

"News of Tya's arrest has spread all over Windhaven, even to Artellia and the Embers. Many of the land-bound have begun muttering their distrust of flyers. Even the Landsmen." He flushed. "The Landsman of the Broken Ring summoned me as soon as she heard, and demanded to know if *I* had ever lied or twisted a message. I was forced to swear my loyalty to her. Even as she questioned me, it was obvious she doubted my word. And she threatened me! She threatened me with imprisonment, as if she could, as if she had the right—" He broke off, and seemed physically to swallow his anger.

"I am a one-wing, of course," he resumed. "All of us are suspect now, but it is worst for the one-wings. S'wena of Deeth was set upon by thugs and beaten after speaking in Tya's defense in a tavern argument. Others have been called names, shunned, even spat upon in Eastern towns. Jem, who is as traditional as can be, was hit with a rock yesterday on Thrane. And Katinn's house on Lomarron was fired while he was away."

"I had no idea it was so bad," said Maris.

"Yes," said Arrilan. "And growing worse. The fever burns hottest of all here on Thayos. Val thinks the mob will come for you soon, so we were sent to bring you to safety."

Evan had returned and was preparing the tea. "Maybe you should go," he said to Maris, concern in his voice. "I hate to think of you in danger. In time, this will blow over, and you can return, or I could come to you."

Maris shook her head. "I don't think I'm in any danger. Perhaps, if I paraded up and down the streets of Port Thayos, crying out my concern for Tya . . . but here in the woods I'm a harmless old ex-flyer, who has done nothing to rouse anyone's anger."

"Mobs aren't reasonable," Arrilan said. "You don't understand—you must come with us, for your safety."

"How kind of Val, to be so concerned with my safety," Maris said, staring at Arrilan. "And how unusual. At a time like this, Val must have a lot on his mind. I really can't imagine him taking the time and effort to devise an elaborate scheme to rescue poor old Maris, who hardly needs rescuing. If Val truly sent you to rescue me, it must be because he's thought of some way I can be of use to him."

Arrilan was plainly startled. "He—you're mistaken. He's very much concerned for your safety. He—"

"And what else is he concerned with? You might as well tell me what you really want with me."

Arrilan smiled ruefully. "Val said you'd see through the story," he said. He sounded admiring. "I would have told you anyway, once we had you safely away from here. Val has called a flyers' Council."

Maris nodded. "Where?"

"On South Arren. It's close, but removed from the immediate hostilities, and Val has friends there. It will take a month or more for the flyers to assemble, but we have time. The Landsman is afraid, and he'll be too cautious to move until he sees what comes of the Council."

"What does Val intend?"

"What else? He will ask for a sanction against Thayos, to be in effect until Tya is freed. No flyer will land here, or on any other island that trades with Thayos. This rock will be isolated from the world. The Landsman will give in or be destroyed."

"If Val has his way. The one-wings are still a minority, and Tya is no innocent victim," Maris pointed out.

"Tya is a flyer," Arrilan said, gratefully taking the mug of tea Evan handed him. "Val is counting on flyer loyalty. One-wing or no, she is a flyer, and we can't abandon her."

"I wonder," said Maris.

"Oh, there will be a fight, of course. We suspect Corm and some others may try to use this incident to discredit all one-wings and close the academies." He smiled over the rim of his mug. "You haven't helped, you know. Val said you picked the worst possible time to fall."

"I wasn't given any choice," Maris said. "But you still haven't said why you came for me."

"Val wants you to preside."

"*What?*"

"It's traditional to have a retired flyer conduct the Council, you know that. Val thinks that you would be the best choice. You're widely known and widely respected, among one-wings and flyer-born both, and we'd have no trouble getting you accepted. Any other one-wing will be rejected. And we need someone we can count on, not some crusty old relic who wants everything like it used to be. Val thinks it can make a big difference."

"It can," said Maris, remembering the pivotal role that Jamis the Senior had played in the Council that Corm had called. "But Val will have to find someone else. I'm through with flying and with flyers' Councils. I want to be left in peace."

"There can be no peace until we have won."

"I'm not a stone on Val's geechi board, and the sooner he learns that the better! Val knows what it would cost me to do as he asks. How *dare* he ask? He sent you to trick me, to lie to me with talk of safety, because he knew I would refuse. I can't bear to see one flyer—do you think I want to be with a thousand of them, watching them play in the sky and listening to them trade stories and finally stand alone, an old cripple, and watch them fly away and leave me? Do you think I'd like that?" Maris realized she had been shouting at him. Her pain was a knot in her stomach.

Arrilan's voice was sullen. "I scarcely know you—how could you expect me to know how you felt? I'm sorry. I'm sure Val is sorry, too. But it can't be helped. This is more important than your feelings. Everything depends on this Council, and Val wants you there."

"Tell Val that I am sorry," Maris said quietly. "Tell him I wish him luck, but I will not go. I'm old and tired and I want to be left alone."

Arrilan stood up. His eyes were very cold. "I told Val I would not fail him," he said. "There are four of us against you." He made a small gesture, and the woman on his right slid her knife from its sheath. She grinned, and Maris saw that her teeth were made of wood. The man behind her rose, and he, too, held a knife in his hand.

"Get out," said Evan. He was standing near the door to his workroom, and in his hands was the bow he used for hunting, an arrow notched and ready.

"You could take only one of us with that," said the woman with the wooden teeth. "If you were lucky. And you wouldn't have time to reach for another arrow, old man."

"True," said Evan. "But the point of this arrow is smeared with blue tick venom, so one of you will die."

"Put your knives away," Arrilan said. "Please, put that down. No one need die." He looked at Maris.

Maris said, "Did you really think you could *force* me into presiding over the Council?" She made a disgusted sound. "You might tell Val that if his strategy is as good as yours, the one-wings are finished."

Arrilan glanced at his companions. "Leave us," he said. "Wait outside." Reluctantly the three shambled to the door. "No more threats," Arrilan said. "I'm sorry, Maris. Maybe you can understand how desperate I feel. We *need* you."

"You need the flyer I was, perhaps, but she died in a fall. Leave me alone. I'm just an old woman, a healer's apprentice, and that's all I aspire to be. Don't hurt me any more by dragging me into the world."

Contempt was plain on Arrilan's face. "To think that they still sing of a coward like you," he said.

When he had gone, Maris turned to Evan. She was trembling, and her head felt light and dizzy.

The healer lowered the great bow he held and set it aside. He was frowning. "Dead?" he asked bitterly. "All this time, have you been dead? I thought you were learning how to live again, but all this time you've seen my bed as your grave."

"Oh, Evan, no," she said, dismayed, wanting comfort and not still more reproach.

"It was your own word," he said. "Do you still believe that your life ended with your fall?" His face twisted with pain and anger. "I won't love a corpse."

"Oh, Evan." She sat down abruptly, feeling that her legs could no longer hold her up. "I didn't mean—I meant only that I am dead to the flyers, or they are dead to me. That part of my life is finished."

"I don't think it's that easy," Evan said. "If you try to kill a part of yourself, you risk killing everything. It's like what your brother said—rather, what Barrion said—about trying to change just one note in a song."

"I value our life together, Evan," Maris said. "Please believe me. It's just that Arrilan—this damn Council of Val's—brought it all back to mind. I was reminded of everything I've lost. It made the pain come back."

"It made you feel sorry for yourself," Evan said.

Maris felt a flash of annoyance. Couldn't he understand? Could a land-bound ever understand what she had lost? "Yes," she said, her voice cold. "It made me feel sorry for myself. Don't I have that right?"

"The time for self-pity is long past. You have to come to terms with what you are, Maris."

"I will. I am. I was learning to forget. But to be drawn into this thing, this flyers' dispute, would ruin everything; it would drive me mad. Can't you see that?"

"I see a woman denying everything she has been," Evan said. He might have said more, but a sound made them both look around, and they saw Bari standing in the doorway, looking a little frightened.

Evan's face softened, and he went to her and lifted her in a great bear hug. "We had some visitors," he said. He kissed her.

"Since we're all up, shall I make breakfast?" Maris asked.

Bari grinned and nodded. Evan's face was unreadable. Maris turned away and set to work, determined to forget.

In the weeks that followed, they seldom spoke of Tya or the flyers' Council, but news came to them regularly, without being sought. A crier in the Thossi village square; gossip from shopkeepers; travelers who sought out Evan for healing or advice—they all spoke of war and flyers and the belligerent Landsman.

On South Arren, Maris knew, the flyers of Windhaven were gathering. The land-bound of that small island would never forget these days, any more than the people of Greater and Lesser Amberly had ever forgotten the last Council. By now the streets of Southport and Arrenton—small, dusty towns she remembered well—would have a festive air to them. Winesellers and bakers and sausage-makers and merchants would converge from a half-dozen nearby islands, crossing treacherous seas in unsteady boats in hopes of making a few irons from the flyers. The inns and taverns would be full, and flyers would be everywhere, throngs of them, swelling the little towns to bursting. Maris could see them in her mind's eye: flyers from Big Shotan in their dark red uniforms, cool pale Artellians with silver crowns about their brows, priests of the Sky God from Southern, Outer Islanders and Emberites whom no one had seen in years. Old friends would hug each other and talk away the nights; old lovers would trade uncertain smiles and find other ways to pass the dark hours. Singers and storytellers would tell the old tales and compose new ones to suit the occasion. The air would be full of gossip and boasting and song, fragrant with the scents of spiced kivas and roasted meat.

All of her friends would be there, Maris thought. In her dreams she saw them: young flyers and old ones, one-wings and flyer-born, the proud and the timid, the troublemakers and the compliant; all of them would assemble, and the sheen of their wings and the sound of their laughter would fill South Arren.

And they would *fly*.

Maris tried not to think of that, but the thought came unbidden, and in her dreams she flew with them. She could feel the wind as she slept, touching her with knowing, gentle fingers, carrying her to ecstasy. Around her she could see their wings, hundreds of them bright against the deep blue sky, turning and banking in graceful, languid circles. Her own wing caught the light of the sun and flashed briefly, brilliantly: a soundless cry of joy. She saw the wings at sunset, blood-red against an orange-and-purple sky, fading slowly to indigo, then turning silver-white again, when the last light vanished and there were only stars to fly by.

She remembered the taste of rain, and the throb of distant thunder, and the way the sea looked at dawn, just before the sun came up. She remembered the way it felt to run and cast herself from a flyers' cliff, trusting wind and wings and her own skill to keep her in the air.

Sometimes she trembled and cried out in the night, and Evan wrapped his arms around her and whispered soothing promises, but Maris did not tell him of her dreams. He had never been a flyer, or seen a flyers' Council, and he would not understand.

Time passed. The sick came to Evan, or he to them, and died or grew well. Maris and Bari worked at his side, doing what they could. But Maris found that her mind was not always in the work she did. Once Evan sent her into the forest to gather sweetsong, an herb he used to make tesis, but Maris found herself thinking of the Council as she wandered in the cool, damp woods. It has started by now, she thought, and in her head she heard the speeches they must be making, Val and Corm and the rest, and she weighed their arguments and set others up against them, and wondered where it would all go, and whom they had chosen to preside. When she finally returned, beneath her arm was a basket of liar's weed, which looks almost like sweetsong but has no healing properties. Evan took the basket and sighed loudly, shaking his head. "Maris, Maris," he muttered, "what am I to do with you?" He turned to Bari. "Girl," he said, "go fetch me some sweetsong before it grows too dark. Your aunt is not feeling well."

Maris could only agree with him.

Then one day Coll returned, trudging up the road with his guitar across his back, some six weeks after he had left them. He was not alone. S'Rella walked by his side, still wearing her wings, and stumbling like one half-asleep. Their faces were gray and drawn.

When Bari saw them coming, she gave a loud cry and ran to embrace her father. Maris turned to S'Rella. "S'Rella—are you all right? How did the Council go?"

S'Rella began to weep.

Maris went to her and took her old friend in her arms, feeling her shake. Twice she tried to speak, but only gasped and choked.

"It's all right, S'Rella," Maris said helplessly. "There, there, it's all right, I'm here." Her eyes found Coll's.

"Bari," Coll said in a shaky voice. "Go find Evan and bring him out to us."

Bari, with a worried glance at S'Rella, ran to obey.

"I was at the Landsman's keep," Coll said when his daughter had gone. "He learned that I was your brother, and decided to detain me until the Council was over. S'Rella flew in after the Council. The landsguard took her and brought her to the keep as well. He had other flyers there, too. Jem, Ligar of Thrane, Katinn of Lomarron, some poor child from Western. Besides the flyers and myself, there were four other singers, a couple of storytellers, and of course all the Landsman's own criers and runners. He wants the word to spread, you see. He wants everyone to know what he did. We were his witnesses. The landsguard marched us out into the courtyard and forced us to watch."

"No," Maris said, pressing S'Rella closer. "No, Coll, he didn't dare! He couldn't."

"Tya of Thayos was hanged yesterday at sunset," Coll said bluntly, "and denying it won't change it. I saw it. She tried to make a speech, but the Landsman would not allow it. The noose wasn't tied properly. Her neck didn't break in the fall, and it was a long time before she strangled to death."

S'Rella pulled away from her embrace. "You were lucky," she said with difficulty. "He might—could have sent for you. Oh, Maris. I couldn't look away—I—it was awful. They wouldn't even let her—have—last words. And the worst—" Her voice caught again.

Evan and Bari were coming, but Maris barely heard their footsteps, or Evan's cry of greeting. A great coldness had settled on her; the same numb sickness she had felt when Russ had died, when Halland had been lost at sea. "How could he dare," she said slowly. "Didn't anyone do anything? Was there no one to stop him?"

"Several landsguard officers cautioned him against it, one high officer in particular—I believe she commands his bodyguard. He would not listen. The landsguard who marched us out were clearly frightened. Several averted their eyes when the trap was opened. In the end, though, they obeyed. They are landsguard, after all, and he is their Landsman."

"But the Council," said Maris. "Why didn't the Council—what about Val, the flyers?"

"The Council," said S'Rella bitterly, "the Council named her outlaw and stripped her wings from her." Anger had pushed her tears aside. "The Council gave him leave to do it!"

"And so everyone would know that he was hanging a flyer," Coll said wearily, "the Landsman put her wings on her. Folded, of course, but still unmistakable. He joked about it. He told her to use her wings to break *this* fall, and fly away."

Later, over cups of Evan's special tea and plates of bread and sausage, S'Rella regained her composure and told Maris and Evan the whole story of the disastrous Council while Coll went outside to talk with his daughter.

It was a simple story. Val One-Wing, who had called the fifth flyers' Council in the history of Windhaven, had lost control of it. He had never *had* control, in fact. His one-wings and allies made up barely a fourth of those assembled, and the three who sat in the positions of honor—the Landsmen of North and South Arren and the retired flyer Kolmi of Thar Kril, who presided—were unsympathetic. No sooner had the meeting begun than angry voices were raised to denounce Tya and her crime, including that of Kolmi himself. "This land-bound girl never understood what it means to be a flyer," S'Rella quoted Kolmi as saying. Others joined the chorus. She should never have been given wings, said one. She had committed a crime not only against her Landsman, but against her fellow flyers as well, said another. She has betrayed her sacred trust, has made all flyers suspect, added a third.

"Katinn of Lomarron tried to speak for her," S'Rella told them, "but he was hooted down. Katinn grew furious and cursed them all. Like Tya, he has seen a lot of war. Some of Tya's friends tried to defend her, at least explain why she did the thing she did, but others refused to listen. When Val himself rose, and tried to put forward his proposal, I thought briefly that we had a chance. He was very good. Calm and reasonable, unlike his usual self. He placated them by admitting that Tya had committed a great crime, but went on to say that the flyers had to defend her nonetheless, that we could not *afford* to let the Landsman have his way with her, that our fates were linked with Tya's. It was a very good speech. If it had come from anyone else it might have swayed them, but it came from Val, and the arena was full of his enemies. So many of the older flyers still hate him.

"Val suggested that the Council strip Tya of her wings for five years, after which she would have to win them back in competition. He also said that we had to insist that only flyers could judge flyers, which meant freeing her from Thayos by threat of a sanction.

"He had people ready to second his proposal and speak in its behalf, but it did no good. Kolmi never recognized us. We were never given a chance to speak. The Council went on most of a day, and I'd say barely a dozen one-wings ever got to speak. Kolmi just wouldn't let us be heard.

"After Val, he recognized a woman from Lomarron, who talked

about how Val's father had been hanged as a murderer, and how Val himself had driven Ari to suicide by taking her wings. 'No wonder he wants us to defend this criminal,' she said. Others like her followed; there was much talk of crime, of one-wings who only half understood what it meant to be a flyer, and Val's proposal got lost in the chaos.

"Then some older flyers put forth a proposal to close the academies. That wasn't popular. Corm spoke in favor of it, but his own daughter rose against him. It was quite a sight. The Artellians were for it too, and some of the retired flyers, and they managed to force a vote, but less than a fifth of the Council voted with them. The academies are safe."

"We can be thankful for that much," Maris said.

S'Rella nodded. "Then Dorrel spoke. You know how highly he's regarded. He gave a fine speech—much too fine. He spoke first of Tya's idealistic motivations, and how much sympathy he had for what she had tried to do. But then he said we couldn't let sympathy or other emotions decide our course. Tya's crime struck right at the soul of flyer society, Dorrel said. If the Landsman could not count on flyers to bear their messages truthfully and dispassionately, to act as their voices in distant lands, then what was the use of us? And if they had no use for us, how long until they took our wings by force and replaced us with their own men? We could not fight the landsguard, he said. We had to regain the trust that had been lost, and the only way to do that was to name Tya outlaw, despite her good intentions. To leave her to her fate, no matter how much we sympathized with her. If we defended Tya *in any way*, Dorrel said, the land-bound would misunderstand, would think we approved of her crime. We had to make our censure clear."

Maris nodded. "Much of that is true," she said, "no matter how grim the consequences. I can see how it might be persuasive."

"Others of like mind followed Dorrel. Tera-kul of Yethien, old Arris of Artellia, a woman from the Outer Islands, Jon of Culhall, Talbot of Big Shotan—leaders, each of them, and highly respected. All of them supported Dorrel. Val seethed, and Katinn and Athen were screaming for the floor, but Kolmi looked right past them.

The talk went on for hours, and finally—in less than a minute—Val's proposal was brought up and voted down, and the Council went on to name Tya outlaw and give her up to the tender mercies of Thayos. We did not tell the Landsman to hang her. At the suggestion of Jirel of Skulny, we went so far as to ask him *not* to. But it was only a request."

"Our Landsman seldom heeds requests," Evan said quietly.

"That was the end of it for me," S'Rella continued. "That was when the one-wings left."

"*Left?!*"

S'Rella nodded. "When the vote was done, Val rose from his place, and his look—I'm glad he had no weapon, or he might have killed somone. Instead he spoke; he called them all fools, and cowards, and worse. There were shouts, curses back at him, some scuffles. Val called on all his friends to leave. Damen and I had to push through to the door, the flyers—some of them I recognized, people I've known for years, but they were jeering, saying things to us—it was *horrible*, Maris. The anger there . . ."

"You got out, though."

"Yes. And we flew to North Arren, almost all of the one-wings. Val led us to a large field, an old battlefield, and he stood on top of a ruined fortification and spoke to us. We had our own Council. A fourth of all the flyers of Windhaven were there. We voted to impose a sanction on Thayos, even if the others would not. That was why Katinn flew here with me; we were to tell the Landsman together. He had already been sent word of the other decision, but Katinn and I were going to confront him with the one-wings' threat." She laughed bitterly. "He listened to us coldly, and when we were finished, he said that we and all of our kind were unfit to be flyers, and that nothing would please him more than never to have a one-wing fly to Thayos again. He promised to show us exactly what he thought of us, and Val, and all one-wings.

"And he showed us. At sunset his landsguard came, and we were marched into the courtyard with the rest, and he showed us." Her face was gray; the recounting of the tale had opened her wounds again.

"Oh, S'Rella," Maris said sorrowfully. She reached out and took her friend's hand, but when they touched S'Rella gave a sudden startled shudder and then, again, began to weep.

Sleep did not come easily for Maris. She twisted and turned restlessly. Her dreams were dark and shapeless, nightmares of flights that ended at the end of a rope.

She woke hours before dawn, in darkness, to the faint sound of distant music.

Evan was asleep beside her, snoring softly into his feather pillow. Maris rose and dressed, and wandered from the bedroom. Bari was resting comfortably, a child's innocent sleep, free of the burdens that weighed on the rest of them. S'Rella slept too, hunched beneath blankets.

Coll's room was empty.

Maris followed the sound of the soft, fading music. She found him outside, sitting up against the side of the house in the starlight, filling the cool pre-dawn air with the quiet melancholy of his guitar.

Maris sat on the damp ground beside him. "Are you making a song?"

"Yes," Coll said. His fingers moved with slow deliberation. "How did you know?"

"I remembered," Maris said. "When we were young together, you used to rise in the middle of the night and go outside, to work on some new tune you wanted to keep secret."

Coll struck a final plaintive chord before he set the guitar aside. "I'm still a creature of habit, then," he said. "Well, I have no choice. When the words scurry about in my head, they do not let me sleep."

"Is it finished?"

"No. I have a mind to call it 'Tya's Fall,' and the words have mostly come to me, but not the tune. I can almost hear it, but I hear it differently at different times. Sometimes it is dark and tragic, a slow, sad song like the ballad of Aron and Jeni. But later it seems to me it should be faster, that it should pulse like the blood of a man choking on his own rage, that it should burn and hurt and throb. What do you think, big sister? How should I do it? What does Tya's fall make you feel, sorrow or anger?"

"Both," said Maris. "That's no help, but it's all the answer I can give. Both, and more. I feel guilty, Coll."

She told him of Arrilan and his companions, and the offer they'd come bearing. Coll listened sympathetically, and when she had finished he took her hand in his own. His fingers were covered with calluses, but gentle and warm. "I did not know," he said. "S'Rella said nothing."

"I doubt S'Rella knows," Maris said. "Val probably told Arrilan not to speak of my refusal. He has a good heart, Val One-Wing, whatever they might say of him."

"Your guilt is foolish," Coll told her. "Even if you had gone I doubt it would have mattered. One person more or less changes little. The Council would have broken with or without you, and Tya would have been hanged. You shouldn't torture yourself with remorse for something you couldn't have changed."

"Perhaps you're right," Maris said, "but I should have *tried*, Coll. They might have listened to me—Dorrel and his friends, the Stormtown group, Corina, even Corm. They know me, all of them. Val could never reach them. But I might have managed to keep the flyers together, if I'd gone and presided as Val asked me to."

"Speculation," said Coll. "You're giving yourself needless pain."

"Perhaps it's time I gave myself pain," Maris said. "I was afraid of hurting again—that was why I didn't go with Arrilan when he came for me. I *was* a coward."

"You can't be responsible for all the flyers of Windhaven, Maris. You have to think of yourself first, of your own needs."

Maris smiled. "A long time ago I thought only of myself, and I changed the whole world around to suit me. Oh, I told myself it was for everybody, but you and I know it was really for me. Barrion was right, Coll. I was naive. I had no idea where it would all lead. I knew only that I wanted to fly.

"I should have gone, Coll. It was my responsibility. But all I cared about was *my* pain, *my* life, when I should have been thinking of larger things. Tya's blood is on my hands." She held one up.

Coll took it and squeezed it hard. "Nonsense. All I see is my sister tearing herself apart for nothing. Tya is gone, there is nothing you could have done, and even if there had been, there is certainly nothing you can do *now*. It is over. Never anguish about the past, Barrion once told me. Make your pain into a song, and give it to the world."

"I can't make songs," Maris said. "I can't fly. I said I wanted to be of use, but I turned my back on the people who needed me, and played at being a healer. I'm not a healer. I'm not a flyer. So what am I? Who am I?"

"Maris . . ."

"Just so," she said. "Maris of Lesser Amberly, the girl who once changed the world. If I did it once, perhaps I can do it again. At least I can try." She stood up abruptly, her face serious in the wan, pale light of dawn, whose faint glow had tinted the eastern horizon.

"Tya is dead," Coll said. He took his guitar and rose to stand face-to-face with his stepsister. "The Council is broken. It's *over*, Maris."

"No," she said. "I won't accept that. It's not over. It's not too late to change the end of Tya's song."

Evan woke quickly to her light touch, sitting up in bed and ready for any emergency.

"Evan," Maris said, sitting beside him. "I know what I must do. I had to tell you first."

He ran one hand over his head, smoothing down the ruffled white hair, frowning. "What?"

"I . . . I *am* alive, Evan. I cannot fly, but I am still who I am."

"It's good to hear you say that, and know you mean it."

"And I'm not a healer. I'll never be a healer."

"You have been making discoveries, haven't you? All this while I slept? Yes . . . I've known, although I couldn't quite tell you. You didn't seem to want to know."

"Of course I didn't want to know. I thought it was the only choice I had. What else was there for me? Pain, only memories of pain and uselessness. Well, the pain is still there, and the memories, but I need not be useless. I must learn to live with the pain, accept it or ignore it, because there are things I must do. Tya is dead and the flyers are broken, and there are things that only I can do, to set things right. So you see . . ." She bit her lip and couldn't quite meet his eyes. "I love you, Evan. But I must leave you."

"Wait." He touched her cheek, and she met his eyes. She thought of the first time she had looked into their deep blue depths, and she felt, unexpectedly strong, a pang of loss. "Tell me now," he said, "*why* you must leave me."

She moved her hands helplessly. "Because I . . . I'm useless here. I don't belong here."

He caught his breath—it might have been a sob or a laugh that he swallowed, she couldn't tell.

"Did you think I loved you as an apprentice, as a healer, Maris? For how much you could help me? As a healer, quite frankly, you tried my patience. I love you as a woman, for yourself, for who you are. And now that you've realized who you are, who you have always been, you think you must leave me?"

"There are things I must do," she said. "I don't know what my fate will be. I may fail. It might be dangerous for you to be associated with me. You might share Reni's fate. . . . I don't want to risk you."

"*You* can't risk me," he said firmly. "I risk myself." He took her hand and held it tightly. "There may be things I can do to help— let me do them. I'll share your burden, share the danger, and make it less. I can do more than just make tea for your friends, you know."

"But you don't have to," Maris said. "You shouldn't risk your life for nothing. This isn't your fight."

"Not my fight?" He sounded mildly indignant. "Isn't Thayos my home? What the Landsman of Thayos decrees affects me, my friends, my patients. My blood is in these mountains and in this forest. *You* are the stranger here. Whatever you accomplish for your people, the flyers, will also affect my people. And I know them, as you cannot. They know me, and they trust me here. Many owe me debts, debts that cannot be paid in iron coin. They will help me, and I will help you. I think you need my help."

Maris felt as if strength was pouring through her, traveling from the firm clasp of his hand up her arm. She smiled, glad that she was not alone, feeling more certain of her way now. "Yes, Evan, I *do* need you."

"You have me. How do we begin?"

Maris leaned back against the wooden headboard, fitting into the curve of Evan's arm. "We need a hidden place, a landing field; a place safe for flyers to come and go without the Landsman or his spies knowing they are on Thayos."

She felt his nod as soon as she had finished speaking. "Done," he said. "There is an abandoned farm, not far from here. The farmer died only last winter, so the forest has not reclaimed the place, although it will shelter it from spying eyes."

"Good. Perhaps we should all move there, for a time, in case the landsguard come looking for us."

"I must stay here," Evan said. "If the landsguard cannot find me, neither can the sick. I must be available to them."

"It might not be safe for you."

"I know a family in Thossi, a family with thirteen children. I helped the mother through a difficult birthing, and saved her children from death half a dozen times—they would eagerly do the same for me. Their house is on the main road, and there is always a child to spare. If the landsguard come for us, they must pass by there, and one of the children could run ahead to warn us."

Maris smiled. "Perfect."

"What else?"

"First, we must wake S'Rella." Maris sat up, moving out of his light embrace, and swung her legs over the edge of the bed. "I need her to be my wings, to fly messages for me, many messages. But one first, the crucial one. To Val One-Wing."

Val came to her, of course.

She waited for him in the doorway of a cramped two-room plank cabin, badly weathered, its furnishings covered with mold. He circled three times above the weed-choked field, silver wings dark against a threatening sky, before he decided that it was safe to land.

When he came down, she helped him with his wings, although something clutched and trembled within her when her hands touched the soft metal fabric. Val embraced her, and smiled. "You're looking well, for an old cripple," he said.

"You're very glib, for an idiot," Maris said back at him. "Come inside."

Coll was within the cabin, tuning his guitar. "Val," he said, nodding.

"Sit," Maris said to Val. "I have something I want you to hear."

He glanced at her, puzzled. But he sat.

Coll sang "Tya's Fall." At his sister's urging, he had composed two versions. He gave Val the sad one.

Val listened politely, with only a hint of restlessness. "Very pretty," he said when Coll was done. "Very sad." He looked sharply at Maris. "Is this why you sent S'Rella to me, and had me fly here at risk of my life, in spite of my pledge never to come to Thayos? For this? To listen to a song?" He frowned. "How badly did that fall injure your head?"

Coll laughed. "Give her half a chance," he said.

"It's all right," Maris said. "Val and I are used to each other, aren't we?"

Val smiled thinly. "You have half a chance," he said. "Tell me what this is all about."

"Tya," Maris said. "In a word. And how to mend what was broken in Council."

Val frowned. "It's too late. Tya is dead. We responded, and now we wait to see what will happen."

"If we wait then it *will* be too late. We can't afford to wait for the flyers to close the academies, or limit challenges to those who promise to ignore your sanction. You've given a weapon to Corm and his kind by walking out, by acting without the support of the Council."

Val shook his head. "I did what had to be done. And there are more one-wings every year. The Landsman of Thayos may laugh now, but he will not laugh forever."

"You don't have forever," Maris said. She was silent a moment, her thoughts tumbling so fast that she was afraid to speak. She couldn't afford to alienate Val. They did understand each other, as she had told Coll, but Val was still prickly and temperamental, as his actions in Council had proved. And it would be hard for him to admit that he had been wrong.

"I should have come when you sent for me," she said after a moment. "But I was afraid, and selfish. Perhaps I could have kept this split from taking place."

Val said flatly, "That's useless. What happened, happened."

"That doesn't mean it can't be changed. I understand you felt you had to do *something*—but what you did may turn out to be a lot worse than doing nothing could have been. What if the flyers decide to strip you of your wings, to ground all the one-wings?"

"Let them try."

"What could you do? Fight them individually, hand to hand? No. If the flyers should decide to take away the wings from all those who participate in your sanction, there would be nothing you could do. Nothing except, perhaps, to kill a few flyers and see a lot more one-wings die like Tya. The Landsmen would support the flyers with all the power of the landsguard."

"If that happens . . ." Val stared at Maris, his face dangerously still. "If that happens, you'll live to see your dream die. Does that mean so much to you? Still? When you know that you can never fly again yourself?"

"This is more important than my dream or my life," Maris said. "It's gone beyond that. You know that. You care too, Val."

The silence in the little cabin seemed to close around them. Even Coll's fingers were motionless upon the strings of his guitar.

"Yes," said Val, the word like a sigh. "But what . . . what can I do?"

"Revoke this sanction," Maris said promptly. "Before your enemies use it against you."

"Will the Landsman revoke Tya's hanging? No, Maris, this sanction is the only power we have. The other flyers must join us in it, or we must stay split."

"It's a useless gesture, you know that," Maris said. "Thayos will not miss the one-wings. The flyer-born will come and go as always, and the Landsman will have plenty of wings to bear his words. It means nothing."

"It means we will keep our word; that we do not make idle threats. Besides, the sanction was voted by all of us. I could not revoke it alone if I wanted to. You are wasting your breath."

Maris smiled scornfully, but inside she felt hopeful. Val was beginning to back down. "Don't play games with me, Val. You *are* the one-wings. That's why I called you here. We both know they will do whatever you suggest."

"Are you really asking me to forget what the Landsman did? To forget Tya?"

"No one will forget Tya."

A soft chord sounded. "My song will assure that," Coll said. "I'll sing it in Port Thayos in a few days. Other singers will steal it. Soon it will be heard everywhere."

Val stared at him in disbelief. "You mean to sing that song in Port Thayos? Are you mad? Don't you know that the very name of Tya raises curses and fights in Port Thayos? Sing that song there, in any tavern, and I'll wager you'll be left in a gutter with your throat slit open."

"Singers are given a certain license," Coll said. "Especially if they are good. The first mention of Tya's name may bring jeers, but after they've heard my song they'll feel differently. Before long, Tya will have become a hero, a tragic victim. That will be because of my song, although few will admit or realize it."

"I've never heard such arrogance," Val said, sounding bemused. He looked at Maris. "Did you put him up to this?"

"We discussed it."

"Did you discuss the fact that he's likely to be killed? Some people may be willing to listen to a song that makes Tya sound noble. But some furious, drunken landsguard will try to stop this singer from spreading his lies, and crush his head in. Did you think of that?"

"I can watch out for myself," Coll said. "Not all my songs are popular, especially at first."

"It's your life," Val said, shaking his head. "If you live long enough, I suppose your singing may make some difference."

"I want you to send some more flyers here," Maris said. "One-wings who can sing and play at least passably well."

"You want Coll to train them for the day when they lose their wings?"

"His song must go beyond Thayos, as quickly as possible," Maris said. "I want flyers who can learn it well enough to teach it to singers wherever they go, and I want them to go everywhere with that song as a message from us. All of Windhaven will know of Tya, and will sing Coll's song of what she tried to do."

Val looked thoughtful. "Very well," he said. "I'll send my people here in secret. Away from Thayos, the song may be popular."

"You will also spread the word that the sanction against Thayos has been revoked."

"I will *not*," he snapped. "Tya must be avenged by more than a song!"

"Did you ever know Tya?" Maris asked. "Don't you know what she tried to do? She tried to prevent war, and to prove to the Landsmen that they could not control the flyers. But this sanction will give us back into the hands of the Landsmen, because it has split and weakened us. Only by acting together, in unison, do flyers have the strength to defy the Landsmen."

"Tell that to Dorrel," Val said coldly. "Don't blame me. I called the Council to act together and save Tya, not to bow down before the Landsman of Thayos. Dorrel took the Council away from me, and made us weak. Tell *him*, and see what answer he can give you!"

"I intend to," Maris said calmly. "S'Rella is on her way to Laus now."

"You mean to bring him here?"

"Yes. And others. I can't go to them now. I'm a cripple, as you said." She smiled grimly.

Val hesitated, obviously trying to put the pieces together in his mind. "You want more than the sanction revoked," he said finally. "That's just the first step, to unite one-wing and flyer-born. What do you have planned for us, if you can weld us together?"

Maris felt her heart lift, knowing that she would have Val's agreement.

"Do you know how Tya died?" Maris asked. "Did you know that the Landsman of Thayos was cruel and stupid enough to kill her while she wore her wings? Afterward they were stripped from her and given to the man she'd won them from two years before. Tya's body was buried in an unmarked grave in a field just outside the keep, where thieves and murderers and other outlaws are customarily buried. She died with her wings on, but she was not allowed a flyer's burial. And she has had no mourners."

"What of it? What has this to do with me? What do you really want of me, Maris?"

She smiled. "I want you to mourn, Val. That's all. I want you to mourn for Tya."

Maris and Evan heard the news first from the lips of a wandering storyteller, an elderly, waspish woman from Port Thayos who stopped with them briefly so the healer might remove a thorn that had lodged under the skin of one bare foot. "Our landsguard have taken the mine from Thrane," the woman said while Evan worked on her. "There is talk of invading Thrane itself."

"Folly," Evan muttered. "More death."

"Is there other news?" Maris asked. Flyers continued to come and go from her secret field, but it had been more than a week since Coll—having passed along his song to a half-dozen one-wings— had taken the road to Port Thayos. The days had been cold, and rainy, and anxious.

"There is the flyer," the woman said. She winced as Evan's fine bone knife sliced the thorn from her flesh. "Careful, healer," she said.

"The flyer?" Maris said.

"A ghost, some say," the woman said. Evan had removed the thorn and was rubbing salve into the cut he had made. "Perhaps Tya's ghost. A woman dressed all in black, silent, restless. She appeared from the west two days before I left. The lodge men came out to meet her, to help her land and care for her wings. But she did not land. She flew silently above the mountains and the

Landsman's keep, and on across the countryside to Port Thayos. Nor did she land there. Since she first came, she has flown in a great circle, round and round again, from Port Thayos to the Landsman's keep and back, never landing, never shouting down a word. Flying, always flying, in sun or storm, day or night. She is there at sunset and still there at dawn. She neither eats nor drinks."

"Fascinating," Maris said, suppressing a smile. "You think she is a ghost?"

"Perhaps," the old woman said. "I have seen her many times myself. Walking down the alleys of Port Thayos, I feel a shadow touch me, and I look up, and she is there. She has caused much talk. The people are afraid, and some of the landsguard say that the Landsman is most afraid of all, though he tries not to show it. He will not come outside to look at her when she passes above his keep. Perhaps he is afraid of seeing Tya's face."

Evan had wrapped a bandage soaked in ointment around the storyteller's injured foot. "There," he said. "Try standing on that."

The woman stood up, leaning on Maris for support. "It pains a bit."

"It was infected," Evan said. "You are lucky. If you had waited a few days longer to come to a healer, you might have lost the foot. Wear boots. The forest trails are hazardous."

"I do not care for boots," the woman said. "I like the feel of the earth and grass and rock beneath my feet."

"Do you like the feel of thorns beneath your skin?" Evan said. They argued back and forth for a time, and finally the woman agreed to wear a soft cloth boot, but only on her injured foot, and only until it was healed.

When she was gone, Evan turned to Maris with a smile. "So it begins," he said. "How is it that the ghost neither eats nor drinks?"

"She carries a bag of nuts and dried fruit, and a skin of water," Maris said. "Flyers often do that on long flights. How do you suppose we could fly to Artellia or the Embers otherwise?"

"I had never given the matter much thought."

Maris nodded, preoccupied. "I suspect they substitute a second flyer by night, secretly, to let their ghost rest. Clever of Val to send someone who looks like Tya. I should have thought of that."

"You have thought of quite enough," Evan said. "Don't reproach yourself. Why do you look so serious?"

"I wish," Maris said, "that the flyer could be *me*."

Two days later, a little girl arrived panting at their door. She was one of that family so indebted to Evan, and for a brief, fearful moment Maris wondered if the landsguard had come for her already. But it was only news; Evan had asked to be sent word of anything heard in Thossi.

"A merchant came through," said the little girl. "He talked 'bout the flyers."

"What of them?" Maris asked.

"He said, he told old Mullish at the inn, that the Landsman is scared. There are three of them, he said. Three black flyers, going round and round and round." She stood up and spun in a circle, her small arms outstretched, to show them what she meant. Maris looked at Evan, and smiled.

"Seven black flyers now," a huge fat man told them. He'd come to their door battered and bleeding, a deserter from the landsguard dressed in rags. "Tried to send me to Thrane," he said by way of explanation, "but damned if I'd go there." When he wasn't speaking, he coughed, and often he coughed up blood.

"Seven?"

"A bad number," the man said, coughing. "All dressed in black too, a bad color. They mean us no good." His coughing suddenly grew so bad he could not talk.

"Easy," Evan said, "easy." He gave the man wine, mixed with herbs, and he and Maris led him to a bed.

The fat man would not rest, though. As soon as his coughing fit had ended, he began to talk again. "If I was Landsman, I'd march out my archers, and shoot 'em down when they flew overhead. Yes, I would. There's some that says the arrows would just pass through 'em, but not me. I think they're flesh just like me." He slapped his ample gut. "Can't just let 'em fly. They're bringing bad luck to us all. Weather's been bad lately, and the fish haven't been running, and I heard tell of people taking sick and dying in Port Thayos when the shadow of those wings touched 'em. Something terrible is going to happen on Thrane, I know it, that's why I wouldn't go. Not with seven black flyers in the sky. No, not me. This is an evil thing, I tell you, and it won't bring us good."

It brought the fat man no good, at any rate, Maris thought. The next morning, when she brought his breakfast in to him, his huge body was stiff and cold. Evan buried him in the forest, among the graves of a dozen other travelers.

"Thenya went to Port Thayos to try to sell her tapestries," reported another of the horde of children Evan had delivered, a boy this time. "When she came back to Thossi, she said there are more than a dozen black flyers now, flying in a great circle from the port to the Landsman's keep. And more are arriving every day."

"Twenty flyers, all in black, silent, grim," said the young singer. She had golden hair and blue eyes, a sweet voice and an easy manner. "They'll make a marvelous song! I'd be working on it now, if only I knew how it was all going to end . . ."

"Why are they here, do you think?" Evan asked.

"For Tya, of course," the young woman said, startled that anyone would ask. "She lied to stop the war, and the Landsman killed her for it. They wear black for her, I'd wager. Many people are grieving for her."

"Ah, yes," Evan said. "Tya. Her story might make a song itself. Have you thought of making one?"

The singer grinned. "There already is one." she said. "I heard it in Port Thayos. Here, I'll sing it for you."

Maris met Katinn of Lomarron in the abandoned field, where slender green ruffians and misshapen dirt-dragons were fast crowding out the wild wheat. The big man with the scylla's-tooth necklace came down gracefully on silvered wings, dressed all in black.

She led him inside and gave him water. "Well?"

He wiped away the moisture from his lips and grinned at her roughly. "I flew in very high, and saw the circle far beneath me. Ah, you should have seen it! Forty wings by now, I'd guess. The Landsman must be drooling at the mouth. Word has gone out, too. More one-wings are coming from all over Eastern, and Val himself flew the word back to Western, so it won't be too long before others join us, too. By now there are so many that it's easy to break away for a rest or a meal without anyone being the wiser. I don't envy poor Alain starting it all. She's a strong flyer, no doubt of that. I've never known her to tire. They've got her resting in secret on Thrynel now, but she'll be back to rejoin us soon. As for me, I'm on my way to join the circle now."

Maris nodded. "What about Coll's song?"

"They're singing it on Lomarron, and South Arren, and Kite's Landing. I've heard it myself, several times. And it's gone to Southern and the Outer Islands as well, and to Western of course— to your Amberly, and Culhall, and Poweet. Heard that it's spreading among the singers in Stormtown."

"Good," said Maris. "Good."

"The Landsman sent Jem up to question the black flyers," said Evan's friend, repeating the news from Thossi, "and it's said that he recognized them and called on them by name, but they would not speak to him. You ought to come to the city and see them, Evan. Whenever you look up, the sky is full of flyers."

"The Landsman has ordered the flyers out of his sky, but they will not go. And why should they? As the singers say, the sky belongs to flyers!"

•　•　•

"I heard that a flyer arrived from Thrane, with a message from their Landsman to ours, but when he met her in the audience chamber to hear it, he turned pale with fear, for the flyer was dressed in black from head to foot. She delivered the message to him as he trembled, but before she could go, the Landsman stopped her and demanded to know why she was dressed all in black. 'I go to join the circle,' she told him calmly, 'and grieve for Tya.' And so she did, so she did."

"They say the singers in Port Thayos all dress in black these days, and some other people as well. The streets are full of merchants selling black cloth, and the dyers are very busy."

"Jem has joined the black flyers!"

"The Landsman has ordered the landsguard back from Thrane. He's afraid of what the black flyers might do, I heard, and he wants his best archers around him. The keep is full to overcrowding. It's said that the Landsman will not go outside, lest the shadow of their wings fall upon him as they fly overhead."

S'Rella arrived with the welcome news that Dorrel was less than a day behind her. Maris kept watch on the cliffs herself all that afternoon, too impatient even to wait at home with S'Rella, and at last she was rewarded by the sight of a dark figure gliding inland. She hurried into the forest to meet him.

It was a hot, still day, bad weather for flying. Maris swiped at attacking insects as she trudged through the tall grass that almost concealed the cabin. Her heart was racing with excitement as she pushed open the heavy wooden door, hanging on its hinges.

She blinked, almost blind in the dark interior after the brilliant sunshine, and then she felt his hand on her shoulder, and heard his familiar voice say her name.

"You . . . you came," she said. She was suddenly short of breath. "Dorrel."

"Did you doubt I would come?"

She could see now. The familiar smile, his well-remembered way of standing.

"Do you mind if we sit down?" he asked. "I'm awfully tired. It was a long flight from Western, and it did me no good to try to catch up to S'Rella."

They sat close together, on two matching chairs that must once have been very fine. But the cushions were impregnated with dust now, greenish and slightly damp with mold.

"How are you, Maris?"

"I'm . . . living. Ask me again in a month or so and I may have a better answer for you." She looked into his dark, concerned eyes, and then away again. "It's been a long time, hasn't it, Dorr?"

He nodded. "When you weren't at the Council, I understood. . . . I hoped that you were doing what was best for you. I was more pleased than I can say when S'Rella came, bearing your message, your request that I come to you." He sat a little straighter in his chair. "But surely you didn't send for me just for the pleasure of seeing an old friend."

Maris drew a deep breath. "I need your help. You know about the circle? The black flyers?"

He nodded. "Rumors have already spread. And I saw them as I flew in. An impressive sight. Your doing?"

"Yes."

He shook his head. "And not an end in itself, I'll wager. What's your plan?"

"Will you help me with it? We need you."

" 'We?' You've sided with the one-wings, I suppose?" His tone was not angry, and did not condemn, but Maris was aware that he had withdrawn from her, ever so slightly.

"It's not a matter of sides, Dorr. At least, not among the flyers. It mustn't be—that way is death, the end of everything we both hold dear. Flyers—one-wing or flyer-born—must not be split up, fragmented, at the mercy of Landsmen."

"I agree. But it's too late. It was too late once Tya declared her scorn for all the laws and traditions by telling her first lie."

"Dorr," she said, her voice coaxing and reasonable, "I don't approve of what Tya did, either. She meant well; what she did was wrong, I agree, but—"

"I agree, you agree," he said, interrupting. "But. We always come down to that. Tya is dead now—we can all agree on that. She's dead, but it's not over, it's far from over. Other one-wings call her a hero, a martyr. She died for the cause of lying, for the freedom to lie. How many more lies will be told? How long will it be before the people forget their mistrust of us? Since the one-wings refused to repudiate Tya, and split away from us, there is talk among . . . among a few . . . of closing down the academies and ending the challenges, returning to the old way, to the old days when a flyer was a flyer for once and for all."

"You don't want that."

"No. No, I don't." His shoulders slumped for a moment, uncharacteristically, and he sighed. "But, Maris, it goes beyond what I want, or what you want. It's out of our hands now. Val spoke the death warrant for the one-wings when he led them out of Council and called his illegal sanction."

"Sanctions can be revoked," Maris said.

Dorrel stared at her. His eyes narrowed. "Did Val One-Wing tell you that? I don't believe him. He's playing some devious game, trying to use you to trick me."

"Dorrel!" She stood up, indignant. "Give me some credit, please! I'm not one of Val's puppets! He didn't promise to revoke the sanction, and he's not using me. I tried to convince him that it would be in everyone's best interest to act in such a way that both flyer-born and one-wings were united again. Val is stubborn and impulsive, but he's not blind. Although he wouldn't promise to revoke the sanction, I *did* make him see what a mistake he had made— that his sanction was useless because it was honored only by a small group, and that this division among flyers was to no one's advantage."

Dorrel looked at her thoughtfully. Then he, too, rose, and began to pace around the small, dusty room. "Quite a feat, to get Val

One-Wing to admit he was wrong," he said. "But what good does that do now? Does he agree that the plan we followed was right?"

"No," Maris said. "I don't think it was right, either. I think you were much too harsh. Oh, I know what you thought—I know you had to repudiate Tya's crime, and you thought the best way to do that was to hand her over to the Landsman for execution."

Dorrel stopped walking and frowned at her. "Maris, you know that was never my intention. I never thought Tya should die. But Val's proposal was absurd—it would have seemed that we condoned her actions."

"The Council should have insisted that Tya be given over for punishment, and then stripped Tya of her wings, forever."

"We did strip her of her wings."

"No," said Maris. "You let the Landsman do that, *after* he'd hanged her in them. Why do you suppose he did that? To show that he could hang a flyer and go unscathed."

Dorrel looked horrified. He crossed the room and gripped her arm. "Maris, no! He hung her in her *wings?*"

She nodded.

"I hadn't heard that." He sank down on his chair again as if his legs had been kicked.

"He proved his point," Maris said. "He proved that flyers could be killed as easily as anyone else. And now they will be. Now that you and Val have split flyers and one-wings into two warring camps, the Landsmen will take advantage of it. They'll demand oaths of loyalty, they'll set up rules and regulations to govern their flyers, they'll execute the rebels for treason—in time, perhaps, they'll claim the wings as their own property, to be handed out to followers who please them. Other flyers could be arrested, even executed, tomorrow. All it will take is for one more Landsman to realize he has the power—that the flyers are too fragmented now to offer any opposition." She sat down and gazed at him, almost holding her breath as she hoped for the right response.

Slowly Dorrel nodded. "What you say has a horrible ring of truth to it. But . . . what can I do? Only Val, and the other one-wings, can decide to rejoin us. You surely don't expect me to try to rally the other flyers in a belated sanction of our own?"

"Of course not. But it's not only up to Val—it can't be. There are two sides, and both of you must make some gesture of reconciliation."

"And what might that gesture be?"

Maris leaned forward. "Join the black flyers," she said. "Mourn Tya. Join the others. When word goes out that Dorrel of Laus has joined the one-wings in mourning, others will follow."

"Mourn?" He frowned. "You want me to dress in black and fly in a circle?" His voice was suspicious. "And what else? What else am I to join your black flyers in? Is it your plan to enforce the sanction against Thayos by keeping all the flyers in formation above it?"

"No. Not a sanction. They don't stop any flyers who bring a message to or from Thayos, and if you, or any of your followers, had to leave the circle, no one would stop you. Just make the gesture."

"This is more than a gesture, and more than mourning. I'm certain of it," Dorrel said. "Maris, be honest with me. We have known each other for a very long time. For the love I still bear for you I would do much. But I can't go against what I believe, and I won't be tricked. Please don't play one of Val One-Wing's games and try to use me. I think you owe me honesty."

Maris looked steadily back into his eyes, but she felt a pang of guilt. She *was* trying to use him—he was an important part of her plan, and because of what they had once meant to each other she had felt certain he would not let her down. But she did not mean to deceive him.

She said quietly, "I've always thought of you as my friend, Dorr, even when we were opposed. But I'm not asking you to do this for me just out of friendship. It's more important than that. I think it is equally important to you that this rift between the one-wings and the flyer-born be healed."

"Tell me the whole truth, then. Tell me what you want me to do, and why."

"I want you to join the black flyers, to prove that the one-wings do not fly alone. I want to bring flyers and one-wings together again, to show the world that they can still act as one."

"You think that if Val One-Wing and I fly together we will forget all our differences?"

Maris smiled ruefully. "Perhaps once, long ago, I was that naive. No more. I hope that the one-wings and the flyer-born will act together."

"How? In what way beyond this odd mourning ceremony?"

"The black flyers carry no weapons, make no threats, and do not even land on Thayos," she said. "They are mourners, nothing more. But their presence makes the Landsman of Thayos very nervous. He does not understand. Already he is so frightened he has called his landsguard from Thrane—and therefore the black flyers have succeeded where Tya failed, and ended the war."

"But surely the Landsman will get over his fear. And the black flyers cannot circle Thayos forever."

"The Landsman here is an impetuous, bloody-minded, and fearful man," Maris said. "The violent always suspect others of violence. And it is not his way to wait for someone else to act. I think he will do something before long. I think he will give the flyers cause to act."

Dorrel frowned. "By doing what? Shooting a flight of arrows to knock us from the sky?"

" 'Us'?"

Dorrel shook his head, but he was smiling. "It could be dangerous, Maris. Trying to provoke him to action . . ."

His smiled heartened her. "The black flyers do nothing but fly. If Port Thayos grows agitated in their shadows, that is the work of the Landsman and his subjects."

"Especially the singers and the healers—we know what troublemakers they can be! I'll do as you ask, Maris. It will make a good story to tell my grandchildren, when they come along. I won't have my wings much longer now anyway, with Jan getting to be such a good flyer."

"Oh, Dorr!"

He held up one hand. "I will wear black as a sign of grief for Tya," he said carefully. "And I will join the great circle that flies to mourn her. But I will do nothing that might be seen as condoning her crime, or expressing a sanction against Thayos for her death." He stood up and stretched. "Of course, if anything should happen, if the Landsman should presume to exceed his powers and threaten the flyers, why then, we should all, one-wings and flyer-born, have to act together."

Maris also stood. She was smiling. "I knew you would see it that way," she said.

She wrapped her arms around him and pulled him to her in an affectionate hug. Then Dorrel lifted her face and kissed her, perhaps just for old times' sake, but for a moment it was as if all the years that lay between them had never been, and they were youths again, and lovers, and the sky was theirs from horizon to horizon, and all that lay beneath it.

But the kiss ended, and they stood apart again: old friends linked by memories and faint regrets.

"Go safely, Dorr," said Maris. "Come back soon."

Returning from the sea cliffs, where she had seen Dorrel launch himself for Laus, Maris felt full of hope. There was sadness, too, beneath it—the old familiar longing had swept over her again as she helped Dorrel unfold his wings, and watched him mount the warm blue sky.

But the pain was a little less this time. Although she would have given anything to fly with Dorrel again, she had other things to think about now, and it was not so difficult to pull her hopeless thoughts away from the sky and think of more practical matters. Dorrel had promised to return soon, with more followers, and Maris enjoyed the vision of an even vaster circle of black flyers.

She was shocked out of her reverie as she approached Evan's house, by the sound of a shriek from within.

She ran the last few steps and threw the door open. She saw at once that Bari was crying, Evan trying in vain to comfort her. Standing a little apart was S'Rella with a boy from Thossi.

"What's wrong?" Maris cried, suspecting the worst.

At her voice, Bari turned and ran to her aunt, weeping. "My father, they took my father, make them, please make them . . ."

Maris embraced the weeping child and stroked her hair absently. "What's happened to Coll?"

"Coll has been arrested and taken to the keep," Evan said. "The

Landsman has seized a half-dozen other singers as well—everyone known to have performed Coll's song about Tya. He means to try them for treason."

Maris continued to hold Bari tightly. "There, there," she said. "Shh, shh, Bari."

"There was a riot in Port Thayos," said the boy from Thossi. "When they came to the Moonfish Inn to take Lanya the singer, the landsguard met with customers who tried to defend her. They beat the defenders off with clubs. No one was killed."

Maris listened numbly, trying to absorb it, trying to think.

"I'll fly to Val," S'Rella said. "I'll spread the word among the black flyers—they'll all come. The Landsman will have to release Coll!"

"No," said Maris. She still hugged Bari, and the child's sobbing had ceased. "No, Coll is a land-bound, a singer. He has no claim upon the flyers—they would not rally together to defend him."

"But he's your *brother!*"

"That makes no difference."

"We have to do something," S'Rella insisted.

"We will. We had hoped to provoke the Landsman, but to make him strike at the flyers, not the land-bound. But now that it has happened. . . . Coll and I discussed this possibility." She raised Bari's face gently with a finger beneath her chin, and wiped away her tears. "Bari, you have to go away now."

"No! I want my father! I won't leave without him!"

"Bari, listen to me. You must leave before the Landsman catches you. Your father wouldn't want that."

"I don't care," Bari said stubbornly. "I don't care if the Landsman catches me! I want to be with my father!"

"Don't you want to fly?" Maris asked.

"To fly?" Bari's face suddenly lit up with wonder.

"S'Rella here will let you fly with her over the ocean," Maris said, "if you're big enough not to be afraid." She looked up at S'Rella. "You can take her, can't you?"

S'Rella nodded. "She's light enough. Val has people on Thrynel. It'll be an easy flight."

"Are you big enough?" Maris asked. "Or would you be afraid?"

"I'm not scared," Bari said fiercely, her pride wounded. "My father used to fly, you know."

"I know," Maris said, smiling. She remembered Coll's terror of flight, and hoped that Bari hadn't inherited that particular trait.

"And you'll save my father?" Bari asked.

"Yes," Maris said.

"And after I take her to Thrynel?" S'Rella said. "What then?"

"Then," said Maris, standing and taking Bari by the hand, "I want you to fly to the keep with a message for the Landsman. Tell him that it was all my doing, that I put Coll and the other singers up to it. If he wants me, and he will, tell him I will turn myself over to him, just as soon as he releases Coll and the others."

"Maris," warned Evan, "he will hang you."

"Perhaps," said Maris. "That's a chance I have to take."

"He agrees," S'Rella reported on her return. "As a sign of his good faith, he has released all the singers except Coll. They were taken away by boat to Thrynel, with orders never to return to Thayos. I witnessed their departure myself."

"And Coll?"

"I was allowed to speak to him. He seemed unharmed, although he was worried that something might have happened to his guitar—they wouldn't let him keep it. The Landsman has said he will hold Coll for three days. If you do not appear at his keep by then, Coll will hang."

"Then I must go at once," Maris said.

S'Rella caught her hand. "Coll told me to warn you away. He said you were not to come under any circumstances. That it was too dangerous for you."

Maris shrugged. "Dangerous for him as well. Of course I will go."

"It may be a trap," Evan said. "The Landsman is not to be trusted. He may mean to hang you both."

"That's a risk I'll have to take. If I don't go, Coll is sure to hang. I can't have that on my conscience—I got him into this."

"I don't like it," Evan said.

Maris sighed. "The Landsman will have me sooner or later, unless I flee Thayos at once. By giving myself up to him, I have the chance to save Coll. And, perhaps, to do more."

"What more can you do?" S'Rella demanded. "He'll hang you, and probably your brother too, and that will be that."

"If he hangs me," said Maris calmly, "we will have our incident. My death would unite the flyers as nothing else could."

The color drained out of S'Rella's face. "Maris, no," she whispered.

"I thought that might be it," said Evan in a voice that was unnaturally calm. "So this was the unspoken twist in all your plans. You decided to live just long enough to be a martyr."

Maris frowned. "I was afraid to tell you, Evan. I thought this might happen—I had to consider it when I made my plans. Are you angry?"

"Angry? No. Disappointed. Hurt. And very sad. I believed you when you told me you had decided to live. You seemed happier, and stronger, and I thought that you did love me, and that I could help you." He sighed. "I didn't realize that, instead of life, you had simply chosen what you thought would be a nobler death. I can't deny you what you want. Death and I wrestle daily, and I have never found him noble, but perhaps I look too closely. You will have what you want, and after you are gone the singers will make it all sound very beautiful, no doubt."

"I don't want to die," she said, very quietly.

She went to Evan and took him by the shoulders. "Look at me, and listen to me," she said. His blue eyes met hers, and she saw the sorrow in them, and hated herself for putting it there.

"My love, you must believe me," she said. "I go to the Landsman's keep because it is all I can do. I must try to save my brother, and myself, and convince the Landsman that flyers are not to be trifled with.

"My plan is to push the Landsman until he breaks and does something foolish—I admit that. And I know that this is a dangerous game. I have known that I might die, or that one of my friends might die. But this is not, *not* an elaborate plan to make a noble death for myself.

"Evan, I want to live. And I love you. Please don't doubt that."

She drew a deep breath. "I need your faith in me. I've needed your help and your love all along.

"I know the Landsman may kill me, but I have to go there, risk that, in order to live. It's the only way. I have to do this, for Coll and for Bari, for Tya, for the flyers—and for myself. Because I have to know, really know, that I'm still good for something. That I was left alive for some purpose. Do you understand?"

Evan looked at her, searching her face. Finally he nodded. "Yes. I understand. I believe you."

Maris turned. "S'Rella?"

There were tears in the other woman's eyes, but she was smiling tremulously. "I'm afraid for you, Maris. But you're right. You have to go. And I pray you'll succeed, for your own sake and for all of us. I don't want us to win if it means your death."

"One more thing," said Evan.

"Yes?"

"I'm going with you."

They both wore black.

They had been on the road less than ten minutes when they encountered one of Evan's friends, a little girl rushing breathlessly up the road from Thossi to warn them that a half-dozen landsguard were on their way.

They met the landsguard a half-hour later. They were a weary group, armed with spiked clubs and bows, and dressed in soiled uniforms stained with the sweat of their long forced march. But they treated Maris and Evan almost deferentially, and did not seem in the least surprised to meet them on the road. "We are to escort you back to the Landsman's keep," said the young woman in charge.

"Fine," said Maris. She set them a brisk pace.

An hour before they entered the Landsman's isolated valley, Maris finally saw the black flyers for the first time.

From a distance, they seemed like so many insects, dark specks creeping across the sky, although they moved with a sensuous slowness no insect could ever match. They were never out of sight from the first moment Maris noticed motion low on the horizon; no sooner would one vanish behind a tree or a rocky outcrop than another would appear where the first had been. On and on they came, a never-ending procession, and Maris knew that the aerial column trailed miles behind to Port Thayos, and extended on ahead to the Landsman's keep and the sea, before curving around in a great circle to meet itself above the waves.

"Look," she said to Evan, pointing. He looked, and smiled at her, and they held hands. Somehow the mere sight of the flyers made Maris feel better, gave her strength and reassurance. As she walked on, the moving specks in the afternoon sky took on shape and form, growing until she could see the silver sheen of sunlight on their wings, and the way they banked and tacked to find the right wind.

Where the road from Thossi joined the broad thoroughfare up from Port Thayos, the flyers passed directly overhead, and for the rest of the journey the walkers moved beneath them. Maris could make out the flyers quite well by then; a few kept high, up where the wind was stronger, but most skimmed along barely above tree-top level, and the silver of their wings and the black of their clothing were equally conspicuous. Every few moments another flyer caught and passed Maris and Evan and their escort, so the shadow of wings washed over them as regularly as silent breakers crashing against a beach.

The landsguard never looked up at the flyers, Maris noticed. In fact, the procession in the sky seemed to make them surly and irritable, and at least one of the party—a whey-faced youth with pockmarks—trembled visibly whenever the shadows swept over him.

Near sunset the road climbed over the last hills to the first checkpoint. Their escort marched through without stopping. A few yards beyond, the path dropped off abruptly, and there was a high vantage point from which the entire valley was visible beneath them.

Maris drew in her breath sharply, and felt Evan's hand tighten in her own.

In the shimmering red haze of sunset, colors faded and vanished while shadows etched themselves starkly on the valley floor. Beneath them the world seemed drenched in blood, and the keep hunched like some great crippled animal made of shadow, impossibly black. The fires within it sent up heat ripples that made the dark stone itself seem to writhe and tremble, so it looked like a beast shivering in terror.

Above it, waiting, were the flyers.

The valley was full of them; Maris counted ten before losing track. Heat beating against stone sent up great updrafts, and the flyers soared on them, climbing halfway up the sky before spinning free to descend in wide graceful spirals. Around and around they moved, circling, waiting; dark scavenger kites impatient for the shadow beast to die. It was a somber, silent scene.

"No wonder he is so afraid," Maris said.

"We are not supposed to stop," the young officer leading their escort said to them.

With a final glance, Maris proceeded down into the valley, where Tya's silent mourners flew ominous circles above the shadowed fortress, and the Landsman of Thayos waited inside his cold stone halls, afraid of open sky.

"I have a mind to hang the three of you," the Landsman said.

He was seated on the wooden throne in his receiving chamber, fingering a heavy bronze knife that lay across his knees. Against a white silk shirt, his silver chain of office gleamed softly in the light of the oil lamps, but his face was at odds with his clothing: pale and drawn and twitching.

The room was full of landsguard; they stood along the walls, silent, impassive. There were no windows in the chamber. Perhaps that was why the Landsman had chosen it. Outside, the black flyers would be wheeling against the scattered evening stars.

"Coll goes free," Maris said, trying to keep the tension from her voice.

The Landsman frowned and gestured with his knife. "Bring up the singer," he ordered. A landsguard officer hurried off. "Your brother has caused me great trouble," the Landsman continued. "His songs are treason. I see no reason to release him."

"We have an agreement," Maris said quickly. "I came. Now you must give Coll his freedom."

The Landsman's mouth twitched. "Do not presume to tell me what to do. By what conceit do you imagine that you can dictate terms to me? There can be no bargaining between us. I am Landsman here. I am Thayos. You and your brother are my prisoners."

"S'Rella carried your promise to me," Maris replied. "She will know if you break it, and soon flyers and Landsmen will know all over Windhaven. Your pledge will be worthless. How will you rule then, or bargain?"

His eyes narrowed. "Oh? Perhaps so." He smiled. "I made no promise to release him whole, however. How well will your brother sing of Tya, I wonder, when I have had his tongue yanked from his mouth, and the fingers of his right hand cut off?"

A wave of vertigo washed over Maris suddenly, as if she stood on the edge of a great precipice, wingless and about to fall. Then she felt Evan take her hand again, and when his fingers twined within her own, somehow she found the threat she needed. "You wouldn't dare," she said. "Even your landsguard might balk at such an atrocity, and flyers would carry word of your crime as far as the wind would take them. All your knives could not long protect you then."

"I intend to let your brother go," the Landsman said loudly, "not because I fear his friends and your empty threats, but because I am merciful. But neither he nor any other singer will ever sing of Tya again on my island. He will be sent from Thayos never to return."

"And us?"

The Landsman smiled and ran his thumb along the blade of the bronze knife. "The healer is nothing. Less than nothing. He can go as well." He leaned forward on his throne and pointed the knife at Maris. "As to you, wingless flyer, I will even extend my mercy to you. You too shall go free."

"You have a price," Maris said with certainty.

"I want the black flyers out of my sky," the Landsman said.

"No," said Maris.

"NO?" He shrieked the word, and his hand plunged the point of the knife into the arm of his chair. "Where do you think you are? I've had enough of your arrogance. How *dare* you refuse! I'll have you hanging at first light, if I so choose."

"You won't hang us," Maris said.

His mouth trembled. "Oh?" he said. "Go on, then. Tell me what I will and will not do. I am anxious to hear." His voice was thick with barely suppressed rage.

"You might like to hang us," Maris said, "but you don't dare. Because of the black flyers you are so anxious to have us remove."

"I *dared* hang one flyer," he said. "I can hang others. Your black flyers do not frighten me."

"No? Why is it then that you do not go outside your halls these days, even to hunt or walk in your own courtyard?"

"Flyers are pledged not to carry weapons," the Landsman said. "What harm can they do? Let them float up there forever."

"For ages no flyer has carried a blade into the sky," Maris agreed, choosing her words carefully. "It is flyer law, tradition. But it was flyer law to stay out of land-bound politics as well, to deliver all messages without a second thought as to what they meant. Tya did what she did nonetheless. And you killed her for it, in spite of centuries of tradition that said no Landsman might judge a flyer."

"She was a traitor," the Landsman said. "Traitors deserve no other fate, whether they wear wings or not."

Maris shrugged. "My point," she said, "is only that traditions are poor protection in these troubled days. You think yourself safe because flyers carry no weapons?" She stared at him coldly. "Well, every flyer who brings you a message will wear black, and some of them will carry the grief in their hearts as well. As you hear them out, you will always wonder. Will this be the one? Will this be a new Tya, a new Maris, a new Val One-Wing? Will the ancient tradition end here and now, in blood?"

"It will never happen," the Landsman said, too shrilly.

"It's unthinkable," Maris said. "As unthinkable as what you did to Tya. Hang me, and it will happen all the sooner."

"I hang who I please. My guards protect me."

"Can they stop an arrow loosed from above? Will you bar all your windows? Refuse to see flyers?"

"You are *threatening* me!" the Landsman said in sudden fury.

"I am warning you," Maris said. "Perhaps no harm will come to you at all, but you will never be sure. The black flyers will see to that. For the rest of your life they will follow you, haunting you as sure as Tya's ghost. Whenever you look up at the stars, you will see wings. Whenever a shadow brushes you, you will wonder. You'll never be able to look out a window or walk in the sun. The flyers will circle your keep forever, like flies around a corpse. You will see them on your deathbed. Your own home will be your prison, and even there you will never really be certain. Flyers can pass any wall, and once they have slipped off their wings, they look like anyone else."

The Landsman sat very still as Maris spoke, and she watched him carefully, hoping she was pushing him the right way. There was a wildness about his puffy eyes, an unpredictability that terrified her. Her voice was calm, but her brow was beaded by sweat, and her hands felt damp and clammy.

The Landsman's eyes flicked back and forth as if hunting for escape from the specter of the black flyers, until they settled on one of his guards. "Bring me my flyer!" he snapped. "At once, at once!"

The man must have been waiting just outside the chamber; he entered at once. Maris recognized him; a thin, balding, stoop-shouldered flyer she had never really known. "Sahn," she said aloud, when his name came to her.

He did not acknowledge her greeting. "My Landsman," he said deferentially, in a reedy voice.

"She *threatens* me," the Landsman said angrily. "Black flyers, she says. They will hound me to my death, she says."

"She lies," Sahn said quickly, and with a start Maris remembered who he was. Sahn of Thayos, flyer-born, conservative; Sahn who two years ago had lost his wings to an upstart one-wing. Now he had them back, by virtue of her death. "The black flyers are no threat. They are nothing, nothing."

"She says they will never leave me," the Landsman said.

"Wrong," said Sahn in his thin, ingratiating voice. "You have nothing to fear. They will soon be gone. They have duties, Landsmen of their own, lives to live, families, messages to fly. They cannot stay indefinitely."

"Others will take their place," Maris said. "Windhaven has many flyers. You will never be out from under the shadow of their wings."

"Pay her no mind, sir," Sahn said. "The flyers are not behind her. Only a few one-wings. Trash of the sky. When they leave, no one will take their place. You need only wait, my Landsman." Something in his tone, beyond his words, shocked and sickened her, and all at once Maris knew why; Sahn spoke as a lesser to a superior, not as equal to equal. He feared the Landsman, and was beholden to him for his very wings, and his voice made it clear that he knew it. For the first time, a flyer had become his Landsman's creature, through and through.

The Landsman turned to face her again, his eyes cold. "As I thought," he said. "Tya lied to me, and I found her out. Val One-Wing tried to frighten me with empty threats. And now you. All of you are liars, but I am cleverer than you think me. Your black flyers will do nothing, *nothing*. One-wings, all of you. The *real* flyers, they care nothing for Tya. The Council proved that."

"Yes," Sahn agreed, head nodding.

For an instant Maris was consumed by rage. She wanted to storm across the chamber and seize the frail flyer, shake him until he hurt. But Evan squeezed her hand hard, and when she glanced at him he shook his head.

"Sahn," she said, gently.

Reluctantly he turned his eyes to meet hers. He was shaking, she saw, perhaps in shame at what he had become. As she looked at him, Maris thought she saw a bit of all the flyers she had ever known. The things we will do to fly, she thought . . . "Sahn," she said. "Jem has joined the black flyers. He is no one-wing."

"No," Sahn admitted, "but he knew Tya well."

"If you advise your Landsman," she said, "tell him who Dorrel of Laus is."

Sahn hesitated.

"Who?" the Landsman snapped, eyes flicking from Maris to Sahn. "Well?"

"Dorrel of Laus," Sahn said reluctantly. "A Western flyer, my Landsman. He's from a very old family. A good flyer. He is about my age."

"What of him? What do I care?" The Landsman was impatient.

"Sahn," said Maris, "what do you think would happen if Dorrel joined the black flyers?"

"No," Sahn said quickly. "He's no one-wing. He wouldn't."

"If he did?"

"He's popular. A leader. There would be others." Clearly Sahn did not like what he was saying.

"Dorrel of Laus is bringing a hundred Western flyers to join the circle," Maris said forcefully. An exaggeration, probably, but they had no way of knowing.

The Landsman's mouth twitched. "Is this true?" he demanded of his pet flyer.

Sahn coughed nervously. "Dorrel, I—well, it's hard to say, sir. He's influential, but, but . . ."

"Silence," the Landsman said, "or I'll find someone else for those wings of yours."

"Ignore him," Maris said sharply. "Sahn, a Landsman has no right to bestow or take away wings. The flyers have united to prove the truth of that."

"Tya died wearing these wings," Sahn said. "*He* gave them to me."

"The wings are yours. No one blames you," Maris said. "But your Landsman should not have done as he did. If you care, if you agree that Tya's death was wrong, join us. Do you have any black clothing?"

"Black? I—well, yes."

"Are you mad?" the Landsman said. He pointed at Sahn with his knife. "Seize that fool."

Hesitantly, two of the landsguard started forward.

"Stay away from me!" Sahn said loudly. "I'm a flyer, damn you!"

And they stopped, looking back at the Landsman.

He pointed again, his mouth twitching. He seemed to be having difficulty finding words. "You will—you will take Sahn, and—"

He never finished. The doors to the chamber burst open then, and Coll was dragged bodily into the room by a brace of guards.

They shoved him forward toward the Landsman; he stumbled to his hands and knees, then rose unsteadily. The right side of his face was a massive purplish bruise, and his eyes were as black as his clothing.

"Coll!" Maris said, horrified.

Coll managed a feeble smile. "My fault, big sister. But I'm all right." Evan went to him and examined his face.

"I did not order this," the Landsman said.

"You said he shouldn't sing," a landsguard replied. "He wouldn't stop singing."

"He's all right," Evan said. "The bruise will heal."

Maris sighed in relief. Despite all their talk of death, it had been a shock to see Coll's face. "I'm tired of this," she said to the Landsman. "Listen, if you want to hear my terms."

"*Terms?*" His tone was incredulous. "I am Landsman of Thayos, and you are nothing, no one. You cannot give me terms."

"I can and will. You'd do well to listen. If you don't, you won't be the only one to suffer. I don't think you realize the position you and Thayos are in. All over this island, your people are singing Coll's song, and the singers are moving from island to island, spreading it through the world. Soon everyone will know how you had Tya killed."

"She was a liar, a traitor."

"A flyer is not a subject, and cannot be a traitor," Maris said, "and she lied to stop a senseless war. Oh, she'll always be controversial. But you'd be a fool to underestimate the power of the singers. You're becoming a widely hated man."

"Silence," the Landsman said.

"Your people have never loved you," Maris continued. "They're frightened, too. The black flyers scare them, singers are being arrested, flyers are hanged, trade has been suspended, the war you started turned sour, even your landsguard are deserting. And you are the cause of it all. Sooner or later, they will think of getting rid of you. Already they know that nothing else will cause the black flyers to leave.

"The stories are everywhere," Maris went on. "Thayos is cursed, Thayos is unlucky, Tya haunts the keep, the Landsman is mad. You will be shunned, like the first mad Landsman, like Kennehut. But your people will only endure it for a short time. They know the solution. They will rise against you. The singers will light the spark. The black flyers will fan the flames. You will be consumed."

The Landsman smiled a sly, frightening smile. "No," he said. "I will kill you all, and have an end to it."

She smiled back at him. "Evan is a healer who has given his life to Thayos, and hundreds owe him their very lives. Coll is among the greatest singers of Windhaven, known and loved on a hundred islands. And I am Maris of Lesser Amberly, the girl in the songs, the one who changed the world. I'm a hero to people who have never met me. You'll kill the three of us? Fine. The black flyers will watch and spread the news, the singers will make the songs. How long do you think you will rule then? The next flyers' Council will not be divided—Thayos will become like Kennehut, a dead land."

"Liar," the Landsman said. He fingered his knife.

"We mean no harm to your people," Maris said. "Tya is dead, and nothing will bring her back. But you will accept my terms, or everything I've warned you of will happen. First, you will give over Tya's body so she can be flown out to sea, and cast from a height, as flyers are always buried. Second, you will make peace, as she wished. You will renounce all claim to the mine that started your war with Thrane. Third, you will send a poor child to Airhome academy every year, to train for wings. Tya would like that, I think. And finally, finally"—Maris paused briefly, watching the storm behind his eyes, and plunged on regardless—"you will renounce your office and retire, and your family will be taken from Thayos, to some island where you are not known, and can live out your days in peace."

The Landsman was running his thumb along the edge of the knife. He had cut himself, but he did not seem to notice. A tiny drop of blood spotted the white silk of his fine shirt. His mouth twitched. In the sudden stillness that followed her words, Maris felt faint and tired. She had done all she could. She had said all that she could say. She waited.

Evan's arm went around her, and in the corner of her eye she saw Coll's bruised lips twist into a slight smile, and abruptly Maris felt almost good again. Whatever happened, she had done her best. She felt as if she had just returned from a long, long flight; her limbs ached and trembled, and she was damp and chilled through to the bone, but she remembered the sky and the lift of her wings, and that was enough. She was satisfied.

"Terms," the Landsman said. His tone was poisonous. He rose from his throne, the blood-smeared knife in his hand. "I will give you terms," he said. He pointed the knife at Evan. "Take the old man and cut off his hands," he ordered. "Then cast him out and let him heal himself. That ought to be a sight to see." He laughed, and his hand moved sideways, so the knife was pointing at Coll. "The singer loses one hand and a tongue." The knife shifted again. "As to you," he said, when the blade pointed at Maris, "since you like the color black, I will give you your fill of it. I will put you in a cell without a window or a light, where it is black day and night, and you will stay there until you have forgotten what sunlight *was*. Do you like those terms, flyer? *Do you?*"

Maris felt the tears in her eyes, but she would not let them fall. "I am sorry for your people," she said softly. "They did nothing to deserve you."

"Take them," the Landsman said, "and do as I have ordered!"

The landsguard looked at each other. One took a hesitant step forward, and stopped when he saw he was alone.

"What are you waiting for?" the Landsman shrieked. "*Seize them!*"

"Sir," said a tall, dignified woman in the uniform of a high officer, "I beg you to reconsider. We cannot maim a singer, or imprison Maris of Lesser Amberly. It would be the end of us. The flyers would destroy us all."

The Landsman stared at her, then pointed with his knife. "You are under arrest as well, traitor. You will have the cell next to hers, if you like her so well." To the other landsguard, he said, "Take them."

No one moved.

"Traitors," he muttered, "I am surrounded by traitors. You will all die, all of you." His eyes found Maris. "And you, you will be the first. I will do it myself."

Maris was achingly aware of the knife in his hand, the dull bronze length of it, the smear of blood along the blade. She felt Evan tense beside her. The Landsman smiled and walked toward them.

"Stop him," said the tall woman he had tried to arrest. Her voice was weary but firm. At once the Landsman was surrounded. A burly bear of a man held his arms, and a slim young woman took the knife from his grasp as easily and fluidly as if she had pulled it from a sheath. "I'm sorry," said the woman who had taken charge.

"Let me go!" he demanded. "I am Landsman here!"

"No," she answered, "no. Sir, I fear you are very sick."

The grim, ancient keep had never seen such festivity.

The gray walls were decked with bright banners and colored lanterns, and smells of food and wine, woodsmoke and fireworks permeated the air. The gates had been opened wide to all. Landsguard still roamed the keep, but few were in uniform, and weapons were forgotten.

The gibbets had been torn down, the scaffolding altered to make a stage where jugglers, magicians, clowns, and singers performed for the passing crowds.

Within, doors were open and halls filled with merrymakers. Prisoners from the dungeons had been set free, and even the lowest riff-raff from the alleys of Port Thayos had been admitted to the party. In the great hall tables had been set up and covered with huge wheels of cheese, baskets of bread, and smoked, pickled, and fried fish of all kinds. The hearths still smelled of roasting pig and seacat, and puddles of beer and wine glistened on the flagstones.

Music and laughter were in the air; it was a celebration of a richness and size unknown on Thayos in living memory. And among the crowds of the people of Thayos moved figures dressed in black—not, by their faces, mourners: the flyers. These flyers, one-wing and flyer-born alike, along with the previously exiled singers, were the guests of honor, feted and toasted by all.

Maris wandered through the boisterous crowds, ready to cringe at any more recognition. The party had gone on too long. She was

tired and feeling a little sick from too much food and drink, all trib-
utes forced on her by admirers. She wanted only to find Evan and
go home.

Someone spoke her name and, reluctantly, Maris turned. She
saw the new Landsman of Thayos, dressed in a long, embroidered
gown that did not suit her. She looked uncomfortable out of uniform.

Maris summoned a smile. "Yes, Landsman?"

The former landsguard officer grimaced. "I suppose I will get used
to that title, but it still brings to mind someone very different. I
haven't seen much of you today—could I have a few minutes with
you?"

"Yes, of course. As many as you wish. You saved my life."

"That wasn't so noble. Your actions took more courage than
mine, and they weren't self-serving. The story they will tell about
me is that I carefully plotted and planned to depose the Landsman
and take his job. That is not the truth, but what do singers care for
truth?" Her voice was bitter. Maris looked at her in surprise.

They walked together through rooms filled with gamblers,
drunks, and lovers until they found an empty chamber where they
could sit and talk together.

Because the Landsman still was silent, Maris said, "Surely no one
misses the old Landsman? I don't think he was well-loved."

The new Landsman frowned. "No, he will not be missed, and
neither will I, when I am gone. But he was a good leader for many
years until he became too frightened and began to think foolishly. I
was sorry to have to do what I did, but I saw no other choice. This
party, here, is my attempt to make the transition joyful, instead of
fearful. To go into debt to make my people feel prosperous."

"I think they appreciate the gesture," Maris said. "Everyone
seems very happy."

"Yes, now, but their memories are short." The Landsman moved
slightly in her seat, as if to shake off the thought. The line between
her eyes smoothed out, and her features took on a kindlier cast. "I
didn't mean to bore you with my personal worries. I drew you aside
to tell you how respected you are in Thayos, and to tell you that I

honor your attempts to keep peace between the flyers and the people of Thayos."

Maris wondered if she was blushing. "Please," she said. "Don't. I . . . had the flyers in mind, and not the people of Thayos, to be honest."

"That doesn't matter. What you accomplished is what matters. You risked your life for it."

"I did what I could," Maris said. "But I didn't achieve very much, after all. A truce, a temporary peace. The *real* problem, the conflicts between the flyer-born and the one-wings, and between the Landsmen and the flyers who work with them, is still there, and it will flare up again—" She broke off, realizing that the Landsman didn't care, and didn't want to know, that this happy ending was no true ending at all.

"There will be no more trouble for the flyers on Thayos," the Landsman said. Maris realized that the woman had the useful ability to make a simple sentence sound like a proclamation of law. "We respect flyers here—and singers, too."

"A wise choice," Maris said. She grinned. "It never hurts to have the singers on your side."

The Landsman went on as if she had not been interrupted. "And you, Maris, will always be welcome on Thayos, if ever you choose to return to visit us."

"Visit?" Maris frowned, puzzled.

"I realize that, since you no longer fly, the journey by ship may be . . ."

"What are you talking about?"

The Landsman looked annoyed at all the interruptions. "I know that you are leaving Thayos for Seatooth soon, to make your home at the Woodwings Academy."

"Who told you that?"

"The singer, Coll, I believe. Was it a secret?"

"Not a secret. Not a fact, either." Maris sighed. "I was offered the job at Woodwings, but I have not accepted it."

"If you stay on Thayos, of course we would all be pleased, and the hospitality of this . . . my . . . keep will always be extended to you." The Landsman rose, obviously concluding her formal recognition of Maris, and Maris, too, stood, and they spoke a few moments longer of inconsequential things. Maris hardly paid attention. Her thoughts were in turmoil again about a subject she had determined was resolved. Did Coll think he could make something come true by speaking of it as fact? She would have to talk to him.

But when she found him a few minutes later in the outer yard, near the gate, he was not alone. Bari was with him, and S'Rella—and S'Rella was carrying her wings.

Maris hurried to join them. "S'Rella—you're not leaving?"

S'Rella grasped her hands. "I must. The Landsman wants a message flown to Deeth. I offered to take it—I have to get home, and I would have to fly south in another day or two anyway. There was no need for Jem or Sahn to go so far when I can take it just as well. I just sent Evan to look for you, to tell you I was leaving. But it needn't be a sad farewell, you know—we'll see each other soon at Woodwings."

Maris glared at Coll, but he looked oblivious. She said to S'Rella, "I told you I would live out my life on Thayos."

S'Rella looked puzzled. "But surely you've changed your mind? After all that has happened? And you know they still want you at Woodwings—now more than ever. You've become a hero all over again!"

Maris scowled. "I wish everyone would stop saying that! Why am I a hero? What have I done? Just patched things over for a bit longer. Nothing has been settled. You, at least, should realize that, S'Rella!"

S'Rella shook her head impatiently. "Don't change the subject. What about that fine speech you gave us about needing a purpose in life—how can you turn your back now on the work you're meant to do? You've admitted you're no good as a healer—what will you do on Thayos? What will you do with your life?"

Maris had asked herself that same question, and had lain awake most of the night arguing it with herself. Now she said quietly, "I will find something I can do here. The Landsman may have something for me."

"But that's such a waste! Maris, you're needed at Woodwings. You belong there. Even without your wings you're a flyer—you always were, and you always will be. I thought you recognized that!"

There were tears in S'Rella's eyes. Maris felt resentful and trapped—she didn't want to be having this argument. She said, trying to keep her voice level and calm, "I belong with Evan. I can't leave him."

"And they say eavesdroppers never hear good of themselves."

Maris turned to see Evan, and there was such tenderness in his eyes that she forgot her lingering doubts. She had made the right decision. She couldn't leave him.

"But no one is asking you to leave me, you know," he said. "I've just been talking with a young healer who is eager to move into my house and take over my patients. I can be ready to leave within a week."

Maris stared at him. "Leave? Leave your house? But why?"

He smiled. "To go with you to Seatooth. It may not be a pleasant voyage, but at least we can comfort each other in our sickness."

"But . . . I don't understand. Evan, you can't mean it—this is your home!"

"I mean to go with you, wherever you go," he said. "I can't ask you to stay on Thayos, just to keep you beside me. I can't be that selfish, knowing you are needed at Woodwings, and that you belong there."

"But how can you leave? How will you live? You've never been away from Thayos."

He laughed, but it sounded forced. "You make it sound as if I proposed to go live in the sea! I can leave Thayos like anyone else, on a ship. My life hasn't ended yet, and until it has, there is no reason why I shouldn't change. Surely an old healer can find some work to do on Seatooth."

"Evan . . ."

He put his arms around her. "I know. Believe me, I've thought this through. Surely you didn't think I was sleeping last night while you were tossing and turning and wondering what to do? I decided that I can't let you walk out of my life. For once in my life, I must be bold, and dare something different. I am going with you."

Maris couldn't hold the tears back then, although she couldn't have said just why she was crying. Evan pulled her close and held her tightly until she recovered.

As they drew apart, Maris could hear Coll assuring Bari that her aunt was happy, that she was crying with joy; and she saw S'Rella, standing a little apart, her face alight with joy and affection.

"I give up," Maris said. Her voice was somewhat shaky. She wiped her face with her hands. "I have no more excuses. I will go to Seatooth—*we* will go to Seatooth—as soon as we can get a ship out."

What began as a few friends walking with S'Rella to the flyers' cliff became a procession, an extension of the celebration within the keep. Maris, Evan, and Coll were the popular heroes, and many wanted to be close to them, to see at first hand what was so special about the flyer, the healer, and the singer who had deposed a tyrannical Landsman, stopped a war, and ended the eerie threat posed by the silent black flyers. If anyone still dared think Tya had done wrong and deserved her fate, it was thought silently, privately, held as an unpopular opinion.

And yet even in this happy, admiring crowd, Maris knew, the old resentments were still buried. She had not banished them forever, neither those between land-bound and flyer, nor the conflicts separating the one-wings and the flyer-born. Sooner or later this battle would have to be fought again.

The journey through the mountain tunnel was not a lonely one this time. Voices echoed loudly off stone walls, and a dozen torches blazed and smoked, making the damp, dark corridor a different place.

They emerged to a dark, windy night, the stars obscured by clouds. Maris saw S'Rella standing near the cliff's edge, talking with another flyer, a one-wing still wearing black. At the sight of S'Rella standing on that too-familiar cliff, Maris felt her stomach clench, and her head reel with dizziness. But for Evan's support she felt she would have fallen. She knew she didn't want to see S'Rella leap from the cliff from which she had fallen, not once, but twice. She was suddenly afraid.

Several youths darted forward now, loudly vying for the privilege of helping S'Rella ready herself for flight. S'Rella half-turned, seeking Maris, and their eyes met. Maris drew a deep breath, steadying herself, trying to empty herself of fear, released Evan's hand and stepped forward. "Let me help," she said.

She knew it so well. The texture of the cloth-of-metal, the heft of the wings in her hands, the firm snap of struts locking into place. Even though she could no longer wear the wings herself, still her hands loved this task they knew so well, and there was a pleasure, even if rimmed about by sadness, in preparing S'Rella for flight.

When the wings were fully extended, the final struts snapped into place, Maris felt the return of her fear. It was irrational, she knew, and she could say nothing of it to S'Rella, but she felt that if S'Rella stepped off that dangerous cliff it would be to fall, just as Maris had done.

Finally, forcing herself, Maris managed to say, "Go well." Her voice was very low.

S'Rella looked at her searchingly. "Ah, Maris," she said. "You won't be sorry—you've made the right choice. I'll see you soon." Then, despairing of words, S'Rella leaned forward and kissed her friend.

"Go well," S'Rella said, one flyer to another, and then she turned toward the cliff edge, toward the sea and the open sky, and leaped into the wind.

There was applause from the onlookers as S'Rella caught a rising current and wheeled above the cliff, wings glinting darkly. Then, rising higher and heading out to sea, she was lost to sight almost at once, seeming to merge into the night sky.

Maris continued to gaze into the sky long after S'Rella had vanished. Her heart was full, but there was a steadfast certainty there, as well as pain, and even a small spark of the old joy. She would survive. Even without her wings, she was a flyer still.

Epilogue

THE OLD WOMAN WOKE when the door opened, in a room that smelled of sickness. There were other odors as well: salt water, smoke, sea mold, the lingering scent of the spice tea that had gone cold by her bedside. But over them all was the smell of sickness, overpowering, cloying, making the room seem thick and close.

In the doorway a woman was holding a smoking taper. The old woman could see its light, a shifting yellowish blur, and she could make out the figure holding it, and another figure beside her, although their faces were lost to her. Her vision was not what it once was. Her head throbbed terribly, as it often did when she woke. It had been like that for years. She raised a soft, blue-veined hand to her forehead, and squinted. "Who is it?" she asked.

"Odera," said the woman with the taper, in a voice the old woman recognized as the healer's. "He's here, the one you asked for. Are you strong enough to see him?"

"Yes," the old woman said. "Yes." She struggled to sit up in her bed. "Come closer," she said. "I want to see you."

"Shall I stay?" Odera asked uncertainly. "Do you need me?"

"No," said the old woman. "No, I'm past healing. Just him."

Odera nodded—the old woman could make out the gesture, though the face was a blur to her—lit the oil lamps carefully with the taper, and shut the door when she left.

The other visitor pulled a straight-back wooden chair across the room, and sat down close to the bedside, where she could see him quite well. He was young. A boy, really, not even twenty, beardless, with a few pale wisps of blond hair trying to pass as a mustache on his upper lip. His hair was very pale and very curly, his eyebrows almost invisible. But he carried an instrument—a kind of rude guitar, square and with only four strings—and he began to tune it as soon as he was seated. "Would you like me to play something for you?" he asked. "Some special song?" His voice was pleasant, lilting, with just the hint of an accent.

"You are a long way from home," the old woman said.

He smiled. "How did you know?"

"Your voice," she said. "It's been years and years since I've heard a voice like that. You're from the Outer Islands, aren't you?"

"Yes," he said. "My home is a little place right at the edge of the world. You've probably never heard of it. It's called Stormhammer-the-Outermost."

"Ah," she said. "I remember it well. Eastwatch Tower, and the ruins of the one that preceded it. That bitter drink you people brew from roots. Your Landsman insisted I try some, and laughed at the expression on my face when I swallowed. He was a dwarf. I never met an uglier man, or a cleverer one."

The singer looked briefly startled. "He's been dead some thirty years," he said, "but you're right, I've heard the stories. Then you've been there?"

"Three or four times," she said, savoring his reaction. "It was many years ago, before you were born. I used to be a flyer."

"Oh," he said, "of course. I should have guessed. Seatooth is full of flyers, is it not?"

"Not really," she replied. "This is Woodwings Academy, and those here are mostly dreamers who have yet to win their wings, or teachers who have long since set theirs down. Like me. I was a teacher, until I got sick. Now I lie here and remember, mostly."

The singer touched his strings, bringing forth a bright burst of sound that faded quickly into silence. "What would you like to hear?" he asked. "There's a new song that's the rage of Stormtown." His face fell. "It's a bit bawdy, though. Maybe you wouldn't like it."

The old woman laughed. "Oh, I might, I might. You might be surprised at the things I remember. I didn't call you here to sing for me, though."

He stared at her from wide green eyes. "What?" he said, puzzled. "But they told me—I was in an inn in Stormtown, just arrived in fact, the ship from Eastern put in the day before yesterday, and suddenly this boy came up and told me a singer was needed on Seatooth."

"And you came. Left the inn. Weren't you doing well enough there?"

"Well enough," he said. "I'd never been to the Shotans before, after all, and the customers weren't deaf or miserly. But—" He stopped abruptly, panic writ large on his face.

"But you came anyway," the old woman said, "because they told you that a dying woman had asked for a singer."

He said nothing.

"Don't feel guilty," she said. "You aren't revealing any secrets. I know I'm dying. Odera and I are frank with each other. I probably should have died several years ago. My head hurts constantly, and I fear I'm going blind, and I already seem to have outlived half the world. Oh, don't misunderstand me. I don't want to die. But I don't especially want to go on like this either. I don't like the pain, or my own helplessness. Death frightens me, but at least it will free me from the smell in this room." She saw his expression and smiled gently. "You don't have to pretend you can't smell it. I know it's there. The sick smell." She sighed. "I prefer cleaner scents. Spices and salt water, even sweat. Wind. Storm. I still remember the smell that lightning leaves in its wake."

"There are songs I could sing," the youth said carefully. "Glad songs to lighten your mood. Funny songs, or sad ones if you prefer. It might make the pain less."

"Kivas makes the pain less," the old woman replied. "Odera makes it strong, and sometimes laces it with sweetsong or other herbs. She gives me tesis to make me sleep. I don't need your voice for my hurts."

"I know I'm young," the singer said, "but I am good. Let me show you."

"No." She smiled. "I'm sure you're good, really I am. Though I probably wouldn't appreciate your talents. Maybe my ears are going too, or perhaps it's just a trick of old age, but no singer I've heard in the last ten years has seemed as good to me as the ones I remember from years ago. I've listened to the best. I heard S'Lassa and T'rhennian sing duets on Veleth a long time back. Jared of Geer has entertained me, and homeless Gerri One-Eye, and Coll. I once knew a singer named Halland who sang me songs a good deal bawdier than the one you were about to perform, I'd wager. When I was young, I even heard Barrion sing, not once but many times."

"I'm as good as any of them," the singer said stubbornly.

The old woman sighed. "Don't pout," she said sharply. "I'm sure you sing splendidly. But you'll never get someone as old as me to admit it."

He strummed his instrument nervously. "If you don't want a song for your deathbed," he said, "then why did you send to Stormtown for a singer?"

"I want to sing to you," she said. "It won't hurt *too* much, although I can't play or carry a tune. Mostly I'll recite."

The singer set aside his instrument and folded his arms to listen. "A strange request," he said, "but I was a listener long before I was a singer. My name is Daren, by the way."

"Good," she said. "I am pleased to know you, Daren. I wish you could have known me when I was a bit more vigorous. Now listen carefully. I want you to learn these words, and sing this song after I'm gone, if you think it's good enough. You will."

"I know a great many songs already," he said.

"Not this one," she replied.

"Did you make it up yourself?"

"No," she said, "no. It was sort of a gift to me, a farewell gift. My brother sang it to me as he lay dying, and forced me to learn all the words. He was in a great deal of pain at the time, and death was a kindness for him, but he would not go until he was satisfied that I had all the words committed to memory. So I learned them quickly, crying all the while, and he died. It was in a town on Little Shotan, not quite ten years ago. So you can see that the song means a great deal to me. Now, if you would, please listen."

She began to sing.

Her voice was old and worn, painfully thin, and her attempt to sing strained it to its uttermost, so that sometimes she coughed and wheezed. She had no sense of key, she knew, and she could not carry a tune any more in her old age than in her youth. But she knew the words, she *did* know the words. Sad words set to simple, soft, melancholy music.

It was a song about the death of a very famous flyer. When she grew old, the song said, and the days of her life grew short, she found and took a pair of wings, as she had done once in her legendary youth. And she strapped them on, and ran, and all of her friends came running after, shouting for her to stop, to turn back, for she was very old and very weak, and she had not flown for years, and her mind was so addled that she had not even remembered to unfold her wings. But she would not listen. She reached the cliff before they could catch her, and plunged over the edge, falling. Her friends cried out and covered their eyes, not wanting to see her dashed against the sea. But, at the last moment, suddenly her wings unfolded, springing out taut and silver from her shoulders. And the wind caught her, lifted her, and from where they stood her friends heard her laughter. She circled high above them, her hair blowing in the wind, her wings bright as hope, and they saw that she was young again. She waved farewell to them, dipped her wing in salute, and flew off toward the west, to vanish against the setting sun. She was never seen again.

There was silence in the room when the old woman had finished singing her song. The singer sat tilted back in his chair, staring at the flickering of an oil lamp, his eyes gone far away and thoughtful.

Finally the old woman coughed irritably. "Well?" she said.

"Oh." He smiled and sat up. "I'm sorry. It's a nice song. I was just thinking how it would sound with some music behind it."

"And with a voice singing it, no doubt—one that didn't wheeze and strain quite so much." She nodded. "Well, it would sound very good, that's how it would sound. Did you get all the words?"

"Of course," he said. "Do you want me to sing it back to you?"

"Yes," said the old woman. "How else would I know if you got it right?"

The singer grinned and took up his instrument. "I knew you'd come around," he said pleasantly. He touched his strings, his fingers moving with deceptive slowness, and the little room filled with melancholy. Then he sang her song back to her, in his high, sweet, vibrant voice.

He was smiling when he had done. "Well?"

"Don't look smug," she said. "You got all the words right."

"And my singing?"

"Good," she admitted. "Good. And you'll get better, too."

He was satisfied with that. "I see you did not exaggerate—you *do* recognize good singing." They grinned at each other. "It's odd that I'd never heard that song before. I've done all the others about her, of course, but never that one. I never even knew that Maris died that way." His green eyes were fixed on her, and the light reflected in them gave his face a pensive, thoughtful cast.

"Don't be sly," she said. "You know perfectly well that I'm she, and I haven't died that way or any way. Not yet, that is. But soon, soon."

"Will you really steal wings again, and leap from a cliff?"

She sighed. "That would waste a pair of wings. I don't expect I could really pull off Raven's Fall, not at my age. Though I've always wanted to. I saw it done a bare half-dozen times in my life, and the last time it was tried the girl had a strut break on her, and she died. I never did it myself. But I dreamed about it, Daren, yes I did. It was the one thing I wanted to do that I never managed. Not a bad thing to say of a life as long as mine."

"Not bad at all," he said.

"As for my death," she said, "well, I expect I'll die here, in this bed, in the not too distant future. Maybe I'll make them carry me up outside, so I can see a last sunset. Or maybe not. My eyes are so bad that I wouldn't see the sunset very well anyway." She made a *tsk*ing sound. "In either case, after I'm dead some flyer will sling my body into a harness, and struggle to get aloft with my dead weight added to his own, and I'll be flown out to sea and given what is widely known as a flyer burial. Why, I don't know. The corpse certainly doesn't *fly*. When it's cut loose it drops like a stone, and sinks or gets eaten by scyllas. It makes no sense, but that's the tradition."

She sighed. "Val One-Wing had the right idea. He's buried right here on Seatooth, in a huge stone tomb with his statue on top. He designed it himself. I never could quite disregard tradition the way Val could, however."

He nodded. "So you would rather have them remember this song than the way you'll really die?"

She looked at him scornfully. "I thought you were a *singer*," she said. She looked the other way. "A singer should understand. The song—that *is* the way I really die. Coll knew that, when he made the song for me."

The young singer hesitated. "But—"

The door to the room opened again, and Odera the healer was back in the doorway, with a taper in one hand and a glass in the other. "Enough singing," she said. "You'll wear yourself out. It's time for your sleeping draught."

The old woman nodded. "Yes," she said. "My head is getting worse. Don't ever fall onto rocks from a thousand feet up, Daren. Or if you do, don't land on your head." She took the tesis from Odera's hand, and drained it straightaway. "Terrible," she said. "You could at least flavor it."

Odera began to pull Daren toward the door. He stopped before he was quite there. "The song," he said, "I'll sing it. Others will sing it too. But I won't sing it until—you know—until I *hear*."

She nodded, drowsiness already stealing into her limbs, the small slow paralysis of tesis. "That would be appropriate," she said.

"What is it called?" he said. "The song?"

" 'The Last Flight,' " she told him, smiling. Her last flight, of course, and Coll's last song. That seemed appropriate too.

" 'The Last Flight,' " he repeated. "Maris, I understand, I think. The song is true, isn't it?"

"True," she agreed. But she was not sure he heard her. Her voice was weak, and Odera had dragged him outside and was shutting the door between them. Some time later the healer returned to snuff the oil lamps, and she was left alone in a small dark room that smelled of sickness, beneath the ancient bloodsoaked stone of Woodwings Academy.

Despite the tesis, she found she could not sleep. A kind of

excitement was on her, a dizzy, giddy feeling she had not known in a long time.

Somewhere far above her head, she thought she could hear the storm beginning, and the sound of rain drumming against weathered rock. The fortress was strong, *strong*, and she knew it would not collapse. Still, somehow she felt that tonight might be the night when, finally, after all these years, she would go to see her father.

About the Authors

GEORGE R. R. MARTIN is the award-winning author of five novels, including *Fevre Dream* and *The Armageddon Rag*. For the last ten years, he has been a screenwriter for feature films and television and was the producer of the TV series *Beauty and the Beast* as well as a story editor for *The Twilight Zone*. After a ten-year hiatus, he has now returned to writing novels full-time and is presently at work on *A Dance with Dragons*, the fourth book of his A Song of Fire and Ice series.

LISA TUTTLE won the John W. Campbell award for best new writer in 1974 and has since gone on to author numerous short stories and novels, including *Lost Futures*, which was short-listed for the Arthur C. Clarke Award, and *The Pillow Friend*. More recently, she has written several books for children.

Texas-born, she now lives with her husband and daughter in a remote area on the west coast of Scotland where the scenery and weather are very similar to the seascapes of Windhaven.

Lands

dhaven

EASTERN

Thrynel

Kennehut
Cheslin

North
Arren

Kite's Landing

South Arren

Lomar

Scylla's Point

WESTERN

Kerres

SOUTHERN

Yethien
Setheen
Hethen
Alessy
Deeth
Veleth